BORN FUNNY

Published in the United States by the Unapologetic Voice House.
www.theunapologeticvoicehouse.com

Some of the names in this book have been changed to protect their privacy.

Identifiers:
Paperback ISBN: 978-1-955090-25-4
eBook ISBN: 978-1-955090-26-1
Library of Congress Control Number: 2022901642

BORN FUNNY

A Comic's Chronicle
Through the Rise
of Alt Comedy

TOM McCAFFREY

ACKNOWLEDGEMENTS

I wrote this book over a four-year period. I first started it as a way to simply recall my experiences in the world of stand-up comedy. It slowly expanded into a sort of origin story of a shy New York City Gen-X'er who knew from an early age that he could make people laugh. I encountered numerous people along my journey that led me to stand-up comedy. Stand-up was not something I jumped into wholeheartedly. It took me many years to finally get the courage to get onstage, but I am thankful I finally did it. It brought me an endless number of experiences and helped me to discover who I was and what my take on the world was.

I first would like to thank my parents Tom and Sarah who made me and who attended my earliest comedy shows that were extremely hit and miss. My mother died only a year into my stand-up career but she did get to see me thrive onstage in her last months alive. My father even agreed to appear on one of my comedy album covers, although I'm not quite sure he knew what he was posing for exactly.

My sister Cindy and Clare for their unwavering support in all my creative endeavors and for helping my album debut at #1 on iTunes.

The New York venue Rififi which served as the centerpiece of the alternative comedy scene. It was there that I developed my voice as a comedian appearing on various shows such as "The Greg Johnson Show", "Oh Hello" and "Invite Them Up". Thanks to Eugene and Bobby for including me on the "Invite Them Up" CD Compilation, an album that to this day is mentioned to me by comedy fans.

Thanks to all the people that contributed their quotes to this book. I truly appreciate you taking the time to write down your memories of the alt comedy scene as it was first taking shape in the East Village.

To Scott Rogowsky for producing my debut comedy album "Lou Diamond Phillips?" an album that completely captured my voice during the alt comedy era and that is still brought up to me to this very day by fans of the album.

Thanks to Erik Bransteen for continuing to co-host the podcast "LE2B" with me for over six years.

To Michael Ferrari and his parents for the fateful ride they gave me in their station wagon when I was just six years old. That ride was truly a defining moment in my life.

To Jacques d'Amboise for giving me my first glimpse into the world of show business and for taking me to the Oscars in 1984, an experience that changed my life forever.

To Irene Cara for dancing with me at the 56th Annual Academy Awards. I know she remembers it as fondly as I do. To Jack Nicholson for telling me I was great at the Oscars (that actually happened).

Thanks to my friends who supported my comedy aspirations all these years especially Rob and Chris who always supported my desire to be funny and laughed at all the right moments.

Thanks to James Depaul the first person to proactively tell me I should pursue stand-up and that I was good at it.

To Lila Glasoe Francese for helping me get this book published. She is the primary reason this is out right now.

To The Unapologetic Voice House team. Carrie Severson who gave my book the chance to finally be seen and for giving me the creative freedom to put it out exactly the way I wanted. And to Amma for helping me shape the final product of this book.

Thanks to Dani Skollar for being the first person to read this book in its earliest stage and give me much appreciated feedback and for helping design the initial cover art. Also, for laughing at things I say that may or may not be that funny, but that probably are funny.

Thanks to Eminem for being a creative genius who motivates me to be myself unapologetically, something I struggle to do every day.

AUTHOR'S NOTE

T HE EVENTS IN THIS BOOK ARE ALL BASED ON TRUE
events as they happened to me. They are retold
to the best of my recollection. While the spirit,
tone of the events, and dialogue are as they occurred,
it is not word for word. Some names, identifying cir-
cumstances, and details have been changed in order
to protect the privacy of various individuals involved.
Some details have been exaggerated slightly for comedic effect, but everything in this book is based on actual
interactions and experiences as they unfolded to the
best of my memory.

CONTENTS

"Don't cry, you're too old for that."
"It's because I am too old. Old and funny."
– Truman Capote's 'A Christmas Memory'

CHAPTER 1:

ONCE UPON A TIME... IN WEST HOLLYWOOD

T HE JOKE APPEARED TO STEVE AS IF OUT OF NOWHERE. He had overheard a visiting LA comic comment backstage about how they loved New York but could never live there. The joke was a response to the LA comic's judgmental utterance.

Steve took his small loose-leaf notebook out of his back pocket. The notebook was almost full of scribblings; some he could hardly read. With the ballpoint pen stuck in the middle of the notepad, he jotted down a short sentence that he knew would help him to recall the idea. Then he placed the notebook back in his pocket and focused on his upcoming set. He immediately knew the joke was good.

This happened to him regularly now. His mind was constantly creating jokes somewhere within the depths of his brain. He had no idea where these bits were coming from, and he had underlying anxiety that one day they would cease to appear. And suddenly, he felt streams of sweat on his back.

He was standing offstage about to tape his first TV appearance, just three blocks down the street from his old high school. It was his thirtieth birthday, and his world domination plan wasn't taking shape as fast as he'd once hoped, although appearing on Comedy Central was a good start. His breathing was shallow and his stomach in knots like it always was before every performance. Petrified, he suddenly didn't want to go out there. It was the same feeling he had each time he was preparing to go onstage. It was an anxiety beyond anything he could explain with words. He'd been told once that doing stand-up caused more trauma than jumping out of an airplane. He couldn't recall who had told him that, but he believed it. Most comedians hated doing stand-up and all comedians had stage fright, all the good ones anyway, though he suspected his was much worse than most. He thought of Carly Simon who, he once heard, experienced intense stage fright throughout her entire career.

Most people would never experience the excruciating fear of doing comedy. Only a select few had endured the ordeal of it. He absolutely hated the feeling and a large part of him despised doing stand-up, yet he was compelled to do it. Sometimes, while lying awake at night, *he thought why had he been blessed with this ability if it often filled him with such dread*? Perhaps God enjoyed watching him suffer, as if it was his very own 'Curb Your Enthusiasm'. After all, Steve was at his funniest when exasperated and annoyed. Maybe Steve was God's favorite show to watch on earth.

He thought about what he'd do if he got onstage and forgot everything. Comedy was a head game. You couldn't overthink it. When you did comedy, you were right on the edge. One misstep and it was all over. Suddenly he couldn't remember his first joke. *Oh no. It was happening.* His worst fear was coming true as if he'd willed it to happen. He heard the famous host start to introduce him.

"Everyone please give it up for...."

Oh shit, he thought. His mind was completely blank. He had two seconds to remember his jokes. He was about to humiliate himself. His first TV appearance was crumbling.

"Steve Collin!" the host announced, gleefully.

Steve turned around, ready to run. No way was he going out there. He could hear the crowd applauding. Steve didn't move...

It was back in 2000, while in LA one February night, that his college friend, Ron, told him about an upcoming performance by David Cross and Bob Odenkirk at a club/bar on Fairfax called Largo. Ron was a complete "Mr. Show" freak. Apparently, there was also another up-and-coming, hot comedian on the lineup. The guy's name was Patton Oswalt. Ron told Steve that Patton Oswalt was on a "whole other level comedically." Ron was a self-proclaimed comedy nerd with obscure and sophisticated taste in pop culture. He loved underground comedy TV shows and weird films, and his favorite director was David Lynch, of course. Like Steve, Ron rejected what was considered the norm, and anything embraced by the masses. For instance, Steve had absolutely refused to watch "South Park" and "Ace Ventura Pet Detective" when they became commercial zeitgeist successes. It felt lame to Steve to like anything everyone else liked, especially since he hated most people.

Later that night, Steve headed over to Largo. He was tired of being ignored at the Hollywood Improv by the asshole manager/booker, Brian, a douchebag actor/model who was a total prick/asshole. Brian didn't like Steve and had never booked him even after seeing him kill it at his audition for the club. He'd told Steve that he was just a white guy with nothing special about him. Steve had already heard this kind of critique a few times back in New York. The Comic Strip manager had once told him the same thing.

Apparently, comedy was the only profession where being a white male was the worst possible thing you could be.

"I mean, yeah, you got laughs up there, but there's nothing unique about you. There are plenty of white guys around. You're a dime a dozen," the Comic Strip manager with frizzy greying hair and dressed sloppily in faded jeans had said to him. She didn't even bother to look directly at him. She'd MC'd the show and bombed the whole night, which made her critique of his comedy sting even harder.

"So, I guess I should work on not being a white guy?" Steve said to her.

"Well, I mean, I don't know what to tell you, Stan," she said this while looking down at the table.

"Steve."

"Steve...Stan, whatever." Then she got up quickly from the tiny booth without so much as a glance in his direction. He'd waited three hours to hear her pearls of comedy wisdom. Steve sat there mortified, he was certain that everyone in the room was staring and laughing at him. That's when he felt the knot in his stomach.

Another comic, a regular at the club, walked past holding a drink in his hand. This short cocky Mexican guy.

"Maybe next time," he said, smirking slightly in his raspy voice.

Steve looked up at the wall. It was covered with the framed pictures of comics who'd performed there. Adam Sandler, Jerry Seinfeld, and Richard Jeni. It looked like some white guys had made it in comedy after all. But he remembered what she had said, he wasn't anything special.

Steve took that comment to heart, and it never left him. He had a hard time letting comments like that go. They never went away. Instead, they nestled inside his subconscious mind along with all the other insults he'd heard throughout his life growing up in Manhattan. Sitting right there in that booth, he had decided to leave New York and move to LA. He had to get away for a little while. No one seemed to give a shit about him in New York. The problem, he decided, was that New York was holding him back. What'd they know anyway?

After all, he was destined for comedy greatness. Didn't they know about the time he was at the Oscars?

Now in LA, Steve was running into the exact same obstacles he'd encountered back in New York, and he was getting even more disillusioned. When Ron showed him the film "Mulholland Drive," he knew he had not been imagining the darkness he felt in LA from the very first day he'd arrived. LA felt like a place where dreams went to die. But Largo felt different from the town of LA.

Largo was packed that night, standing room only. It was dark with dim red lights illuminating the bar in a way reminiscent of "The Shining." The ceilings were low, and all the chairs and booths were full, forcing Steve to take a spot at the bar.

He had never seen the Comedy Store or the Improv this packed on a Monday night. How had he not heard about this show before? From the bar, he could see the audience, made up of mostly LA types, dressed casually but cool. Steve had seen "Mr. Show" a few times in the last year and, although he thought it was a funny show, he wasn't a total fanboy or anything of the sort.

The Sklar brothers were onstage hosting and were doing pretty well. Steve had performed with them a few times on bringer shows in New York. They were new to the scene but were quickly moving up the ranks. The show was unlike any other comedy show Steve had been to. The comics didn't perform with the desperation of being approved by a late-night show booker or with the hopes that the crowd would approve. They simply did whatever they wanted and whatever they thought was funny.

This place had a different vibe from the Comedy Store, which felt haunted by demons. And the Improv on Melrose was the complete embodiment of Hollywood, a place for pretentious asshole agents and managers to have "important" meetings with people who weren't important at all. Largo had no drink minimum and the cover was a paltry five dollars. Everyone was there because they wanted to be, not because they were tourists from Wisconsin who'd stumbled into a "real comedy show." This place was for actual aficionados going to watch underground comedians who weren't stars ... yet. This was clearly *the* cool place to see comedy, not just a place to be seen standing near famous people. Being famous in this place seemed lame.

"Mr. Show" was five months off the air and every person in the room was a disciple. The room was full of devotees who were the equivalent of music groupies watching their favorite band that hadn't been discovered by the masses yet. Steve imagined the punk rock scene of the '70s being similar. The comedians here weren't famous. Oh, most of them would be hugely famous one day but it would seem like it was almost by accident. This was a place where hacks came to die. Survival of the funniest.

The blue lighting onstage was dull. In the middle of the stage was a small black frail music stand comedians placed their notes on as if they were in the New York Philharmonic. There was an unspoken requirement that comics did material that was new and not worked out. Notes onstage were not only expected but were also embraced here. This detail especially appealed to Steve who was constantly writing jokes and didn't know what to do with most of his unpolished material he couldn't perform given the little stage time he was able to manage. He was usually given five minutes at best. Steve also had a hard time sticking to a script and was constantly writing bits that he'd scrap after doing once. Another comic had once described him as "prolific as hell." The official rule in stand-up was to do a joke three times and, if it didn't work by the third time, abandon it. Steve's rule was to do a joke one time. If it didn't kill immediately then never do it again and write something that *would* kill.

A thirty-something-year-old male comic named Nick went up first at Largo. Steve had never seen him live, so his heart jumped at the chance to see him in such an intimate venue. He'd seen the comic do a set on Conan a year earlier and was blown away by his naturalistic style. Nick walked onto the small Largo stage with his chest out. He wore a black t-shirt and jeans, his body oozing with confidence. He placed his notes on the music stand and then awkwardly started his set by thanking the audience and asking how they were.

"Hello, how are you? It's weird to be here because I um...fucked all your moms," he said.

"I'm just kidding, I didn't sleep with your moms. Relax. I fucked your dads though."

He did about seven bits that Steve had never heard him do before and would never hear him do again. They were all unbelievable jokes, each with absurdly original premises. Each brand-new bit killed. One bit was about starting a service where people could hire celebrities to tell their dying parents that they loved them. "Hey man, your daughter doesn't love you, but I love you...I'm Brad Pitt!"

For three months, Steve had seen the regulars at the Improv do the same acts verbatim every single time they went up. This unassuming comic had just done a brand-new ten-minute set that was superior to most comedians' "A" material sets. He was like a comedy superhero and in Largo, he was a god.

The next comedian was a surprise, a drop-in. His name was Mitch Hedberg. Steve had seen him on Letterman a year earlier. He was rising fast on the comedy scene after his Letterman appearance. He was a shy, unassuming, good-looking, extremely likable guy with an affable presence. He had long blondish hair and wore red-tinted glasses due to his insecurity. He was an uncomfortable stoner hippie with charm; shy and never looked out at the crowd. He had an original cadence delivery and even his missteps drew roars from the crowd. He looked like a rock star and in there he *was* a rock star. He did quick one-liners.

"So I used to do drugs. I still do but I used to also. They say you can't please all of the people all of the time and last night all of those people were at my show."

The crowd ate up every word and nuance. Steve wanted to be in his position. To have a roomful of people listening to him. Mitch Hedberg and the other comics weren't following the same rules everyone else in town was following. They didn't start with a personal relatable joke about themselves, something Steve had been told by every industry insider was an absolute necessity. They just told jokes about absurd little things. They sounded like they were making things up on the fly. Hedberg fumbled with his notes in the middle of his set which also drew laughs. He was getting laughs for being clumsy and messing up. It was as if being unprepared got you more respect there. This was mind-blowing to Steve. You would never be allowed to bring up notes at the Improv, you'd be banned by Brian the asshole manager. The rawness of Hedberg's act made it seem more organic and in the moment. Nothing was phony. Steve immediately made a mental note: *being too prepared in comedy came off as disingenuous.*

Bob Odenkerk and David Cross went up, individually, and basically fucked around onstage for 30 minutes each. Neither seemed much interested in getting laughs. In fact, Cross seemed to want the audience to not like him. It was "hack" to be liked in this room. At one point he berated the audience for laughing at a joke he felt was stupid.

"Yeah, of course, you laugh at that one. The stupidest joke I've ever written is the one you like. Figures, this is fucking Hollywood where shit thrives and gets sitcom deals," he said.

The comedians were in charge here and set the rhythm. In clubs, it was the exact opposite, the audience was king, and you had better make them laugh or you would never get booked again. In Largo, funny was all that mattered. No jokes about being Russian here or being half Irish and half Scottish and being Jewish. Steve responded to the aloofness of the comics. A bunch of people just hanging out watching smart and funny people talk. He thought of that time in the back of the station wagon. The image came into his head often now that he was trying to do comedy as a career. There had been something prescient about it. He felt it then and he felt it now. The station wagon moment had somehow led him here.

Steve had been uncomfortable and mostly miserable in LA. He was constantly told he had to conform to a certain type of comedy style. The place drained him. Many LA comedians and managers treated stand-up comedy like a math equation that could be manipulated and solved. In LA, stand-up was simply viewed as a way to get on TV. He'd been told after a set by an agent that he had to completely change his act and pretend to be a "character" onstage that the industry could sell. Steve was new to stand-up, but he wasn't buying this whole bullshit "character" narrative. He hadn't found his voice yet, but he knew that his voice wouldn't come from some douchey LA industry guy with coke eyes. LA was a fucked-up place.

The comics at Largo weren't pretending to be anything and it felt more dangerous somehow. The mainstream scene seemed lifeless. It was failing to adjust to the changes in the comedy industry. Many comics in the clubs were doing a slightly altered version of '80s comedy that wasn't working anymore. Times were changing. This room wasn't trying to conform to some idea of what stand-up was. It was making its own way and was being ignored by the industry, for the time being.

Bob Saget dropped in, and his set didn't jibe with the energy of the place. He was the most famous comedian there and had the worst set. He went up without notes, not a good start, and did hacky polished jokes about "Full House." He did one bit about wanting to sleep with the Olsen twins which bombed horribly. This was probably the only place in LA where being famous wasn't going to buy you any credibility, especially if you were famous for hosting a show where people got kicked in the crotch repeatedly. If you sucked, it didn't matter who you were. Saget flubbed his way through his set and finally left the stage with his head down.

Patton Oswalt went up last and destroyed it. It was unlike anything Steve had ever seen before. He wasn't just having a good set, he had everyone right in the palm of his grasp. Everyone had been good, but this guy was in an alternate universe. Oswalt was a comedy equivalent of Lebron James, Kobe Bryant, and Jordan in one. He was short and somewhat pudgy. He was a bit of an awkward guy, none too good looking but he too was a god up there.

Oswalt did about thirty minutes of what didn't even seem like jokes. He was just kind of talking. No real setups or punches. It was almost like a magic trick. It was like he was killing it without even really doing anything at all. He finished his set with a long story about Yoshinoya Beef Bowl being a shit hole that must have gone on for ten minutes. The story didn't get a lot of laughs, yet everyone hung on to every word. He was killing it without getting many laughs. How was that even possible?

Although he was a comic, watching stand-up comedy often bored Steve, especially as a kid. When he watched Eddie Murphy's "Delirious" at age ten, he'd become restless twenty minutes in. That didn't happen with Oswalt. He wasn't just telling jokes. He was doing a new style of stand-up that was seamless. Patton Oswalt wasn't doing a character he'd fabricated to get on TV, he was simply hilarious. Steve knew he could be that funny if only he could somehow get out of his own way.

He left Largo that night and got into his Toyota Tercel. Then he started the car, sat there and put his head down, and started to cry.

CHAPTER 2:

OSCAR NIGHT

THE OSCARS WERE WINDING DOWN AND STEVE SAT onstage with his friend from PS 40, Mike Ferrari. He was tired since it was past midnight in New York although only 9:20 p.m. in California. Johnny Carson stood near him talking to Shirley MacLaine. He noticed a table of Oscars offstage about fifty feet away.

"I bet I could grab one of those," a short kid with curly brown hair, a baggy blue sweatshirt, and over-confidence, named Adam said.

"Oh, man! I dare you!" a taller kid named Andre said.

These two kids were the loudest troublemakers in the group. The show was over, and they were all still in a sort of adrenaline daze having just performed in the Oscars an hour earlier. They were surrounded by Hollywood legends and all amped up. Steve watched Adam stride confidently over to the Oscar statues sitting on a shiny black table. He looked around cautiously with wide eyes. Then he turned and looked back, smiling a mouth full of large silver braces. His two crony friends egged him on. "Yeah! Adam! Do it, Adam!"

Adam picked up an Oscar and put it under his sweatshirt while his friends hooted and hollered and clapped.

"Oh shit! He did it!" Andre cackled while lifting his arm in a sign of victory.

An older man in a tuxedo appeared out of nowhere and grabbed Adam by the arm and scolded him. Adam quickly put the statue back down and ran off. Steve shook his head and rolled his eyes. He didn't like Adam all that much. He wasn't an awful person; he was just too brash. He couldn't believe the kid had tried to steal an Oscar during the Oscars. What a delinquent. Returning to the group, Adam breathed heavy short breaths and smiled broadly. His braces blocked any semblance of teeth when he smiled.

"Did you guys see that shit?!" he said.

"You see what I did Steve?! Fresh, right!?"

"Yeah, sure. Dope," Steve said turning to look straight ahead into the auditorium which was now emptying of people. Steve made it clear that he wasn't impressed and turned to his left. A slightly overweight woman with reddish short curly hair dressed in a fancy black dress sat just a few feet away on the steps. She was the only adult there also sitting on the steps with them. His friend Mike giddily told him that it was Shirley Temple.

"Isn't that cool?!" he said smiling.

She smiled and Steve shook her hand when she offered. Just then, he spotted an older man donning red-tinted sunglasses walking toward him. The man was smiling. Steve thought it was cool that the guy was wearing shades indoors at night. That's how he would do it if he were a star, he thought to himself. He recognized the guy from the movies, mainly "The Shining" and a boring movie called "Reds" that his parents had taken him to see. The man stopped in front of Steve and looked at him. He was a towering presence.

"You kids were fantastic!" he bellowed.

"First time at the Oscars?" he said looking down at Steve.

"Ahh....yeah," Steve said.

"What's your favorite movie?"

"Um...Raiders of the Lost Ark. I prefer comic books."

"Is that a fact?" he said with a chuckle.

"Yeah. They should make more superhero movies."

"Not likely, my friend. Not likely."

"You ever been in a superhero movie?"

"Ahh...I'm not quite the superhero type," he whispered, leaning closer.

"Maybe you could play a bad guy," Steve offered as the man walked off clutching his trophy.

The man stopped suddenly and smiled. Then he looked down at Steve again.

"Welcome to the big-time, kid," he said, just before disappearing.

The next day, after the Oscars, Steve noticed that the world seemed obsessed with the event. There were pictures of celebrities from the show on the cover of every newspaper. Steve didn't understand what all the fuss was about. He was only ten, but it was clear to him that these "famous people" as he knew them now, had some kind of superhuman quality that made them different from regular people for some reason. He'd seen it all up close and the whole thing hadn't seemed like that big a deal. Seeing it all through a child's eyes made it seem a bit absurd, which it was. He'd even noticed himself being treated differently by his friends and teachers at school, especially his science teacher Mr. Sachs. Just being near these people had given him something. Maybe their power had somehow seeped into him making him more interesting. Steve who'd never felt seen in his life, relished this newfound fountain of attention, which was short-lived like a crack high.

It was clear to him now that in American society, being famous was critical and Steve quickly took mental notes. He liked the attention and, once that door was opened, there was no shutting it again. That same door had been inched slightly open just two years earlier, except that then, Steve hadn't been aware of it.

It was at Mike Ferrari's birthday, June something, 1980. All Steve remembered was that school was out so it must have been about June 24th. The party which, as he recalled, had been fun had taken place in Central Park. Mike's parents were dropping kids off at their respective Manhattan apartments in the family station wagon. The car was packed to capacity with Steve cramped way, way in the back where there weren't any seats available. A bunch of kids, mostly girls, were in the front singing "99 Bottles of beer on the wall!" He'd never heard it before and immediately hated the song which seemed pointless.

More room was becoming available in the back as kids were being dropped off. It was now Steve, Mike, Arvin, Peter, Nicky, and at least two others. The awful singing had finally stopped, and the kids were now telling jokes. Everyone seemed to have one at the ready. Arvin yelled one out confidently.

"What's brown and sits in the attic?! Diarrhea of Anne Frank!" the kids laughed.

Nicky yelled one out that he didn't understand at all. "What did the midget say to the woman when he walked into her? Gee your hair smells terrific!" Everyone howled. Steve soon realized they were all just reciting jokes from the "Truly Tasteless Jokes" book that was popular in his school.

The more jokes they told; the more Steve felt left out. Suddenly, at the perfect moment, a joke popped into his head out of nowhere. He'd heard it from one of his older sister's mean friends, Betsy Palmer. The joke didn't seem very funny, but it was short and at least he'd be taking part in this activity.

"I have a joke," Steve finally chimed in. Everyone got quiet and looked at him. Mike Ferrari had a flashlight in his hand and shined it directly on his face. With the bright light in his face, Steve squinted. What if they didn't like it? He barely even understood the joke he was about to tell. Fuck, why hadn't he just kept his stupid mouth shut? The car was quiet. Now he was forced to deliver. Stage fright kicked in. He was frozen and couldn't remember the joke. He'd felt this before whenever people looked directly at him. Steve was an intensely shy kid yet at the same time craved attention since he barely got any at home.

"Knock, knock," he said, remembering the joke.

"Who's there?" everyone asked in unison.

"Joe."

"Joe who?" they asked.

"Joe Mama!"

There was a second of silence and then the entire station wagon burst into hysterics. Mike doubled over holding his stomach as if the joke were hurting him. Steve was amazed but more importantly relieved. The reaction was way bigger than he'd ever anticipated. He hadn't even expected to get a laugh. He noticed even Mike's parents laughing. He'd made adults laugh? This was big.

"That's s-o-o-o hilarious!" Mike said, still laughing.

Steve felt a sudden rush of warmth throughout his body that he'd never felt before. He didn't even know what it was exactly. All he knew was that he enjoyed the feeling. A few minutes ago, he had just been sitting back not saying anything and now he was the star of the moment. He was almost embarrassed at how well the joke had done.

Nicky tried to follow up with a knock-knock joke and it bombed something awful. Everyone mocked Nicky who glared at Steve. He felt bad for Nicky but was confused by his animosity. It turns out Nicky was jealous of the attention Steve was getting and quickly turned on him. Mike took the flashlight and shined it back on Steve who was now officially the funniest one in the car. The god of the station wagon.

A shift happened that night. It changed the way people saw Steve. The change was almost instant. Steve was funny. And being funny got people to pay attention to him. And just like a surfer searching their entire life for the perfect wave, Steve was hooked from that moment on. He had found his perfect wave.

"Ladies and gentlemen, introducing Steve Collin!" Mike Ferrari announced Steve by imitating Ed McMahon.

Everyone in the car clapped. This would be the only thing he remembered from that entire year. Years later, others present in the car would recall that moment to Steve too, illustrating that the size of the moment wasn't just in his head. Something palpable had transpired in that tiny brown station wagon in the middle of Manhattan. Steve discovered that comedy was power.

A year later, he saw a movie with his father about a military school called "Taps." They showed a trailer before it for the John Belushi movie "Neighbors," a film which ended up being a notorious misfire and critical disaster. The trailer for it, however, was funny. Steve's father laughed heartily during the trailer. This got Steve's attention and he unconsciously made a mental note that never fully went away.

His father liked comedy and that was a way to get his attention, especially given that his father was a member of the silent generation. He wasn't affectionate and never gave much overt encouragement. Never hugged him or told him he loved him, but Steve knew that he laughed at funny things. It was these two moments that subconsciously put him on a path of sorts.

That day, in 1981, Steve unconsciously decided he was going to be a comedy star. Perhaps, one day, his father would watch him and laugh at what Steve was doing and saying onscreen. It was a simple plan really. Just become a comedian who stars in movies and gain approval from the person closest to you. Oddly, Steve would come to realize that this is probably how most comedians decide to become comedians. Inattentive parents at the movies with their kids were funneling the entertainment industry with showbiz hopefuls. It never even dawned on Steve that he wouldn't be a star. Why would he not be? After all, how hard could it be to become a comedy star? He was already the funniest kid in his grade.

CHAPTER 3:

A SMALL DARK ROOM IN THE BACK OF SOMEPLACE

S TEVE WAS IN THE MIDDLE OF YET ANOTHER AWFUL Bumble date. He had been single for about four years and was now a lawyer. At 45 years old, his 47-year-old date, who didn't look anything like her pictures, babbled on about herself. None of her life stories were intriguing. She had no idea of this, of course. Every time Steve commented on not being familiar with something she said, she would make a pained face and shake her head.

"I went skiing in the Champs-Élysées," she said.

"Oh, where's that?"

"You don't know where that is?" she replied as if he'd asked her what a shoe was.

Steve was finding this common lately. Meeting unattractive women in their late forties who were neither interesting nor pleasant to be around. It was mind-blowing. There was something about New York that gave women a sense of entitlement and delusion. He'd seen it over and over on the apps. Forty-four year-old women who said they "definitely wanted to have kids." Surely, a 44-year-old woman must be aware of how biology works.

Then he'd meet the women and realize they weren't living in the real world and perhaps were hoping to find a sorcerer. And he was meeting a lot of such women. Women who were exasperated that he wasn't ready to get married by the second drink.

"Do you want to get married?" one woman asked him within ten minutes of meeting him. When he said he wasn't sure, she got up and left, saying it wasn't going to work. That seemed a bit forward. Many of them seemed disgusted by Steve's inability to commit after three minutes. As if he'd been stringing her along for ten years. He was starting to think he'd be single for-ever and maybe that wasn't a bad thing nowadays.

So here he was with another one of these single, never-married, 47-year-olds, with no kids, who wasn't even trying to be charming in the slightest. No one seemed to have manners anymore, especially since dating apps were now giving people the illusion of end-less options.

The cold woman with no manners sipped on her third vodka and blabbed on about herself and never asked him anything. Whenever Steve tried to talk about himself, he was shot down.

"I was on the Oscars once," he commented.

"Huh?" she said narrowing her eyes as if to say, "How dare you have the audacity to interrupt my fascinating story about buying a hat!"

"Huh?" she said again when Steve didn't answer. It was the fifth or sixth 'huh' to come out of her, especially since she hadn't given Steve much of a chance to speak. Anytime he said something, she replied "huh?" as if she hadn't heard him. By the fifth time she did it, he couldn't stand it. He almost asked if she was hard of hearing.

"So, I have to ask you something. I googled you and I found this clip of you from Comedy Central. Are you a comedian or something?" she asked with a pained face.

"Ummm...I used to be," Steve replied.

"Really? I mean, no offense but you haven't seemed very funny this whole date."

Steve finished the last of his soda and said he had to go. She looked at him blankly. He had made a rule to get out of these dates as fast as possible if they went awry, which this one had quickly.

"I have to go home."

"Huh?"

Steve didn't repeat himself. He was done with that. If she didn't get it on the first shot that was that.

"Fine, okay then. I have to go too," she said, gulping the drink she hadn't even thanked him for. Getting free drinks was obviously her birthright, not something to be thankful for in the slightest.

"Can you at least call me an uber?" she moaned.

"Huh?" Steve responded.

The woman walked off in a huff. Had he been that bad? Why was she so upset with him? He started to realize that maybe he wasn't the problem after all. He was relieved she was gone. One more "huh?" might have sent him into a rage. Now he could go home and just lay alone in his spacious bed. He was older now and a good night's sleep was often more enjoyable than sex.

He ordered another drink from the older tattooed bartender with her huge rack shoved up to her chin. He'd heard she used to do porn. He noticed the TV above the bar was playing the Robert Redford film "The Natural" with no sound. Steve stared at the screen with his mouth agape. It was the scene in the hospital where Robert Redford was lying in bed talking to Glenn Close. He knew the scene well. *Things sure turned out different,* Steve heard the words run through his head and turned away from the TV as if it pained his eyes to look directly into the bright screen.

In his periphery, he spotted a young woman wearing a hooded sweatshirt. She was holding a notepad and reading it as she walked. She had on glasses and a serious expression. He knew this look. Surely, she was a comedian and a new one at that. He watched her walk through a red curtain in the back of the place. It was almost like something right out of a David Lynch film.

Steve stood up and walked slowly over with his soda water. He didn't want to keep going, but he couldn't help himself. He peeked his head through the curtain and saw about ten people sitting on stools with notepads. All of them were sloppily dressed, mostly in hoodies and jeans. Yeah, these were comedians all right. They all had on the unofficial uniforms. A young Asian guy wearing a crumpled red t-shirt, faded jeans, and old Adidas sneakers stood in the corner holding a mic. There was a small spotlight on him that barely lit the top of his body. He was telling jokes that barely garnered a reaction. Steve stood back just outside the threshold of the room as if entering would drag him back years. The sound came through a shitty beat-up-looking speaker right next to the comedian. Every now and then, the mic would go out and then come back on. It always threw the comics when it shorted. Steve hadn't been in a room like this in years. He'd left all this behind years ago. As bad as the Asian comedian was, he was more enjoyable to listen to than his awful 47-year-old Bumble date. The words "so close" echoed in his head. The station wagon flashed in his head again. It'd been months since he'd thought of it and now there it was. It kind of bummed him out. He watched the Asian comic struggle through his set and Steve felt sad.

CHAPTER 4:

A CITY OF BAD CHARACTERS

S TEVE STOOD IN THE MIDDLE OF A SMALL COFFEE shop in the Valley. He was seconds away from going up on "stage," for lack of a better word, to do his three minutes in front of about twelve other comedians. He was twenty-six and had been in LA for only four weeks. He was still figuring it all out as best as he could. The city was vast and hard to navigate, and he felt overwhelmed most of the time by its largeness and the lack of driving skills Angelenos possessed. It was as if everyone there was constantly stoned and took forever to do anything.

There was a dark vibe to the city that he couldn't quite get past. The city seemed to be haunted by the ghosts of broken dreams and desperation. It wasn't the glamorous city he'd been promised by the media. His overweight, hairy, next-door neighbor always left his blinds open for everyone to see the hundreds of pictures of nude women pasted all over his walls. The guy sat in his underwear and read porn nonchalantly every night as if he were reading "The DaVinci Code." The guy had clearly murdered people. Possibly a failed actor or comedian who'd lost his mind and was now consumed by the darkness behind some dumpster in a parking lot. If news cameras showed up to interview Steve one day about his serial killer neighbor Steve knew what he would say.

"Yeah, I knew he was a murderer. He seemed exactly like the kind of guy who would murder people. I was sure he was killing hookers."

Everyone in LA wanted to be seen, so it made perfect sense that Steve had ended up there. LA was like one big, neglected, child-support meeting. It wasn't surprising that the porn industry had begun there. The town was full of people desperate for attention in any capacity. The type of people who could be persuaded to have sex on camera for money. Steve had seen the HOLLYWOOD sign on his fateful childhood ride to the Oscars and knew he'd live there someday. He didn't know how tough it would be though, but very few did. LA wasn't full of stars; it was full of perverts like his neighbor. Lucky for Steve, he was way too shy to ever do porn, at least for now. Who knew what could happen in the city of broken dreams?

He had accidentally discovered an open mic scene that got him out of his tiny Hollywood studio apartment which only had a futon, two pieces of lawn furniture, and a tiny TV screen with HBO. Everyone at the coffee shop open mic was about Steve's age, save for a 50-something-year-old woman with grey hair who'd decided to try and pursue comedy after a failed marriage and a midlife crisis. Most people seemed to go into stand-up after failing at everything else.

Steve watched a tall blondish guy finish his set. He was very animated, and his voice was punchy. The guy did well and seemed to be a regular since the crowd supported him. The MC took the mic from his hand.

"Give it up for Daniel Tosh!"

The host was a young, blond, arrogant Russian guy who was way too confident for what he looked like. Steve immediately disliked the guy because of his extreme arrogance but he also reminded him of the Russian teacher who'd fucked him over his senior year of high school. The Russian comic's whole act consisted of corny jokes about being from Russia. They were hacky and completely stolen from the '80s Russian comic, Yakov Smirnoff the "what a country" guy who was considered a hack even back in 1985.

The surly Russian with confidence was Dan Kinno, a 19-year-old kid with swagger, and a manager who sat watching in the back of the room.

"In America, you need a nice car and expensive house to get women. In Russia, if you have toilet paper, you're the king. The women flock to you!" was one of his punchlines. All his other jokes were basically the same.

He brought Steve up to the stage with a snarky insult because being an asshole was his shtick. "This guy is really making a name for himself in comedy. You've probably seen him....over there before."

It amazed Steve how cocky the guy was at such a young age. LA was the perfect place for him. A young comic with confidence *and* a unique hook was gold there. Talent was completely irrelevant in this town, something Steve had yet to discover. Steve walked onstage to barely any applause from the other comics and did three minutes of newish jokes. Some drew small laughs, and some drew nothing.

"I um...I used to date this girl; she could have been a model. Yeah, she was that stupid," Steve said and got barely any reaction. He heard one guy laughing. It stood out since he was the only one laughing and also because his laugh sounded like a slow moan. It was the most unique laugh Steve had ever heard. The guy was sitting in the front row. He was thin, with leathery skin and sharp facial features. He died laughing after every joke Steve told.

"So, what else? I'm writing a weed-themed horror movie right now. It's called 'I Have No Idea What You Did Last Summer'."

The laughing guy spasmed wildly in his chair and applauded loudly as if he were having a heart attack. Steve told his last joke.

"So um...you ever seen a girl that's so hot you get mad at your girlfriend? Then you see your girlfriend and you can't tell her why you're in a bad mood. It's like 'honey what's the matter?' You can't say, 'well I didn't appreciate the way you weren't this girl I wanted to have sex with'," Steve said, causing the guy to stand up and clap while rocking his body back and forth and contorting his face uncontrollably. The rest of the room stared as the guy jumped up and down. Steve may not have had the entire room, but he had one guy in hysterics which, looking back, was the best kind of comedian to be.

If everyone liked you, then you were probably a hack. If only some people loved you, then you were most likely a genius. Like Darryl Hall said after their album went to number one on the charts; "Number one? I thought we were better than that."

Steve finished and the Russian hack made another dig at him. The lone laughing guy was on next. He stood on the stage with the mic held about a foot from his face, his right arm held up, and began his set. He spoke loudly and punchy. His jokes were funny but extremely dark. It was as if he wanted the audience to hate him.

"Hello, ladies and gentlemen! My name is James Painter, and I am ahh...filled with hate!" he said in a booming voice that bordered on psychotic.

"I don't understand the Special Olympics. One thing I can tell you about the Special Olympics is that they were not a retarded person's idea dammit! I can't imagine some retarded guy waking up one day and saying to his friend, 'well let's see, seeing as how I lose control of my bowels every time I bend over to tie my shoes, I think I'll try pole vaulting today!'" he yelled. The room was silent.

"Uh....man, that ate shit didn't it," he said, staring down at his feet. He ended his set with a joke about masturbating to Britney Spears.

"Oops! I did it again dammit! Sorry Britney!" he yelled to no reaction and got off the stage with his notebook in hand. The crowd barely applauded. He smiled a painful smile and hurried out the back door.

Steve stood outside on the back patio sipping on a Corona he'd been forced to buy in order to perform. James Painter approached him slowly.

"Ahh...Dude, I just wanted to say ahh....that was fucking hilarious. How long have you been doing comedy?" he asked in a slow drawl, his arms folded tightly.

"Oh, thanks. Ummm...about a year."

"Man, a ye-e-e-ar? Wo-o-o-o-w!" he said stomping his foot down. "Du-u-u-de, you're really, really funny. That really cracked me up," he added while leaning his torso back uncomfortably. This had happened to Steve at various stages in his life. Occasionally, someone would be blown away by his humor. They wouldn't simply think he was a "funny guy," they'd be almost astonished by his humor. Steve felt he was getting better, but this guy was making him rethink things. Maybe he *was* good.

Steve had moved to Cali after kicking around New York City for about a year doing bad open mics here and there. He hadn't moved there to make it big, more to just get away from New York City after his mother died suddenly. He just needed to get away. Her death had changed everything for him. And although he wasn't enjoying LA, he was happy to no longer be in the apartment where he had watched her die.

"I don't know why the hell no one was laughing. You're am-aa-zing," the guy continued.

"Thanks," Steve answered, appreciating the praise but not completely comfortable with it either. He wondered why everyone else wasn't laughing too. Comedy and showbiz were all about getting everyone to like you right? Steve always found new and creative ways to beat himself up.

James was friendly and funny but also had a manic energy that was off-putting. He had a kind of Quentin Tarantino, coke-like energy and constantly rambled on, usually about comedy. Steve was wary of the guy at first as he often was with people.

A tall Jewish guy went up a few minutes after Steve. He wore thick glasses and had long curly hair. He held the mic lightly and slumped over a bit. His name was Ari Shaffir, and he did a lot of jokes about being Jewish. There were hard and fast rules to stand-up in LA. First of all, you had to make a joke, up top, about yourself, usually your ethnicity. This was a way to explain to the crowd who you were at the start to make them comfortable. Then you had to do some quick jokes that told the crowd what your persona was. You had to make it clear right away. Were you the nervous Jewish guy with no confidence, the cocky Russian, the strange nerdy guy who had trouble with women, the dorky married guy, who were you? The audience had to know, and they had to know fast. This was how you got a late-night spot, which was extremely hard for newbies to come by in 2000. Comedy had boomed just years earlier and now there weren't many outlets for stand-up since it had gone cold. If you wanted to do stand-up in the early 2000s, then you really had to *want* to do stand-up. At the time it was the equivalent of opening a members-only jacket factory.

Back in the comedy heyday of the '70s and '80s a "Tonight Show" appearance could catapult a comic to superstardom overnight and get them a sitcom. Those times were long gone. Johnny had retired and been replaced by the lame Jay Leno, and a "Tonight Show" appearance would now maybe get you more road work and some weekend spots at the Improv. There were also Conan and Letterman, but those shows rarely used stand-ups and they didn't make you a star. Some guys who'd done Letterman over 20 times weren't household names. Most late-night appearances now just led to more late-night appearances.

Comedy Central was developing some stand-up showcase shows, but, for the most part, comedy opportunities were few and far between in 2000. The only way you got a late-night spot was if you had been doing it for a long time. Which meant new comics had to compete against comics who had been in the business for 20 years.

Steve often heard comics talk about the lucrative development deals doled out to comedians in the early '90s like tic tacs. By the late '90s, the practice of handing out large development deals to stand-ups was long gone and had come to a complete halt by 1999, the year Steve started. His timing was impeccable.

Every new stand-up was trying to develop a marketable act that might get them on a sitcom.

"You have to be a character they can just stick into a TV show," the slick co-owner of the Improv who managed his friend, Kjell, once said. The manager provided loads of unrequested advice to Steve about how to make it as a comedian. Steve was wary of his "tips" usually offered in a patronizing manner. The guy seemed a bit slimy and "showbizzy" for Steve. Not surprising since he was part of the Hollywood industry.

The manager was a huge Johnny Carson fan and name-dropped a lot. It was obvious from his unwanted "tips" that he was clinging to an old style of comedy that was stale to Steve. He even dropped odd names, once introducing Steve to a fidgety, short, bald guy outside the Improv as the guy who had given Freddie Prinze the gun that he used to kill himself.

Steve was confused. Was this supposed to impress him? LA was a weird place for sure. There were porn stars doing stand-up after their porn careers had dried up. Stand-up was a backup plan to porn? Stand-up was not high on the Hollywood food chain. It was more like a thing people did simply to get a foothold in showbiz and launch their acting career. No one out there was actually working at improving their stand-up, almost no one.

And what did it even mean to "be a character?" Steve was just trying to be funny and comfortable and himself onstage. Was he not supposed to be himself? Wasn't just being funny enough? All the greats seemed to be completely natural up there. And that's what he wanted to be too.

"What?! What's being funny have to do with it?" Kjell's sleazy manager once said to Steve while squinting his eyes and shaking his head. In LA, being funny wasn't even a factor comedians were at all concerned with. Everyone just wanted to be a specific marketable type, the jokes were secondary. Steve had seen a young, pretty Asian girl who barely spoke English perform regularly on the highly coveted Saturday night show at the Improv. The girl had no jokes. Everything she said was a play on Asian stereotypes. The gag seemed to be that she couldn't speak English. This town made no sense to Steve. He knew one thing for sure now. There were two types of funny. There was funny and then there was "LA" funny, meaning *not* funny.

Steve occasionally hung around the Comedy Store to watch and study the comics to see exactly what they were doing. He still barely knew what he was doing up there and figured that to learn he should watch more seasoned comics. He'd made some comedian acquaintances who worked the door such as Ari, the lanky

Jewish guy from the coffee shop open mic and a newer friendly comic with a growing rep and some "industry heat" named Bob Oshack. Oshack took a liking to Steve after watching him perform at the Valley coffee shop open mic. This upped Steve's comedy cred a great deal. Oshack had offered to refer him for an audition to become a paid regular at the Store, a highly coveted designation. Oshack was essentially a made-man at the Comedy Store and he was vouching for Steve.

He often sat in the back and watched Andrew Dice Clay, Paul Mooney, and Pauly Shore perform. Seeing "Dice" was a thrill to Steve since the guy was a giant icon when he was in high school. One night, "Dice" followed Steve on a show in the Belly Room which made him feel like he'd made it to the big time or at least had an interesting showbiz story he could tell his friends back in New York. The Store was well past its prime in 2000. Ari said it had been *the* place for comedy in the '80s. That was no more. It felt void of energy and had no spark. Comedy seemed to be in the midst of an identity crisis. Change was coming. After all, it was the millennium.

One night Steve was hanging out at the Improv bar with some of his closest comedian friends, who now included Kjell from Minnesota, James, the laughing guy, Bobby, and a pretty redhead named Kristen. The five of them often hung out at the Improv's bar area pretending to be in showbiz.

The Improv had the most Hollywood vibe out of all the clubs. Most nights, there'd be huge celebrities and comics just standing around. Agents and managers would stand at the bar chatting with the likes of Carrot Top, Emo Phillips, and Adam Sandler. That made the Improv the place to be seen. It also meant that the place was full of vampires ready to suck the life out of healthy bodies to stay afloat. No one in LA was interested in being good, they just cared about being seen talking to Matt Dillon.

Brody Stevens was a New York comic new to the LA circuit. He walked out of the showroom wearing a serious expression and rubbing his buzzed skull intently. He was exactly the kind of 'character' they wanted at the Improv, with his white button-down shirt, crisp jeans, and thick beard.

"Collin, Bjorgen, Painter. How are you fellas?" he said, stopping abruptly.

"Hey Brody, how was the show?"

"They did not seem to get on board with me. No, not a good set for me. But that's okay. Can't get them every time."

"Brody. You were great at the Store last night. You really killed," James commented with folded arms.

"Thanks, Painter. Fellas, excuse me, I have to talk big showbiz stuff. My friend Judah Friedlander is here. Also, I'm taping 'Comics Unleashed' next week. Big things are happening. Huge things. *Huge*," he said, nodding his head sharply. Brody was odd but friendly to new comics.

He walked up to a thirty-something-year-old-looking man holding a fancy cocktail and donning a fancy blue shirt, glasses, and a smile who congratulated Brody on his set even though he hadn't actually seen his set. He looked like a manager.

Brody had just done "The Craig Kilborn Show" and killed it. He now had a lot of "buzz" around him. Steve had heard, from Brody himself many times, that he was friends with Zach Galifianakis, another comic who was gaining steam fast. Being close friends with a famous comic was a huge advantage in the industry; it was almost a necessity if one wanted to move up in the ranks. It gave a comic a lot of cachet in the industry. Of course, it helped if the famous friend actually tried to assist you, which most didn't. Steve was finding that all the trite LA cliches were completely true.

Steve, Kjell, and James stood in the middle of the bar area sipping the cheapest lagers available. Since Kjell was managed by the shady slick co-owner, they felt a bit more welcome there. They, at least, had a connection to the place, a shoestring connection. Steve spotted a man with a worn-looking white Vanderbilt University hat on. He was a hacky comedian from South Carolina always shadowing Steve and his friends.

He was irritating as hell and spoke way too loudly, a pet peeve of Steve's.

"Oh fuck, there's Charlie Goodnights," Steve said.

"Ahh!" James laughed, his body jerking back in a sudden spasm.

"Just, pretend that you don't see him," Kjell said.

"It's too late for that, dude. He's looking right at me," Steve said.

"Fuck. What's his fucking problem?" Kjell asked.

"I don't know. He's so awful. How does he not know that? He bombs every single time he performs. How can he be that bad and keep going?" Steve said, causing Kjell and James to burst out laughing again.

Mark, the Vanderbilt hat guy, made his way across the room in their direction. He had ketchup on his cheek, a stained shirt, ripped pants, and some food on his face.

"Aww, man. I just killed at Mixed Nuts. I killed it. The room was on fire m-aa-n. I felt like I was flying," Mark said in a southern accent. He always told anyone who would listen about how hard he'd just killed, which was odd to Steve since he'd never seen him once kill, ever.

"Yeah? That's awesome," Steve said.

James laughed and Mark looked at him.

"Man, relax Painter," he said. "Did you get up tonight?"

"Ahh...yeah we did Jennifer's Coffee," Steve said.

"Yeah? I killed there last week," he said.

"Really? What a surprise," Steve said, sending James into hysterics.

"Ya know, I just tried out this new bit about how I'm losing my hair. It killed."

"Yeah? That's something else," Steve said with a blank expression.

Comedians were often exhausting to be around. Mark was one of those obnoxious comics who was always "on." Sometimes, he would try to be slick and shoehorn his awful bits into conversations. It was pathetic how transparent he was. He had ruined Steve's weed high with his vibe. As Mark went into his stupid new balding bit, Steve looked to his left and sighed audibly, trying to convey that he didn't want to hear his hack joke. Mark was completely oblivious to people not wanting to listen to him. He was stuck in his head all the time.

"I mean, it's like I'm losing my hair, ya know? It's like man I have a really shitty barber named god," he said.

"Get it?" he added.

"Yeah. That's great. I think you're really on to something," Steve said not even cracking a smile. James laughed audibly and put his hands over his face. He was shaking with laughter right next to Mark.

"You like it?" Mark asked Painter who just howled and spasmed.

"Yeah, I think he likes it," Steve replied with a blank expression.

"Ya know, I'm featuring at Charlie Goodnights next week," he said.

"Yeah. I know," Steve said.

"How'd you know?"

"You told me like three times already," Steve said.

James jerked back and clapped his hands.

"You wanna hear another joke I wrote?"

"Um...ya know, I can't really hear you that well. It's loud in here," Steve said.

"Oh. Okay."

"So, you know that guy the crocodile hunter?!" Mark yelled.

Mark's thickness was angering Steve now. He'd somehow thought the problem was the volume of his voice. Of course, Mark had a crocodile hunter bit, it was the go-to hack premise of the time. Every shit comedian in 2001 had a crocodile hunter joke. It was kind of an amazing phenomenon in retrospect.

Mark looked down the bar after finishing the bit that Steve hadn't listened to.

"Is that Adam Sandler?" he asked loudly.

"Ah...I guess," Steve said, praying that Mark wouldn't embarrass him.

"My friend once met him at Charlie Goodnights. I'm gonna try to talk to him," he said and walked off.

"Yeah, that's a good idea man," Steve said.

"Thank god. That guy's unbearable," Steve said after Mark walked off.

"He's such a dick. Now he's going to harass Adam Sandler?" Kjell added.

"Charlie goodnights! I heard last night he had a Charlie bad night!" Steve said in a mock southern accent causing James to crack up yet again.

"Du-u-u-de! Aa-ah!" James doubled over and stomped his foot on the ground.

"Fucking crocodile hunter jokes? Fuckin' of course," Kjell added cracking James up even more.

A thin woman with a long angular face walked in and nodded when she spotted Kjell.

"Noataro," Kjell said.

"He-e-e-ey Bjorgen," she answered, drawing out her words.

Steve said hi to the woman. He'd met her the week earlier when he killed at a club in the Valley owned by a psychopath who'd yelled at him for using the wrong bathroom. The owner was a failed comic, a trait most comedy club owners shared.

"Hey, you were really funny. Do you perform around here a lot? How come I've never heard of you?" she'd asked Steve after the show the week before.

"Um...I'm not sure. I haven't been in LA long," Steve had replied.

She'd praised Steve for about five minutes before telling him her name. Tig. She'd made him feel better. Tig performed at Largo regularly and it blew his mind that a Largo comic would compliment him. Largo was gaining popularity, especially among his group of comics who, like Steve, were new and huge comedy fans.

"Hey, I know you," Tig said while staring at Steve for a few seconds with no expression. It was like she had a constant resting poker face.

"Yeah. I met you at 'Ha Comedy' last week," he said.

She again stared at him for a few seconds before answering. She never answered right away as if she were on a slight delay or something.

"Yeah, right. You were funny as I recall," she said finally nodding slowly.

"Yeah, that's right," Steve said.

"Did you just agree with me that you're funny? That's pretty egotistical," she said, staring hard into his eyes.

"Um...I don't know. I mean...I guess so."

"Keep an eye on this one," she said to Kjell, pointing her finger at Steve and still looking in his eyes.

"He's hilarious," Kjell said.

"Yeah, so I've heard. From him. Apparently, he has trouble using the correct bathroom though," she said.

"Is Sarah here?" she asked.

"Sarah?" Steve asked.

"Yeah. Sarah Silverman. We're close friends," she said in a deadpan tone while turning her head to him with a smirk on her face.

"I saw her in the room earlier," Kjell said. "I think she might be on now."

"Cool. Did you talk to her?"

"I said hi," Kjell said.

"Cool. You guys still...talking?"

"Well, we might hang out next week. Her friend's having a party."

"Kjell, Kjell, Kjell," Tig said, shaking her head. She walked off toward the showroom.

"What a bitch," Painter said after she left. "Dude, she didn't even say hi to me. Her stand-up sucks too. She's one of those alt assholes," he exclaimed with a pained expression on his face while waving his arm in front of him.

James assumed everyone hated him. He had a real confidence issue, and it was clear that like most comics he hadn't been seen as a child. Steve found it funny the way that James constantly shit on everyone. His vitriol did get a bit overwhelming at times though. At first, Steve had thought his outrage was sort of a joke until James said that a random drive-through guy at Burger King hated him just because he screwed up his order.

"He forgot my fries! That guy fucking hates me!" he had yelled, while spit mixed with fries flew out of his mouth. "I didn't do anything to that fucking guy! Why would he hate me so much?!"

Brian approached Kjell and asked him if he wanted to go next since a comic had just canceled their appearance. Brian was the douchey house room manager who secretly wanted to be a comic, his only obstacle being that he had no talent. He was one of those comedy manager/booker types, usually bitter wannabe comedians who couldn't hack it, so they used their power to spitefully fuck over new comics who were actually putting themselves out there. Brian was one of the worst of the lot, if not *the* worst. LA was an entire town built and run on spite.

Kjell agreed and took out his small loose-leaf comedy notebook from his back pocket quickly, something every comic had with them almost at all times. Comedy notebooks were a comedian's weapon of choice.

"Oh man, dude that's awesome. Fucking Improv spot. Nice." James said, leaning back.

Steve immediately felt nervous for Kjell. He also felt a ping of jealousy since Kjell was actually getting some breaks. He was set to appear at the Montreal Comedy Festival in a month, a huge steppingstone for comics. Kjell wasn't funnier than Steve, but he had a likable and easy-going presence. His material wasn't that strong, but he was charming and good-looking with a warmth that came through onstage. Everybody liked Kjell. Painter was the complete opposite and Steve was somewhere in between.

They all walked into the crowded showroom and sat in the comedians' section in the back. Sarah Silverman was onstage in the middle of a bit about Chinese people, racism, and getting out of jury duty. She wrapped up with a joke about her friend asking her to check him for testicular cancer. "He asked me to check his testicles for lumps. I check them for him once a day, but only until he comes." The crowd laughed loudly, and she got off.

The young unfunny host with long blonde hair ran onstage. The guy was a known hack around town. He went into an impression of Beeker from "The Muppets" shaking his head up and down and mumbling gibberish. The crowd ate it up. Painter groaned loudly and Tig shook her head at the next table.

After the host did a horrible bit about Chris Farley playing Batman, he brought Kjell up. Steve couldn't help but feel jealous. He hated being jealous. After all, Kjell was his friend and he wanted to be happy for him. Unfortunately, in comedy, it was all but impossible to not be completely self-absorbed. If being supportive and happy for others came naturally to him, he would have joined the Peace Corps, not pursued comedy. Comedy was a competition when it came down to it, and there weren't many spots to go around.

Kjell had a pretty strong set. His jokes weren't great, but he had good banter with the friendly crowd. He knew how to get a crowd on his side, which was the most important thing in LA comedy. Steve had great jokes but struggled with letting the audience in. He was loose onstage but often felt the audience was secondary and that it wasn't important that they like him. Most of the time, he didn't even want the audience to like him. He never wanted to pander to anyone. Kjell, however, got crowds to like him without pandering. He was exactly what the industry wanted right then.

After the show, Kjell, Steve, and James sat with Tig and Sarah Silverman in the bar area at a U-shaped booth. Sarah flirtatiously commented a few times, saying that Kjell had bombed horribly. Kjell was drunk and simply laughed the comments off.

"Seriously Kjell, you should give up after that set. Just go back to Minneapolis with your tail between your short stubby legs."

"How bout you two?" she asked staring at Steve.

"What?" Steve asked.

"What?" she said, mimicking his voice.

"Do you do comedy?" Sarah asked.

"Ahh...yeah, we do," James said with a serious expression.

"Okay, you don't sound too sure," she said.

"Ahh...no I am sure," James replied with serious eyes.

"Are you funny?" she asked, looking into Steve's eyes.

"He's great," Kjell said.

"Really? Great, huh? That's great. You seem fun. More fun than this one," she said, nodding her chin in James's direction while taking a sip from her glass.

"Ahh...yeah, great," James said, with a tense expression.

"Relax bro, just a joke. Get this guy some coke huh?" she said.

"Dude, okay, I'm relaxed, yeah," he said, fidgeting with his hands.

Although by industry standards, Steve wasn't making any kind of headway in LA, he *was* starting to get positive feedback from other comedians and was developing a reputation among the open mic scene as being someone who always had new jokes. James often marveled at Steve's comedic ability. It was almost as if James were his publicist the way that he talked Steve up to others.

Since Steve had nothing to do in LA except go out and do open mics, he had begun to "find his voice" as they say. And in his brand-new class of comedians at the bottom of the LA comedy scene, this meant Steve was becoming a standout. He killed almost every time he performed. He became a favorite in the smaller rooms around town. Sure, they weren't good shows, but he was getting noticed by some of the best new comics around who were regulars at the Store and Largo.

But he had been in LA for two years, and Steve was growing impatient. He didn't feel like he fit in there. He had moved up from the open mic circuit a bit and was now a semi-regular at comedy clubs, including shows at the Comedy Store's Belly Room. He had once watched Bob Saget destroy in the Original Room at the Store which, to him, was indicative of the disparity between the clubs and this new comedy scene outside the clubs.

One night, Steve was hanging out in a dark booth watching Damon Wayans in the back of the Original Room, when Ari, who was now a paid regular at the Store, told Steve he was going by another big show on the Strip down from the Store at a bar called Dublin's. Ari invited Steve to check it out since it was one of the "hottest shows in LA," featuring the best, new, stand-ups in town and was packed every Monday night.

Steve drove over to the trendy and too cool Sunset Strip bar and thought it seemed lame. There was something off about it. Dublin's had a showbiz comedy club vibe. The place was flashy, with green neon lights, and plenty of beautiful women all hoping to fuck Ben Affleck. Dane Cook, who was just starting to blow up, was now the main draw every week.

Cook closed out the show every week and the crowd adored him. Ralphie Mae was killing when Steve walked in. He told jokes about his weight and spoke in a confident southern drawl. This guy was a character the industry knew what to do with. The show was hosted by a surfer-type, good-looking, blonde dude by the name of Jay.

After the show, Steve was introduced to Jay by a female comedian he'd met months earlier at a show on Pico. She'd approached Steve after he killed and asked him to help her write jokes. The woman was excited to see Steve there. She was a fan and a Yale grad who'd studied Shakespeare and was now doing stand-up. She seemed out of her mind and desperate for fame. Steve guessed her parents hadn't shown her any attention growing up either.

Jay flirted with the woman before agreeing to book Steve, which made Steve believe he had scored the booking mainly so Jay could get into the woman's pants. Either way, this was a huge deal and Steve felt like this might break him to another level. He also thought she might sleep with him which she didn't. But she did think he was funny and talked him up to Jay.

"Oh my God! You're a genius! You should be on TV! You're a star!" she kept telling him later at a bar in the Valley. She sucked back vodka sodas and asked if he wanted to get high.

"You will kill Dublin's! You will kill! Agents and managers are always there!" she proclaimed loudly.

She kept touching Steve's leg but then told him she had a boyfriend, sort of.

The night he showed up to do his set, he was surprised to find the room at Dublin's almost empty. He walked up to Jay and told him he had been booked. Jay looked at him with a blank expression and then told him he'd be going on second. He was a lot less friendly this time. Jay turned his back and went back to hitting on a blonde chick with her breasts hanging out of her tight pink tank top which read "MY BOYFRIEND'S OUT OF TOWN." She wore a scowl on her face like most of the women in LA did. Steve found it amusing that she would wear a see-through shirt with such a provocative statement and then act annoyed to be receiving attention.

The show started at 7:30 p.m. There were about thirty people there. Most of them were talking or didn't pay attention to the comics because they weren't Dane Cook. Steve watched the first comedian, a tall and very handsome guy with huge arms, short thick hair, and square geeky glasses. He looked like Clark Kent or a '50s matinee idol and had an accent that sounded Canadian. He performed to the crowd that barely cared. The mic looked tiny in his giant hands, it was almost comedic how small he made the mic look. This was just the pre-show to the main event. These newer comedians were the ones who performed as people took their seats and got drinks. This was LA and if you weren't "somebody" then why would anyone pay attention? It made Steve feel right at home in a way.

Steve watched the big Canadian guy perform. He had impressive jokes even though no one was laughing or listening. At first glance, he seemed to be your typical LA comedian. Good looking and confident. Most comedians in LA were really just actors who couldn't get their foot in the door and were trying stand-up as a sort of backdoor entry. But this guy had well-written jokes, a rarity in LA comedy.

Steve watched him closely. Every single joke had a good premise and punch. The guy was an actual comedian. Another thing Steve had discovered over the years was that if a comedian thought another comedian was funny, they didn't laugh at their jokes. They'd just watch in total silence and appreciate them. But if a comic thought another comic was okay *then* they'd laugh. The less a comic laughed at another comic, the more likely it was that they actually admired them.

When the Canadian giant was done, he got off and Douchey Jay took the mic. "Give it up for Lachlan Patterson! Yeah!" Then he introduced Steve, getting his name wrong, of course. This made sure Steve knew he meant nothing in this room.

Steve went up to tepid applause which ended before he even got to the mic. No one was listening, but he powered through his set. He started out by shitting on the room commenting on how no one was paying attention. He did his jokes and the three or so people accidentally listening chuckled since he went off-script. The rest of the beautiful vapid crowd full of fake tits just talked and drank. He was given the light after about 7 minutes and got off again to hardly any applause. This was his big Dublin's debut? It wasn't exactly Elton John at the Troubadour. He wasn't going to be a star overnight. He was funny, but how the fuck was anyone going to ever know if they wouldn't pay attention?

After his set, Steve ran into a friend from high school at the bar who was now a somewhat successful film actor. He'd been in a few movies that had become huge cult hits. The friend was with a famous movie actor who was surprisingly friendly.

Every so often, one of his old, high school friends turned movie star would call him to hang out but that happened less often with every passing year. They were on a whole different plane now, and in LA it was important to only surround yourself with those who could benefit your career. He knew a bunch of other aspiring comedians and actors in their mid-'20s who were ready to take on the world and were simply waiting for their chance to realize the dreams that had manifested when they were just kids. They each probably had their own station wagon moment that had propelled them to move to LA and follow the new American dream of becoming famous and showing everyone that they were wrong about them.

"Hey Steve, I saw your set, funny man."

"Thanks," Steve replied.

"He's fucking funny man," Steve's high school friend said.

"How long have you done stand-up?" the movie actor asked him.

"About two years."

"That's great. I did improv with Del Close in Chicago," he said.

"Oh yeah?" Steve said, not knowing who that was.

"I always wanted to try stand-up but was too scared," he said.

"Really?" Steve said, squinting his eyes.

"Yeah. It looks like the scariest thing in the world," he replied.

The affable movie actor bought Steve a drink from the busty tan waitress and Steve hung out with them for the remainder of the night at their table in the corner. He enjoyed the perks of hanging out with a movie star. This included endless attention from women and bar staff. Jay, of course, was a lot friendlier too, which made Steve hate him even more. At the end of the night, the movie actor hugged Steve hard and told him they should stay in touch and hang out sometime. He seemed overly intrigued by stand-up comedy and seemed to want to be a part of it in some way.

Three weeks later, Steve ran into the movie actor guy at the Comedy Store and was ignored by him.

"Hey there, I'm Roy's friend. Remember? We hung out a few weeks back," Steve said extending his hand.

"I don't know who you are man," he said, turning away in a hostile manner, basically telling Steve to fuck off with his body language. The famous movie actor wasn't nearly as warm as he'd been that first time and Steve immediately decided that the guy sucked. It was yet another Hollywood encounter that Steve was now accustomed to. It was no wonder that Steve enjoyed watching the movie actor's career go south over the next few years. How dare he have the nerve to blow him off.

CHAPTER 5:

THE SCOOMIES

S TEVE KEPT DOING THE OPEN MICS. HE'D DISCOVERED one in Westwood at the Brewco. It was the most popular mic in town with celeb drop-ins. And it was extremely cliquey, almost like a gang, a passive-aggressive gang. Anyone could sign up, but there was a judgmental inside crew that watched every performer. If they didn't know you, it wasn't pretty. They'd make sure you didn't get laughs from anyone on the inside. This mic was theirs and they weren't just going to let in newbies. Steve went there every week with Kjell, James, and now Lachlan, the Canadian giant. They'd become friends since the time Steve saw his last show. Sometimes, Ari would also join them, and they'd all sit together in the unofficial visiting section on the right side of the room.

Steve had a good set. He did his "A material." This was a room where you had to bring out your big guns.

You had to show them you meant business. If a new comic made people laugh, it was usually by accident. You had to be so funny that people had no choice but to laugh, almost involuntarily. Steve did one of his strongest bits at the time. It was about the '80s Lionel Richie video "Hello" where Lionel Richie falls in love with a blind girl who sculpts his head and it looks exactly like him. Except that Lionel Richie barely has any reaction to the sculpture done by a blind woman that looks exactly like him. Steve comments that that had happened to him once. He had fallen in love with a blind woman who sculpted his face and it looked exactly like Lionel Richie.

He finished on a laugh and got off. He had done well, and the room knew it. A female comedian who came on after him made a snarky comment about Steve's material which didn't go over. A big shock. The female, a big shot there who would later become the spokesperson for a national insurance company for the next 15 years, had taken a shot at Steve and missed. Her dig at Steve wasn't even appreciated by her own clique, which meant he had impressed them.

A month later, Steve found out he'd been nominated for a scoomie award. The awards show was held at the Brewco open mic and was supposed to be tongue in cheek, but on some level was not tongue in cheek at all and actually completely out of cheek. The show mirrored the actual Hollywood awards shows with a long red carpet, photographers, and comedians acting as interviewers holding microphones and calling comedians over. Everyone was dressed up as if for the Oscars. It was all supposed to be a joke but there was a feeling that it wasn't a joke at all.

Steve was shocked to learn that he'd been nominated for two awards. Just months earlier, he'd barely been acknowledged at the place. Still, he had performed regularly at the open mic for the last few months as some act of defiance to show that he wasn't intimidated by this cliquey open mic. They actually challenged him. Killing there meant something.

He was asked to present the award for "Most Improved Comedian." He was told by the producer in an email that being asked to present was a huge honor. As aloof as Steve tried to seem, he was secretly ecstatic for the recognition. The "Most Improved Comedian" award was a backhanded compliment to the recipient. It was the Brewco higher-ups throwing a bone to their oddball diehard supporters of the show. Steve presented the award with a girl named Wendy. She'd written a skit for them where she admitted to having a crush on him and awkwardly tried to kiss him. It went over well in the room.

Later in the show, Chris Hardwick, the biggest name there at the time, presented an award for "Best Male Stand-up." Chris Hardwick read Steve's name as a nominee and then looked up and shook his head with his mouth agape. Then he turned to Steve who was sitting in the front row.

"Who the hell are you?! I don't know you! You come here?!" he exclaimed pointing at Steve.

The room got eerily silent except for some uncomfortable laughter in the back. Steve was mortified by the whole thing but didn't say anything. He smiled and raised his hands in an "aw shucks" kind of way to convey he was unfazed. Luckily, he was wearing sunglasses, something he picked up from Jack Nicholson that time at the Oscars, so any embarrassment was undetectable. He played it cool, aloof. Hardwick was their messiah and was none too pleased by Steve's acceptance into *his* tribe. He was still riding on his fast-fading MTV fame. Hardwick was currently hosting a dating show on Fox about people forced to be on a cruise together and was somewhat of a comedy snob. Which was perplexing since he wasn't currently doing A-list comedy work.

Still, Hardwick was currently the biggest big shot at the SCOOMIES, and he had just displayed his insecurities for all to see. He obviously felt threatened by this new guy who was getting some buzz. Buzz? Steve hated that term. But could it be that he had some? For the king of the place to be rattled by Steve was the highest compliment one could get at the Brewco. Steve knew something had shifted.

Steve didn't win in his award categories. To cover up his faint disappointment, he got drunk and smoked a joint outside with Wendy and another girl named Carol. A few of the Brewco regulars approached him and apologized about Hardwick.

"That was very rude of him, and I told him so," one feisty girl with braids and wearing a kilt said. One thing was certain, Steve was being noticed and he liked it. Ari, dressed in a cheap blue suit and a yarmulke as a joke, walked over to them and didn't miss a chance to dig into someone when they were down.

"That was funny when Hardwick called you out and embarrassed you in front of everyone," he said smiling and laughing to himself with his arms folded in front of him defensively.

"Yeah, okay," Steve replied not looking at him.

"Come on man, don't be such a little faggot," he said.

"Faggot?"

"Come on. You're being a real pussy. Don't take things so seriously," Ari said, grabbing the joint from Wendy's hand.

Steve laughed it off on the outside while stewing on the inside with rage that washed through his body. He was ultra-sensitive and had never felt comfortable with the roast culture of the stand-up scene. He sometimes felt he was way too emotionally fragile for comedy and showbiz or maybe even for life in general. A disrespectful comment could trigger him and send him into a fit of anger as it had in the past, the worst being back in kindergarten when he had rammed a kid's head into a wall after the kid insulted his sister.

Ari took a few more jabs at Steve before hitting on Wendy who was reacting to his advances favorably. He asked if she'd give him a hand job in the bathroom and she laughed. Ari got off on pushing people's buttons, but his act was becoming more and more confrontational. He now often used racial epithets onstage and had recently started taking his dick out just to piss people off.

A month later. Steve drove back to New York City. LA was taking a toll on him, and he couldn't seem to get anywhere in comedy. All but ignored by the industry, his weed habit was spinning out of control. LA just had a way of making you feel awful about yourself. He'd met people in LA who'd spent ten years there and had nothing to show for it. And he didn't want to end up just another broken dream.

Before he left LA, a few comedians threw a party/roast for him. During the party, James took him aside at the Ye Rustic bar in Los Feliz afterwards.

"I hope you continue to do stand-up man."

"Yeah, I think I will," Steve responded.

"No, I'm serious. You can't give it up. I think you could like change people's lives with your comedy. I've never seen someone like you before. You could be something really great. I'm serious."

"Thanks, man, I really appreciate that."

"Well, I'm only saying it because it's true."

Steve felt uncomfortable and looked at his drink. He knew James meant it. It wasn't just a passing compliment because James wasn't some phony who gave people empty compliments. James hated most people, but here he was, completely opening up and spilling his true feelings. The equivalent of someone telling them they loved them.

Between comedians, this was the exact equivalent of that. This moment always stayed with Steve. He knew that he had the power to get inside some people's heads. He didn't have the obvious in-your-face talent that the entertainment industry was drawn to. He had a more subtle quality, and if you liked him, you loved him.

Steve always felt deep down that he had something but most just didn't see it. And every so often, he'd feel like someone had seen it too. This was one of those times and Steve knew it was real. James wasn't just a fan of his comedy in the general sense, he had been deeply affected by Steve's comedy. This was what good art could do to people. It had the power to move them and leave them changed and Steve had done that, and he knew it.

CHAPTER 6:

LOST IN NEW YORK

S TEVE MOVED BACK TO MANHATTAN WITH RENEWED confidence. He still had a feeling that he wouldn't be able to stick it out in comedy much longer. He was going to give it another go in New York but only for eight months. After that, he'd walk away and never look back.

Three weeks later, two airplanes crashed into the World Trade Center two miles from his dad's apartment. It looked like it wasn't going to be easier in New York City after all.

The 9/11 attacks had dampened the New York comedy scene and sets were few and far between, especially for a comic who was new to the city. And Steve was restless. His father had never been talkative and was now even less so as a widower. It made Steve uncomfortable living there again.

This was the exact energy he'd received his entire childhood, which was why he was now pursuing stand-up so desperately. Steve needed attention from not just his father but from everyone else. He was going to show them all what he was capable of and then they'd all be sorry they'd ever overlooked him.

There was a part of him hidden somewhere deep down that wouldn't just let him sit back and be happy with where he was. No, he had to show everyone that he had worth. Once he proved to everyone that he mattered then he would tell them to go fuck themselves like a scene out of a movie. It was clearly a master plan that had absolutely no holes in it. He constantly felt like time was running out and that made him antsy to get attention.

There was an open mic he'd heard about from a friendly comedian from Virginia named Roger who had also just started on the New York scene. Roger was a good-looking guy with a good vibe. The mic was called the Trainwreck and took place in the backroom of a rundown dive bar down on Houston. The neighborhood which used to be a seedy area full of homeless crackheads wasn't too dangerous anymore, but the bar was still a shit hole. And yet, this mic was rumored to be one of the better and more productive ones.

There was also a weekly mic at Surf Reality downtown on Sunday nights. It wasn't so much an open mic as much as it was a place where drug addicts got on stage and took off their clothes and babbled incoherently. One night, Steve listened to a woman who just danced and cried about the 9/11 attacks for 8 minutes straight. Yeah, it wasn't easy to follow a heroin-induced mental breakdown with short observations about toothpaste and dating.

The Trainwreck mic was dark, spacious, and full of other comics. The vibe was however better than other mics since it was run by two comedians who were actually good and laid down very strict rules for the show. People listened there and well-known comics often dropped in to perform. He watched a few comedians get brought up by the very ecstatic and likable host Joey Gay. The guy had a lot of positive energy and was usually as high and drunk as most of the people there were. It was a supportive environment with a bunch of drunk and stoned people.

The first comedian to go on the first night Steve stopped by, was a young wiry guy wearing glasses who looked like a geek but also not a geek in the old-fashioned sense of geekiness. Like Chris Hardwick, this guy was the new breed of geek, the cool geek. His name was Ed Helms, and he destroyed the room with his awkward but confident demeanor and absurdist jokes. Steve had overheard a loudmouthed comic say that the guy had just booked a regular gig on "The Daily Show" and was on the brink of going "next level."

Next up was a tall and lanky guy wearing jeans, New Balance running shoes, and a black t-shirt. He had a long nose and a neatly coiffed Beatles-type haircut. He placed his worn notepad down on the stool next to the mic and threw out one-liners that were carefully and economically crafted.

"I saw a sign in a restaurant men's room that said 'all employees must wash hands...especially Carl'."

He did all non-sequiturs and each one did pretty well. The ease he displayed was amazing. These were all new jokes, yet they weren't sloppy or all over the place like most new jokes usually were. They needed some cleaning up, but the premises were all fully formed. The guy clearly had a unique point of view. Steve just watched without laughing since the guy was really good. It was like watching a basketball phenom just shoot three-pointers during practice and effort-lessly nail most of them.

The guy mentioned in a joke that he was a law school dropout. Steve later heard that the guy had a genius-level IQ. He was gaining traction fast and had just gotten back from the Montreal comedy festival. There was serious "heat" on the guy, as they say in "the biz." He'd just done a TV spot on Conan, a huge deal for a new comic. The idea of going on TV and doing comedy for 5 minutes was mind-blowing to Steve.

After the guy got through his set, he walked off, which meant that Steve had to follow him. Steve always dreaded going onstage, yet he was compelled to do it. He always had massive stage fright that he hoped would eventually go away. It never did. The level of anxiety varied according to the weight of the show, but even small shows and open mics frightened him to the point of feeling sick to his stomach. It was as if he didn't have a choice in the matter. But something else was driving him up there. He had no idea what it was even though, in a way, he did.

The energy in the room was positive. Steve walked up the steps to the high stage with his pad and read off his very unformed ideas. The first bit didn't quite land but got a few minor chuckles that sounded genuine. There were no pity laughs at an open mic. After a few more bits he ended with a joke that got a big reaction. He hadn't felt like he killed but the overall set was about a B.

Steve was confident in the last bit ever since he'd first thought of it. It involved the film "The Texas Chainsaw Massacre" and how he'd seen a man at a Blockbuster video store reading the back of the DVD cover to get the plot synopsis. Steve felt it didn't make sense to get a plot synopsis of "Texas Chainsaw Massacre" since it was pretty clear what you were getting in that movie. Was someone going to rent "Texas Chainsaw Massacre" and be shocked by what they saw? Man, there sure was a lot of chainsaw massacring in that. That one guy was obsessed with it. It's like all he did.

Steve left the stage. Joey the friendly host was supportive and told the crowd to give it up for him. It didn't feel like an average open mic which was usually awful. Everyone was there because they wanted to do comedy. A roomful of people who'd failed to be seen by someone close to them growing up. These were the people showbiz attracted. No one knew deep down why they were doing this, they just knew they had to for some inexplicable reason.

The outside world would be severely puzzled to find out why anyone would ever take the time to do this bullshit for no money. But inside, it made perfect sense to everyone there. This was who they were and what they were passionate about. That was it. No money, no fame, just jokes. Steve felt like he fit in there and that actually kind of bothered him.

He was leaving the bar later that night when a tall, skinny guy with sharp features and wide eyes stopped him.

"Hey man. That Texas Chainsaw Massacre joke is amazing. I love it."

"Oh, thanks."

"Is that new?"

"Um...yeah. I mean, I've done it once before."

"Once? Well, it's pretty much done. I'm Carl Hodson."

"Hey. Steve....Collin."

Carl was friendly and seemed chill, which put Steve at ease. Most comedians were high-strung and had an energy that seemed a bit off, but Steve could tell that Carl was like him; a somewhat normal person who did comedy because they were funny and had some flaws under the surface.

Carl asked Steve how long he'd been doing comedy (always a sign that the person thought you were good). This inquiry was a tactic often used to size up another comic. If you were good but had been doing comedy for over five years, then that was a relief because it meant you were good but not *that* good since you were no longer improving. Steve told Carl he'd been doing it for two years. Carl just nodded with a blank poker face.

"Two, huh? Cool," he said.

Yeah, this meant Carl had immediately sized him up as good which was both good and bad. Comedians liked other funny comedians, but they didn't want them to be funnier than them. There wasn't much room for other comics since there was barely enough to go around.

"How long have you been doing it?" Steve asked.

"Almost four years," he said.

He made sure to stress "almost." That made it clear he was also fairly new but not quite as new as Steve.

Carl ordered a PBR from the bartender with tattoos completely covering her neck and arms. Then he told Steve about a show just down the street on Ludlow that featured the best comics in town. It was called Luna Lounge. He told Steve to stop by there the following Monday since Carl was on the show. Carl bought him a two-dollar beer. Then he went through Steve's other jokes and told him which ones he liked and gave suggestions for others.

Steve appreciated Carl's suggestions but was also a bit annoyed since he hadn't asked for any help. But comics couldn't help themselves, they loved coming up with tags for other people's jokes. It was a completely reflexive action done unconsciously, comedy turrets. In this case, Carl was simply trying to come off as a more seasoned comic, and Steve let him have his moment.

The following night, Steve did a horrid open mic on West 41st Street in the basement of a mostly empty biker bar blasting old '70s rock music and lacking in décor. The clientele was there mostly to get drunk or to hide from the police. The host was a smug asshole with hipster glasses and a doughy frame named Dennis. He had a lot of jokes about growing up rich. They were well-written jokes, but he was hugely unlikable causing most of his material to fall flat. It was like listening to Chewbacca try and sing "Wonderwall."

Dennis co-hosted with a thin girl sporting a prominent nose and a thin frame. Her name was Stephanie. Stephanie's stage persona was almost identical to that of her co-host's. She was snarky, sarcastic, and obnoxious. She was funny, but she also came off as incredibly mean and not in a good, funny ha-ha way. She looked like the kind of person who would cut you to pieces if you dared to cross her. She rubbed Steve the wrong way. Other people there seemed to like her though.

Steve had seen this many times before. Every now and again, he'd meet someone who rubbed him the wrong way but who had everyone else fooled. It first happened when he was eleven and met one of his sister's friends, Bernie. Bernie was a cocky, hairy, Jewish guy whom Steve hated immediately. He was constantly insulting Steve and ridiculing him in front of his family to everyone's delight.

Steve's family loved Bernie. He was perplexed that no one saw through the guy's bullshit façade. Years later, his family finally turned on Bernie after he insulted them beyond repair. Meanwhile, Steve had seen through the guy from day one and had been made to feel like an asshole psychic or something. He could tell you immediately if someone was an asshole or not. "Asshole-dar" if you will. A completely useless skill.

Stephanie exuded confidence, and that went a long way, especially in stand-up. That was about 70% of the battle. She had an air of being completely too good for the room which may not have been a bad thing.

After telling a few jokes, Stephanie brought up a female comedian with a narrow face, goofy smile, and a weak chin. She was wearing a red dress with floral prints that didn't fit her well, and she spoke with a slight lisp and sounded like a young child. She almost came off as mentally challenged which seemed to be done for effect. As part of her presentation, she put on a British accent and pretended to work for the "Antiques Roadshow."

She wandered around the room examining items and pricing them accordingly. There were only about 11 people there, but they all loved it. She was fully committed to what she was doing in a dank basement in the middle of Times Square. *It's only a matter of time*, Steve thought to himself. The city seemed to be rampant with small dark unassuming rooms full of huge talents. It couldn't be contained much longer.

"Everyone give it up for Kristen Schaal!" Dennis said when the woman finished.

Steve was on next. This was not going to be easy but because he was so over the room and its shittiness, he kind of didn't care what happened, and that's exactly when he thrived. He had a bad habit of overthinking and getting in his head when he cared too much. When he did that, the 'funny' didn't come out right because he wasn't being himself.

He walked onto the stark stage completely relaxed and picked up the metal mic with a few dents on the top of it as if it had been flung across the room a few times. Then he nonchalantly did a few throwaway jokes that didn't go over well. But he didn't panic or get in his head. He kept going. He was comfortable with the silence and stood completely still.

He'd watched good comics take their time and settle into their rhythm. Bad comedians, on the other hand, got antsy when the crowd didn't react. Doing that let the crowd dictate the pace, and Steve wasn't going to do that anymore. Just because they didn't laugh at first didn't mean the jokes were bad, it just meant that the crowd needed more time to get on board. And nothing got the crowd on board like an attitude that said you knew something they didn't just yet.

A set was like a first date. At first, audiences weren't quite sure whether or not they could trust you. So you had to come off like you'd be fine no matter what they thought. If you showed any weakness early on, it was over. The key was to not worry about the results. Get in your zone like in "Legend of Bagger Vance," and see the field. He could hear Will Smith's wise voice; *See the field Junuh. I can't take you there. You need to find it for yourself.*

He adopted the attitude of someone casually hanging out with his friends and trying to make them laugh, like the station wagon kid. There were no aspirations beyond the next laugh. Steve didn't take his set too seriously and by the end of his set, he saw the field. The crowd which was once dead was now alive and laughing.

But something felt different about this set. He felt lighter standing there and lost himself in the moment. He felt like he'd stumbled onto something by accident, by not thinking. He'd found his voice. This was who he was onstage. He didn't have the desperate vibe so many comics had. Most comics told the crowd, with their attitudes, that they had to kill. Killing felt almost hack to Steve now. It wasn't cool to want to kill. It wasn't cool to want anything. It was less about jokes and more about the comic's unique view. Old school stand-up was all about the crowd and being liked.

Steve embraced this newer style of comedy. It was a persona he'd grown up trying to emulate. Big laughs were overrated. Growing up, all his heroes had been laid-back slackers who didn't look like they were trying at all. Bill Murray never looked like he was trying. Trying was a sin. And like Kanye West once exclaimed, "when you try hard that's when you die hard."

Steve had always been very aware of how he was coming off to others. Under all his bravado, he was terribly shy. Acting as if he didn't care was his defense. It was a way of making up for his fear and over-sensitivity. After he'd had his heart broken a couple of times, he'd made damn sure that no one would ever catch him caring again.

And now, he channeled that aloofness he'd cultivated from a young age. Trying was for suckers. Maybe the clubs weren't the way to go after all. Every new comic was fighting to get seen by the clubs. Steve thought that maybe there was another way. Maybe there was something new coming beyond the clubs that were inhabited by older comics who never hit it big. Maybe he could do this after all. Just maybe.

CHAPTER 7:

BILL MURRAY SAVED MY LIFE TONIGHT

"YOU'RE A FAILURE," HIS MOTHER BARKED AT HIM. Steve didn't respond. He just kept his head slightly down at the dinner table, staring at the meatballs covered in tomato sauce on his plate.

Steve didn't answer. He felt the warm wave flow through his head and body as if he could feel the blood pouring out of his skull. The comment was a punch to his gut.

"I wish someone else was my son. You're going to end up a mooch if you keep this up!"

Steve now felt the shame with which he'd become familiar in the last couple of years. There was a giant knot in his stomach, and he felt like puking. He'd screwed up again. His mother was like a kettle that overheated from time to time. Now dinner had been ruined and he felt responsible. He could barely look up from the table.

Steve was in the 8th grade at a private school down on 11th street, and he had been struggling academically. The curriculum was a lot more demanding than it had been in his previous public elementary school. But he was extremely popular with his classmates because he made them laugh. Humor had always gained him friends.

Earlier that day in school, Steve had discovered that he'd missed a Latin quiz the day before because he was at home, sick with bronchitis. His teacher, Mr. Southern, was willing to let him take a make-up test, but Steve was not prepared and couldn't afford any more bad grades. He was already walking a thin line at his new school. His last report card had been a total disaster and had seriously angered his mother. Steve was terrified of her when she was angry, and a bad grade in Latin would surely provoke her.

Steve got up to walk to the library when one of his friends, Cliff, handed him a small paperback Latin vocab book with a smile. Cliff made a crack about the Chevy Chase movie "Spies Like Us." There was a hilarious scene where Chevy Chase takes a test and brings in a cheat sheet stuffed into his crotch. They'd seen the movie a week earlier and Steve got caught up in the bit.

Chevy Chase was one of his idols and if he did it in a movie, then so could Steve. Life was just like in the movies, right? Steve stuffed the book down the back of his pants while coughing into his hand. A few of his friends laughed as he sloppily shoved the book into his khakis, hamming it up with great physical comedy stolen from Chevy Chase. The laughter encouraged him to play up the bit even more. Soon, he was milking the book in the pants routine for all it was worth. He wasn't even considering using it during the test. The whole thing was supposed to be a joke.

In the library, Steve sat down and felt the sharp edges of the book digging into his side. He shifted it around with his hands as best as he could without drawing attention to himself. The library proctor walked over as Steve was contorting his torso awkwardly arching his back. The bespectacled, short, bald man with a pointy nose walked up just as Steve was hunched over in a ridiculous position, his hand on the book. He asked Steve what was in his pants with a tense face.

"In my pants? My um...underwear," Steve said.

"That's very clever. Do you have something in there?"

Steve shrugged, trying to feign ignorance which didn't work like he'd hoped. The proctor asked for the book and took Steve back to his classroom. The energy in the room was nothing like the scene from "Spies Like Us" and Steve was suspended for a half day. Not really the end of the world, but when word got home about it, his mother completely lost her shit. Steve, now terrified of his mother's angry outbursts, debated never going home again. Maybe he could just run away.

Maybe he'd die and then she'd be really sorry. He imagined how sorry everyone would be if he'd died. Oddly, the thought cheered him up.

For some reason, she took his suspension personally, as if he'd gotten her suspended from school. On TV, Steve had seen sitcom characters get in trouble, and it never seemed to be a big deal. Everyone got over it in twenty minutes or less. Most times, it was also funny, and by the next episode, everything would go back to normal. That is what TV had taught him from day one. But that's not how it worked in his house. There was no laugh track in his apartment that lightened the situation. In his house, there was just tension and anger if anyone messed up. His mother berated him when he got home, and the problem didn't magically evaporate in twenty minutes. In fact, he beat himself up about the incident for years. He felt like this was the end of his life. He'd cheated on a quiz, though he actually hadn't, and was now doomed to a life of failure. That's what his mom told him over and over anyway.

Steve was yanked from the private school and enrolled in a new school the very next day. He tried his best to move on. As the year progressed, he became obsessed with emulating his heroes onscreen even more since they were an escape from his life which he now hated. He became more detached as the year wore on because he'd decided that he couldn't show anyone how he felt deep down ever again. That kind of vulnerability would kill him. Detachment was now a matter of survival.

After the Latin quiz incident, his mother seemed more on edge. He'd get yelled at for little things like leaving the milk out or forgetting an appointment or leaving a towel on the floor. The quiz was dug up over and over and used against him. It seemed like every little thing he did got scrutinized after that. He'd sensed from an early age that his mother didn't want him around. Had he been a mistake? New York City was a rough place, especially in the '80s. Perhaps his mother was struggling herself and didn't know how to handle it. The vibe he'd felt throughout his childhood was eerily reminiscent of the dark energy he would feel in LA years later when he sensed that the town didn't want him there. LA seemed to draw people that felt alienated.

Meanwhile, his father was completely off the grid parenting-wise, hiding away from the family as much as he could. He rarely sat with the rest of them at the table when they ate dinner. His father acted like he'd been tricked into having a family and didn't know how to get out of it. Instead of abandoning the family he just spent most of his time in the other room.

One night, when Steve had made a comment his mother didn't like, she snapped again and poured a glass of ice water over his head at the dinner table. Covered in freezing tap water, he stood up slowly and walked to his room in silence. He shut down, closed his door, and lay on his small narrow bed. He didn't cry although he wanted to. He breathed heavily into his pillow, which had a weird smell, Steve tried to calm himself down.

Then, he went about plotting some kind of revenge. One day, he'd show her, he thought to himself. She never came to apologize which he hadn't expected but had secretly hoped for. Instead, he bottled his anger, rolled over, and turned on the TV which was his only escape from his painful reality. TV and movies were where he drifted off to when he couldn't handle the world. TV and movies understood how he felt and tried to cheer him up. They were friends that listened to him and told him everything would be okay. He hated how his mother had made him feel and was going to show her that he was worth something.

That night, he flipped around his plastic and broken TV dial which only got about five channels. "The Natural" was playing on channel 11. They kept making a big deal about it being the "Exclusive TV World Premiere." He watched the last hour of the film about an older baseball player. Then Steve watched as Robert Redford talked to a woman while laid up in the hospital bed.

"Things sure turned out different," Redford's character said with his head down.

"In what way?" the woman asked with a smile.

"Different. For 16 years, I've lived with the idea that I could be...could have been the best in the game."

"You're so good now."

"I could have been better. I could have broken every record in the book."

"And then?" she asked.

"And then?" he asked looking into her eyes confused and somewhat angry.

Steve had never seen the movie and barely paid attention to it as it played. He'd heard it praised as one of the best movies of the last few years, but he didn't see what the big deal was. It was kind of boring to him and he didn't understand why Robert Redford was so depressed the whole time.

When the movie ended, he flipped the channel and stumbled upon an interview on Fox 5 with Bill Murray. Bill Murray was sitting across from a female newscaster with his legs crossed as they discussed his new movie "Ghostbusters." Of course, Steve was a huge fan of Bill Murray's by this point. He'd heard about the new film coming out and was excited since "Stripes" and "Caddyshack" were now his favorite movies.

In the interview, Bill Murray was shy and awkward. He kept looking down and smiling and didn't say much. It amazed Steve that Bill Murray seemed so unsure of himself. He'd always appeared totally in control and larger than life. In the middle of the interview, he made a comment that caught Steve's attention. He said when he was younger, he was a shy class clown type, desperate for attention. What? Shy and desperate for attention? That sounded vaguely familiar. Steve sat up and watched intently. He tried to mimic his body language.

Steve soon felt better deep inside. He even managed to smile.

Later that night, he heard his mother walk to her room. And once she was inside, he could hear her voice coming as she talked to his father.

"He's a total mess! And you're not doing anything to help out!"

That comment took root in his mind and would never leave him, ever. That one comment would gnaw at him whenever he felt low. He felt like nothing sitting there in his cramped room.

Steve got to his feet and looked at himself in the full-length mirror attached to his closet door. He mussed up his hair just like Bill Murray's and imagined himself being interviewed by the newscaster about *his* latest film. He was the biggest comedy star of the moment and just like that Steve was in his self-made world where he mattered. He may now have been too gone to ever come back fully into reality. If he wasn't going to receive positive feedback from his parents, he'd have to get it from everyone else in the world. Once that happened, he was sure that he'd finally be happy. It was a simple plan really. He knew he was up for the challenge. How hard could it be to get the world to like you?

For as much as Steve and his mother didn't connect, there were moments through the next few years when he felt deep empathy for her. He often caught her looking distant and sad. He recalled walking in on her sitting alone in their kitchen one day, just staring out the window, lost in thought. She looked a million miles away at times.

But the moment that stood out to him the most was the time in fourth grade when he spotted her mouthing along to the words of the Les Misérables song "I Dreamed a Dream" in the back of their car. With her eyes closed, she looked completely caught up in the song the way he would often get lost in TV and movies. Her expression seemed wounded, and she looked like she was on the verge of crying, but not in a sad way. That's when he realized that maybe he wasn't so different from her after all. Maybe she'd also felt unseen.

Steve was only nine years old then, but he knew there was a deep longing somewhere in her. He'd never seen her like that before. She seemed less like his mother and more like a human being. He thought that one day they'd sit together and joke about all the disagreements they'd had over the years. He thought there'd be time for that one day. Surely there would be time for them to truly connect.

Steve's personality began to take shape around age 11, at least he felt like it did. Now a full-blown pop culture junkie, he started to take on certain personality traits of those he watched on TV. The experience at the Oscars had taught him that those were the people everyone looked up to. The first and foremost influence was of course Bill Murray. He figured out the best way to get through life was to act nonchalant and to never show anyone that you cared. Caring was death. Being a kid in '80s New York City almost demanded that you appear as if nothing got to you. If anyone ever caught you caring, you were dog meat. He'd witnessed many "sensitive" kids get pounded in his neighborhood.

New York kids could smell weakness a mile away and being sensitive was not cool, it was weak. You had to be Bill Murray or better yet Jason Bateman's character, Matthew, on the short-lived NBC TV series "It's Your Move." Matthew was everything Steve wanted to be, charming, smart, funny, witty, sarcastic, and also likable but not in a pandering way. Most importantly though, he was funny. The funniest guy in any room he was in. And funny was key.

Matthew was the prototype for many young male teenage icons who emerged in the late '80s. The funny con man with charisma for days; Ferris Bueller, Mike Seaver from "Growing Pains," Anthony Michael Hall in "Sixteen Candles" and Bart Simpson. These weren't the all-American "nice guys." They were cocky, arrogant, smart, and always had a funny comeback at the ready, never at a loss. These were the role models Steve was inundated with as a pre-teen. He took the bait more than willingly and knew this was who he wanted to be.

The rest of his family loved "The Cosby Show," but Steve didn't think Cosby was very funny. Cosby seemed transparently phony to Steve and kind of creepy. He wondered why no one else saw what he saw in Cosby. His "asshole-dar" went off with Cosby. What he hated most about "The Cosby Show" was that there were life lessons to be learned in each episode.

That didn't seem authentic to Steve. His family wasn't at all like that. His parents weren't supporting him or encouraging him or even hugging him. They weren't monsters or anything, but they sure weren't lip-synching and dancing in the living room like the Cosbys were doing.

And the more Steve felt ignored as the years passed, the more he found Jason Bateman's "It's Your Move" character relatable to his life experience. The young kid had to hustle and didn't care what people thought of him. He was like a modern-day Tom Sawyer in a tough modern-day world.

As he approached high school, his generation's identity became defined by the pop culture landscape. He felt right at home as a member of Gen X, the ignored child generation. An age bracket that felt marginalized and overlooked as they grew up. They were the little brothers and sisters watching their older siblings get all the attention and praise while they settled for the back seat. His entire generation's feelings of detachment developed gradually with every passing year. Unsupervised kids raised by TV, thrown into the world to fend for themselves. Of course, Steve had no idea about this at the time, but, with some perspective, it would all make sense later.

CHAPTER 8:

LUNA

S TEVE STOPPED BY THE LUNA LOUNGE TO CHECK out the show Carl had told him about. The room was tiny and jam-packed with lazy boy chairs in the front of the room near the stage. There were also couches on the sides of the room. Every seat was occupied, and about twenty people stood in the back pressed close together. Steve squeezed his way into the back and uncomfortably stood right next to a tall man wearing a scarf and trucker hat with his arms folded.

On the stage was a popular comic whom Steve had seen on Conan numerous times. The comic was ranting about teenagers. He was sort of a comedy icon, and Steve thought he was funny even though he was a bit too angry for Steve's taste. He seemed to be pissed off about everything, even things that didn't seem bad. It all felt a bit put on to Steve.

Was this guy really that angry about buying stamps? Steve was angry too, but he didn't like showing it to people. Showing any emotion was way too vulnerable and you could never let anyone fully see you. Being aloof and seemingly detached was the best way to go through life. Yet, this comic wore his anger like a shiny medallion. Steve was nervous standing in the crowded room which was quiet except for the sound of the comedian's booming voice. The audience was well-trained as if they were watching an orchestra at Lincoln Center. It somewhat resembled the inside of a church with bright lights shining onto the stage.

The angry comic was comedy royalty at Luna, and yet he still seemed unhappy. At one point, he said if you've never been on Conan then you're still in high school. Steve despised bullies more than anything in the world.

Luna reminded him of Largo but with more of a rough-around-the-edges vibe. It had more substance to it, something New York City inherently delivered to any establishment. What it did have in common with Largo was that it wasn't a comedy club. It was a tiny unassuming room with a distinct energy that Steve's potent intuition instantly picked up on.

Steve spotted Janeane Garofalo lounging on a sofa to the left of the room, in what seemed like an unofficial VIP section. Garofalo was currently the biggest figure in comedy. She'd become an actual bona fide movie star, something most comedians could only dream of. Most importantly, she'd done it with seemingly no effort, making her seem even cooler. She had the whole 'not trying' attitude down cold, making her the perfect Gen X icon.

After screaming at a guy in the front row for talking, the comic stormed off the stage. Carl from the Trainwreck went on next and had a solid set. It was impressive since following the last comic wasn't an easy thing to do. Carl seemed comfortable and the crowd liked him. His jokes were pretty solid for some- one who was only four years in.

David Cross went up next and killed since he was now a comedy legend. He did his usual thing, acting as if telling jokes was beneath him. He wasn't some clown who was going to entertain people. He was in charge of the room and if you didn't want to come along with him, well, so be it, your loss. He sometimes seemed to be punishing the audience with his comedy, an approach that went over well in places like Luna.

Steve approached Carl at the bar. He was sitting on a stool and drinking a PBR.

"Hey man, great job," Steve said.

"Hey, thanks. You made it. How are you, man?"

"I just came from an open mic," Steve said, adjusting his black ski hat.

"Oh yeah? Which one?"

"40th Street and 9th Avenue."

"Yeah, Tagine."

"Yeah, that's the place."

"Yeah, that place can be fucking brutal."

"It was okay."

"Did you do Texas Chainsaw?"

"Ahh...yeah."

"I was telling someone about that joke yesterday. I'm so jealous of it."

"Yeah, me too."

Carl laughed.

A couple of cute girls in their early twenties and oozing sex approached them. One was a stunning brunette with her hair pulled up. She had sharp high cheekbones and full lips covered in shiny red lipstick, something Steve found irresistible. The other girl was a little heavier but still attractive. Her voluptuous body was slumped over a bit, and she didn't wear much makeup.

"Hey Carl, great job. You *killed* it," the hot brunette said.

"Cooper! Thanks for coming out girl."

"Hi," Steve offered after Carl failed to introduce him, a pet peeve of his.

"Oh, girls, this is Steve," Carl said.

"Hey," Steve said.

The girls barely glanced at him and didn't say a word. They looked right through him, making his skin tingle and his head fill up with blood. He hated not being acknowledged more than anything.

The hot brunette moved closer to Carl who put his arm around her waist playfully. She whispered into his ear and giggled. Carl smiled and put his other hand on her thigh. Steve immediately felt a sting inside that he immediately recognized. It was what he'd felt the night his mom had poured water over his head. He wasn't good enough and was nothing. This feeling had been there, hiding under the surface of his emotions.

Steve felt the rage. He didn't understand why this had set him off so quickly, but he could feel himself losing control of his emotions as he'd done in the past.

She'd be sorry someday. She'd be begging for his attention one day. Then it would be too late for her and she'd be kicking herself. She'd regret ever ignoring him one day. He'd make them all regret ignoring him. He told himself this whenever he felt rejected. The brunette touched Carl's stomach with her hand and leaned into him smiling. The heavier one stood back awkwardly, staring ahead with a frown, and holding a glass with clear liquid and a red straw.

Steve leaned in and asked her if she was a comedian. She replied with a sharp dismissive no and didn't bother to even look at him.

Just then, the angry comic walked over and stopped next to them. The heavier girl stared at him with wide eyes that now sparkled.

"Kris! Hi Kris," she said lighting up.

"Yeah, yeah, hi," the angry comic said not looking up.

"Great job tonight."

"Yeah, thanks. So um...how are you doing hon?"

"I'm great. We met at Rififi remember?"

"Yeah. Shirley, right?"

"Shelly," she said smiling.

"Shelly. Yeah, I totally remember now," he said, looking Steve up and down as if trying to place him.

"How ya doing?" he said with a tense frown.

"Good. Thanks."

"What's your name?"

"Steve."

"Yeah, okay," he said turning to Shelly.

Shelly proceeded to laugh at everything the angry comic said even though he wasn't being very funny offstage. Steve was invisible to both of them. He uncomfortably scanned the bar area which was mostly full of young women dressed in sweatshirts and tight vintage T-shirts.

Steve sipped on his PBR and stayed close to Carl who now had his arm around a different brunette who was wearing a fake crown for some reason. Carl shook various people's hands as they left the place. Everyone there seemed to know him. He introduced a few people to Steve, including a short girl wearing fake elf ears.

Steve noticed Janeane Garofalo right next to him at the bar. He said hi and she responded but with a serious guarded expression as if she were thrown by Steve addressing her. There was an unwritten rule there that you didn't annoy the place's royalty. He'd seen one comic get into it with David Cross one time at Largo after getting a bit too overexcited and needy. Steve smirked at her, nodded his head, and turned away.

Steve walked out of the place after Carl became completely preoccupied with the first brunette who was now sticking her tits in his face. He was out of place there. He was surely funnier than all of the people there or at least just as funny and yet they all thought they were hot shit. Even the girl wearing plastic elf ears had acted superior to him. He thought about that feeling he'd had in the station wagon many years ago and wondered why the world wasn't cooperating with his life plans. It was hardly fair.

He was twenty-nine and had yet to learn that the world didn't accommodate your plans just because you wanted it to. His thoughts wandered to the hot brunette at Luna. He didn't even like her, yet he desperately wanted her to see him. He despised her now.

He realized right then that, like most comics, although he was confident, he was also insanely insecure. He sometimes wondered if he'd transformed his deep insecurity into overconfidence as some sort of defense mechanism like rappers did. He'd convinced himself that he was great, even though deep inside he felt less than.

He wanted to be in Carl's place. He wanted to have the women all over him, not even to sleep with them but just so he knew that he could if he wanted to. He wanted all women to notice him. Deep down, he knew this had to be linked to his mother somehow. All this overthinking made him more depressed, and he felt himself spiraling again in a way that had been prevalent the last few years. He stopped at a bar on 14th Street for a few whiskeys.

As he got drunk alone, he told himself that he could still get what he wanted and prove himself. He talked himself into a better place as an old Pet Shop Boys song played. *There's a lot of opportunities if you know how to make them you know!!* He finally went home.

A BRIEF ORAL HISTORY OF ALT COMEDY PART ONE: IN THE BEGINNING

I reached out to comics, friends, comedy fans, waiters and bartenders. I wanted to hear from everyone that was there to witness the alt scene as it grew in the aughts in New York City and finally culminated into a comedy movement of sorts. Many people didn't get back to me, not that I'm bitter mind you. I very much wanted to include something in the book told directly from the people who were there as it unfolded, so I broke down this brief oral history into four separate parts, each covering the different stages of this alt era.

"Throughout the 2000s New York's East Village used to house one of the most peculiar, albeit entertaining, comedy clubs. Named Rififi it became the stomping grounds for the East Coast's so-called alt comedy scene. A low attendance comedy club turned into a hotbed for many of the key players of the second comedy boom."

— Vulture Magazine

"I was a huge standup comedy fan when I first moved to New York City's East Village in 2000. On any given night I could go see a show for free that featured literally some of the best stand up comics of all time at the beginning of their careers. Comedy fans were spoiled and then everyone else discovered them. It was great for me. I always liked funny guys."

— Wendy
Comedy Fan

"The caliber of talent that went through some of these places was astronomical. You'd be doing a room in front of ten people in the East Village and Dave Chappelle would just drop in and do an hour. Then you'd have to follow him. It was nuts"

— Sean Patton
Comic

"I worked at one of the popular Lower East Side bars that started hosting these small comedy shows. There were a lot of comics that came through there. some were famous already and others would become famous later. Most were cool. Some of the guys were creepy though especially one that later got canceled. Also, there was this one female comic who was soooo rude to everyone. She's sort of big now and was on a popular TV Series. Can you not use my name?"

— Anonymous

"Kabin became popular for a few crucial reasons: the booze, the hang, & the show itself. Kabin was the last place in the East Village where you could snag a $2 can of Pabst. Much to the chagrin of many a bar owners, comics are known for milling about and not spending money. The lineup was part of the excitement, too, because--thanks to Sean Patton & Rebecca Trent--the show always felt fresh due to the wide variety of comics who were booked on the show. From established New York comics, up-and-coming comics looking to prove themselves, to the best comics from across the country—."Club" or "Alt" comics, it didn't matter: we booked comics who we thought were funny."

— Chesley Calloway
Comic and Producer of *Comedy as a Second Language* at Kabin

"The term alt was one people didn't like. It grew out of frustration with the club scene and what seemed to be stale. It started in small rooms like nothing"

— Barron Vaughn

"I discovered the alt comedy scene after 9/11 when things were bleak and I just started writing these odd things like songs. The alt comedy scene was similar to the Velvet Underground, kind of like the Velveeta Underground"

— Ben Kronberg
Comic

CHAPTER 9:

RIFIFI

ONE DAY, STEVE WAS SIGNING UP FOR A SET WHEN the surly co-host, Damian, complimented his comedy. He was doing the Trainwreck every Monday night and had started to kill regularly. "Hey man, I've been watching you the last few weeks, funny shit," Damian said.

"Oh, thanks," Steve said.

"Yeah. How long you been doing comedy?"

"Ummm...two years."

"Oh yeah? Cool."

The compliment meant more to Steve than he cared to admit. The host wasn't a friendly guy who doled out compliments, so it meant something to Steve. The Trainwreck was just an open mic where you had to pay to get up, but he at least stood out. It was kind of like being the best-looking guy at an Iron Maiden concert.

Steve had a hard time giving himself any credit and was constantly downplaying any type of success he had, another common comic trait. But little comments like that encouraged him to keep doing comedy a little longer, something he debated quitting almost daily now since nothing was clicking. He was getting better but what did it matter in the long run if he couldn't get on any good shows?

He felt in danger of just becoming a good open mic'er. The thought of that terrified him as he looked around and saw many people well into their thirties and forties doing an open mic in the back of a dive bar.

A piece in the New York Times had called them deluded. It was an article about New York's open mic comedy scene and how it was full of oblivious people who couldn't accept reality. The reporter had even mentioned the Trainwreck show and some of its regulars had been singled out.

Steve passed by a short man in his forties with long fingernails and beat-up black jeans. The guy always carried a backpack, even onstage. And he was awful. He had been doing stand-up for over ten years. Steve swore to himself that would never be him.

After that night at the Trainwreck, Steve started branching out to other open mics downtown. One decent one was at a small hipster bar on 3rd Street and Avenue B called B3. The downstairs room was tiny and dark with a small bar in the middle of the room. The host was a super friendly and likable young black guy from New York named Romey. He had a sharp fashion sense and was always smiling and laughing. He exuded an infectious exuberance. And he was funny too.

He called the show "The Love Below" since he strikingly resembled Andre 3000. The energy there was extremely positive, so positive that it didn't even seem like an open mic. Steve started going there every week. Most other open mics had a terrible vibe as if someone had just died.

He'd first heard about "The Love Below" from a young, new comedian just out of Georgetown whom he'd met at the Trainwreck. The guy, Nick Kroll, who had wavy, almost curly hair and donned glasses, had complimented Steve after one of his better sets. Like so many comics around New York at the time, Nick was sort of a nerd, but with loads of confidence and charm. In addition to being a comedian, Nick was also an aspiring actor who took improv classes at the UCB, a place Steve had heard about a few times but had never been to since he wasn't a fan of improv comedy. There was an almost unspoken rivalry between the two camps of comedy; improv and stand-up.

Nick and Steve hit it off almost immediately. Nick was the kind of guy who made you feel like he was genuinely interested in you. He'd also clearly been raised well since he was polite to everyone. He was a climber but not in a bad sense. He was just ambitious. Nick was funny in everyday conversation but wasn't obnoxious like those comedians who were "on" all the time. Most comedians always had to one-up you with a clever quip. The majority of comics were intolerable to Steve, so when he met a normal one, he made a point of making friends with them.

At The Love Below, Steve met another new comic, a skinny white guy with a long sharp nose, called Neal. Neal had been hanging around with Nick and Roger a lot more lately. And Roger was beginning to find his voice. He too was starting to get noticed due to his sharp writing and likable presence. Steve gravitated towards Roger because he was another friendly, normal-ish person.

Neal wasn't super friendly though. It was like he had a sort of invisible wall up around him all the time. He was unassuming yet cocky, and he often looked down at his tennis shoes and shook his head if a joke didn't land. He rarely smiled but when he did his face kind of lit up. Steve watched Neal's set carefully. He didn't do very well, but not because he wasn't good. He commented on how dead and stupid the crowd was. They were a bad crowd. And his comedy was aloof as hell, definitely a Gen X'er.

"I know you guys don't like me but, believe me, the feeling is mutual. It's not you, it's me, I hate you," he said while grinning at one point after a joke ate shit.

He was acerbic and his jokes were sharp and well crafted. He clearly knew what he was doing. Steve wondered if the guy had just moved to New York City from another city since he wasn't a newbie. Like Stephanie from Tagine, Neal had the bravado of someone who hadn't made it yet but knew that he would. He seemed angry that he had to pay his dues in shitty basement rooms like B3, and he had the attitude of a prisoner wrongfully convicted and who was complaining that they didn't belong there.

Steve told Neal he'd done a good job when he walked past. Neal looked at him and obnoxiously snickered at the comment.

"Yeah, whatever man. They suck."

After leaving The Love Below, Steve, Roger, Nick, Romey, and Neal went together to a bar across the street. They settled into a large U-shaped booth with ripped upholstery and ordered drinks. Roger was sitting close to Steve and told him that Neal had written a popular stoner movie with Dave Chappelle a few years earlier. The movie had bombed when it was first released but was now a cult classic. Steve had seen it a few years earlier. This small factoid perfectly explained Neal's detached demeanor.

Neal had just left LA and was trying his hand at stand-up. And although he'd had big success as a writer, he had to start at the bottom of the stand-up ladder like everyone else. One thing about stand-up, you couldn't fake it like other things in showbiz. It didn't matter who you knew, if you sucked at comedy, there was no amount of celebrity connections that could hide the fact that you sucked. Neal knew this and was diving into the trenches of stand-up. He was frequenting the same mics as Steve, Roger, and Nick and was beginning to warm up a bit, after Steve killed in front of him a few times.

One cold night in November, Steve performed at The Love Below after bombing something fierce at Tagine. He'd barely garnered a laugh out of the shit Tagine crowd and Stephanie made a wisecrack about his set. For someone with such thin skin, it was a sort of sick joke that he nightly put himself in a position to be bashed by strangers.

"Let's hear it for the comedy of Steve. That was really something Steve. Top-notch, man!" she said, making the okay sign with her hand and winking sarcastically. It set him off.

Tagine was one of the hardest rooms in the city, but Steve kept going back like a battered wife refusing to leave an abusive husband. There were only about ten people at The Love Below. Fed up with everything and tired of trying new bits, he simply went up and scrapped his jokes and just talked about what had pissed him off that day.

At a recent show, an audience member told a comedian sitting next to him that he'd had a great set. The audience member said nothing to Steve who had also just performed. That had triggered him, and Steve ranted about it. It wasn't a joke it was just him being honest about something he was angry about onstage. He was angry but not aggressive. He was more annoyed, and he made it funny. One thing Steve knew was that he was at his funniest when he was genuinely pissed off, which he was after that awful Tagine set. Stephanie's snarky comment had echoed in his mind the whole night.

He then talked about how someone in front of him in line earlier at Starbucks wouldn't leave the counter area after paying. It fucking drove him crazy when idiots stood there squatting the counter, refusing to move on. These weren't even formed jokes, but they drew huge laughs mainly because Steve hadn't cared how they went over. If you didn't like them, then well, fuck you. Steve felt different during his set. This was beyond just clever, well-written jokes. There was something behind the jokes. A point of view. When he got off the stage, all the comics congratulated him. He spotted Stephanie from Tagine standing in the back, and even she smiled and told him good job. He thanked her and felt vindicated. Something was different. He had let go up there and was in the moment. That night was the first time he genuinely didn't care what happened onstage and he felt lighter because of it.

Later, Steve went with Roger, Nick, and Stephanie to a spot called Rififi nearby in the East Village on 11th street.

"Rififi? Is that a bar?" Steve asked on the way there.

"Yeah. They have a back room where they do shows," Nick said. "My friend Mike is on the show tonight."

Rififi was dark, empty, and cold. The backroom could fit maybe eighty-five people. There were about fifteen there when they arrived. When they walked in, Demetri Martin was onstage doing jokes out of his notebook on a stool. Steve had seen him do most of these jokes a month earlier at the Trainwreck but now they were polished. The small crowd ate him up.

He often chuckled to himself after a joke didn't land. He wrapped up his set after about ten minutes when he ran out of jokes on the page. The host came on clapping. He was a good-looking, affable redhead wearing a tight blue polo shirt and glasses. He didn't do jokes but rather riffed onstage. At one point, he took out a bag of coke that he said he'd found in his apartment and didn't know how old it was. Then he snorted some and gave the bag to a female audience member in the front. Steve had never seen someone do that in a club. It was like Luna or Largo but with no crowd. There was no cover charge here and the drinks were dirt cheap. Four dollars for a Jack on the rocks, which was insane in Manhattan. It felt like a beatnik club or a private clubhouse for comics. A secret speakeasy that no one was aware of. It would not remain a secret.

Nick's college friend, Mike Birbiglia, went on next. Steve had heard about him in the scene and had seen him on Comedy Central's Premium Blend, the new stand-up showcase. Mike was short and stocky with short dirty blonde hair. Good looking in an all-American way but not traditionally handsome. He was also of the geeky yet confident school. This was a trend Steve was noticing back in New York. Confident, awkward, nerds seemed to be multiplying. Birbiglia's act was self-deprecating, and he often addressed his social awkwardness in everyday situations. He was odd but had a presence and some of his jokes bordered on absurdity. His TV credits placed him in a league above Steve and his circle of open-mic friends.

These were the up and comers. Not yet famous but on the cusp. The next big things. These guys were the best in New York and yet Steve strangely didn't feel intimidated. He actually felt like he could perform alongside them and not embarrass himself. Steve had always maintained an air of cockiness about him and was getting more in touch with it the more that he performed. He didn't care as much anymore. He literally had nothing to lose and was tired of being meek and afraid. He was a New York City kid after all.

Later at the bar, Nick politely introduced Steve to Mike who spoke quietly and nodded a lot while smiling. His eyes disappeared when he grinned. He was with a young woman, also a new comedian and Georgetown alum. It wasn't clear if she was Mike's girlfriend, but they stayed extremely close together. The young girl was pretty and smiled a lot. Her name was Jacqueline Novak.

Steve ordered a whiskey and spotted Carl leaning against the bar. He was talking to Bobby, the host, who was from South Carolina and spoke with a twang. Bobby wore tinted glasses that were borderline sunglasses. Carl introduced Steve to Bobby and a few other comics including a large guy named Eugene Mirman who was drinking a pint of Guinness.

Eugene seemed standoffish, and Steve took it personally as he often did. Even so, the vibe wasn't quite as exclusive as it was at Luna. There seemed to be an unwritten rule that because Steve was new, he wasn't welcome in the circle. Not that this was a huge circle or anything. It was just a bar show with less than twenty people in attendance. Comedy was kind of like the mob, comics had to see you kill before they'd trust you fully.

"Steve's a funny comic," Carl told Bobby, but Bobby didn't seem to care who Steve was or if he was funny. He quickly walked off to talk to a comic who had just entered the bar wearing a bulky ski coat that was too big and a dark blue knit hat. Steve recognized the guy with a long face from a 90s TV series and a movie that had become a cult classic of sorts. The man had wide eyes, a long nose, and a tense mouth, it looked as if he had just taken a swig of something sour.

Steve had grown up less than ten blocks away from the place, so that made him feel more confident being there. This was his turf. No one there was actually from Manhattan. He was the only true New Yorker in the room and yet he felt unwelcome. Maybe it was just his paranoia or maybe he was yet again picking up on the place's energy like he often did. Still, it wasn't as uncomfortable as it was at Luna. Rififi still felt like neutral territory not run by industry big shots. It was just a comic's hangout which explained the slight tension similar to a high school cafeteria.

Nick, Roger, and Steve stayed for a while drinking at the bar which had now cleared out. Birbiglia walked over and put his arm around Jacqueline. Steve told him that he liked his set and Birbiglia nodded and thanked him. He stood with them for a while not saying a word the whole time. Nick and Roger were drunk and being loud but not in an irritating way. They talked about old teen sex movies they'd grown up on and tried to decide which was the best one.

Then Nick and Roger went outside to smoke weed leaving Steve alone with Mike and Jacqueline. Steve immediately felt uneasy. He didn't know these two and they didn't seem outgoing. Steve sipped on his whiskey and just stared ahead. He could sense they were also uncomfortable. Jacqueline tapped her foot against her stool.

"So...." Steve started.

"Yeah?" Mike interjected fast.

"Oh, um. Nothing."

"Do you do comedy?" Jacqueline asked Steve.

"Ahh...yeah, I do," Steve said.

"Really?" Mike said, looking directly into his face now.

"Yeah. I do."

"Where?" Mike asked, staring at him even more directly now.

"Well...I just moved here from LA actually. I just do a lot of open mics really." He hated how his last sentence had come out.

"Oh? Cool. Where'd you get up in LA?" Mike asked.

Suddenly, Birbiglia seemed much more interested in Steve than he did before. It was like he was sniffing Steve out and inadvertently exposing his irrelevance in comedy in the process.

"Um...the Comedy Store," Steve said, knowing he sounded unsure.

"I do that place all the time...when I'm there," Mike said.

"Oh cool. I did the Belly Room a lot."

"Oh, I've never done that room. I do the Main Room usually. Do you know Mitzi?"

"Oh, um. Well, no. I mean..." Steve stammered and took a sip of his drink. Mike and Jacqueline were looking dead at him. He had to pull this together or he'd come off like he didn't belong. He went into aloof mode.

"I was supposed to audition for her before I left. My friend Bob Oshack set it up, but Mitzi was sick, so I didn't get to do it."

"Yeah. I know Oshack. He's great. He recommended you?" Mike asked.

"Yeah."

"I love the Store. Where else did you get up?"

"I did a lot of open mics and stuff. I also did the Improv here and there."

"Yeah. They book me there a lot," Birbiglia said.

Steve took another sip and felt the blood rush from his head. His face went numb. He already felt out of place. Now he felt like he was being completely taken down by this guy. Steve hated how comedians constantly got into pissing matches always trying to outdo each other.

"I did a few shows there when I was out there doing Kilborn," Mike added.

"Yeah, I saw you on that. That was great," Steve said.

Birbiglia's face changed as soon as Steve said that. Then he relaxed and slumped over a bit, his chest not as puffed out as it had been a minute earlier. Steve hadn't seen him on Kilborn, but he knew that you could disarm a comedian or actor if you complimented them. It was their Achilles.

Suddenly Birbiglia was a lot more open and friendlier. He had just been trying to make sure Steve knew he was one of the big shots in New York comedy. Once Steve conceded the point, all was okay. Birbiglia even bought him a drink after that. Nick and Roger walked back over with their eyes glazed over. Nick put his hand on Steve's shoulder.

"This guy is a fucking riot. You guys need to see him," he said.

"Hey, I have my moments," Steve said, making Birbiglia chuckle.

"Yeah?" Mike said.

"Yeah, sure," Steve said, before ordering another drink.

CHAPTER 10:

THE NEW STYLE

A FTER ABOUT THREE MONTHS OF DOING THE OPEN
mic circuit regularly in New York, Steve was starting to lose his patience. His weekly routine was;
the Trainwreck on Monday, Tuesday was The Love
Below, and Wednesday was Tagine. He did a few other
small shows in Brooklyn where you had to be booked,
but other than that he wasn't making much headway
and he was getting down on himself again. His inner
critic was getting louder lately. His depression seemed
to have taken hold and he knew he couldn't fight it. He
would stop by Rififi on Wednesdays after Tagine for
Invite Them Up more often.

Carl would usually be booked since he was Bobby's
roommate. AD Miles was another regular since he
and Bobby had known each other for years. AD was
another geeky type with confidence coming out the
ass. His self-assurance bordered on arrogance. Nerds

had definitely changed. He didn't do straightforward stand-up but rather told stories with almost unparalleled confidence.

Zach Galifianakis showed up and went on regularly when he was in town from LA. Zach had grown up with Bobby, and Steve kept hearing Galifianakis was on the verge of "blowing up." He'd recently started incorporating the piano into his stand-up which only made it better.

The room was noticeably more packed every week. There were about fifty people when Steve stopped in. The word was getting out about this bar with the strange name that now drew celebrity status comedians. It was a way better alternative to the comedy clubs which targeted unwitting tourists to come in and spend upwards of 100 dollars for drinks. Comedy clubs hired aggressive barkers to hustle people into their clubs off the streets. The barkers often lied about the club's lineups. "Chris Rock and Adam Sandler are performing!"

Rubes from out of town would then be forced to sit through a show of complete unknowns, most of whom were terrible. Many times they'd demand their money back from the club. They never got a refund though. It was a total racket.

Steve had performed on a few of these club shows that were full of angry mid-westerners expecting to see Robin Williams. One night an angry patron complained that George Carlin wasn't on the lineup. Someone had to explain to them that George Carlin was dead.

Rififi had none of that club bullshit. Many clubs still looked like they were stuck in the '80s while Rififi felt modern with its bareness. They didn't bark people in because there was no cover charge, and they didn't have to. The vibe was more relaxed and was well, "alternative." This of course was not a new term. Steve had heard the phrase "alt-comedy" years before, but it was used negatively. He'd heard club comics bad mouth this new breed of "alternative comics." They were dismissed as unfunny comics who didn't know how to write a joke. They weren't considered "real" comedians. Janeane Garofalo had come to unofficially represent what the alternative scene represented. She was now the alt breakout star since she seemed hip and didn't do traditional stand-up. She told jokes but they weren't jokey jokes, they were just kind of stories about herself with some funny parts. Comics often denounced her comedy.

"She docsn't do stand-up!" he'd heard a club comedian declare angrily.

Comedians, of course, loved to tear apart other more successful comedians. It was something you couldn't avoid. Talking shit about more successful comedians was just a part of it all, although some comics were more gifted at shit-talking than others. But when it came down to it, "alt-comedy" was simply different from what had come before it.

People don't like things that are different, especially not at first. And comics hated other comics surpassing

113

them. Club comics felt these "alt comics" weren't funny, so the fact that some were getting attention and success pissed them off. It was assumed that the "alt" thing was a fad that would soon disappear, just like rap music. There was no future in these sparsely attended alt rooms. Many comics asked Steve why he was even hanging out at these places. What was the point? The clubs were "where it was at" he was told over and over. Steve was wasting his time.

But the more Steve frequented these downtown shows, the more confused he was by people's judgment of them. The comedians there *were* telling jokes. Sure some of them did weird different types of things like tell stories or tap dance during their sets but for the most part, the stand-ups were just doing comedy. It just wasn't hacky stuff like Bill Clinton impressions.

People told jokes about obscure old pop culture things like '80s rock videos or '70s rock songs with inane lyrics. It was what Tarantino would have talked about if he'd been a stand-up comic. They told jokes about things that Steve actually wanted to hear about. The topics weren't universal and broad but acutely specific. Their acts were also less polished. In fact, being polished was frowned upon. The crowd reveled in something that felt fresh. They could tell when a comedian was taking a risk with something completely new. It was more fun watching someone walk the tightrope with no net than it was to listen to someone on autopilot spitting out old jokes. It was exciting and in the moment.

In the clubs, most comics had been around since the '80s and hadn't written a new joke in 15 years. They were still making funny observations about airplane food.

The comics in the downtown rooms were creating a new style. It was now next to impossible to break into a club and become a regular. There were no open slots since the older comics refused to leave. Steve liked the fresh and detached style of the alt rooms. He was at his best when he didn't think too much. Like Tom Cruise in "Top Gun." "You don't have time to think. If you think you're dead." Stand-up could always go horribly wrong at any moment if you got in your head. The last thing you wanted was to be thinking too much.

Steve was tired and hungover. All these crappy open mics were wearing him down, plus his father seemed angrier every day that Steve was staying with him. He was scrambling around for an apartment but wasn't having much luck. New York City had gotten a lot more expensive in the last few years since no one was afraid to live there anymore. The best he'd found was a spare room in Astoria for $1000. The train ride was 45 minutes out.

When Steve headed out to Tagine, he could feel that something was getting ready to blow, and not in a good way. He thought about his mother and her bursts of anger that appeared seemingly out of nowhere. This was a trait he was relating to more and more as he grew older. His anger was a problem at times and there were moments when he felt like he couldn't control it.

Dennis was hosting Tagine alone now. She was still doing spots on the show every week though. She always made it clear when she went on that she hated the audience and felt like she was above them.

She was desperately trying to break into the alt rooms and had been able to get onto *Invite Them Up* because she was good friends with Bobby, and was apparently sleeping with Carl. Nick and Roger were now hanging around her more and more. Stephanie was a master networker, but Steve still didn't get why she was so well-liked. He realized much later that she was different with different people. It all depended on who you were. She saw people as opportunities and since Steve had nothing to offer her, she did not need to treat him with respect. She was a shark.

Steve once heard someone say that Stephanie would "kill her own mom to become famous." It was meant as hyperbole, but Steve now believed that remark. She was going to get what she wanted no matter what she had to do to get it. Fame would make a person who needed to be seen do crazy things and he had a feeling she was even more insecure than even he was.

Steve went onstage and picked up the mic. There was now electrical tape at the base of the mic. It looked like it had been treated like shit. It was fitting that such a damaged mic was being used for damaged people who did stand-up. He placed his notepad on the stool next to him and did a quick joke that got nothing. Not even a chuckle and it felt like a punch to the gut. He'd expected the crowd would be bad, but this was on a whole new level. The room felt abandoned and angry. Steve noticed two twenty-somethings, a guy, and a girl, in the back. They were talking at conversation level as if there wasn't a comedy show happening right in front of them.

At first, Steve ignored it. He tried another joke that had worked many times in the past. It got nothing. Dead silence. It sounded even more silent than silence. There's no silence like the kind that comes after telling a joke on stage. It's a cruel and mocking silence that's worse than heckling. It's like the crowd hates you so much they can't even be bothered to insult you.

When the third joke bombed, the young man and woman talking seemed much louder amid the immense quietude. Their chatter made things worse. Not only was he bombing, but a couple was having a full-on conversation in the middle of his set. Ignoring him. It wasn't a good thing to ignore him, and Steve felt a wave move through his body. He wasn't angry yet, but he knew he couldn't fight it off much longer.

He asked them what they were talking about.

"You're not funny," the woman turned and said without missing a beat. It was almost as if she had prepared the comment beforehand.

Then she went right back to talking. It stung Steve hard, and the energy went from hollow to almost dangerous. He remained calm and aloof.

"How do you know I'm not funny? You're not even paying attention," Steve said.

She turned to him again, this time with a pained face. "I feel sorry for you," she shot back at Steve. Then she went right back to her conversation.

That made him snap. He could feel the blood rushing to his head and knew another part of him was taking over. It must have been a primitive thing. It was as if a part of his DNA felt like its life was being threatened. That part of him took hold and popped out as if to say; "I'll take it from here Steve. You just sit this one out."

Steve didn't think of himself as a tough guy, but when he was pushed too far, he pushed back, hard. He knew this part of him that usually lay dormant was about to push back hard. The aloof cool guy was gone, now replaced by a cornered animal who would do anything to survive.

He put the mic in the stand slowly so he could have his hands free. Then he listened to the man and woman talk for a few more seconds. He looked out at them and asked the guy if that was his girlfriend.

"Fuck off. You suck," he said to Steve without looking at him. The woman laughed.

The comment was harsh, but what enraged Steve the most was the casual way in which it was being done. They were completely stripping him of his dignity in a room in the freest and easiest way as if shooing away a fly. Steve realized that he was a mere thirty feet away from them and could just walk over to them. There was no protective glass or anything. But Steve figured he'd give them one last chance.

"What are you guys doing here? Did you know there was a show going on?"

They just ignored him.

"Oh. So you're just going to ignore me now? Okay. Well if you want to ignore me then let me ask you this. Can I fight you when I get offstage?" The man glanced over at the stage, not as casually this time. This had gotten his attention.

"Thanks, everyone. I'm done. I'm gonna go beat the shit out of this guy," Steve said, while calmly stepping off the stage.

The other comics laughed, trying to diffuse the situation. He heard one guy say, "Hey! Come on man! Just let it go!"

Steve slowly walked directly to the guy who was still talking. The guy didn't quite know what to do. The fly he'd tried to kill was a full-grown man ready to pounce. Steve was in a rage and knew he couldn't stop himself. He had nothing to lose. Adrenaline flowed and his entire body shook. Even if this guy was fucking Mike Tyson, Steve felt he could knock him out. He felt like a mom who would lift a minivan to save their trapped baby.

The last time he'd felt the rage this strongly was as a thirteen-year-old when he went after John Keefe, a bully from his camp. Keefe had kept on needling Steve until he snapped and punched John in the face until he fell to the ground bleeding. John Keefe had the same blank expression this guy now had. Realizing too late he'd picked the wrong guy.

Steve felt the past two years of snubs and shitty open mic crowds and insults channel their way through him as if a spirit had taken over his body. He didn't even give a shit about comedy anymore. As he walked over to confront this asshole, he knew he was done with all this bullshit for good. Fuck it. He didn't need this shit anymore. He was going out with a bang. The guy was an embodiment of every person who'd treated him like crap while doing comedy. He was ready to take it all out on him in this dark basement.

Two comedians grabbed at Steve's arms when they saw that he was serious and wasn't stopping. This wasn't a joke. He had a fire in his eyes. The hands he felt on him were weak and did nothing to stop him, they were the equivalent of a weak spiderweb. Steve was three feet away and about to grab the guy's head and shove it into a nearby wall when he was grabbed by strong hands that felt much bigger. These hands weren't weak, and they clearly didn't belong to a comic.

This place has a bouncer? he thought to himself. Suddenly the fierce rage transformed into mortification and shame as the hands dragged him almost comically and easily up the narrow staircase and hurled him out the front door like a towel being tossed onto the floor.

It was like something out of the Patrick Swayze movie "Roadhouse." Steve was now outside on 40th Street in the freezing cold. He stared at the blank steel door for a minute then turned to his left. There was a homeless man picking food out of a trashcan. The homeless man shook his head as if he were embarrassed for Steve. Yeah, that settled it. He was officially done with stand-up. He wanted to burst out crying. Fuck this shit. If they didn't want him then he didn't want to be a part of it anyway. He was tired of trying to win approval from people he didn't even like. He'd be better off anyway. He'd tried, nothing had worked. The world didn't deserve his comedy. It was their loss he thought to himself.

CHAPTER 11:

JOHN WINGER WALKS INTO A BAR

TEN MINUTES AFTER BEING THROWN OUT OF TAGINE, Steve got a call from Nick who said he was headed to The Love Below and asked Steve to meet him and Roger there. Steve was ready to go to a bar and get wasted on whiskey but knew that wouldn't help anything at all.

When Steve arrived, the place had maybe eight audience members. Roger was onstage trying out some brand new one-liners. He was slowly developing a solid rhythm as a comedian. Nick whispered to Steve that Bill Murray was upstairs in the restaurant eating with his kids and that he'd asked him to come down and watch his set. Steve was blown away by Nick's balls. Bill Murray, Steve's childhood hero, the very guy who'd inspired him, possibly even saved him that awful night in his room after getting screamed at for cheating on that dumb Latin quiz was actually there? Murray was his entire generation's hero. In reality, if you were a comedian in 2002 in your twenties, Bill Murray was most likely the reason why.

Nick was set to go on next. Bill Murray hadn't come down and Nick's disappointment was showing. Then Steve noticed a pair of black dress shoes heading down the twisty staircase that led to the basement room. The figure that emerged wore a dark blue suit and no tie. His grey hair was long, straggly, and combed back. His face was reddish with a deadpan expression. Even though the place was dark, Steve swore Murray was glowing as if a light was surrounding his body. He stood in the way back by the bar. The sparse audience didn't even notice him. Nick shot a quick wide-eyed look to Steve and mouthed the words; "Holy shit." Steve gave him a thumbs-up as a way of wishing him luck.

Meanwhile, Romcy stood onstage oblivious to the fact that Bill Murray was at his open mic in a basement, in the East Village, on a Wednesday, watching him. He introduced Nick who took the mic and began to nervously rush through his set, stammering over his words. His timing was completely thrown. Steve thought of Top Gun. Tom Cruise's voice echoed, "If you think up there, you're dead." It was amazing how applicable this line was to stand-up comedy. It was strange to think that being a fighter pilot and a comedian was in any way similar.

In some ways, being a fighter pilot was probably easier. After all, no one was judging you the whole time. The worst fear a fighter pilot had was dying. Steve knew now that being yelled at by drunk strangers and being humiliated in front of a crowd was way worse than being shot down in a fighter jet.

The small crowd was non-reactive to Nick's first bit about his cat. Steve glanced over at Bill Murray who was stone-faced and still as if waiting in line at the DMV. The more he didn't get laughs, the faster Nick's delivery became, and soon he was sinking fast.

Steve suddenly felt like he was bombing in front of Bill fucking Murray. It was the worst bomb a comic could have. It was like watching an animal die. Some bombs were fun to witness. There was nothing enjoyable about this kind of a bomb. It wasn't just unfunny, it was gut-wrenching. The worst part was that Nick had brought it all on himself by asking Bill Murray to be a part of it. That was the thrill of stand-up. You knew at any moment it could go horribly wrong. One misstep and it was over.

And Nick was having a whole set of missteps as he fumbled around with his notebook looking for more jokes to do. He did about six minutes that felt like ninety-six and got off to barely any applause. He walked past Steve with his head down to avoid eye contact. Bill Murray walked up to Nick by the bar and shook his hand while saying something Steve couldn't make out. Nick shook his hand, smiling, and looking down. Then

Bill Murray turned and slowly walked toward the stairs that led out of the basement.

Steve felt like he had to at least try and say something to Bill, even though his heart was racing, and he didn't have any idea what to say. He got up and slowly walked over while trying to think of something good to say. He tapped Bill Murray on the shoulder. Bill turned and looked at Steve.

"Yes?" he asked.

"Um...Mr. Murray. I just wanted to tell you I'm a....ahh... huge fan. I've been a fan since I was a young kid growing up near here. I used to watch you a lot on TV, a lot."

Bill Murray looked back at Steve, still expressionless.

"Well, okay then," he said back in his unique Bill Murray inflection.

Steve could hardly believe that Bill Murray was looking at him. He was just a person who looked tired, not a ghostbuster. And he seemed to simply be an older man who didn't want to be bothered. Steve's pinnacle childhood moment meant nothing to this guy who simply turned away from him and went back up the winding stairs.

Steve felt slighted. It had been a rough night in his little comedy world. Part of him died that night. But maybe it was a good thing. Maybe something inside had to die so something else could take over.

"Oh, fuck. Fu-u-u-u-ck me," Nick said. "Fuck me, fuck me, oh shit," he added.

"Hey, it wasn't that bad," Steve said.

Nick laughed abruptly.

"Pffftt! It wasn't that bad? Yeah, neither was Hiroshima. What the fuck was I thinking asking him to watch me here?!" he said chuckling about it.

"I went to Hiroshima last year," Steve said.

"What?"

"Hiroshima. I went there. It was the bomb," Steve said.

Nick laughed again.

"Maybe I should have used that," Nick said.

Nick's laughter made Steve laugh. Nick was taking the whole thing well which made his situation seem like nothing. Yes, Steve had bombed horribly at Tagine and been violently thrown out of the place, but not in front of his comedy hero. Maybe Steve had been taking this comedy shit a bit too seriously. Maybe he just had to enjoy it more like he did when he was younger. Ever since he'd started stand-up, it seemed the innocence, fun, and playfulness of it had been removed.

Steve went on a couple of comics later and killed since he didn't give a shit. The bad set at Tagine had drained him of any fucks to give. Besides, he'd already decided that he wouldn't be doing this anymore anyway.

Neal went on and, of course, couldn't resist calling out what happened in the room.

"Hey, Nick. Good set man. Went off without a hitch," he said.

Nick laughed and clapped. The tension hanging over the room that needed to be drained was now diffused. Neal went on kicking Nick while he was down.

"Don't worry Nick. He probably didn't even notice. Plus he's not even that popular anymore. Damn man. Bombing in itself sucks but you did it to the next level. You literally bombed in front of one of the biggest comedy icons of all time! That may have been the biggest bomb in the history of bombing. After a bomb like that, I only have one question. Who you gonna call?!"

"Ghostbusters!" everyone responded as if it had been pre-rehearsed.

After the mic, Steve, Nick, Roger, and Neal, and some girl Neal had just met at the show went to a dive bar called Double Down, across the street. Neal hit on the cute girl who was dressed in jeans, a tight blue spandex top, and a hoodie sweatshirt. She was downtown hot, not dolled up too much, and not flaunting her looks. When she went off to the bathroom, Neal commented that he was running out of showbiz stories with which to impress her. He said he'd already mentioned his friendship with Dave Chappelle and having written "Half Baked" but that she was still freezing him out.

"Maybe I should take her home and show her the new pilot I just shot with Chappelle," he said as an almost throwaway line.

"You guys finished it?" Nick asked.

"Yeah. You guys wanna watch it? We're pitching it to some networks in a few weeks."

Of course, everyone wanted to see it. What a ridiculous question. They finished their drinks and all went over to Roger's to watch the very first episode of his new still-untitled show starring Dave Chappelle. Neal was hoping this would seal the deal with the downtown girl.

They all found it cool that Neal had shot a TV pilot and that it might actually be on TV, nothing beyond that. Someone from their scene might actually have a TV show on the air. That was cool and maybe they could all secure parts in it. Steve asked what they were thinking of calling it.

"We're still thinking about it," Neal said, putting the DVD into Roger's player.

"All right. Let's check out this Chappelle Show," Steve said putting his feet up on Roger's wooden coffee table which was littered with books and dirty ashtrays.

"Yeah, well, enjoy," Neal said while looking up slightly as if contemplating something important.

Neal left with the downtown hot girl who now seemed a bit more open to Neal's advances. He smiled at them and winked as he walked out behind her.

Steve thought the pilot was funny. Really funny actually. Of course, he didn't think he was watching a show that would soon dominate the TV landscape and end in a national story culminating in Oprah asking Chappelle about what happened with Neal. It was just a 20-minute pilot with some funny sketches.

"That blind racist skit was pretty good I thought," Nick said, lighting a one-hitter.

"Yeah, that one and the one about black reparations. I wonder if they'll sell it to anyone," Steve said.

They got high and riffed with each other while watching late-night TV for a couple of hours. Weed loosened up his mind and sparked some funny premises. All Steve did now was to look around for new bits. He was in full comic mode all the time now and it was hard to simply turn it off. Steve came up with some of his best jokes while high and talking to comics. At one point, Nick commented that they should record their convo and put it online somewhere. It sounded like a cool idea, but they doubted anyone online would want to listen to a few comics simply talking. Just then, a commercial came on for a product to get rid of genital warts. A voice on the TV said: *Do you have unwanted genital warts?*

"Unwanted genital warts? Shouldn't that just say 'do you have genital warts?' Isn't that enough? Isn't it implied that if you have genital warts that you don't want them? That's like saying 'do you have unwanted diarrhea in your mouth?'" Steve said out loud in a weed haze.

Nick and Roger burst out laughing. Roger was mid-sip and almost spit out his beer.

"Oh man, you have to do that as a bit," Roger said.

"Yeah?" Steve answered.

"That will destroy," Nick said.

"Yeah. Maybe," Steve said, sipping on a Heineken bottle.

And just like that, a joke from the ether made Steve decide to give comedy one more shot. Hell, who knew what might happen? *If you had one shot or opportunity to seize all you ever wanted, would you capture it or just let it go?* He heard one of his heroes in his head as if speaking right to him. It was just a small moment, but that funny thought he decided to say out loud kept him alive.

Roger flipped around on his TV. The Yankee game was over, and he flipped to HBO. The movie "Stripes" was showing. They all went silent as they watched the screen.

"Well, good show tonight huh?" Nick said.

"Yeah. Pretty run of the mill though," Steve offered.

"Yeah, I'm gonna need more weed," Nick said.

CHAPTER 12:

CHAPPELLE SHOW

A WEEK LATER, THEY WERE ALL AT A BAR ON 14TH Street. The room had a huge stage raised about three feet high. It was a music venue and there were drums and mic stands set up all over the stage. There was barely any light in the square room. A new likable pothead comedian named Tim had started a show/open mic a few weeks earlier and had given Roger, Nick, and Steve spots on it. Neal arrived in the middle of the show with two friends in tow. One was Chappelle and the other was Mike D from the Beastie Boys. Chappelle wasn't a comedy phenomenon just yet, though he was a recognizable comedian.

After Neal performed, Chappelle walked over to Tim and asked if he could go up. Tim was flabbergasted and nodded his head.

"Um...yeah, of course. I would have offered but I assumed you wouldn't wanna do it," he answered smiling widely.

He knew this story would find its way around the scene and possibly turn his show into a hot spot. That's all it took. One celebrity pop in and your show would most likely pick up steam and get a coveted listing in TimeOut NY.

Chappelle went on after Steve and did an hour. He riffed his entire set talking about the room and what he'd done that week. At one point he got into the DJ booth at the back of the stage and started scratching records. He finally got off the stage after apologizing for going on too long.

After the show, Steve glanced at Chappelle who sat at the bar quietly smoking cigarettes with Neal and Mike D. No one bothered him since they didn't want to drive him away. Steve, Nick, and Roger all sat at a back table drinking whiskey and beers and getting drunk. Occasionally one or all of them would retire outside to smoke and get high. It was on one of these trips outside while smoking on a camel he'd bummed, that Steve spotted Chappelle smoking alone. Steve's stomach dropped but he didn't flinch although he began to panic on the inside. He hated being around celebs, they made him uncomfortable, and he always felt like he couldn't be himself around them. There was always an unspoken tension with celebs. You couldn't let on that you knew who they were, but it was also completely clear that you did know who they were. Being around celebrities was like a masterclass in phoniness. Chappelle looked up.

"Hey man. How ya doin?" he asked, lighting up, his eyes looking at the flame.

"Hey, I'm good," Steve said, immediately feeling like an asshole and judging his response. *Hey, I'm good! What the fuck kind of answer was that?! Stupid!*

"Hey, funny shit man, for real," he said to Steve, taking a long drag.

"Oh, yeah. Um...thanks, man. You too. I liked your set," Steve said, again feeling like everything he said was wrong.

"Thanks, man. How long you been doing it?"

"Oh. About two years."

"Aww man, you a baby," he said, laughing.

"Yeah, I know. I ahh....I'm a really big fan by the way... of you."

"Thanks, man. I appreciate that. Where you from man?"

"I'm from Manhattan," Steve said.

"Manhattan huh? Cool."

"Can I ask you something?"

"What?"

"You still like doing it? Comedy, I mean."

Chappelle took another drag and looked down at the sidewalk thoughtfully.

"Hell yeah, man. I love it. I mean, it can get tiring at times, and this industry can really fuck you up and drain you. But the comedy part, the stand-up, that part I love. Being funny, man. I loved it as a kid, and I love it now. The rest I can live without though. Just be careful. There's a lot of people out there who don't give a shit about you. Sometimes I feel like I just need to get away from it all you know?"

"Get away?"

"Yeah. Like maybe I could just walk away and go somewhere and disappear for a while."

"Like where?"

"I don't know. Australia maybe," he said looking down at the street, his eyes glazed over. He was thinking about something.

"Australia? I've never been there. My sister lives in Africa and she says it's beautiful and totally relaxing," Steve said, beating himself up inside again for everything he said.

"Africa, huh? Yeah. That sounds dope. Who knows man?" he said after a long pause.

"I saw that show you and Neal did. It was great."

"You saw it? How?" he said turning his head to Steve. Uh oh. Was he not supposed to tell him this? Fuck. He'd blown it. Why was he so stupid?!

"Oh, I saw it with Neal. He....um...had a copy of it."

"Neal had a copy huh? And what? He just showed it to you?!" he said shaking his head.

"Oh. I mean, I'm sorry. I didn't," Steve stammered.

Silence. Steve took a drag.

"I'm just playing man," Chappelle said, smiling and blowing smoke out of his mouth.

"You looked fucking terrified boy," he added and walked inside.

Steve stood there just staring straight ahead. His heart beating fast now, almost out of control. He took a drag, his hand shaking, still rattled a bit by what had just transpired. When he calmed down a bit, he stomped out his smoke and laughed to himself. Had he just recommended vacation destinations to Dave Chappelle? Like Chappelle would ever listen to his advice on anything.

Back in the bar, Steve got drunk with Nick and Roger. At one point later in the night, he heard the song "What a feeling" playing over the speakers from the bartender's iPod shuffle. Steve was right back there again just like he always was when the song came on.

"Hey, I ever tell you guys about the time I was at the Oscars?" Steve asked full of adrenaline and weed and booze.

CHAPTER 13:

TURN AROUND
BRIGHT EYES

"A HH...I'M NOT QUITE THE SUPERHERO TYPE," JACK Nicholson whispered, leaning closer to Steve.

"Maybe you could play a bad guy," Steve replied.

"Steve, this is Shirley Temple," Mike Ferrari said to him while tapping his shoulder, smiling.

"Isn't that cool?" Mike then remarked.

This was the same Mike Ferrari in whose station wagon Steve had been that fateful night years earlier. Now here he was yet again during one of Steve's pivotal moments in life. Maybe Mike was his good luck charm or something.

They were sitting on the black shiny steps to the stage while all the night's biggest stars and winners mingled together just a few feet away, reveling in their awesome lives as cameras flashed in their faces.

Jack Nicholson still stood close to Steve's side while clutching an Oscar for "Terms of Endearment". He'd stopped his forward momentum after hearing Steve's throwaway comment.

"Welcome to the big-time kid. Enjoy it while it lasts because it never does," he said in his inimitable voice and smiled widely. He then slicked back his hair with his hand, and walked over to kiss Shirley MacLaine. Christie Brinkley walked past right after and smiled a white smile.

"Hey handsome," she said and walked off. Steve watched her as she glided across the stage. Had Christie Brinkley just called him handsome?

As Steve looked around, he realized that he barely knew who most of the people on stage were. He was only 11 years old, and showbiz had never been important to him. He loved comedy movies, but he didn't follow the Oscars or anything.

What intrigued him about this whole appearance at the Oscars was the loads of positive attention he'd received from everyone leading up to it. Even his mother seemed impressed. Grownups and teachers were nicer to him now. Even his notoriously mean science teacher, Ms. Marx, had started treating him better. She'd hated him just months earlier but being at the Oscars had changed that.

"Get used to people being mad about your success," the choreographer, Jacques D'Amboise, had once told the group after rehearsal one day.

Now here he was. He'd performed at the Oscars and stood at a podium with the rest of the group of kids during a director's award acceptance speech for Best Documentary Short. He'd recount this night endless times over the years.

The following Monday, kids at school and grown adults had asked him over and over what it was like to have had that experience, with a spark in their eyes. Who did you meet? Did you see Michael Jackson there? Lots of kids asked about Michael Jackson, it was 1984.

"Did you see Michael Jackson?!" a boy named Alexis asked.

"Ummm...no. I think he was there, but I didn't see him. I did meet Tito Jackson though," Steve said.

"Tito Jackson? Who's that?"

"His um...brother?"

"Who gives a fuck about him?"

"Well, he looked like Michael."

"Man, I heard Michael Jackson has this huge house with huge rides and video games all over the place. Sometimes he even lets kids stay over in his room as long as they want. I would love to stay over there. It must be paradise," Alexis said.

"Yeah. I guess so," Steve said.

"What do you mean you guess so?"

"Well, I mean I don't know if I'd want to stay over there in his room."

"Why not?! What could go wrong?!"

This was during an era when actual access to celebrities was almost non-existent. Pre-internet and social media and podcasts. In 1984, seeing a celebrity or meeting one was a huge deal that didn't happen to most people. It was like seeing Bigfoot. So Steve felt special to have had that kind of experience.

At the Oscars, he had casually conversed with the cultural icon, Shirley Temple, who sat just feet away from him. She was famous, but she wasn't the biggest celebrity of the time, and it was clear from her body language and lack of people to talk to that even she felt out of place. Next to her sat the tiny Oscar she'd been given as a tribute to her career. It was slightly smaller than a normal Oscar. It was as if done intentionally to make it clear that she hadn't won a *real* Oscar.

"Where are you guys from?" she asked Mike, leaning in.

"Manhattan," Mike offered.

"Oh, that's wonderful? What grade are you in?"

"Sixth. We graduate in a few months," Mike said.

"That's just great," she added.

Steve noticed the host for the night walk past. Johnny Carson rubbed his forehead and dragged his feet a bit. He held an unlit cigarette between his fingers. He looked a lot older in person, and Steve could see that he was covered in heavy makeup. Steve knew who he was because "The Tonight Show" was a staple of American television and his dad watched it sometimes. Steve had even seen his father laugh at Carson a few times.

Sitting there on that stage, Steve had a quick flashback of what had happened in the backseat of Mike's station wagon back in 1980. It just popped into his head out of nowhere. He remembered the huge laughs he'd gotten. Johnny Carson was a real comedian and Steve was right near him. Suddenly, Steve pictured himself hosting the Oscars one day. After all, his friends at school thought he was hilarious, plus he was already at the Oscars. How hard could it be really? How hard could any of this showbiz stuff be?

"Do you like being at the Oscars?" Shirley Temple asked Steve, inching a bit closer toward him on the steps.

"Yeah, it's okay," Steve said, shrugging his shoulders.

"Okay?! Is that all?"

"Well, it's had its moments. Nothing to write home about."

"You're funny," she remarked, chuckling at his nonchalance.

"Yeah. I've heard that," he said.

"You've heard that?! That's great! You're a doll!"

She laughed and cocked her head back slightly with her mouth open. "Oh, honey. You have really got this Hollywood thing down. That's the way to play it. Who knows? Maybe you'll be back one day to pick up one of these little awards," she said, wiping her eye with her finger as if he'd made her laugh so hard that tears had come out.

"Yeah, maybe," Steve replied.

He wasn't aware of it of course, but that moment was one he'd be chasing for the rest of his life. Maybe his mom scolded him for telling jokes and teachers punished him for "goofing off" but Shirley Temple told him he was funny. Maybe being funny was something he could use later in life.

All he knew of jobs was from his father who always looked tired and annoyed when he came home. His father was the only adult who hadn't been too impressed with his Oscars trip. Even that didn't get his attention. But Steve knew he was on the path to something that might make his father take notice. He thought about that time when his father had laughed at the funny movie trailer years earlier.

A week later, Steve showed up at his little league practice. He had missed the first game because of the Oscars. When he showed up, all the kids were standing around the fat, bald, bearded coach who was wearing big silver mirror sunglasses. Steve only knew one other kid on the team, the rest were strangers. When Steve arrived, the coach wasn't exactly welcoming to him.

"You Steve Collin?" he said, scratching his crotch a bit too long.

"Yeah?"

"You missed the first game, pal. Your friend Nicky told me it's because you were at the Oscars huh?" he said loudly with barely any inflection.

"Yeah. Nicky was right. I was," Steve said, grinning and expecting a compliment or some sort of praise.

"I watched them, I wasn't real impressed," he replied, sending a few members of the team into hysterics.

One ugly, freckle-faced kid wearing an Iron Maiden shirt with grape juice stains on his mouth, shook with laughter as if this were the funniest thing he'd ever heard. The laughter made Steve's stomach and chest tense up. He got knots in his gut, a sensation he was all too familiar with in moments such as this. He was frozen. The red-headed kid laughed so hard he looked like he was having a seizure. Was it *that* funny? It wasn't. The kid was trying to rub it in. Steve felt a wave flow through him. He immediately hated the kid.

How had his Oscar moment been used to embarrass him? Now he was supposed to be ashamed of being on the Oscars? This didn't make any sense. Who did this piece of shit coach think he was talking to?

Steve watched the red-headed punk laugh his ass off bent over as if he was about to fall. His laugh was a high-pitched cackle that sounded like Jabba the Hutt's evil little monster sidekick in "Return of the Jedi." "Why are you laughing? Did you just see your penis for the first time?" Steve zinged. Another part of him took over and somehow created this line at just the right moment. The Oscars thing had given him some confidence.

As years passed, this freckled kid would become the subject of many awful neighborhood stories, like the time he stomped a baby pigeon to death or how he liked to hang stray cats for kicks. Even years later, when Steve heard that the freckled kid had died in a car crash, all he could remember about him was his evil cackle.

After the Oscars buzz had settled, Steve harbored a sort of secret that he didn't let out of the bag to anyone, including himself. He had an undeniable feeling that he had something and would someday end up in showbiz. He had no idea how this feeling had manifested. Maybe it was because celebrities had spoken to him as if he belonged there. He had no idea that one day he'd later reflect on the whole Oscars experience as the worst thing to ever happen to him.

AN ALT ORAL HISTORY
PART TWO: THE BUZZ

"Doing *Invite Them Up* was like doing a spot on 'The Tonight Show' definitely. That's not hyperbole. It was real nerve wracking and could change your career."
— Roger Hailes
Comic

"I did *Invite Them Up* once and I thought it would be my big break since the lineup was sick. It was Aziz, Galifiniakis, Hannibal. I showed a video I had made that had been mentioned in the New York Times and it bombed horribly. Not one laugh. I felt like complete shit afterwards. It was like I wasn't cool enough or something."

— Ray Devito
Comic

"I worked with a band in New York and they had me come out to write music with them. While I was out there I started to do standup at a place called Rififi on a night called *Invite Them Up*. Everybody performed there and I met a lot of people. When I performed there, it immediately felt like my family. I knew that if I moved, I had friends and a place to perform and it would all work out."

— Reggie Watts
Comic

"I f****d a lot of comics in the Rififi bathroom."

— Wendy
Comedy Fan

"The alternative comedy scene of the early aughts was very similar to (and had all of the positive aspects of) the alt music scenes of the late 20th century, in that it largely consisted of talented friends getting together for the sole purpose of creating things that entertained each other. Rififi was a locus of the scene in that era"

— Jack Vaughn
Comedy Central Records Producer

"I went up and was lost and ate shit. I was terrified after that. It took me a year to get the nerve to get back on"

— Paul Gilmartin

Comic

"Rififi was a neat place. There was always great energy for the comedy shows and also for drinking. There was a large pillar in the middle of the room. I'd always hide behind that pillar so I didn't have to pretend to laugh at jokes I wasn't into. It was a great pillar. The audiences for shows were always incredible. You could really try things and experiment and still feel the support of the crowd simply because they were just nice people. I'm happy to have experienced it for a couple of years and very grateful for the sets and shows and people I met there."

— Kenny Zimlinghaus

Comic

"It was around the fourth year of the Kabin show that we started to get more comedy legends dropping in: Todd Barry, Jim Gaffigan, Colin Quinn, Janeane Garofalo, Eugene Mirman, Maria Bamford, Mike Birbiglia, Patton Oswalt, John Mulaney, Brody Stevens, Louis CK, Reggie Watts, and more. I got to bring up Zach Galifinakis--he'd always been a hero of mine. I also distinctly remember when Aziz was putting the finishing touches on his material for a special so he came and closed the show with a half-hour set and just crushed the whole way

145

through. I've always been bummed that David Cross-
-another personal comedy hero--never did the show.
I actually met him one time at some other Lower East
Side bar and I tried to tell him about the show and
he blew me off. David, if you're reading this: Go fuck
yourself! (just kidding, I still love you)"

— Chesley Calloway
Comic and Producer of *Comedy as
a Second Language* at Kabin

"One time Louis CK was standing alone at the bar. I told
him I was a huge fan and he told me to get away from
him. It was great. I felt like I was flying."

— King Ace
Co-Host of *Stand-Up Apartment*

CHAPTER 14:

ALLOW ME TO INTRODUCE MYSELF, MY NAME IS STEVE COLLIN

S TEVE HAD JUST PERFORMED A SET IN A DRAFTY basement down on West 4th Street. The room was empty except for maybe six people. He'd been there once before. It was a new open mic run by a short older guy with glasses who loved Steve almost as much as James Painter the LA laugher guy did. He'd invited Steve to do the show many times guaranteeing him a spot whenever he wanted.

A douchey-looking, frat-type with short blond hair was onstage. He wore a tight-fitting flannel shirt and was good-looking and cocky in the worst way. He made fun of the room and called all the other comics "losers" for doing a show in a basement. His two friends, who looked exactly like him, sat at the bar and laughed at everything he said. Steve thought it was funny that the guy was insulting them for doing a show he was currently on.

"If I were you guys, I'd kill myself. This place is depressing," he said from the stage. "At least I'm good-looking," he added.

Steve was on next. And though he tried, he couldn't resist calling the frat guy out.

"It's funny, you said we should all kill ourselves. Good tip. I actually did want to kill myself listening to your jokes."

The frat guy stared daggers at Steve and threatened him from the audience. "I'm gonna kick your ass you faggot ass!"

The comment caught Steve's attention. He had a flash of the freckled-faced, red-headed kid who was now dead and tried to stay calm and not take the bait. The guy kept hurling insults. Whenever Steve was about to finish a joke, the guy would yell over the punchline.

Finally, he was asked to leave by the burly Irish bartender. But he didn't go quietly. He went out yelling various insults about how the room was full of pathetic losers. The show had bummed Steve out, so he went to get a drink with Nick and Roger afterwards. They had asked him to meet them at Molly's where they had gathered to watch the Oscars.

Once there, Steve went to the bar which smelled like beer and some kind of cleaners like ammonia or something. There was puke on the floor at the end of the bar. The place was almost empty since it was a Sunday night. The old color TV over the bar played the awards show with the sound off.

They were presenting Best Actor and Steve watched with a knot in his stomach as a guy he went to LaGuardia with won. He watched as the excited guy grabbed a famous actress and ambushed her with a kiss. This was well before the me-too movement so the whole auditorium cheered him on as he kissed this woman seemingly against her will. Even then, Steve found it creepy.

Steve sipped his whiskey and watched the guy talk with no sound coming out. He had his mouth open and held his skinny arms out at his sides. Watching a guy he once knew make history as the youngest Best Actor in history made Steve feel small and not special at all. He looked down at the bar and chuckled to himself. He could picture the lanky Adrien back in school trying way too hard to act tough. Every huge star in the world was applauding him while Steve was replaying the time when the guy had farted loudly in the middle of Mr. Eldo's math class.

The whole thing was a bullshit façade. The guy later dubbed "the math farter" by some kids was now Hollywood royalty. Of course, Adrien never forgave Steve or his friends for ditching him in the middle of Central Park that one night in 1990. He didn't have any idea back then that the guy who farted in math class would someday win an Oscar. The farter had the upper hand now. Well-played math farter, Steve thought to himself.

Steve joined Roger and Nick at the table as Nick excitedly told them about a new MTV prank show he was booked on with another rising improv guy named Bret Gelman. Nick was now part of the UCB improv scene. He and Birbiglia had their own show there now, a huge deal.

Nick wasn't crazy about stand-up even though he was good at it, so Improv was clearly a better fit for him. During that same conversation, he also mentioned that he and a new comic from NYU named Aziz were doing some comedic short films together too.

Steve had heard the name Aziz mentioned a few times in the last month but had yet to see him perform. People were talking about him as if he was some basketball phenom out of college about to be drafted. Steve was quiet as he listened to the chatter around him and tried not to think about the fart Oscar winner. He was slowly being pulled into one of his depression spirals and he didn't even try to fight it off. Instead, he numbed himself with whiskey and weed.

Steve's flip phone rang while he was sipping his third drink. He felt hazy now and didn't recognize the phone number, so he didn't answer it. He rarely answered his phone anyway. It was never good news. It was usually a bill collector or a different bill collector.

The next day, while hungover and ordering a five-dollar Chinese food lunch item that he'd been ordering for two straight months now, he noticed that he had a message on his phone and listened to it with a sense of foreboding dread. Who did he owe money to now?

"Hi, Steve, this is Suzanne from Comedy Central," the caller announced, "just calling to congratulate you on being selected to compete in the Laugh Riots Stand-up Competition. The semi-finals will be at Gotham Comedy Club on May 5th. Congratulations again, and we'll see you on the 5th!"

Steve stood completely still in the Chinese take-out place. The surly Asian woman behind the counter barked at him impatiently. "Next! What you like?!"

Steve listened to the message again.

"Sir! What you order?!" the woman yelled.

Steve looked up and ordered his dish and then listened to the message three more times just to be sure. No way had he just gotten good news about comedy. After listening to the message for the tenth time, his takeout was ready to go, and he went off to get a drink down the street to celebrate alone. He was happy until it sunk in that he still had to compete and who knows what would happen then. The odds were that he wouldn't win and that would be it. He'd be right back to open mics and cheap Chinese takeout.

A few drinks loosened him up though and he thought that maybe, just maybe, there was a possibility that he could win. Who knows? In the bar, "What a Feeling" played and Steve enjoyed it. It was a good omen.

Two weeks later, the night of the contest finally arrived. There were eight up-and-coming comedians on the bill. The room was packed, and the crowd was hot. There were a few reputable comics in attendance, comics Steve had been fans of for years. This was definitely a big deal. At the bar area, the competing comics drew pieces of paper with numbers written on them from a clear bowl. This determined where they'd go in the lineup.

Steve drew the number eight spot, which meant he was going up last. That was at least better than being the first, but it wasn't an ideal slot. It could easily backfire. The crowd could be dead by the end and that would be that. He tried not to think about it but of course, that was impossible.

The first seven comedians went on and Steve actually felt good, calm even, or at least as calm as he could be. He didn't put a lot of pressure on himself. If he placed in the top three, he would be happy. There were three winning slots. A tall nerdy confident guy with glasses was killing as Steve waited to go on. The guy ended on a big laugh from the audience and walked past Steve with a cocky grin.

Steve was introduced and his fear all but disappeared. He fumbled with the mic when he first got up there. Not a good start. The room felt tense, so he took a breath and went right into his first joke, which luckily connected. He had eight minutes to do this, and he already felt like he had them. All he had to do now was keep them. The crowd was hot, so he didn't get too excited. It was best not to get too comfortable doing stand-up.

Stand-up was like life, you wanted to be comfortable but not too comfortable. And starting strong and ending weak was the worst possible thing you could do. It was easy to get cocky when a set started well. Steve knew now that in stand-up everything could shift just like that.

Steve went straight to his next bit about seeing relatives that hadn't seen him since he was a baby and how they were shocked that he was no longer a baby.

"Wouldn't it be more shocking if after 28 years I still *was* a baby?"

The bit landed and before he knew it, he was five minutes in and still crushing. Everything he said drew laughs, even adlibs. He was completely relaxed as he went into the last bit that he knew was strong and had a feeling would do well. Even so, he was not prepared for the reaction. He'd been doing well up to this point, but this joke changed the room. It brought down the house and Steve could barely even finish it due to the laughter that never stopped during the entire bit.

The entire last minute of his set was one big laugh break. It was one of those dream sets where everything worked perfectly. It was like a perfect golf swing. He felt like Bagger Vance was watching him from the back and proud that Steve had found the field. There hadn't been a single misstep. He'd been in the zone the whole time. When he walked offstage, he felt light on his feet and knew he'd done well, really well. Everyone else knew it too. The other comics didn't look at him as he passed. He felt he would at least place so he was proud of himself.

When they announced the winners, Steve was by the door. They called the first runner-up, the nerdy guy who had gone just before him.

"Dammit!" the guy shouted, hitting himself in the leg with his hand.

It was then that Steve realized he'd won the contest. The host called his name. Steve wasn't exactly excited but stunned. He didn't show any reaction on his face since he was self-conscious about being stared at by everyone. The entire smiling crowd turned to watch him walk in. A couple of the other comedians smiled and shook his hand, but the nerdy guy scowled at him. Steve walked onstage and took his prize which was just a piece of paper. He was now off to LA for the finals. He was excited to be going back to LA, this time with a reason to be there.

I'M GOING BACK TO CALI...CALI....CALI

Word got out fast about the Laugh Riots contest results. Steve noticed people being much friendlier to him at the various mics. He even got booked on some shows that hadn't been welcoming to him before. When he stopped by *Invite Them Up*, Bobby congratulated him.

"I heard about Laugh Riots. I'm gonna give you a spot, man," Bobby said smiling.

"Oh great. Thanks, man," Steve said.

This was a huge deal and Steve relished it, though he acted his usual aloof self. *Invite Them Up* had gained more traction in the last few months but was still not as popular as Luna Lounge was.

Bobby booked Steve on *Invite Them Up* the following week. When Steve arrived, it was the most packed he'd ever seen it. It was standing room because the lineup was full of huge comics. Steve was the only non-name on the bill. His hands were shaking even as he first walked into the place. He headed straight to the bar and got himself a Makers on the rocks from the pretty blonde bartender named Lindsay. He paid with the drink tickets Bobby had given him when he walked in.

Welcome to the big-time, drink tickets as payment. Enjoy it while it lasts. He sucked the whiskey down like water and felt calmer as the whiskey buzzed him and numbed his nerves. He hated how nervous he always was before performing. It wasn't getting any better especially as his career progressed. His hands were steadier now. Alcohol helped, which he knew wasn't a great path to get on. His stomach was still in knots and no amount of whiskey was going to make him forget all of his shortcomings or the fact that his mother and father, for most of his life, hadn't seen who he truly was.

He knew that he'd be okay as long as he could just stay out of his head. He was starting to believe he was actually good at stand-up and that he deserved to be there.

He looked around the room and saw the hot brunette who had hung all over Carl at Luna a few months earlier. She was of course with the heavy girl. They were standing at the end of the bar drinking with serious expressions on their faces as if they were casing the joint. Bobby approached and hugged them both flirtatiously and Steve turned away. He didn't want to think about them because doing so made him angry.

The show started and Bobby informed him he was up next. Steve finished his whiskey and carefully squeezed into the back of the room which was dark and packed to the back wall. He anxiously waited to be called up with a piece of paper in his hand, his set list. Of all people, Nick, the comic from Largo was performing. He tried not to psych himself out. The biggest hurdle to stand-up was remaining calm in a situation fraught with tension. Stand-up was like trying to relax while on fire during a prison riot. He tried not to think about how just two years prior he'd walked into Largo in LA as a brand new open mic'er, a complete unknown watching this comic perform. Nick was now the absolute top tier in comedy and Steve was now on the same bill as him in a room packed just like Largo and now, he had to follow him. No big deal. He tried not to overthink any of this as he watched Nick kill. It was such a ridiculous scenario that it almost made him more relaxed. He finally chuckled to himself about the ridiculousness of the whole thing. He was in an almost impossible situation, and part of him felt that he was being given the hardest set on the show on purpose as a sort of test. He told himself, "Fuck it. Just be yourself.

If they don't like it, who gives a shit? Be Bill Murray in the '80s." And just like that, he wasn't nervous, he was annoyed. He was at his funniest when annoyed.

He spotted a famous actor in the crowd from one of his favorite films. Nick ended on a big laugh, but not huge, which was good for Steve. Bobby gave him a welcoming intro that was almost like an induction into an exclusive club.

"This next guy is new to the New York scene, but he's been tearing it up lately. He just won the Comedy Central comedy contest. Let's make him feel at home and give him a warm welcome. Steve Collin!!!" The crowd applauded and Steve walked up the four steps leading to the high stage. The crowd seemed like they wanted him to do well. He took the mic out of the stand and riffed on the room which got a small laugh from pockets of the room.

One thing he'd noticed about alt rooms was that it wasn't a great idea to just go right into your act. It seemed phony. You didn't want to sound like you were giving a speech you'd rehearsed. You wanted to sound like you were just making this shit up as you went. He would realize years later that the comics that sounded unrehearsed were actually the most rehearsed of all. These rooms could smell a polished set and that was death. If you think up there, you're dead.

He looked down at the mic and knew his first joke. The room was dead silent now. The crowd consisted of comedy fans yes, but they still needed to know you had the goods. He was completely unknown to them. They weren't just going to put out like a bunch of comedy whores. Steve was going to have to prove that he was funny, something that he resented. Fuck it. Who cares about these pricks!

He looked out at the dark room, the lights on him were bright and many, and he couldn't make out the faces of anyone past the second row. The silence conveyed that they were waiting for Steve to start being funny. The shy kid from Manhattan who hadn't been noticed most of his life and who at the age of six decided to tell a joke in a station wagon was onstage at the hottest comedy room in New York City. He remembered those great sets at Tagine and B3 when he didn't give a fuck. Just have fun.

"Ya know, this is my first time on this show, and I invited a girl here. This is totally true. It's our first date ... so ummm ... please laugh. Don't be a bunch of fucking cock blocks. If I don't get laid, it's on you." This got a good response and now Steve knew he could just do what he'd planned.

Steve did his set and got off on a huge laugh. His closer had done better than Nick's. He knew as Bobby walked up that he'd passed their test. Bobby smiled widely at him and hugged him. It was like the Johnny Carson of the alternative comedy scene had called him over to the couch. His first time on a real legitimate alt-comedy show with bona fide comic legends and he'd done it. He felt a huge relief as he walked through the smiling crowd all still applauding and making eye contact. The girl he'd referred to during his set smiled warmly as she approached him. In all honesty, he wasn't on a date. He had casually mentioned the show to a woman he'd met a week earlier. He wasn't sure she would even show.

"That was incredible! Let Steve Collin hear it again! Great first time! Our next comedian was on the show last week for the first time and he absolutely destroyed so this week we have him doing 30 seconds of stand-up! Please welcome back Aziz Ansari!" The crowd applauded wildly. A short and good-looking Indian kid who was not more than 23 years old walked up and took the mic. He wore a plaid shirt and a brown hoodie sweatshirt. He began to speak with a punchy southern drawl.

"Hey ya'll. It's ahh ... good to be here again. Thank you. Thank you so much." He did a joke about a senator talking about fucking a box turtle. The joke did well and, when he finished, Steve admired the bravery of this young kid putting himself out there and trying. The kid had spirit.

Aziz walked off and Steve shook his hand. "Great job man," Steve said.

Aziz nodded his head and thanked him with wide eyes and a small smile. "You too man. Hey, I wanna ask you something," he said.

They walked out of the room.

"Hey man, I'm starting a show at UCB next month, do you wanna do the first one?" he asked.

"Yeah man. Of course. Thanks," Steve answered.

"Cool. Gimme your email address man. I liked your stuff a lot man."

"Oh, thanks, you too. I've actually heard about you from Nick Kroll."

"Oh yeah? Nick's a cool guy," Aziz said.

"Yeah, I think he's super funny too," Steve said.

"Me too," Aziz said looking around the room with his eyes wide.

"What'd you say?"

"I said, *me too*!" Aziz shouted, leaning closer.

This was before the age of social media where one could find someone and easily contact them. Steve gave his email to Aziz who then walked off to talk to Zach Galifianakis. The kid was friendly and eager, with a manic energy that wasn't off-putting. He was young and hungry. Soon, Steve would be seeing him all over the city. This nervous-looking kid was to be the next darling of the comedy industry.

Steve walked to the bar and ordered a Makers on the rocks. He felt like he'd done what he wanted and now he was going to reward himself. He used his drink ticket and felt a tap on his shoulder. It was the hot brunette from Luna and her friend.

"Hi there, I'm Sarah," the brunette said. "I just wanted to say that I loved your set. That last bit about the genitalia manipulation had me dying," she said.

"Oh, thanks," he said.

"I've never seen you before. Are you new to New York?" she asked.

"Ahh...yeah. Yeah, I just moved here like six months ago."

"Hi, I'm Shelly," the heavy one said, offering her hand. Steve shook it.

It was almost comical. Months earlier they wouldn't even look at him and here they were borderline hitting on him. The hotter one offered to buy him a drink and he accepted her offer. Just then, a pretty young redhead walked up and introduced herself. She was wearing a tight sweater and high-waisted jeans, and she had a raspy voice.

"Hi there. Great set," she said smiling and offered her hand.

"Oh. Thank you," Steve said, shaking it.

"Where are you going to perform next?"

"Ummm...not sure. Why?"

Aziz was standing nearby.

"He's doing my show at UCB in a few weeks," he said.

"Great. Can you let me know about it?" she said.

"Ummm...how?"

"Well, I can give you my number," she said.

"Yeah. Well, that would be one way to do it," Steve said.

"You're funny," she said, touching his arm.

Then she took out a pen from her notebook in her bag and wrote down her number on a white cocktail napkin and handed it over. The notebook told Steve she was a comic. The woman he'd invited to the show walked up to him. She smiled at the redhead and the other two women and said hi.

"Oh, sorry. I hope I didn't cock block you," the redhead said and walked off.

"Well, it was great to meet you. See you around. We're going to be like your groupies now," the brunette said.

"That was really great," the woman commented, pulling Steve close to her and marking her territory.

"I don't want those other women to get the wrong idea," she said and kissed him right there.

Steve smiled. Wow, things were different. One great set and things were different. He thought about those two women from Luna who were now talking to Aziz. Yeah, this was different. He ordered another Makers on the rocks and went home with the woman he'd invited to the show.

Later, while in bed with her, he closed his eyes and pictured the two brunettes from Rififi.

CHAPTER 15:

WHAT'S THE ALTERNATIVE?

A FEW WEEKS AFTER STEVE'S SET ON *INVITE THEM Up*, Steve showed up at UCB on 26th Street and 7th Avenue. The space was nice and large. It was directly under a Gristedes. Steve had been to the old location a year earlier, it was much smaller with barely even a room. UCB was moving up fast. Steve stood in the back row of the packed house. There was rap music playing, and Aziz was DJing in the booth to the left of the stage. He was mixing Gang Starr into De La Soul. He spotted Steve and waved. Then he walked out from the booth to meet Steve.

"Thanks for doing the first show man. You're first," Aziz said.

Steve figured this would be the case. He was, after all, lowest on the comedy pole in this scene. The other established; comics Leo Allen, Whitney Cummings, and Heather Lawless weren't going to go first. Steve was gaining a rep, but he was still new.

"I just put you first because you're so strong."

This was a common statement made to the comedian given the dreaded bullet spot. The comment played to a comic's ego. It was flattery offered in return for doing the toughest spot. Steve knew it was a bullshit line, but he actually didn't mind going first. He saw it as a challenge and, even better, as a win-win scenario. If you went first and killed, then you were considered amazing. If you went first and bombed, well, you were first and maybe the crowd wasn't warmed up yet. Plus, Steve was getting more and more confident about his ability and felt he could handle it better than most.

The audience settled into their seats, and Aziz took the stage with comedian Jessi Klein, a pretty brunette with glasses and a lot of confidence who was a bit awkward but charming. She was right out of central casting of what a female alternative comic was. A sort of Janeane Garofalo-esque look and attitude but more personable.

She was co-hosting, and the two of them started a bit about how much they hated Coldstone Creamery. The crowd was electric, and they killed from the start. There was no need to win them over. Everyone was there to see Aziz and they could not have been happier. Steve had only seen Aziz the one time a few weeks earlier at Rififi but now he got to see an entire set. He didn't love his material but was blown away by Aziz's comfort level. He owned the stage and, more importantly, loved being up there. He was a lot more comfortable onstage than he seemed to be in life. Literally at home onstage. All comics liked the attention, but Aziz basked in it. Steve tried to find holes in Aziz's stand-up, but it was clear that Aziz had something you couldn't fake. He had presence. The Coldstone bit was funny and killed but it kept going and going with no end in sight. The longer the bit dragged on the more anxious he became waiting offstage.

"Another thing about Coldstone Creamery is the size names...they got a size I Gotta have it! What the fuck kind of crackhead size is that?!" Aziz said.

Soon, there was tension in the room. The audience also seemed uncomfortable with how long the bit was dragging on. Steve looked at his watch. They'd been onstage for twenty-five minutes. A twenty-five-minute opening? Damn.

His stomach was no longer in knots. He was calm now, calm, and angered by their refusal to bring him on. Steve knew he was the funniest when he didn't have any need for approval. After thirty-five minutes, they finally got around to introducing Steve. He sat on the side of the black box theatre and walked up slowly with his notepad in hand. He could feel the energy of the packed young crowd now focused on him. It was the same energy he had felt at Largo that very first night he'd gone there. Now he was on the other side.

He took the mic out of the stand, placed his notepad on the stool next to the stand, and thanked Aziz and Jessi. He wasn't sure if he should address what had happened. The bit they'd done was insanely long. Had anyone else noticed it? Fuck it.

"Great job you guys. Thanks. You might wanna tighten that Coldstone bit though. Get it down to a tight 45 minutes." The crowd erupted with laughter. It even shocked Steve how well it did. Steve laughed with the crowd. He knew some recognition was necessary. There was an awkward tension that needed to be released. He had them now. They were completely on his side, and he went into his A-list set. He killed. It was a good feeling, but it was more of a relief than anything. He'd proven that he hadn't just gotten lucky at Rififi. He wasn't a fluke. He was a comer now.

After a few more comics performed Steve approached Aziz and Jessi in the green room.

"Hey, thanks for having me on," Steve said to Aziz.

"Yeah, man. Great job. I guess we went on a little long with that Coldstone bit," he said with a slight frown.

"I was just kidding around. I thought it was funny."

"Yeah. Yeah, I know."

"Steve, that was amazing," Jessi interjected. "Sincerely you're great. Ya know I saw you at Rififi the other night. After the show, I was talking to Zach Galifianakis and he kept saying how funny you are," she said.

"Oh yeah? Thanks. I'm a fan of yours. You were really great tonight," Steve said.

Maybe he'd made a mistake by calling out the long Coldstone bit. Maybe Aziz had taken his comment personally and was miffed. He couldn't read him since he was always friendly on the surface. Jessi smiled and hugged Steve. Steve left to get a drink with Roger and Nick who'd come by to support with Stephanie.

At McManus Pub down the street, Nick said that Birbiglia had just gotten Letterman. It was a huge deal given how young he was. Twenty-five!

Nick kept going on and on about it to the point where it became irritating. It was clear Birbiglia was gonna be on the next level soon, and Steve was immediately jealous even though there was no reason to be. Birbiglia had been around longer. Envy was an affliction that had always plagued Steve from a young age. He always felt behind everyone else, like he was always playing catch up. Everyone was *beating him to it,* and he took other people's successes way too personally. Unfortunately, the type of personality that would do stand-up comedy and pursue a career in showbiz was prone to jealousy and competitiveness. Steve didn't like that he had this trait. Once he had some taste of success, it got even worse, which he hadn't expected. Wasn't success supposed to make you feel good, not more jealous?

Aziz showed up to McManus with some people from the show. A young, hot brunette about twenty-one, who would repeatedly use the phrase; "we partied like rock stars" throughout the night, even when it didn't fit what she was saying, introduced herself to Steve and sat closely next to him. She bought him a drink and told him about a documentary she was working on. Steve listened and tried to act interested. At one point Roger tried to move in on the girl too. He was sitting on the other side of her and started chatting her up with aw-shucks energy. Steve knew what he was doing though. Roger tried to play the naïve southern guy, but he was also a comic, which meant he was a cock block at heart. Roger soon gave up after Stephanie began flirting with him.

"Last night, I was closing up the restaurant I work at, and we just partied like rock stars the whole time we were cleaning up," the brunette said, sticking her chest out.

"How can you party like a rock star while cleaning up a restaurant? That's not really how rock stars party," Steve said.

"Yeah! You're funny!" she said slapping his shoulder with her hand.

"You're an alien," she said at one point.

"What?"

"You're an alien. You're not of this earth. You're from somewhere else far away," she said, laughing and lighting a cigarette in the bar.

She meant it as a compliment, but it made him self-conscious and made him feel like he didn't belong, something he'd always grappled with.

He got the feeling she wasn't that into him until they ended up back at her place nearly an hour later. They drunkenly made out on her sofa until her roommate came home, forcing them to go into her tiny room. She told him she thought he was really funny and put on her stereo. From her iPod shuffle, she played Billy Idol's "Dancing with Myself."

Steve didn't have a condom and figured it was better he didn't sleep with her since he wanted to go home. She told him she didn't mind, and, in his drunken state, he went ahead. Afterwards, she asked him if she could come to his next show. He told her he'd let her know when his next good one was and that he'd call her. He ran into her again a week later and hooked up with her again. This time she seemed a little more annoying and hinted that she had slept with Aziz. That freaked him out a bit, but she was 21 and hot so, ya know, what was he supposed to do?

CHAPTER 16:

YOU NEVER FORGET YOUR FIRST TIME

S TEVE WAS ENDURING HIS SOPHOMORE YEAR IN college in the middle of Dallas, Texas. He wasn't enjoying it much since he hadn't been prepared for the city of Dallas. It was nothing like New York City and he didn't fit in. He was a huge fan of rap music, no one there seemed to understand that about him. The campus was full of frat boys and sorority girls donning cowboy boots and listening to Garth Brooks while he wore Doc Maartens and Adidas Stan Smiths, before it was cool.

He hated most of the people there and found them completely uninteresting. What he hated most was that he wasn't popular. He was being completely ignored all the time and it was getting to him. He often felt his rage deep inside when he was alone in his dorm room. It got the best of him at times.

What made things worse was that during this time, he watched as some of his classmates from his arts high school moved ahead in their careers. He'd just received a call from a high school friend telling him about their mutual friend getting cast in a new film. Meanwhile, he was feeling helpless and out to sea in Dallas. Yes, he was still studying acting since he still harbored his dreams of one day becoming a successful actor, but he didn't even have a plan on how to make that happen.

One day, in drama class, his large, soft-spoken, Buddha-like, acting professor, James DePaul, informed the class that they all had to prepare a stand-up comedy act to be performed in class.

"Stand-up comedy is one of the hardest things in the world to do, maybe *the* hardest thing. It's a good lesson in what it's like to be alone onstage with only your wits to protect you. It all comes down to you and you alone."

This got Steve's attention. After all, he'd been funny his whole life. However, the idea of being a stand-up comic seemed completely ludicrous to him. He had been trained at the Fame school to be a movie star like so many other grads. Stand-up seemed beneath him. But at least for a moment, it pulled him out of the homesick depression he'd been experiencing with no outlet. He hadn't joined a fraternity and was thus looked at as some sort of social outcast. This made him take on even more of an aloof defensive attitude. He had few friends and was lonely all the time even though he never showed it. He still strutted around campus like he had everything figured out.

He got started on his stand-up act that night in his dorm lobby even though he had no clue how to even approach a comedy routine. It was like being asked to prepare a monologue in Chinese. How the fuck did you do something there was no actual guide for? There were no books in the library about writing jokes. He jotted down a few things he could remember from over the years. Steve had always had a knack for critiquing pop culture tropes. He was a TV addict with a keen sense of absurdity especially when it came to TV and movies. As much as he was addicted to pop culture, he constantly noticed the ridiculousness of it all and took pleasure in picking it apart. He watched the awful teen sitcom "Saved by the Bell" for the sole purpose of mocking it. He often enjoyed what he considered bad entertainment because it made him feel better about himself.

The week before his professor brought up the assignment, Steve had seen a news show about a serial killer on death row dubbed, "The Night Stalker." The killer had murdered over ten people and a woman had still fallen in love with him and married him while he was waiting to be executed. She left him when she found out he was cheating on her on death row. Steve thought it was funny that a woman would marry a guy named Night Stalker and then be shocked when he turned out to be a liar. Really? You didn't see any red flags when you started dating The Night Stalker? A serial killer also turned out to be a cheater?

When the day came, he watched the first few people go on and perform their odd acts. The whole class seemed confused about what to do and were all terribly unfunny. They wanted to be serious actors, not comedians. They did monologues. One girl named Heather simply re-enacted an SNL sketch as if that were a stand-up act. One guy danced with his pants down for a minute. It was extremely awkward to watch. Steve's body felt tight as he waited since he'd actually prepared jokes which he thought was what stand-up was supposed to be.

Then finally it was his turn. He opened with a quick one-liner joke.

"I used to date this girl. She could've been a model. She was that stupid," he said. The class laughed loudly since he'd formed a real joke. Compared to them, he was fucking Richard Pryor. He then went into a bit he felt was sort of funny. It was about the "Friday the 13th" movies and how he didn't understand how Camp Crystal Lake in those films remained open after numerous summers where kids were murdered. It did well and at the culmination of the joke, he got an applause break. It stunned him.

An applause break? He followed it up with a bit about not remembering people's names who remembered every detail about your life and trying to trick them into telling you their name again without asking.

This killed even harder and as he walked off the bare stage, he felt a shift in the class. People settled in and took notice. He'd been the best one, no doubt. It wasn't even close, and everyone knew it.

He was actually embarrassed at how well he'd done compared to everyone else. It felt unfair to them. They were out of his league. He was Shaq and they were a bunch of third graders. He thought about the station wagon moment for the first time in years. It felt like that again when he saw another kid in class scowl at him. It had been the only time on stage that he'd felt completely like himself.

The professor walked up to him after class smiling widely.

"That was great, man. You're really funny," he said.

"Thanks."

"No," he said looking at Steve directly. "You are *really* funny. You should do that as a profession."

"Yeah, I thought it was pretty good," Steve answered modestly.

"Pretty good? Yeah, I mean you were only the best one in the whole class. You need to do that," he said and then lit a clove cigarette in the hallway. Other classmates congratulated him as they walked past including this one arrogant prick whom he couldn't stand.

"That was...really...really good man. Really," he said, staring at Steve.

It was the first time in a long time that he felt like he was good at something. He hadn't exactly been a breakout at the Fame school where he had trouble standing out since everyone there was a star in their own right. He thought maybe he actually could do stand-up.

Unfortunately, the thought of ever doing it again terrified him. Steve had suffered intense stage fright from the very start.

His professor asked him if he wanted to get coffee at La Madeleine down the street. Steve agreed even though he was taken aback. No professor there had ever seemed interested in him before now, at least not enough to get coffee with him.

They sat outside on the patio.

"So what're you going to do this summer?" James asked him, smoking a clove.

"I don't know. I'm gonna be in the Hamptons," Steve answered.

"Ya know, I think you really have something. A natural gift for comedy. I think that could take you somewhere," he said.

"Yeah?"

"I think you should do comedy and not worry about anything else."

"What do you mean?"

"I can see you. I see you grasping for attention yet trying to remain unseen. You have this air about you. You have a sheen up that you use to keep people out, yet you want people to see you. You need to be careful in this business. Don't lose sight of the work and what you're doing. What's important is that no matter what you're doing, if it's work you're proud of, nothing else matters. As long as you know what you want to say and are honest about how you're saying it they can't take that away from you. Don't worry about results. That's the key to it all."

Steve was taken aback by his professor's forthrightness. What did any of it mean? Know what you want to say? Steve was a little overwhelmed but at the same time, it seemed that James had seen him. James had been the first person in a long time to see something in Steve. But Steve wanted to be an actor, not some goofy stand-up comic. This was all a load of bullshit he decided. He wasn't a stand-up comic. What did a stand-up comic even do anyway? Steve loved comedy but he'd barely ever paid attention to stand-up comedy.

That whole week, Steve thought about what James had told him about being honest. It must have taken root down in his subconscious and stayed there. He didn't quite know what he meant by it, but he never forgot it. Maybe he'd understand it later like a movie you didn't get at first but years later clicked with you. Similar to how Steve had experienced the film "Field of Dreams," which seemed pointless when he first watched it at age 16. A movie about a middle-aged man whose dreams hadn't come true seemed downright silly to Steve. He understood it fully years later though.

CHAPTER 17:

THE NEXT BIG THING?

S TEVE TAPED HIS FIRST TV COMEDY SET IN AUGUST on his 30th birthday. The taping took place right down the street from LaGuardia High School. He felt like the plan was starting to take shape. Soon, the world would love him, and so would his father.

Steve was backstage, about to go on. He was calm, calmer than he thought he would be. He tried not to think about what a big deal this was. He talked himself down as he stood there breathing heavily. He was about to have one of the biggest moments of his life and he was well aware of it.

"It's just your first TV spot, what's the big deal? It's just your life. Know what you want to say and be honest about it," Steve told himself over and over, recalling his meeting with his professor James from years ago.

Comedian DL Hughley was getting ready to introduce him. His father, sister, and brother-in-law were in the audience. This TV taping was such a big deal that even his father had shown up. His father never came to his shows mainly because he hated crowds and people. Steve was shaking and his stomach muscles twitched involuntarily. He could never seem to shake his intense stage fright no matter what he did. He thought about Carly Simon's stage fright. If she could do it, then he could do it too. The thought made him feel a little bit better.

"You're so vain, I'll bet you think this song is about youuuu! Don't youuu! Don't youuuu!"

There was another comic on his episode, a short cocky guy with curly hair from Austin. He was yet another nerd with confidence, now a full-on movement in stand-up comedy. The Bill Murray era of comedy seemed to be waning. They didn't much like detached wise guys anymore. There was currently a 'nerdais-sance' happening. The comedy industry creamed their shorts for cocky weird dorks like this guy. He'd over-heard the guy telling a Comedy Central exec that he was moving to LA the following month. Another comic told Steve there was a lot of "heat" on the guy. Austin nerd was thought to be the funniest comic on this epi-sode, and he'd just signed with a big manager who also represented Zach Galifianakis. Everyone there was kissing the guy's ass.

He told Steve to relax when Steve was anxiously pacing backstage. He said it like he was some old, sea-soned comedian like he was Lenny fucking Bruce or something. The guy was 24 years old, younger than Steve was. Steve hated that the guy was so calm. He also hated how wound up he always got while performing. Sometimes the stage fright became unbearable and every time he did stand-up, he wondered why he was doing it. Those moments just before walking out there felt like an eternity and were excruciating. Most would never know that feeling. It felt like being forced to jump into a pit of fire.

The nerdy Austin guy went on second and struggled to find his rhythm. The crowd had been instructed by the audience warm-up comic to applaud as often as possible. Turned out that was a bad thing for this guy since it made it harder for him to get through his long jokes. The frequent applause breaks completely threw off the guy's timing and he soon became frustrated shaking his head. He raised his hands sharply when they interrupted his closer. Then he slammed the mic into the stand and walked off staring at the floor with a frown on his face. He kicked a door backstage that led to the green room.

"What the fuck?! They wouldn't let me get any of my fucking jokes out! Why the fuck were they applauding so much?! What's wrong with them?! I wonder if they'd let me do it again. They should let me!" he said to Steve but more to himself.

He was livid that he hadn't destroyed like he was supposed to. Comedy was like that. There were no sure things. A set could go either way no matter who you were. No one was immune to a bad set. It was the great equalizer. The guy may have had "heat" on him but that didn't matter during his set. Steve liked that about stand-up. It was all a gamble, sometimes you got Blackjack but the potential to bust was always in the air.

The cocky Austin guy wouldn't pan out like expected in the next few years. The next time Steve ran into him in LA, the guy looked haggard and worn down. He actually commented on how bad the audience was when they taped Premium Blend years earlier. Steve was amazed he was still holding on to it. Yeah, it was a tough biz. One misstep and it was all over.

"Making his TV debut, please give it up for Steve Collin!" DL Hughley exclaimed. Steve walked out to the full theatre applauding wildly. He walked up to the mic stand and noticed that there was no mic. Fuck! This was not a good start. No mic? That seemed like something they would have warned him about. He was now going to have to do his debut TV set with no mic? What the fuck? This was a nightmare!!

He turned to see DL Hughley walking off the stage with the microphone still in his hand. Steve ran over to him and tapped him on the shoulder. DL turned, confused, and then realizing his mistake, handed the mic to Steve as if this was no big deal. Yeah, no big deal, I just need the fucking thing that you talk into. The incident felt like it had spanned three minutes but in actuality, it was a mere five seconds when he watched it later on Comedy Central.

Now with the mic in hand, Steve began his set. "Hey everyone, how are you? I'm glad DL finally decided to hand me the mic, that'll help my stand-up." This drew a huge reaction. Almost too big. Steve knew right away this was going to be a fucking turkey shoot. He settled into himself and proceeded to kill for 11 minutes. He'd learned from watching the Austin guy bomb that he had to take his time. There was an applause break after every joke, hell there were applause breaks after joke set-ups.

"You guys ever go to a family reunion and see people who hadn't seen you since you were a baby and they're shocked you're not a baby?" Ten seconds of applause.

"It's like, wouldn't it be more shocking if after 28 years I still *was* a baby?" Ten-second applause break. At one point in his set, he spotted his father's face, and he was laughing. Before he knew it, he was in his last joke, and just like that, he was done.

He walked offstage and the next comic waiting, a short guy named James, told Steve with a blank face that he'd done a good job. The guy looked like he didn't want to follow Steve. Steve walked back into the green room now full of comics waiting to tape their episodes. There was a huge screen playing the show. Comics watched it with blank faces. Some comics looked at him as he entered. None said anything to him even though he knew some had watched him on the monitor. He passed the cocky Austin nerd who was sitting with a serious expression talking with an older man in a suit.

He looked up at Steve and shot him a sour look similar to Nicky's in the back of the station wagon years earlier. Steve now knew for sure that he'd done well. Fuck that Austin nerd. As Steve passed, he said out loud over his shoulder towards Austin nerd, "Great crowd huh?"

Back in the green room, a few comics asked him how it had gone. He told them it went well. No one seemed happy for him. No way could you support another comic on the same show you were on. Everyone was trying not to psych themselves out of this big opportunity. Steve was relieved and fell into a cushioned leather chair located next to a young guy with long bushy hair. The guy had a goofy face and a crooked nose. He was friendly and smiled at Steve, showing very huge teeth. He seemed a bit more chill than the others.

"Hey, good job. I saw it on the monitor," he said.

"Thanks. They're great. When are you on?"

"They start taping my episode in an hour. I'm nervous," he responded.

"Good luck. You'll be great. I'm Steve Collin."

"I'm Andy Samberg," the guy said, nodding.

Andy told Steve he was from California and currently was in LA. They knew some of the same people. He even knew James from the Store. He told Steve that he and his two friends made short comedy films and recorded raps songs. They talked about their favorite rappers when they discovered they were both huge fans.

Steve left after about an hour of hanging about and watching a few comics on the monitor as if he were a skier making sure no one beat his time. But eventually, he grew tired of the vibe in the tense green room and left.

"Nice meeting you, man," Steve said to Andy.

"You too, man. You're lucky you're all done. What're you gonna do now?"

"Maybe go have a drink. I'm looking forward to getting some sleep tonight since I couldn't last night. I just wanna have an easy Sunday tomorrow and wake up in the late afternoon. A nice lazy Sunday," Steve said.

"Yeah, a lazy Sunday. That sounds like a good idea," he said.

Steve walked down the street to get a look at the Fame school located just up the avenue. He looked into one of the ground floor windows. The building was dark, but he could make out a few school jackets hanging on the wall. He was amazed at how little it had changed. He had one of those cliché flashbacks and "where did it all go" moments. Steve was always prone to sentimentality. He knew deep down that he was way too sensitive for the world and this industry. All of a sudden, he was depressed. It confused him since he'd just done something huge. It was a huge step in his career and yet he didn't feel good. Why was he even doing this? He didn't know why he was so adamant about all of it. He knew there was a void inside and that getting the things he thought he wanted wasn't going to fill that void. That scared him.

He went to get a whiskey at a bar downtown after walking around his old school's neighborhood for an hour or so. He thought about how the "Fame" school sandbagged him in his last year there and he regretted ever going there. Maybe if he'd never gone there, he'd have found happiness more genuinely. Maybe he'd now have a normal life as a lawyer or something. Maybe he'd like himself more and wouldn't worry all the time about who was beating him or who was funnier. Showbiz fed on insecurity, and he was now fully invested.

Oddly, getting this break in comedy also gave him more perspective on how much he'd been struggling. He texted the hot 21-year-old brunette after a few drinks and asked her to meet him. She told him she would, and he suddenly felt a bit better. Then his mind went to the senior showcase and the spiteful Russian prick.

CHAPTER 18:

RUSSIAN MEDDLING

S TEVE HAD TAKEN THE CITYWIDE STANDARDIZED test that was given to all 8th and 9th graders across New York City. He felt like he'd done well after spending months preparing for it. He didn't feel certain about the results, but he was confident he'd get admitted to Stuyvesant High School, a prestigious academic school.

On a lark, he had been told by a drama teacher that he should also audition for LaGuardia High School of Performing Arts. The cherubic, supportive, drama teacher had taken an instant liking to Steve after he did a skit in class that killed. She thought he was funny and had charisma, so she set up the LaGuardia audition for him. Steve was taking drama because he liked the attention, but it was just for fun, nothing beyond that.

Soon he found he could get laughs more easily than anyone else in the class. Others in drama class aspired to be legitimate, serious, dramatic actors. Not Steve. He was playing strictly for laughs. After all, if you were straight-up acting, you couldn't tell how you were doing. With comedy, you knew right away how it was going. Once he'd gotten that first huge laugh in that station wagon, he had never stopped trying to get it back. He wasn't even aware how hooked he'd become at that age.

He showed up for his audition at the school not feeling nervous at all since he didn't expect anything from it. After all, he was convinced he'd be going to Stuyvesant the following year. He had his whole plan mapped out already. This acting thing was just a sort of dream that he knew was a total stretch. He hadn't expected to actually go anywhere with it. He certainly didn't expect to get into this prestigious school on the strength of two dramatic monologues that he'd memorized 16 hours earlier. He was competing against kids who'd studied with acting coaches for months in preparation for this. He was way out of his league, and he knew it.

He was led down a white winding hallway. The school looked brand new and huge. The hallways seemed to go on for miles. He sat in the hallway and was handed three scripts by a pretty blond girl with a spandex top that accentuated her huge breasts. She had on ripped jeans and black shoes. Steve tried not to look at her enormous tits that were perfectly shaped by her tight top.

186

"What's this?" Steve asked while glancing at the scripts she'd handed him.

"They're scenes you have to read with another student in there."

"No, I prepared monologues."

"You have to also choose one of these scenes in addition to the monologues," the blonde student told him, smiling.

He looked at the three scenes that were about a page each. There were two serious dramatic ones and then one sort of funny one. He immediately chose the funny one. He went over the lines and, as he did, he heard someone screaming from inside the audition room.

"Chino!!! Chino!!!" a boy yelled in a deep booming voice. It sounded like James Earl Jones was in there.

Chino? What the fuck was the guy yelling? The guy sounded like he was crying. And on command? Steve wanted to leave before he humiliated himself. The door opened and a tall black boy emerged full of bravado. He sat down next to Steve. An effeminate student walked up wearing a black turtleneck.

"How'd it go?"

"Well, my big mouth must have paid off, they want me to come back."

Come back? For what? Steve took a deep breath. This kid next to him seemed like some trained Broadway actor. He was crying and being asked to come back. Steve had no idea what coming back even meant.

He sat there fidgeting with his hand. He tried to go over his first monologue in his head. He just prayed he remembered it. This was a huge mistake. He figured he'd do his best to remember the monologues, do this stupid scene and get the fuck out.

"You're up honey," the hot busty blond said.

He walked into the huge room that had a mirror on one side of the wall and a wooden dance bar. The room smelled clean and new. Three adults were sitting behind a table in folding chairs, and two teens sat in chairs off to the side, one male and one female. Steve said hi and they all smiled politely at him.

"Hello there Steve. How are you?"

"Um...I'm good. How you doing?" Steve was now in knots. He hadn't expected a committee facing him.

"Are you ready?"

"Um...yeah. I don't think I can yell as loud as that last guy though," Steve said.

They laughed at this comment which relaxed him. A laugh was good.

"That's okay, just do what you want. We just want to see you," a male with dark curly hair wearing a tight black t-shirt said.

"What monologues are you going to do?"

"Ummm...one from *The Glass Menagerie* and one from this play called um...*Evergreen*."

"I don't know that play," one older man said.

The younger dark-haired guy chimed in. "I've heard of it," he said.

Steve went into his first monologue, delivering it to his right. There was a huge mirror there which made him more at ease since he'd practiced it in the mirror in his living room. He got through it with the energy he had at home, and he didn't forget any words which amazed him. Then he did the next one which he also remembered perfectly.

After that, he read a scene with a student in the room. The scene was funny, and Steve got some big laughs which he hadn't expected at all. Laughs made him feel more confident, for him laughs were like spinach to Popeye. Once he heard laughs inside the audition room, he knew he had them. He had no idea how the monologues had been since there had been no reaction, but the scene was good because he heard them respond. He was asked to do the monologue again to the female student and then he was done. He was told to sit out in the hallway for a minute.

After about three minutes, they called him back into the room. He was a bit confused since he thought he was done. He sat in front of the committee behind a long table. The young, dark-haired guy looked at him smiling.

"Steve. We decided we'd like you to come back for the next phase of the audition."

"Oh...okay," Steve answered nonchalantly.

There was silence for about three seconds before the man added. "Are you excited about that?"

Suddenly it dawned on him that this was a big deal or something.

"Ahh...yeah. I'm very excited," he said putting on a smile since they seemed to be expecting one as if he'd just won "Star Search." He felt a wave through his body and his leg began to shake a bit. They laughed at his ignorance of what was happening to him. Most kids auditioning would have been thrilled to be called back, but Steve wasn't, which seemed to intrigue them even more. His severe detachment had worked to his advantage for once. He was like the guy who didn't want to sleep with the hot girl who was begging him to bang her.

"Okay, well great. Congratulations and good luck."

Steve left the room and was congratulated by the student. He told his parents who were waiting for him outside. His mom was surprised and skeptical.

"They want you to come back? Are you sure? What did they say exactly?" she asked with a stern face.

Then she smiled widely and seemed happy. He waited in the drama department's office for about two hours and then did a group audition with seven other kids. They did theater games, and he performed his monologue again, this time in front of a bigger group on a large theatre stage. He was sure he'd blown it after he left but he decided it didn't really matter. He didn't even care about any of this bullshit. A month later he was rejected by Stuyvesant and accepted by LaGuardia. And that was that.

Steve started LaGuardia more excited than he had been when he auditioned. The school was huge and intimidating. Most of the kids there seemed determined and mature. Some kids in the drama department already had agents and had already been on TV and in movies. It was crazy. There were a few kids who were recurring cast members on "The Cosby Show." Steve was star-struck when he saw one of them. There was a bona fide TV star walking the hallways with him. What the fuck had he walked into here? There were hot girls all over the place dressed in tight spandex leotards and they all seemed to have giant chests as if Russ Meyer was in charge of admissions. Steve had a hard-on for about two years straight.

He made friends with a few kids who were hell-bent on becoming famous. One of them guaranteed him he'd be in movies by 21. The guy was off by a year. Another obnoxious loud kid there had three older brothers whose TV show had just become a phenomenon. Steve had been fascinated by TV and movies his entire childhood. Before this, he'd thought fleetingly about maybe being an actor but, in this school, it seemed like an actual possibility. In fact, the faculty encouraged it. In the hallways, there was a board of famous alumni called the "Wall of Fame." Steve passed by it every day and then it began to sink in that getting on that wall was a top priority. If you didn't make it up there, then it was like you didn't even exist. His acting teacher commented often about the importance of getting up there.

One day, Steve was down in the South Street Seaport with his friends Jonesy and Rob, both savvy drama majors, when they spotted a girl walking past. She was cute with dirty blonde hair that was coiffed perfectly. She wore jeans and brown stylish boots that went up to her knees. She was thin with pleasant energy and confidence.

"Yo! Jen!" Jonesy bellowed at her walking towards her with his arms wide.

"Hey," she stopped and looked over with her eyes tight.

"It's me, Jonesy, from Performing Arts. Remember?"

"Oh my God! Jonesy! How are you?!"

"I'm great," he said, leaning in and kissing her cheek.

"You remember Rob Hayden?"

"Oh yes! Of course!" she said and hugged him.

"And I don't remember you though," she said, looking at Steve.

"Oh, I'm Steve. I wasn't there when you were," he said.

"Oh, I'm Jen. So what're you guys up to?"

"We're graduating soon."

"Oh my God. It flies by huh?"

"What're you up to?"

"Well, I've been acting. I just did this movie called 'Leprechaun'. It's like a horror movie. What about you guys"

"Just trying to get that break," Jonesy said.

"How's school?"

"Great. Are you in touch with anyone still?"

"Ummm...well, I talk to Sasha Marrison still, but no one else really. I didn't have that many close friends there, to be honest."

After a couple of minutes, she said she had to leave because she was meeting a guy for a first date.

"Oh, you're not still with Ted?" Jonesy asked.

"No, no actually. I mean we're kind of 'on a break' as they say," she said making air quotes with her hands.

"Oh. Okay. It was great seeing you," Jonesy said, kissing her again, something he did to every woman he met. She walked off and Jonesy and Rob went on and on about how she had been the hottest girl in school a few years back.

"She was easily in the top five back then, easily," Roy said.

"Top five?!" Jonesy answered.

"What?"

"She was in the top one bro!"

"What about Denise Adams?" Rob shot back.

"Get the fuck out of here! Denise Adams? What was so great about her?"

"Double D Denise? Ahh...her huge tits and ass," Rob said, letting out a laugh.

"Dude! Her body was good, but her face was trash," Jonesy said.

"It wasn't trash. Besides the body is more important," Rob said.

"Dude, whatever. No way can you even put Denise Adams in the same category as Jen Aniston. It's like comparing apples and carrots," Jonesy said, getting the saying wrong. Jonesy often got things just a bit wrong.

"Apples and carrots?" Steve said.

"What?"

"Apples and oranges you idiot," Steve said causing Rob to break into hysterics.

"Whatever," Jonesy said, waving his hand as if shooing a fly away.

They walked to Joe's Pizza on Seventh Avenue and decided to smoke a joint and go see "The Naked Gun" on Eighth Street. Rob went on about the new agent he'd signed with that was sending him out for the new Oliver Stone movie. Steve tried to hide his jealousy as Rob bragged about his recent breaks in the biz. He'd just filmed a part on a new series, and it had boosted his ego.

Steve's mother wasn't so sure of his new aspirations and told him many times he should just go to law school and forget showbiz. She was probably just worried, but she undermined his confidence with these comments. His classmates' parents meanwhile all wanted their kids to be in showbiz and hit it big.

As his senior year drew to a close, Steve had done well for himself. The big Senior Showcase was just a week away and he knew he was a lock. He was also dating a super-hot girl that most of the guys there wanted. He liked that they were jealous of him.

"Dude, if you kill it in Senior Showcase, things can really happen for you. That's how Helen Slater got discovered. She signed with William Morris after that," his friend Adrien from Queens told him. The kid acted like a tough guy even though he wasn't. Steve liked

him even though his friends thought he was pretentious. They referred to him as the "math farter" now
and would never let it go.

"I mean, I already have an agent, so it doesn't matter
for me, but it could really help you man," the tall, lanky,
handsome guy with a crooked nose said sitting in front
of a wooden piano in the main drama classroom. The
guy had already been in a movie and was a standout
talent there. He was good and he knew it. Adrien put
his fingers on the keys lightly and pressed down. He
played a simple piece that sounded like the theme of
the movie "Halloween."

"Do you play the piano?"

"Not really. I mean....my mom made me take lessons
as a kid but I'm not that good. I mean I'm not going to
win any awards for being a pianist or anything," he said,
smiling while continuing to fiddle with the ivories.

Steve was all set to go. He knew this was his chance
to finally get his career going and become what was his
destiny. He was going to live forever, people would see
him and cry...Fame! Baby, remember my name! FAME!
Just like the stupid song said.

There was just one thing standing in the way. To get
into the senior showcase, you first had to audition your
scene in front of the committee of teachers. The day of
the auditions was happening on Wednesday afternoon.
The whole senior class did their scenes in front of
the entire drama department and faculty. There were
three teachers on the judging committee, including

a petulant Russian teacher who had a reputation for aggressively playing favorites.

Steve's scene partner was his friend Todd, a funny actor with a sort of nerdy sensibility. They were doing a scene from the Neil Simon comedy, "Broadway Bound." It was a scene they'd performed back during their sophomore year, and it had destroyed. Some kids still brought it up to him. Steve had been told specifically by his sophomore acting teacher to do the scene for the showcase. "That scene was great. You guys will get work from doing that scene," he told Steve.

Todd wanted to do the scene also, but the Russian teacher Yusim warned Todd not to do the scene with Steve. Yusim despised Steve for some inexplicable reason. Todd ultimately did the scene with Steve defying the spiteful Russian. They rehearsed for a few weeks and had it down cold. They performed for the department and committee and the scene killed. When it was over, Todd and Steve hugged in the hallway.

"That was great man," Steve said.

"You killed it, man," Todd said.

The lanky kid, Adrien, walked past and congratulated them.

"Yo, that shit was fucking dope man. You guys are definitely in," he said slapping Steve's hand.

Then the list for the Senior Showcase picks went up in the hallway and Steve's stomach tightened up in knots. There was something wrong with the list. It was wrong of course. After all, it didn't include Steve and

Todd. It included a couple of scenes that had bombed during the auditions. The worst actor in their grade had somehow been chosen for the showcase. One guy who wasn't even audible onstage had been chosen over Steve. There was an uproar of sorts, and some students actually went to bat for Steve and Todd voicing the blatant unfairness of their scene not being selected.

"Fucking Yusim," Todd said shaking his head outside the school smoking.

"What?"

"He did it to get back at me since he hates you," he said.

"How...how can he...I mean that's not fair," Steve said without an ounce of irony. He wanted to cry right there on Amsterdam Avenue that sunny Friday.

The showcase happened the next week and a few people got signed by agents and went on to have successful careers. Three of them made their film debuts almost immediately. And then it was all over. Steve was told not to worry about it by his friends and his hot girlfriend. He'd have other opportunities, she said, as they lay in her parents' king-size bed. He resented the school, and now he hated Russians. He watched the film "Red Dawn" with a newfound fervor after that.

Steve met with a few agents through some contacts, but his aloofness didn't translate well to industry people. They weren't impressed with his detachedness. They saw it as laziness or shyness. One talent agent said that he didn't seem to want it "badly enough." Didn't want it badly enough? Was he supposed to walk into the office begging the agent like some chump?

His mother had never been enamored with his ambitions of becoming some dumb actor. It all seemed ridiculous to her, and she kept planting seeds that he should be a lawyer although she wasn't saying that much anymore.

Lately, she was commenting that he would have to settle for being a fireman now. The comment was meant to demean him. He recalled one of his sisters laughing after she said it which made it hurt even more. His mother used to dismiss his natural sense of humor. She described it as something that alienated others. His natural comedy sense was a hindrance in school. He was dubbed a class clown a few times. The message was clear, his sense of humor was something to stifle and be ashamed of. It made other kids laugh but, in the end, there was no real merit in being funny. And life was all about making yourself into something so that you could later rub it in everyone's face.

His mother's hopes now seemed to be pinned mainly on his oldest sister and a little less on his other sister. His mother was going to make sure her daughters excelled as a sort of vendetta against male chauvinism. She often made comments about how men had destroyed her chance at a career. The comments made Steve feel like her unhappiness was somehow his fault. He often felt like he was on his own to fend for himself. No one was guiding him, and his showbiz hopes were all but gone after the senior showcase snub. All this built inside Steve's mind and his detachment and resentment grew stronger. He couldn't count on anyone but himself. He felt alone most of the time. He dreamt about the station wagon weeks later and in the dream, he was now completely alone in the car without a driver.

CHAPTER 19:

DOWNHILL RACER

S TEVE QUICKLY BECAME A REGULAR ON *INVITE THEM Up,* as well as on Aziz's wildly popular Crash Test show dubbed "the biggest comedy show in New York City" by the Times. The tide had shifted fast and now Rififi and UCB were the biggest alt rooms, not Luna.

Serena Williams had sneakily eclipsed her older sister and was now kicking her ass. Luna was still a popular room, but it was more corporate and uptight and thus not cool anymore. Luna had alienated people with its shitty exclusive vibe and so most people had stopped going there. Rififi and UCB were more fun and laid back.

The people had spoken. Rififi was cool, Luna wasn't. Luna was like the older comedian that had overnight become like your unfunny dad. Luna was Friendster and Rififi was Facebook. It was like Chevy Chase's awful piece of shit talk show that made clear how completely out of touch he had become. UCB was the new cool kid in town who didn't give a fuck what people thought. Luna was acid-wash jeans now.

Steve had finally done Luna months earlier. It was more of a hurdle he'd had to jump over since it represented an alternative comedy milestone like graduating college. If you didn't do Luna, you weren't officially in the New York Comedy scene. Even some of the top comedians failed to garner a spot. Luna had at least bought him some cachet around New York. Now some of the biggest names in New York comedy knew who he was.

One night at Rififi, he was asked to audition for the prestigious Aspen Comedy Festival by a TV producer who was on the festival panel. Aspen was a huge deal and had launched many comedy stars. An appearance could lead to huge opportunities and TV appearances. The comedian TJ Miller had just broken out there a year earlier. Steve knew he was ready. Two years earlier he'd been doing bringer shows at Stand-up New York, doing three minutes, and now he was back there auditioning for the hottest comedy festival in the world. The audition lineup featured all the hottest new comedians in the city.

The competition was fierce. Aziz, Anthony Jesselnik, Pete Holmes, Whitney Cummings, and Jenny Slate were all on the show. The room was only half full and was mostly made up of industry people. Comedy industry people were known to be averse to enjoying comedy. They weren't there to laugh at you but to judge you quietly.

Steve sat at the bar being careful not to interact with the other comics. He didn't want to psych himself out. He went on after Kurt Metzger who was quickly climbing up the club scene. Kurt was an aggressive strong comedian with acerbic wit, a strong presence, and a unique point of view. His confidence was off the charts. He was like a freight train due to the physical dominance he lorded over the room. He commanded a room.

Steve's hands shook a bit as he sipped his whiskey and soda slowly. He didn't want to get wasted. This was the absolute Top Gun of New York comedy, and he knew it. *If you think up there, you're dead.* He was honored to just be included. It was an awkward position for the comedians, they all knew each other but were also in direct competition. Everyone was fighting to get ahead and at the end of the day, your goal was to beat the other crabs climbing up the walls of the comedy bucket. This dynamic made for a very awkward time in the cramped bar area where everyone was preparing to destroy everyone else while also trying to remain cordial. Steve felt a bit out to sea. Almost every comic there was flanked by their manager, something Steve had yet to secure.

Aziz was sitting at the end of the bar with his "people." He was now hot property and had a team of agents and managers making moves for him. The industry was going to make sure Aziz happened. Pete Holmes stood in the corner talking intensely to a short Jewish man. They looked like they were planning a military coup. Pete Holmes was a friendly unassuming guy, but he wasn't just some clueless rube from the mid-west. He was a driven, business-savvy, shark navigating the industry and doing everything he could to get to the next level. In other words, he was a comer. TJ Miller sat at the bar sipping a large cocktail and talking loudly to a striking young blond whom Steve assumed he was fucking. He was merely there as a spectator. TJ and Pete were close from back in Chicago. They were of the same breed and seemed determined to get to that next level.

Steve watched Kurt who was doing well but, surprisingly, not killing like he usually did. This made Steve feel a bit better. Kurt was usually a powerhouse but was having an off night. Anything could happen in comedy. Steve knew he was the underdog which felt like a better position to be in. There was no real pressure on him. He didn't have wily managers over his shoulder telling him what to do like needy girlfriends. He could do whatever the fuck he wanted. He suddenly felt the way he had at his LaGuardia audition. No expectations. These managers all looked like stage mothers, the way they creepily doted on their investments. They were like Jewish mothers constantly fixing their kids' hair.

Steve watched Kurt rush through his final bit. The red light was flashing furiously. He was going over and

203

he was panicking since he was having a hard time turning the crowd around to him. Kurt's last bit didn't land at all. There was sparse laughter in the way back and silence everywhere else. He waved his hand up out of frustration and got off with his posture slumped. As Kurt walked out of the room Steve told him, "good job." Kurt chuckled sarcastically. "Yeah right," he answered with his head down wiping his forehead. He added "Good luck, they stink" in a dismissive way that Steve knew was meant to psych him out. He was acting just like the cocky Austin nerd had when he ate shit.

Steve just smiled. He was calm now. He spotted the producer who had asked him to audition sitting way in the back, alone. She smirked at him warmly and shyly and waved. He nodded his head at her. He now felt like she was on his side. She'd been very supportive of him ever since his TV spot aired on Comedy Central. His TV set had come out great and many had commented on it to him. He told himself just to have fun like he did when he was the funniest guy in school and comedy wasn't a career option.

Steve walked up calmly after the older and surly MC wearing outdated baggy jeans introduced him. He opened with his quickest one-liner in his joke arsenal.

"Hey everyone thanks a lot. Big night. I was just dating this girl and she was really into playing sex games. There was this one she used to like to play all the time called...sleep with my friend Rob." The crowd laughed loudly.

Steve completely relaxed. He was loose and killed. Only one joke in the middle received a tepid response, but he saved it with an adlib which killed. He was so loose that he never once got too in his head which is what he'd seen take Kurt down. He got off on a huge laugh.

None of the other comics made eye contact with him at the bar, which confirmed that he'd had a good set. The other comics actually looked mad. One comic sat at the bar with his head down. He mouthed the words to his set with a pained look, the same pained look Nicky had in the back of the station wagon after Steve killed. Steve had oddly experienced every aspect of the comedy business when he was a 6-year-old.

The comic stopped mouthing his set and stared up at Steve. Then he got off his stool. Steve smiled. The comic did not smile back at Steve.

"I heard everyone's bombing," he said instead, looking at Steve with a tense look before heading into the room. Then just a few seconds later, he walked back to the bar area. "Fuck me!" he yelled.

The older rude waitress shooshed him.

"Don't shoosh me! This is bullshit!" he yelled and stormed out of the place.

Steve looked into the room, the audience was on its feet applauding as the MC brought Robin Williams up. The Aspen showcase was now over for everyone else. Pete Holmes walked past Steve and told him he liked his set with a goofy smile that made his eyes disappear into his face.

A few days later Steve received an email from the Aspen committee producer telling him he was in the next round of auditions. Metzger and some other heavy hitters hadn't even been called back. Steve tightened his set a bit more at The Love Below and Trainwreck to prepare for the final audition back at Stand-up NY.

He didn't like Stand-up NY since he rarely got booked there and it was a weird room. The setup and dynamic were hollow. It was a room that took some getting used to, so he felt like he already had a few strikes against him especially since the other comics were regulars there. It was like he was playing an away game and the others were the home team.

He had a solid set again and afterwards, the Aspen producer told him the committee of other judges liked him. He wondered on his subway ride home back to Brooklyn how Aspen would change his career. He imagined it would be a great experience and could finally make him relax a bit. He had killed in all his auditions so logic would dictate that he'd go to Aspen. I mean, that's how life works right? Just ask that asshole Russian.

A day later, Steve received a call from the female producer from the Aspen Committee. She asked him to meet her for a drink. Steve felt maybe this was bleeding into the not professional territory, but he figured she was just being friendly. When he showed up to meet her, she was dressed up more than usual. She was a lot looser also and he saw an empty wine glass next to a full one. He'd been warned months earlier by Carl that she had "a thing" for new male comics and often held out her influence. Steve felt a bit defensive going in and immediately picked up on the strange vibes. He immediately regretted meeting up with her.

They drank for a couple of hours, and she dropped a lot of famous comedian names. She was slurring her words and her eyes looked tired. She promised Steve spots on shows that could change his career. She mentioned she was considering booking him on a huge music and comedy festival that had launched many comics. If this producer thought that he was funny, then he must be doing something right. At the end of the night, they stood outside the bar on 17th Street talking about nothing in particular.

Steve was drunk. Something weird was in the air. The producer stared at him smiling. What was going on here?

"You look cute," she said, smirking and putting her hand on his arm.

"Oh, thanks," Steve responded crinkling his brow.

"Everything okay?" she asked stepping closer.

She finally leaned in and kissed him gently. Steve pulled back abruptly and let out a breath. She pulled back, looked down at the sidewalk, and giggled. She sort of hemmed and hawed and finally walked off without saying anything. Steve wasn't sure of what had happened and just watched her walk off in a sort of diagonal pattern. Maybe it was just a drunken thing. Not a big deal.

After that night, the producer stopped contacting him and returning his emails. All the promises she'd made had apparently come with an ultimatum. Steve got the feeling she'd felt snubbed. This was years before the me-too movement, and during a time when this was simply part of the business. If you didn't play the game, well there were plenty right behind you who would. Steve had no power and he felt no one would have cared in the end about his story anyway.

"Steve, this is Nicole from Aspen. I just wanted to tell you that it was close. So close. If we could have taken one more comedian, it would have been you. I want you to know that. You really impressed everyone, but this just isn't the year."

So close. Steve knew these words had probably haunted many showbiz hopefuls over the years. So close was probably what many people who didn't land the role in a movie that would go on to become a block-buster heard. That's what the guy who almost got the part of Chandler on "Friends" probably heard from the casting people. The words were meant to make him feel better, but they had the opposite effect. So close. Great. Live with that for the rest of your fucking life.

The worst part was that their decision hadn't been based on anything fair. It came down to who was repped by the most influential management, and Steve had no one fighting for him. He wondered if the female producer had also had a hand in it. There was no way to know for sure if she'd sabotaged him, although it seemed suspicious since she'd now completely cut him off after being so friendly. Just like back in LA, Steve felt like the industry was now infiltrating the alt scene. Soon, the whole festival circuit would come down to powerful managers and favors. Ironically a huge comedy sex scandal would take place at the festival that same year, the festival would launch Aziz and Anthony Jesselnik to the next level of comedy.

CHAPTER 20:

HEAT

STEVE SAT IN A BAR, ALONE, ON 23RD STREET, getting drunk on whiskey. He needed to take his mind off of Aspen. Aspen would have given him the boost he so desperately needed. His heat had recently cooled considerably, and his TV credits were in danger of expiring. In comedy, you were always on the brink of becoming irrelevant. You had to constantly look over your shoulder for new comics who were lining up to replace you. A year without a significant TV appearance was about the equivalent of no TV credits. He felt in jeopardy of becoming a has-been. He thought of a comedian he'd heard killed himself a couple of years earlier. The guy had become a kind of comedy cautionary tale as to what can happen when a comic goes off the rails. The guy named the "Chicken" had massive heat after appearing at the Montreal Comedy Festival. He was supposed to be the next big thing. And after he fell short of expectations, he killed himself.

Steve drank his whiskey fast and looked at the clock. It was almost 8 p.m. He stood up and walked over to Rififi. A younger comic from Boston had asked him to appear on a new show he had started a few weeks before. *Invite Them Up* was *the* show there but other shows were now popping up at Rififi left and right since the place had a following. The Boston comic named Greg Johnson was extremely funny and likable with an infectious laugh that made you like him immediately. He often clapped when he laughed to accentuate how amused he was. Steve liked Greg right away.

Greg was hosting this new show, and Steve waited at the bar drinking his usual when he was approached by a tall and good-looking guy with a kinetic presence and thick curly hair.

"Hey, Steve?"

"Yeah, hey."

"I'm Ryan Palmer. I met you once through Phil."

"Oh yeah, how's it going?"

"God, man. You're on the show?"

"Yeah, I am."

"Awesome! I can't wait to see you. I saw you at the Aspen auditions. You killed it."

"Oh, thanks."

"So, when do you find out?"

"Ummm...well. I already found out."

"You're going right?"

"Ummm...not actually."

"What?! That's bullshit. You were the best on that show. I'm not even kissing your ass. I mean it."

"Thanks. Maybe I was just *too* funny."

Ryan laughed. "Yeah! Probably!"

Steve had heard of Ryan Palmer for the past year. He was new to New York and making a big splash. He'd gone to Aspen an unknown and left with a TV show. Now he was in a popular new movie and was doing the New York circuit more now with his Chicago friends Hannibal, Kumail, and Phil. They were all new to the city, but they would not be new for long. They had their sights set high and soon took the scene completely by storm.

Thanks to his recent TV credits and regular appearances on the best UCB and Rififi shows, Steve was now a downtown legend of sorts and most new comics that came through the alt scene were aware of him. He had been branded an "alt comic" even though he didn't consider himself one. He was just a comic. What the fuck did that even mean? Alt comic? He wrote funny jokes and that was it.

"Alt comic" was fast becoming a disparaging term used to describe comedians who meandered and phoned in their weakly crafted jokes. Maybe Steve was falling into that trap a bit more lately, but he was a great joke writer. Nevertheless, he decided to embrace the label and not run from it. He knew some alt comedians could be lazy and rest on their laurels while others described themselves as storytellers just to escape the pressure of having to write jokes.

Steve wasn't like that. He was a good comic. The alt comic label was just meant to take him down a peg; comedy was full of people who didn't want you to succeed. They were waiting for you to fall on your face. And Steve hadn't realized yet that one had to be careful who they let close. These people could be friendly, but they weren't true friends. They were "comedy friends." Everyone was after the same thing, and some would stop at nothing to get the brass microphone.

"Ya know, I know this comedian in DC, and I told him I met you and he told me that you're his favorite comic," Ryan said.

"Oh really?"

"Yeah, the guy got all excited when I told him I knew you. I told him I didn't know you that well but that I had met you once."

Ryan was super charming. His quick rise didn't surprise Steve. He had a way about him. He bought Steve a whiskey even though Steve got all his drinks for free anyway. Steve found himself getting a little defensive, there was something off about this guy. It wasn't normal to be this friendly, this was comedy, and everyone in this industry had an ulterior motive. Steve was learning slowly that when people in comedy were nice to you out of the blue, there was usually a reason.

For years, he'd been ignored by almost everyone. Now he was constantly being approached by comics who were new to the alt-comedy scene as if he was someone to know. He grappled with his resentment that these people were all paying attention to him now. It was a good sign that opportunists were sucking up to him, but it still pissed him off and was completely transparent to him. Steve liked the attention more than he cared to admit. Ryan went up before Steve and crushed the room. Ryan was a killer, a born performer who had a rep for ruining an audience for the next comic. He was hard to follow.

Word was that Ryan was months from blowing up. He had a great rep as a comic even though he also had a rep for being a bit boisterous. Steve had also been told by Nick Kroll that Ryan had blown an audition for a big TV series by getting drunk beforehand. The bad press didn't matter though, it actually helped him in the long run. Ryan was becoming a breakout alt-comedy star.

Ryan did a bit imitating a dumb frat guy hitting on a cop. It was killing, but Ryan seemed distracted by something happening in the crowd to the left of the stage. The socially awkward alt comic from the cult military school movie was talking to a woman next to him. He was talking a bit too loudly on purpose to flaunt his status as if he were King Henry the 8th. He was a geek but in this alt world he was the high school quarterback and Ryan was just a freshman. Ryan finally addressed it.

"Hey, man, can you talk louder during my set? It really helps me out! Come on! Christ dude!" he bellowed, banging the mic stand on the floor. The alt-heavy took issue with Ryan's flippant comment.

"What?"

"Everyone can hear you, man! Come on! Shut up!" Ryan said while smiling slightly.

"Do you have a problem with me?!"

"Yes! You're loud as fuck, dude!"

"Just do your act man! What's your problem?!" he said glaring at Ryan.

"Okay, thanks. I'm just fucking around man. Are you actually mad at me?"

"Fuck you! How dare you call me out! I did nothing to you! Nothing!" the man yelled, pointing his finger at Ryan sharply.

"Are you for real? I can't tell if you're mad or if this is a bit," Ryan said to laughter.

"It's not a bit! You're a fucking asshole!" he yelled and stood up. "How dare you! How dare you!" he yelled over and over.

"Okay. This is weird. Dear diary. Tonight I was berated by one of my comedy idols."

"Fuck you!"

"Fuck me? What? Why?" Ryan responded with his arms held out to his sides.

The alt king stormed out of the room and slammed the door. It was tense and quiet.

"Okay. Well, I'm just glad that didn't get awkward. And on that note, I think I'll end my set and see if my career is over."

Ryan went to the bar and was approached by the alt guy who immediately started shouting in his face. Ryan was flustered and tried to calm him down as everyone stared at their pissing contest. The idea of two alt-comics getting into a physical altercation was ludicrous. The alt king had a temper and often acted like a spoiled kid. Everyone around him enabled his behavior since they wanted to be close to him. He was like the cruel little kid with magic powers from that "Twilight Zone" episode. The King Joffrey of alt-comedy. He intimidated people into respecting him.

Eventually, the alt king left Rififi, and Ryan simply drank at the bar with his head down. Steve walked over and told him not to worry about it.

"What?" he said.

"That guy can be kind of a dick," Steve said.

"Yeah, okay. Fuck, man," he said looking away and shaking his head.

It seemed as though Ryan was now angry with him for some inexplicable reason, so Steve left him alone.

Just two months later, Ryan Palmer's new movie was a hit. Steve spotted him at a UCB show one night and approached him to say hi.

"Hey, Ryan, how are you? Congrats on your movie, man," he said.

Ryan simply stared at him with his mouth open. "Mmmm...thanks, what's your name?"

Steve chuckled, thinking he was kidding. But when Ryan failed to laugh Steve realized he was dead serious.

"Ummm...what's my name? John Coktosten," he said.

"Cool John, glad you liked the film," Ryan shook his head and looked away. He walked off to talk to the alt king he'd almost come to blows with at Rififi just a couple of months earlier. They'd seemed to have resolved their problems. Having success seemed to unite them. Ryan was now on the next level. And that was that. Ryan had turned a corner in comedy and didn't need to be charming anymore. Now he could act however he wanted with no consequences whatsoever. Nothing would ever bring him back down to earth, save for some cosmic cultural shift.

Comedy was not for the weak, and no one was nice in this business for no reason. Steve had respect, but once others surpassed him then they ceased to act respectfully toward him since there was no use in having him as an acquaintance anymore.

Steve knew he couldn't control his success in comedy. The only thing he had any control over was how good he actually was. So he got back to the business of being good. Fuck all these phony assholes. At the end of the day, they couldn't deny that he was great.

"Hi Steve, I'm Amy. Amy Schumer," the young pretty blonde said, smiling at him and leaning back on her heels a bit. Steve said hello back politely, but she must have read something in his expression. They were standing near the bar at Rififi before *Invite Them Up*, which that night boasted a huge lineup including Zach Galifianakis, Jessi Klein, and Aziz.

Steve was talking with a cute brunette with a slender frame and a large bosom. The cute brunette was a new comic who had asked Steve to get a drink with her. She was also sleeping with Greg, so he didn't think anything of it beyond her seeking advice. Yet there she was, flirting with him hard, laughing at everything he said and touching his stomach a little harder with every laugh. And now, this blonde was interrupting and cock blocking.

"You never remember meeting me," she said, still smiling while eyeing the cute brunette. "We've met like three times at the mic on Houston" she added.

"Yeah. The Trainwreck," Steve said.

"Right, the Trainwreck. I forgot the name of it."

"Yeah, I remember, I just didn't at first. Amy, the Trainwreck," he added.

"Wait, did you just call me a train wreck?"

"What? No. I was just saying I remember you from there," he said.

"Just kidding. You're right. That actually might be a good way to describe me, a train wreck. I'll have to write that down. Maybe I'll use it."

"Just remember who gave you the idea," Steve said, smiling.

She offered to get him a drink and then talked to him and the brunette who was now frowning. Steve remembered meeting her now, though it had taken him a second to place her face. She was almost brand new, one year in, and Steve had met her after Greg's show weeks earlier. She was bubbly and held herself with confidence. He hadn't seen her do stand-up yet, but a friend said she was good and that she was a climber. She eventually asked him for a recommendation to the booker of *Invite Them Up*. Steve introduced her to Bobby who was skittish and headed out of the place with Jenny Slate. Steve offhandedly mentioned to Amy that he was filming a rap video the next morning at a comedy club on the West Side.

Online videos were the latest platform that comics were using to get seen. The recent success of Human Giant, Lonely Island, Whitest Kids U Know, and Derrick Comedy had made short comedy vids, the latest launching pad every comic was trying to capitalize on. One viral video could get you noticed now. Amy smiled and pulled Steve's shirt with a tug.

"Oh, can I be in the video!?" she asked bouncing up and down.

Steve was taken aback by her enthusiasm and told her he'd love to have her and any other friends she might want to bring. Amy excused herself and went to talk to the alt king from the cult movie. The cute brunette was still standing there. She asked him if he wanted to get a drink at her apartment and they left.

Steve and the cute brunette lay in her bed staring at the ceiling in silence. He was sweaty and out of breath. It was dark and he could smell the smoke from her cigarette. His head was spinning, and he had a headache. He was tense and wanted to get out of there. This was his least favorite part. After about an hour or so he said he had to leave since he had to shoot the video the next morning. She leaned over on her bed and asked if he wanted to hang out again. She then smiled and asked if she could blow him again. He was putting on his shirt and almost out the door. He glanced at her on the bed playing with her hair. He sat on the bed already mad at himself.

Steve was flabbergasted when the young comic Amy actually showed up early the next morning with three comedian friends dressed up like rap video vixens. The women, all comics, gamely acted as his groupies. Amy went above and beyond of course. In the middle of a shot, she grabbed Steve and pretended to make out with him and then passed out on the floor.

"Steve, I think for this next shot I should do coke off your dick," she said.

"I don't have any coke, unfortunately," he said.

"Well, okay then just take out your dick and we'll pretend to snort. You want this to look real right?" she said with a sarcastic chuckle. He knew she was only being crass since that was her shtick, and she was always saying provocative things. She may have been flirting for real, but it was hard to tell.

When the video came out, it quickly garnered attention on the comedy scene. It was even featured on Comedy Central. This got the attention of an independent music producer who offered Steve a contract to record a whole album. Steve hadn't anticipated getting a record deal from doing a video, but he decided to do it. After all, he'd done one rap song, he was ready to produce an entire album.

A month later, Amy appeared on the reality comedy competition show. The show was considered corny and frowned upon by many comics in the scene, especially alt-comics, but it didn't matter, she was now a contender and was on her way. When Steve overheard some comedians talking shit about Amy at Rififi, he knew she had officially graduated to the next level. People only talked shit about you when you were a threat. One comedian called her a hack with no talent. The comedian dishing about her was a total hack himself with absolutely no originality. That's usually how it went in comedy and in life. Once you put yourself out there you were instantly a target and there were plenty of people ready to take aim.

AN ALT ORAL HISTORY
PART THREE: THE HEYDAY

"I'd worked years to get myself into the mainstream comedy clubs because that was how it had been done in the past and then one day this small scene became the hottest thing in town. Soon the biggest shows were in the back of dive bars. It definitely became a thing almost overnight and most of the people were pretentious a**holes. They thought they were so cool."

— Erik Bransteen
Comic

"There are times when I felt like hmm....well I guess they didn't want me to be a part of that. There were various shows where you had to follow John Mulaney who'd just destroyed."

— Jim Gaffigan
Comic

"Eugene and Bobby came to see if we (Comedy Central Records) wanted to do an album of the show. The idea was massively appealing (and if memory serves I said yes in the room), because it's always fun to capture a special local movement like this, share it with the world, and preserve it as a time capsule. It was a massive three-CD and one DVD set, which offered a lot of real estate on the package for art, and it was important that it reflect the mood of the scene. The album wasn't for everyone, but the people who got it loved it and more people bring up that album to me than most of the other records I've produced. The idea of having fun making art with your friends is one of the most irresistible notions in the galaxy."

— Jack Vaughn
Comedy Central Records Producer

"The 00's will likely be remembered as the era "alternative comedy" broke. After the boom and bust of the 80's a new generation of smartasses arrived to stretch the limits and help redefine it"

— The Onion AV Club

"The UCB had some of the most killer shows I'd ever seen. Aziz had a show at 11pm on Monday nights that were packed with people actually sitting onstage. You'd see Gaffigan, Garofalo, TJ Miller, Louis, Patton Oswalt on the same fucking show! It was a crazy time"

— Joe List
Comic

"I'd just moved to New York from Louisiana and was nobody. I would go to this little place called Rififi and there'd be Zach Galifiniakis, David Cross and Louis CK. It was all just right there in a small room. It was beyond exciting. Getting on the show at UCB was like a huge moment. You had a feeling anything could happen. TJ Miller would show up and eat paint thinner. You'd be at Rififi and be like 'Tom McCaffrey looked at me!' It was a crazy time. Sean Patton turned to me during a UCB show once and said 'Don't you tell me dreams don't come true!'"

— Mark Normand
Comic

"One time I saw David Cross at the bar. I told him I liked his set and he shook his head angrily and shooed me away."

— King Ace
Comic

When I stepped onstage for the first time during college in January 2005, I had never heard the term "alt comedy." I knew there were different styles of comedy... one-liners, storytellers, observational, confessional, prop... but only when I took my first dip into the comedy waters 'below 14th Street' on that summer's break from college my eyes were opened to the world of what was described as 'alt'. I was 20 years old and instantly seduced by what I perceived to be a burgeoning new scene. Rififi in the mid 00s seemed like CBCG in the 70s or Cafe Wha in the 60s. I felt like I was 'in it', being treated to intimate performances from the most brilliant minds doing the most inventive things I had ever seen on a stage: Demetri Martin's easel paper, Jon Glaser's party subs, Brett Gelman's 1,000 Cats, Reggie Watts' infinite loops, Kristen Schaal's horse, Andres du Bouchet's unhinged character monologues, Nick Kroll and John Mulaney's Gil Faizon and George St. Geegland. What a time to be alive!"

— Scott Rogowsky
Comic/Producer/Celeb Host

"I wanted to do my show where the 'cool kids' were doing their shows. I thought it would help me get more exposure. *Invite Them Up* was the focal point of the alt scene back then. It was amazing the people they had perform there. We were the nerdy Tuesday show. On Thursday there was a show Nick Kroll did with Jessi Klein and then with John Mulaney. It was a pretty amazing array of talented people that were performing there in the mid 2000's. Rififi was the first place I saw Patton Oswalt perform and the third or fourth place I had sex with my wife."

— Andres Dubouchet
Comic and Writer for 'Conan'

"One time Eugene Mirman told me to stop bothering the comics at the bar."

— King Ace
Comic

"Another favorite moment at Kabin is when Tom McCaffrey—another absolute favorite comic of mine and one of our most-frequently booked comics—happened to be on show the same Thursday that Michael Jackson died. Tom took the opportunity to do all of his Michael Jackson material. After the first joke the audience groaned and Tom asked 'Too soon?'. The answer didn't matter because he continued to pile on one well-crafted joke after another until the audience had no choice but to laugh at Michael Jackson jokes just a couple hours after his death had been announced. Legendary performance!"

— Chesley Calloway

CHAPTER 21:

COMEDY 54

THE CUTE BRUNETTE STEVE HAD BEEN CASUALLY sleeping with showed up to Greg's show, one Friday night, with a somewhat famous comic from LA. She stood by the LA comic the whole time. Now and then, Steve glanced at her because he could feel her gaze on him from across the room. He didn't want to be jealous, but he couldn't help himself. Greg told him that the famous comedian was dating her now. She performed on the show and didn't do very well. She was new and didn't know how to write jokes. She told two jokes that Steve had helped her write months earlier. Steve thought that was pretty ballsy.

She was ignoring him but also doing his jokes in front of him. She even told a joke that seemed like it was aimed directly at him. He wasn't sure though, it could have been aimed at anyone. It was such a common comic move. Comics often passive-aggressively attacked other comics with jokes that were indirect jabs. Her new boyfriend went up right before Steve. As he watched from the back Steve realized the brunette comic had slept with every comic in the lineup. Her new boyfriend had no idea of this fact of course.

Comedy was an incestuous place, and it was a bad idea to get involved with someone mixed up in it. If things went wrong, which they usually did, then the person would have a myriad of ways to retaliate against you. This brunette comic knew too much about Steve, who he hated in the scene, what his biggest insecurities were, and how to push his buttons. Comics had no ethics or boundaries when it came to women or exes. Every woman was fair game, even if you were currently dating her. Steve had been warned early on by a comic to never bring your girlfriend around a roomful of comedians. Someone would undoubtedly try to fuck her. All was fair in love and stand-up.

Steve stood at the bar sipping his Makers when a young comedian with a short-cropped afro and light skin walked into Rififi after *Invite Them Up* wearing shorts and a Wu-Tang t-shirt. Steve had brought him onstage a few weeks before at a show in the village in a bar. The guy's name was Erik Andre. Steve had gotten his name wrong and brought him onstage as Erik Alexander weeks earlier, but the guy wasn't a jerk about it. He apologized after the guy's set when he realized what had happened, and Erik took it in stride which surprised Steve since most comedians were total egomaniac psychopaths who would bite your head off in that situation.

The guy seemed chill, Steve liked him. He smiled widely when he saw Steve and walked up laughing in a deep register.

"Hey, man! Steve Collin! My man!! How the hell are ya?" he bellowed.

He had intensely goofy energy and a happy face.

"Hey, Erik! What up? Where you coming from?"

"I just did the lantern down on Bleecker. It was fucking shit man."

"Yeah?"

"Yeah, they were shit. The guy who runs it yelled at me for wearing fucking shorts. Fuck that guy."

"Yeah? That's funny."

"How was this show?"

"It was great."

"Is that Ellen Wichtel?" Erick asked, looking over at the brunette.

"Yeah," Steve said.

"Is that her boyfriend now?"

"I don't know," Steve said, shrugging.

"I hear she gives great head."

"Cool."

Erik looked right into Steve's eyes and laughed a loud hearty laugh that drew stares. It was almost uncomfortable how loud he laughed.

They drank for a while and Steve overheard a comedian talking shit about Aziz. The comedian was a smarty-pants who wasn't funny but thought he was smarter than everyone else just because he'd gone to Yale. He was talking loudly about Aziz being an asshole to him which astonished Steve. After all, this was the center of the comedy scene and Aziz was a big shot here. The guy was clearly doing it to antagonize people. It was clear he didn't feel accepted in the scene and was going to shit on it loudly.

"That guy doesn't care for Aziz, huh," Erik said.

"Guess not."

"Did you hear about his show?"

"Yeah."

"It's really fucking good," Erik said.

"That's what I hear. I haven't seen it yet. I don't watch MTV."

"It doesn't belong on MTV though, it's too smart. It's fucking great."

"I heard it was good."

"It's genius," Erik added.

Steve was actually kind of sick of hearing about how great Aziz's show was. He was sure it was, but he didn't want to see it and then have to admit that it was. He figured it probably was amazing.

"Are you talking about 'Human Giant'?" the obnoxious guy who was shit-talking Aziz interjected aggressively.

"Yeah, why?"

"You like it?!" he asked, exasperated.

"Yeah, why?"

"Why?! It's crap! It is a sinking ship! It is going down faster than a stone in water!" he added.

Steve and Erik kind of ignored him, hoping he would move on from them, which he did. Steve didn't want to draw a scene, especially not here. This was the hub of the alt-comedy scene and Steve had already experienced what it was like to get on the wrong side of the wrong person with status in this extremely small scene. This business was steeped in landmines and Steve had stepped on a few already and paid a price. He didn't need to make things harder for himself. This drunk guy was poison here and Steve and Erik didn't engage.

Rififi was now packed and in full swing. There were comedians and young women all over the place. In the showroom, the DJ was now pumping house music as everyone danced. The drinks flowed freely, and people were smoking all over the place which was unusual in New York City. Sam and Trevor of The Whitest Kids showed up and Steve spoke to them briefly. They ordered shots of whiskey and smoked a joint in the back of the place.

Trevor had just released a film starring him and Zach from the Whitest Kids and it wasn't being well received. The film had opened the day before, and Steve mentioned that he wanted to see it. Trevor made a pained face and told Steve not to bother.

Steve then started talking to a cute, short, blonde girl wearing a t-shirt and shorts. She looked to be pretty young, sort of voluptuous but also a bit timid. She meekly sipped on vodka and told Steve he was really funny. Steve asked her if she was from there and she told him she was from Virginia but was at school at the School of Visual Arts. She was 20 years old. Steve told her his age, but she didn't seem to mind. It was amazing the power of comedy even though Steve didn't truly think she was into him because of comedy. He'd already forgotten the dry times of his life where no one would look his way at a bar. He had convinced himself that he was just charming and handsome now and women were just responding. He would learn the harsh truth later on.

The college girl was named Meg, and she was with a friend from school; a Latina girl wearing a green dress. The Latina was a bit overweight and pretty and down for having fun. She was speaking to Erik, and they seemed to be hitting it off, which was perfect. As Steve got drunker on whiskey, he started freestyle rapping for the girl who thought it was funny how he couldn't do it very well while drunk. With each whiskey shot and laugh from the woman, Steve got more and more confident.

After about an hour, he made his move and started to make out with the college girl at the crowded bar. The Latina who was now hanging onto Erik suggested that they all go back to the girls' apartment.

Once they were back at their apartment in the East Village, they all smoked from a vape bong. Erik and his girl began making out on the small red sofa, and Steve and Meg followed suit. He figured Erik and the Latina would go to another room, but she took off her dress right there in the living room and straddled him. Soon, Erik and the Latina girl were full-on having sex right next to Steve and his girl. She looked at Steve while they did it and had her mouth open, and she was loud. Steve stared at her, frozen.

"Oh, I want to get fucked by your friend too!" she yelled.

"Oh yeah? I want you to fuck my friend!" Erik said.

"Oh, please fuck me too!" she screamed, looking at Steve.

She waved him over and Steve walked over slowly. She grabbed him by his face and pulled him towards her. She squeezed his face way too hard with her bony fingers. So hard that Steve felt her fingers dig into his cheeks. She was screaming.

"Oh, yes! Fuck me!" she yelled.

Steve was confused and in pain.

"Are you talking to me?" Steve asked.

"What?!" she yelled.

"The fucking thing, is that for me? Or are you just saying that?"

"What?! Oh, yes!!!"

"Is that a yes like you want me to fuck..."

She squeezed his face harder, and Steve wailed in pain and winced.

"Ahh-h-h-h-h-h!" he yelled.

She slapped Erik and then Steve. Steve backed off and massaged his jaw. Then Meg took off her shirt and pushed Steve onto the sofa and straddled him. Her friend kept yelling, saying that she wanted to fuck Steve, which he tried to ignore. It made him nervous. He finally ended up taking Meg into her room. They rolled around on her bed for a while. He didn't sleep with her after she threw up in a garbage can next to her bed, after which she passed out halfway on his chest and began to snore loudly. Steve lay still and listened to Erik and his Latina continue to have sex. She wasn't asking for him anymore, so he decided not to go back out.

CHAPTER 22:

BATON ROUGE!

ONE NIGHT AT *INVITE THEM UP*, STEVE WAS approached by a female comedy producer wearing a short afro. She wore glasses and a hooded sweatshirt, and she was friendly and awkward and spoke like a valley girl with her vocal fry.

"Steve, hi, I'm Randy, I loved your set. I'm a fan. I wanted to ask if you wanted to appear on a show that I produce for FUSE TV."

Steve was getting asked to do a lot of things now just from performing at Rififi all the time. Steve agreed to do the show which Randy said was a music/comedy show hosted by Amy Schumer and Mark Hoppus of Blink 182. They featured comedians on a panel every episode.

The day of the taping of the FUSE TV show, Steve showed up and saw a dressing room with his name on it, misspelled of course. It seemed people were always mispronouncing or misspelling his name. He took it personally because it seemed so avoidable. It took like three seconds to google someone. A producer of a TV show didn't have google?

The other panelist on the show was not a comedian but a DJ. Steve found that odd since the panel was supposed to be a segment where the panelists could riff with each other and make funny comments about pop culture events in the news. They had spent three weeks on the phone with Steve making sure he had funny things to say. Steve assumed this DJ guy must have been funny and had a good personality or something.

Right before the start of the show, the producer walked Steve and the other panelist to the completely quiet set. The audience was well out of sight, which seemed strange. Steve and the DJ sat right next to Mark Hoppus and Amy Schumer. Steve greeted Amy who responded with a smile. Mark Hoppus didn't even acknowledge Steve. Steve introduced himself and he just stared the other way. That helped Steve to relax.

Right before they taped, Steve noticed that the DJ was fidgeting with his hands. His head was down, and he had a pained look on his face. He was also very quiet and didn't come off as someone funny at all. In actuality, he seemed like he hadn't ever spoken in front of people before. Randy, the producer who had invited Steve to the show, leaned close to Steve about ten seconds before the cameras rolled. "Try and be high energy, your co-panelist seems shy. I don't think he's been on

TV before," she whispered. "Good luck! Just have fun!" she continued, smiling and giving the thumbs up with both thumbs.

Steve was thrown and suddenly became self-conscious. He forgot what jokes he was even supposed to say or what pop culture events he was supposed to discuss. Steve was not a high-energy personality in the slightest and Randy knew that. She'd just told him right before taping not to be himself.

The stage manager counted down and pointed to Mark Hoppus who turned to Steve with a wide smile, having suddenly transformed into a ball of energy. He asked questions about current events in pop culture. They had been prepped beforehand about topics such as Nicki Minaj and Kanye West doing something weird. He had some jokes about how Kanye was always interrupting people. The bit involved Kanye interrupting Taylor Swift's wedding toast. Hoppus asked them about Britney Spears, something the producer hadn't prepared them for. His co-panelist continued to fidget with his hands on the desk and stammered as he answered. He was barely audible and didn't get any laughs.

"Okay, well what about you, Stan," Hoppus said getting his name wrong.

"Ummm....well, Britney Spears, I mean come on. What's her problem, right?" Steve said thrown by the fact that he'd gotten his name wrong.

"Yeah, okay," Hoppus said.

It was dead silent, and the segment was bombing. He looked to his left and saw Randy with her mouth agape. She was motioning her arms wildly telegraphing for Steve to pick up the pace. Steve was blank. Suddenly he remembered a Britney Spears joke he'd written years before.

"So, nothing else on Britney, Stan?" Hoppus asked.

"Yeah, well I like Britney, but she's confusing to me. She was always claiming to be a virgin for so long but then all her songs were really sexual. Also, she had that song 'I'm not a girl not yet a woman.' That was confusing. It's like, can you figure out what you are, so I know what I'm masturbating to?" Steve said.

"Yeah! Right, Stan!" Hoppus said.

"Also, it's Steve."

"What?"

"My name is Steve, not Stan."

Silence. Hoppus's expression dropped and his eyes narrowed. He looked like Steve had told him he'd just fucked his sister.

"Oh, sorry, *Steve*," he said.

For the remainder of the segment, Steve tried to overcompensate with high energy while the DJ guy just sat there looking down at the table, frozen like Cindy Brady on that game show. The Blink 182 guy seemed unpleased by Steve's demeanor and never got past being corrected. He furrowed his brow as Steve improvised about other topics. Steve's arms felt numb, and it soon became like a bad set.

Hoppus went onto another topic that Steve had been prepped on.

The DJ mumbled an answer and Hoppus asked Steve for his take. Steve's heart was pounding now. He waved his arms around trying way too hard and thus bombing. He was thinking too much. *If you think up there, you're dead.* One misstep and it's over. Things went like that for about seven minutes, and, after the segment, Mark Hoppus glared at Steve. It was funny because before the segment he couldn't be bothered to even turn his head in Steve's direction and now he looked as if he were trying to read Steve's mind.

"Great job STAN!" he yelled, before storming off the set. Steve felt his whole body freeze. So he was angry at Steve for fucking up *his* name? The producer appeared and rushed them off the set in a frenzy. It was a debacle, but at least he had another TV appearance under his belt and that's all that mattered.

Steve promoted his appearance on the show all over Facebook. He wanted to make sure that everyone was aware that he was back on TV again. He thought maybe he'd get the attention of some people on Facebook and maybe get laid. That was the whole point of Facebook after all. He also figured it would buy him a few more weeks with the star-fucker he was sleeping with again. The cute brunette. She had broken up with the famous comedian and began contacting him again. He'd tried to avoid her, but she was super aggressive, and he was only human. It was next to impossible for Steve to turn down a hot woman showering him with attention, which she did. It was obvious that he had issues with women and fell for any tricks they threw his way. The woman was a love bomber but all he knew was that someone beautiful told him he was great and so he was all in.

Meanwhile, Steve was tired of seeing everyone else's posts promoting their career achievements and was happy to finally have an achievement to rub in people's faces. That afternoon, he received an email from Randy, the producer, informing him his segment had been cut from the show and, just like that, his latest TV credit disappeared. His stomach tightened. She claimed the bit was too long even though it was at best five minutes.

He had needed it badly since he felt he was quickly being forgotten and left behind by a new class. He was clinging to any relevance he may have had and was starting to lose his grip. All anyone cared about on social media these days was what you were doing now. What you did last month didn't matter at all. They'd all loved him and wanted to be his friend when he was hitting home runs, but now that he'd had a few bad games, they weren't coming around as much. Steve could feel himself getting left behind and had no clue what to do, so he drank more. That had to help right?

CHAPTER 23:

THERE'S A NEW KID IN TOWN

NICK KROLL HAD BROUGHT A FRIEND OF HIS FROM Georgetown to B3 to do a set with him. The friend was a couple of years younger than Nick and wanted to get into stand-up. The guy was thin and tall with thick straight black hair that he combed back. He sort of looked like a little kid with no hair on his face, and he spoke in a distinct voice that was slightly effeminate. He sounded like a guy from a 20s Gatsby party.

He and Nick did a bit together in front of about fifteen audience members. The new guy shyly held the mic close to his mouth and looked down the whole time. They were winging it and it wasn't going very well. It was eating shit mainly because the new guy was so unsure of himself and barely audible.

Nick's friend approached Steve after the show. His name was John Mulaney. He was soft-spoken and friendly. He'd just graduated from Georgetown even though he looked about 15 years old.

"Oh, hello, Steve. I met you last summer at Rififi. Good to see you. I loved your set on *Invite Them Up*."

"Thanks, man. How have you been?" Steve replied, not remembering meeting him.

"I'm great, just great. I'm John Mulaney. I'm new in town."

He spoke in a punchy way.

"John Mulaney? Huh, I loved you in 'Sex, Lies, and Videotape'," Steve said.

"Hmmm...I haven't heard that one before," John said, smiling and nodding his head in a way that said he was being completely ironic. Steve could never resist pointing out a pop culture reference and someone having the same name as an iconic film character was low-hanging fruit. Steve felt like he should have kept his mouth shut.

After the show, Steve, Roger, Nick, John, and Neal all went to Niagara on 7th Street and Avenue A and got hammered. John was an entertaining and engaging drunk. He held court after some cocktails and drank the rest of them under the table. He seemed to like his liquor. And the more he drank, the louder and punchier his cadence became. He was like some kind of machine you could put words into so they would come out sounding funny.

"Hello there, young lass!" Mulaney bellowed at the young blond waitress with huge tits.

"Hello there," she said back.

"Oh, hello!" Mulaney said in his unique voice.

"I quite like your huge cans, m'lady," he said, bowing his head. The waitress laughed at that.

Kroll and Mulaney spoke of their old sketch group at Georgetown that featured Birbiglia and their friends Ed Hero and Jacqueline Novak. The entire group was now in Manhattan doing comedy. They had their own gang in town which Steve would later notice was how to make it in comedy. Comedy was sort of like a prison. You needed to be part of a gang to survive. Steve was completely solo in comedy. He hadn't known one person doing comedy before he started, and the friends he had made were most loyal to their gang. Going it alone would be the death of you. Comedy was full of little posses from various cities. The Georgetown posse would soon be making moves in a big way.

They all ended up at a diner down on Avenue B at 2 a.m. Steve ordered a sandwich and picked at it. It tasted awful to him. Like most New York diners they had put way too much into the sandwich making it hard to eat.

"Something the matter with your food?" Mulaney asked.

"It's okay. It's just...they gave me too much tuna," Steve said.

"Too much tuna?! That's great!" Mulaney said and laughed.

A few months later, Nick and John started a show at Rififi called "Oh Hello" which quickly became the hottest new show in town due to its star-studded lineups. They seemed to know every major comic in New York. They hosted as two older Jewish men who complained about everything. The show featured comedians who they'd then interview after their sets.

Nick asked Steve to be on the first "Oh Hello" show. It featured a powerhouse lineup; Birbiglia, Aziz, Pete Holmes, and Jessi Klein. They interviewed Steve onstage after his set as their characters and Steve riffed well with them even though it made him a bit uneasy doing an improv exercise with such seasoned improv guys. Steve did a good job holding his own.

Steve got off and was leaving the room to get his usual whiskey on the rocks when he stopped sharply at a sound. It was the sound of John Mulaney's voice which seemed way different than he'd recalled just months prior. His voice had been low and almost a mumble. It was now completely confident and authoritative. He was just doing stand-up as himself now, but it came off as a character. What stopped Steve in his tracks was the sheer presence he exuded. It was like Steve had no choice but to stop and pay attention to Mulaney. It was like some kind of force turned him around involuntarily. Steve had seen this many times. This, however, was more of a revelation than the others. There was no denying this guy's talent. He was so good it was almost like he was cheating or something.

Steve watched Mulaney confidently stroll through long and winding bits that went into seemingly endless tangents. They were like jokes wrapped up in riddles. It was like watching an impressive magic trick. His voice was now more like a 20s gangster. It was a character but not really. This was just how Mulaney talked. Was this the same guy he'd seen months ago at B3? He'd found his voice in a matter of months. Surely it was a fluke. It must have been an old set, or he had just gotten lucky with a good crowd. There had to be an explanation. This was what Steve told himself to appease the jealousy and inadequacy he harbored. If someone was better than him it felt like it exposed all his flaws to the world.

Mulaney destroyed the room completely with his chest out and his voice completely steady with no hesitation. Steve had heard many club comics comment that alt comedians were sloppy and didn't have jokes. Well, Mulaney was a comic on the biggest alt stage at the moment in front of an alt crowd and he may have been telling the most well-crafted jokes Steve had ever heard.

Later on, Steve was sitting on a wobbly stool at the bar when he saw Mulaney and told him how great he'd been. John had a tall whiskey and was already in the bag. He thanked Steve and drunkenly pushed him back gently with his hands. He was doing it to be funny, of course, as if he were still his old Jewish "Oh Hello" character. But when he pushed Steve for the third time,

Steve pushed him back. John whipped his head with a surprised look and stared at him through glassy eyes his thick eyebrows raised.

"And who do you think you are Mr. Fancy? How dare you lay a hand on me," he said in his Mulaney cadence.

"I don't like people pushing me."

"And so what? Who the hell are you? Don't talk to me unless you have some blow!" John responded while sipping his vodka.

"What?" Steve asked.

"Be gone with you!" he said.

Mulaney pushed him again, this time a bit harder, causing Steve's drink to spill. Steve looked up at Mulaney whose expression had become blank. Mulaney wouldn't look at him now.

"Get me another one," Steve said, standing up off the stool.

"What?" Mulaney asked still looking off into the distance at nothing.

"Makers on the rocks. Get me another one, now," Steve said again, standing just inches away from him. This guy was talented, but Steve wasn't going to let himself be pushed around.

Mulaney turned his head and stared Steve in the eye with a steady gaze and soft eyes. Then he turned without changing his expression and ordered Steve a Makers from Lindsay while slumped over the bar. Nerds may have had confidence now and were in control of the comedy landscape and were becoming stars, but one thing hadn't changed, nerds couldn't fight. Steve made it clear he wasn't some sycophant.

John quieted down seeming to realize he was being boorish. One thing was certain about this whole comedy scene, you had to play the game, something Steve had always struggled with. He'd made the mistake of thinking that comedy was just about being funny. He was learning slowly that being funny was about 20% of it at best.

Carl entered Rififi at about eleven o'clock and informed Steve almost immediately that Mitch Hedberg had died from an overdose. Steve had never actually met the man but remembered that first night at Largo when he saw Hedberg kill, it was a night forever cemented into his memory. He felt much sadder than he expected he would. That was another thing about Steve. He took things very hard and had a hard time letting go of the pain. He was much more emotional than people knew.

The news about Hedberg got around Rififi within a half-hour and darkness hung in the room, making it feel colder. Maybe it was just a coincidence, but the place's energy felt off to Steve like the weird island in "Lost." Bobby walked up and told him he'd had a great set while patting him on the back hard. Hedberg's death felt like the end of something that night and Steve sulked in his drink the rest of the night.

"Hey, don't mention this to anyone but I wanted to ask you to perform on our live taping for a CD and DVD that Comedy Central is producing," Bobby said.

"Ahh....yeah. Of course. That sounds great," Steve answered trying to hide the excitement but not doing a great job.

"Okay, great. I think you're gonna open one of the shows. We're all excited to have you involved man. You're one of my favorites now," Bobby said, smiling.

This was a huge deal. *Invite Them Up* was now *the* show not only in the alt scene but in the entire city. Luna was gone now. Now he was being asked to be part of the *Invite Them Up album*? It felt like being made in the mafia, minus having to murder anyone. All he had to kill was a roomful of comedy fans.

CHAPTER 24:

INVITE HIM UP

T HE *INVITE THEM UP* TAPING WAS SCHEDULED FOR Monday and Tuesday nights at Pianos on Ludlow Street in the East Village. Steve was slated to appear on the Monday night show. Comedy Central was producing the album and there were write-ups about it in various New York papers and popular blogs, including Rolling Stone.com. This was a major event on the comedy scene, and it was an honor to be involved. He was still relatively new to the New York City comedy scene, so he knew this was a big step in his career. The hottest up and comers were featured, thus making him also an up and comer and possibly one of the "next big things."

The cute brunette star-fucker was contacting him again which was a good sign. She was like a heat barometer. When she wanted to fuck you, it was because you were doing well.

Steve walked into Pianos about an hour before the show and hung out with Carl and a couple of other regular female comedy fans, Ann and Pepper. He'd met them before at Rififi. Pianos was full of big comedy fans. All the current New York heavy hitters were there in various parts of the room. Demetri, Aziz, David Cross, Mike Birbiglia, David Wain, Stephanie. Some hadn't yet become what they soon would become, but there was a buzz in the air that this was the new wave of comedy. This was like alt comedy's graduation party and Steve was opening the ceremonies.

Steve was nervous of course, but he'd gone over his set many times, so he felt prepared even though he never felt fully prepared when he performed. He wanted to be as prepped as he could even though this was an alt show which was meant to be loose. He had a Makers on the rocks at the upstairs bar which was the unofficial green room since only performers were there. He'd promised himself he wouldn't get too drunk beforehand and blow it even if his nerves got out of control.

He was first on the lineup and wanted to wait to drink after he finished. He was trying to stay cool and not overthink. He heard words in his head berating him with insults. They were trying to sabotage him. These comments always came when he was most nervous. They jumped out from his brain attempting to throw him. The voices had long been his worst enemy and they were especially strong on this particular night. He got a sudden flash of the station wagon, where he was sitting in the back of the car nervous to tell a simple knock-knock joke.

This was a long way away from that night. This was a big deal, maybe the most important show of his life, and he knew he was in the deep end with the sharks. As a kid, he'd thought about maybe doing comedy. Now, here he was in the middle of the current comedy movement, an actual part of it. He had a flash of Johnny Carson at the Oscars. It was all coming together. It was fate, right? His hands shook and he suddenly regretted ever telling that joke in the back of the station wagon. And as he took a sip of Makers he was filled to the brim with terror. The voices in his head had gotten him. He ordered another whiskey, breaking the promise he'd made to himself. He just wanted to calm the voices a little more.

He always felt like he'd earned his drinks after performing. But the more he became known in comedy, the faster and more often the drinks came. He felt he needed them to get through this whole comedy thing which wore heavily on his nerves. As funny as people thought he was, he found the whole environment anxiety-inducing, and the more success he got the less comfortable he was in his skin and the less he felt like himself. The alcohol, pills, and weed were a way to not have to worry about it. He knew it was a cliché, but he also didn't think he'd ever have to depend on any of it especially after he made it.

He entered the smallish showroom. The place held maybe sixty people, a bit smaller than Rififi. Its intimate vibe was deliberate, meant to capture the vibe of an alt room. Bobby was onstage wearing jeans and a golf shirt and tinted glasses, his unofficial uniform.

After about five minutes, Steve was introduced. The crowd was supportive and excited. He only had to do about twelve minutes which wasn't too long, but twelve minutes could be an eternity if things went south. He started his first joke which he knew was good and thought it would do well. And it actually did, which made him relax. Just when he felt on track to a great set, a drunk guy yelled out something unintelligible. Of course. Why would this huge moment in his life be easy? Nothing was ever easy for him. Steve was going to have to deal with a drunk asshole during one of the biggest sets of his life.

"What'd you say?" Steve asked calmly.

"Yeah, you are you, man!" the guy yelled.

There was tension in the room. Similar to the tension in the station wagon. Steve stayed calm. The last thing he wanted was to get too mad and ruin the vibe. He'd learned the hard way that once you go over that line it was impossible to get back on track.

"Yeah, cool man," Steve said, with a chuckle.

The crowd laughed and the guy yelled out again.

"Ha! Yeah man! You do it!"

"I'm not sure if you're heckling me or cheering me on. Either way, it's super helpful. I was hoping some drunk guy would yell out at me in the middle of my big comedy taping," Steve said.

The crowd laughed louder. Steve was calm and they could sense it. Once it was clear the guy wasn't throwing Steve off his game, they felt at ease. Comedy is all about tension and release. The crowd tenses up and as long as the comic can release the tension, everyone has a good time. Steve knew he'd handled it as well as he possibly could. The guy was quickly told to shut up by Bobby and Eugene, and Steve was able to get through his set. He received three full applause breaks, a huge accomplishment. When he got off, he realized it was over and he had actually done it.

Steve immediately got drunk afterwards to celebrate. He'd survived yet another day in comedy. That's what comedy was like. Every show was its own battle, and it was only a matter of time until your luck finally ran out and you were discovered as a fraud. As much as he was gaining success, he wasn't enjoying himself and often felt only one bad set away from losing it all. He told himself it didn't matter right now that he was unhappy all the time. All that mattered was making it to the next level. Once he got there, then he could relax. That's what he told himself as he drank his bitter whiskey on the rocks, the unofficial drink of the alt-comedy scene.

He was surprised by how few people came up and spoke to him after the show. He thought since he was on the show that more people would be friendlier. A few were pleasant to him like Demetri and Aziz who congratulated him on his set, but it seemed like everyone else was uptight and focused on what this show would do for them. The whole thing was high school when it came down to it. They were all in their late twenties or thirties, yet they acted like insecure seventeen-year-olds.

The most popular kids here were the socially awkward nerds. The jock, confident types were the ones ostracized here. And bro frat type would be the lowest level being there. Bizarro high school. To be in this club, you had to be smart, quick, and a bit awkward. Steve felt out of place there. He wasn't a jock, douche, frat boy but he wasn't a geek either. He was somewhere in the middle, a place he often found himself.

While standing alone at the bar, Steve was approached by a brunette female comedian, who was also on the show. He'd met her a few times in passing through mutual friends. She smiled widely as she spoke. She asked him how his set had gone. He told her it went well as she played with her hair and smiled. She was cute but more importantly, she was friendly. She was getting ready to go on and do Thirty Seconds of Stand-up, a sort of novelty of the show that was meant as a weird shtick type of thing.

After all, this was alt-comedy, so it had to be different from club comedy. She went on and yelled her act with excitement. She wasn't much of a stand-up, but more of a quirky actress type. She mainly made her living doing commercials.

Steve left Pianos early and went to get a drink nearby at Magician Bar. He felt good about how it had gone and called Roger and Nick. They met at a bar on Seventh Street and Avenue B. They asked him how the show went, and he told them it had gone really well. They all toasted him, and Nick told him he deserved the attention. He felt he was finally starting to get some recognition. He just wished he was enjoying it more.

Nick mentioned that he'd just booked a part on a new series based on the Geico cavemen ads. He was going to be a series regular. The show sounded like an awful idea, but Nick didn't seem to mind. After all, this was an actual TV show on a real network, NBC. Nick pondered the idea of the show getting picked up and lasting for years. A caveman TV series? Steve didn't voice his concern to Nick, but it sounded like something that could destroy someone's career.

They all sipped their whiskeys and got drunk without a care in the world. Everything was starting to roll their way and it was only a matter of time before they were where they wanted to be. What could go wrong from here? As a young New York City kid, Steve had been told over and over by various kids' shows that if you followed your dreams everything would fall into place. Steve loved making people laugh so of course, everything would work out in the end as it did for everyone who followed their dreams.

Nick talked ad nauseam about Aziz's new show that he'd just done a bit part on. He went on and on about how genius it was. Steve was tired of hearing about what a wonder-boy Aziz was, so he just listened and didn't comment. Roger sipped on his third Hoegaarden.

"That kid is going to be huge. Enormous," Nick said.

"Yeah? You think so?" Steve asked.

"Yes. He is a monster. He just auditioned for a new show on NBC with Amy Poehler."

"What show?"

"Not sure. It's the same producer of 'The Office'. Believe me. You'll see. He's on the brink. I heard he might be hosting the MTV Awards," Nick said.

Now that was a huge deal. The MTV Awards? Damn. Some kid from the alt scene hosting an award show on MTV? The alt scene was going mainstream, no longer just existing in small dark back rooms of dive bars.

Nick went on about this girl he was seeing. He then mentioned that Bobby was dating Jenny Slate. Jenny had been around for a few years, and it seemed every comedian was obsessed with her. They gossiped for a while about the hottest female comics in the scene. Steve mentioned he was sleeping with the star-fucker again. Nick mentioned that she was also sleeping with a hugely successful comic Steve worshipped. Steve didn't know if that was true, but he didn't much care, especially tonight. Sleeping with the same woman his comedy hero was sleeping with had to mean he was doing something right in a sort of fucked up way.

Nick mentioned his new book coming out about camp. He said it was going to get a release in major stores. He then told them how Mulaney had met with Tina Fey about possibly writing for SNL. Mulaney was a kid who had just moved to NYC. Was he that good? I mean, Steve had thought he was talented but was he so talented that he'd just jump over everyone else that fast? Apparently, he was that good.

Steve got another drink. Still riding high from the *Invite Them Up* show and full of confidence, he hit on the blond girl sitting at the bar who looked tired and drunk. She seemed into it as he talked to her, but he grew tired of her when she got belligerent. He told her he was a comic and she asked him if he was funny with a sneer. That was the most dreaded question a comic could hear from someone. Almost every person asked this same question as if they had been the first to ever think up such a witty retort. She then commented about how he didn't seem very funny and turned away. He gathered himself and went back to the booth since she'd royally pissed him off.

"What happened with that chick?" Nick asked Steve.

"Nothing. I mean, she's totally hot for me."

"That's what your mom said last night," Roger quipped.

"Ha!" Nick retorted sarcastically and they began to play slap each other. Steve watched them and sipped his whiskey. He felt something inside coming up and he hoped the whiskey would stop it. It didn't work though.

CHAPTER 25:

I HAD A DREAM

I N MAY OF 1998, STEVE'S MOTHER WAS DYING. IT WAS clear that the chemo was slowly killing her. He woke up almost daily to her wailing in pain. He was 24 years old, and it was all happening quickly. She'd first informed him that she was sick about a month earlier, and now it wasn't looking very good. He was trying to pursue a career as an actor but wasn't having any luck.

What made it worse was that many of his former Fame High School classmates were getting opportunity after opportunity, making him feel even worse. Sometimes he tried to remember why he had even wanted any of this in the first place. Of course, he didn't have enough perspective to really know. All he knew was that he wanted that initial feeling he'd had from that first moment in the station wagon and at the Oscars. What a feeling.

He'd met with an agent recently who had told him he was okay looking but that there was nothing special about him. The agent's comment had stayed with him and shook his confidence and now his mother was nearing the end of her life. He was having a hard time keeping up with the negative thoughts racing through his head. The voices never seemed to tire out like an Olympic marathon runner. His mind was now chipping away at his self-esteem, never taking a break.

Why couldn't life be like it was on TV or in the movies? Life seemed so much easier on TV. Life was how it actually *should* be on TV. At the end of each "Diff'rent Strokes" episode, everything was completely resolved. All of the Drummond's problems were fixed in a half-hour segment unless it was a two-parter. The actual actors in "Diff'rent Strokes" weren't as lucky as their counterpart characters. In real life, they were total train wrecks addicted to meth and going around murdering people. (Google it.)

As a young latchkey kid in Manhattan, Steve became a full-blown TV and movie junkie by the age of eight. Parents in the '80s simply plopped their kids in front of TV sets and let the TVs raise them. Steve had learned everything about love and relationships from 80s TV shows, movies, and rap videos. On TV, love and intimacy were crammed into 22 minute long intervals with perfect endings. Even if someone died in an episode or was molested by a bike store owner, the characters were always completely over it by the next week with no mention of what had happened ever again. In one brutal two-part episode of "Diff'rent Strokes," Kimberly had almost gotten raped and, by the next week, she was fine as if nothing had ever happened. Just a week later, she was bubbly and making wisecracks at Arnold and Willis, no therapy or anything. To Steve, TV was a magic world where no problem was too big to resolve in thirty minutes or less. These shows never depicted the hard parts of life and relationships. The simplicity of it all was what had first attracted him to TV.

Later on in his life, when he encountered difficulties, he was dumbfounded by their very existence. What was this? He hadn't seen any sleepless nights, emotional manipulation, or lying on "MASH," "90210" or in Beastie Boys videos. On TV, good was rewarded and bad was punished, and the world was always a fair place. Sex was fun, light, and uncomplicated. No one ever got hurt and righteousness always won out in the end. This was why Steve had first aspired to become an actor. He wanted to live in that world where everything worked out the way it should. Deep down, he didn't really want to be famous, he just wanted to live in this better-looking world where people actually saw you.

He related to the films where a huge star would be ignored in the film world they inhabited. Like in "Heathers" where Christian Slater was supposed to be the outcast no one likes, even though in reality it was clear he was the coolest guy in the world. This was how

Steve felt, he was a star stuck in a film where no one knew he was a star.

He had been doing stand-up off and on for three months when his mother told him, one Wednesday night, that she had lung cancer. She was only 61 years old, and he knew the second she told him that life would never be the same again. His mother cried in front of him in her pink robe. She looked scared, and that terrified him. He was more scared than he'd ever been before in his entire life. She was to start chemo in a week. The doctor said things didn't look good since they'd caught it in its advanced stages. Steve thought about the time when Valerie Harper died on her sitcom. Two weeks later, the family was over it. He knew it wouldn't be like that and that made him even sadder. TV had lied to him.

The next few months were a blur for Steve. One memory that always stood out was when he drove her to the hospital for chemo. He surprised her with a tape for when she got out. It was an Abba album, He played "Dancing Queen" when he picked her up. She wept in the back seat and thanked him through tears. A week later, her hair began to fall out and she shaved it all off herself, something he knew she hated doing.

About two months later, she was wearing a wig and was unable to get around on her own. He woke up most mornings to the sound of her screaming in pain for over an hour as he lay in bed frozen, not knowing how to handle it. He often lay awake at night trying to think of jokes. Stand-up was his only escape now. Jokes were what kept his mind off his mother. If an idea popped into his head that grabbed him, he'd write it down in a small notebook he'd bought. He soon had about ten pages of ideas that were unformed but seemed funny enough to at least try. His notebook became his lifeline.

Steve had a show at New York Comedy Club. He'd only performed stand-up about twenty times by this point. All the sets he did were only five minutes long making it almost impossible to improve. New York Comedy Club was a shit hole room. It was dark, the wobbly tables were crammed next to each other, and it smelled like mildew. The place looked as if it had never been mopped. The owner was a mean, heavy guy who was a failed stand-up comic. He of course treated all the comics at the club like crap. He was known for ripping off comics, especially new comics. He often stiffed performers of their pay just to save thirty bucks. Steve was doing a bringer show there. He'd done bringers before, and it was already getting harder to get people to come and see him perform. The novelty of his stand-up career had worn off fast and no one was all that interested in coming anymore.

This particular night, Steve's father and mother had come to the show and Steve went on in the middle. He was given seven minutes, two more than usual since another comic had canceled. At this point, he'd had a few good sets but, on this night, he killed for the first time in front of a real audience. He received applause breaks and the crowd cheered him loudly when he finished. One excited audience member high-fived him as he walked offstage. The MC told him he'd had the best set of the night and asked him how long he'd been doing stand-up.

Afterwards, his mother walked out with a cane she used to get around now and told him he'd done great with a serious face. She had tears in her eyes, so he knew she meant it. It had gone great, and he felt light on his feet. Steve recalled that she herself had been an aspiring writer. She told him one time years earlier about the time she had almost secured a book deal. When she told him this, she stared to the left in a deep trance. Almost looking at a future that never was. "Yeah, I was close," she said quietly, almost to herself.

Seven weeks after that night at New York Comedy Club, she was dead. The morning she died; he recalled the time he saw her singing to the Les Misérables song in the back of the car.

What would he do now? His life had changed in an instant. When something like that happens, people are nice and sympathetic but only for a short period.

And just as surely as he'd expected everyone soon moved on. They expected Steve to move on too, whether he was ready to or not.

After three months, no one wanted to hear about it anymore even though he wasn't anywhere close to being over it. Three months was supposed to be sufficient time for something like that? One thing that never left him was the fact that his mother had written letters to his sisters before she died but hadn't written anything to him. He thought perhaps she meant to but ran out of time. Still, he was never able to fully move past it and he just stockpiled it on top of every other thing that gnawed at his feeling of inadequacy and further fueled his desire to be seen. He knew his craving for approval from strangers was not healthy, but he had no idea how to get out of that mind frame. He simply poured alcohol on the problem and hoped his deep-seated intimacy issues would magically disappear, though he knew they wouldn't.

CHAPTER 26:

OUTSIDE IN

T HE WEEK AFTER HIS *INVITE THEM UP* TAPING, THE quirky friendly woman he had met there messaged him. She invited him to Sunday brunch at her apartment and made it a point of telling him that Carl was going to be there. Steve told her he would stop by but then forgot about it completely.

The morning of the brunch, he was hungover from a show the night before at UCB. She messaged him a friendly reminder and he responded that he couldn't make it and was sorry. Carl called him immediately and demanded that he come over. Steve was confused by Carl's insistence that he be there. What was the big deal? He barely knew this woman.

Two hours later, Steve arrived to find that most of the people were already gone. Steve was greeted at the door by the female comedian and Carl. Her roommate sat with his legs crossed at the end of the long table in the spacious living room that had empty dishes strewn all over it. The roommate, a big-shot, intimidating alt comic (she'd told him weeks earlier, unprompted, that they were just friends) didn't bother to greet or even look at Steve as he walked in. He wore a slight frown, and his black straight hair was mussed up in a sloppy way that seemed deliberate. The guy was a sort of indie celebrity from his cult movie about military school. Steve had never encountered him directly, but he'd seen him around the scene and been told by some that he was "an arrogant prick." He had a rep for being moody and difficult but was still regarded by many comedians as a comedy legend. He was the same guy who'd had a sort of odd altercation with the phony comic Ryan months prior. Steve assumed he was probably like most comedians, socially awkward, and a bit egotistical, which was normal for creative types. He seemed harmless.

There were three other people seated at the picnic-shaped table. Steve didn't know any of the others, although everyone there was friendly in an almost fraudulent Stepford-type way. Steve was offered whatever food was left.

The aloof roommate didn't acknowledge him until Steve had been there for almost an hour, which pissed him off. Steve commented about something, and the guy laughed. Everything at the brunch seemed like an unofficial test. It was like some invitation into an exclusive club, and he felt he was being judged in an interview or something. He guessed this was supposed to be some kind of big honor, like being called over to the 'cool' table in the lunchroom or being invited to the cool kid's party in high school. Steve's complete disinterest in even showing up had only seemed to make him more intriguing to them. Who was this guy? Did he turn down a chance to be around us? Thousands would kill to be in his position, rubbing elbows with an indie film star.

Steve spoke to Carl about the UCB show he'd done the night before. Carl was the only one Steve knew so he clung to him. Steve wasn't completely sure how he'd ended up there. The big shot comedian chewed on his toast at the end of the table with a blank expression. He was about thirty-seven, but he acted almost like a child. Anytime he made a comment everyone laughed and complimented him.

"That's so true! You are so funny!" one woman exclaimed repeatedly every time he spoke.

He was kowtowed to by the others around him out of a sort of fear.

At one point, Steve made a random comment about how the movie title "Good Will Hunting" was a double entendre. The aloof comedian's eyes widened as he frowned and vehemently disagreed with Steve's comment as if he were effortlessly blocking someone's jump shot. The whole table stared quietly at Steve, waiting for his response.

The same tension arose that was prevalent in comedy rooms when a comic was heckled. How would

Steve handle this? When Steve nonchalantly offered support for his case everyone chimed in and dismissed him agreeing instead with the comedian. Steve eventually conceded since he didn't want to be rude, and the vibe rubbed him the wrong way. He was one-hundred percent positive he was right, but he let the king of the table have the win. This was the guy's apartment and his weird party, so he figured he'd let it go. After all, Steve didn't want the guy to turn him into a jack in the box and banish him into the cornfield.

Later that night, Steve googled "Good Will Hunting" to find that it was common knowledge that the title had a double meaning. It was official, he'd been gaslit by the comedian and made to feel like a moron. It was like he'd been pulled into some sort of impromptu Asch experiment. The brunch had existed in an alternate universe where normal rules didn't apply. Steve had made the mistake of disagreeing with an alt world leader.

A short guy with glasses sat close to the big shot comedian and at one point asked him to watch a film he'd just shot and finished editing. He agreed to watch it and the glasses guy smiled and thanked him wholeheartedly. He remained close to the big shot the whole time as if guarding him.

Slowly everyone retreated from the brunch except for Steve and the woman who'd invited him. She kept offering him food and coffee to get him to stick around. Even the celeb guy finally grew bored and dramatically announced he was taking a nap in his room as if he were a prince or something.

Steve and the woman decided to take a walk to get coffee and Steve was surprised by how much he'd started to like her. She was funny and better looking than he'd first thought she was. She was wearing a tight dark top that brought out the curves in her body. He enjoyed her somewhat goofy personality and affable charm a great deal. She had something for sure. She was charismatic as hell, something he'd always responded to in women since the fourth grade. At the end of the day, he refrained from trying to kiss her since he didn't want to get into a weird situation. He was new in the New York comedy scene and didn't need any further obstacles or complications like an awkward hookup with a fellow comedian. He'd seen this backfire for many other comics such as Roger who was currently going through it.

He finally left and she contacted him the next day. They hung out again after a show at Rififi. This time she made it clear that she liked him by repeatedly touching his arm and leaning close to him when she laughed. He got caught up in the moment and finally succumbed.

He couldn't fight that there was something between them. They made out in his car on and off for a couple of hours. He could see himself dating her for a long time, so he figured it was okay. He was confused because the feeling came quickly and before he knew it, he'd fallen for her.

Things were good at first, but they soon got weird. He'd kind of anticipated this but when it actually happened, he freaked out since the vibe became somewhat malevolent. He'd been dating the woman for a couple of months, and it was clear that she was a member of this inner clique, not unlike the Westwood Brewco Mic clique.

Steve had always despised cliques, even ones he'd been a member of. He hated exclusion culture even when he wasn't being excluded. The idea of hiding behind a clique brought out his rage. He remembered times when he had felt excluded and didn't like when he saw it done to others. Cliques felt cowardly to him, which they were.

He now felt awkward and uncomfortable around her roommate and the other various hangers-on around. Even Carl acted differently around him now. He felt blowback everywhere, even from comedy friends who were kept outside the clique. Some people distanced themselves from him. He thought maybe he was simply imagining this invisible barrier that had formed until things got particularly odd one night.

Steve had been hanging out with a comedian friend near the woman's apartment. When he called her to tell her his friend was going to stop by with him, she pushed back hard and way too aggressively which felt like a slap in the face.

"Why are you bringing him here?" she asked in a stark voice.

"Well, we're hanging out down the street, and he needs to call a car and wait for it."

"Don't let him in here," she said sternly.

"What? Why not?"

"I don't trust him," she said.

"What?"

"I mean...is he coming here to ya know get close to my roommate or something?" she asked.

This was incredible to Steve. He was speechless for a few seconds. Steve made up some lame excuse to his friend about his girlfriend being sick. He wasn't sure the guy bought it since he had a sour expression. It was clear that some people were not welcome in this world, and they were going to do their best to police those who didn't belong. The sentiment was that he'd been allowed inside, and he'd better not do anything to upset anyone, or he'd be ousted immediately. It made him physically ill and his perception of her changed that night.

He was often ignored by her friends, a longtime trigger for Steve. Being ignored wasn't something he simply disliked, it was a direct threat to his core and things could get bad quickly if someone ignored him. For Steve, being ignored was the equivalent of having his life threatened.

They were ignoring him to illustrate to him that he was expendable and not an integral part of their world. He was simply there because his girlfriend was one of them. He was not. He could be cut off at any time. Of course, Steve knew his girlfriend would never turn her back on him. After all, they were in love. Right? Love was stronger than comedy.

Others from his comedy class acclimated themselves to this inside scene. Stephanie and Nick were embraced, playing the game perfectly. The clique members seemed constantly suspicious of Steve's intentions, however. Just like every other aspect of comedy and showbiz, there were huge political undertones and though he was now on a higher plane he was having zero fun there. He was around the cool group in high school and hated every minute of it. He told himself to suck it up, comedy wasn't just about fun, it was about making it. That's all that mattered right? But he found it odd how unenjoyable professional comedy seemed to be. As a kid, comedy had been the pinnacle of fun.

One night, Steve was excluded from a gathering at his girlfriend's apartment. Things had come full circle. He went from being summoned months earlier to being deliberately excluded. It was unfathomable that his girlfriend would exclude him from a party she was throwing. It seemed his membership had unofficially expired like a work visa in a foreign country. When he confronted her about the slight, she coldly told him that he was overreacting. She claimed that he hadn't made any effort to fit in with everyone. Steve again felt like that kid being told he wasn't enough.

And that's when the voices came at him in his head. Comedy was supposed to be his solace, to save him and make him feel like he was something. The popular clique had used their status to make others feel less than and now they'd done it to him. Steve felt bullied and he hated bullies more than anything. He asked her for an apology.

"An apology for what?" she asked, genuinely surprised. "*You* owe *me* an apology."

"I owe you an apology for not inviting me to your party? Explain that logic to me. I really want you to tell me how that makes any fucking sense. Are you really that deluded or are you actually aware of how insane you sound?" Steve said.

"Did you call me deluded?"

"Yes. You're deluded in this world of people who treat everyone like shit. Doesn't that bother you? Does it at least bother you that they treat me like shit?"

"I think you make them feel uncomfortable," she said.

She slammed the lobby door in his face and left him out there in the cold night. Steve got the message. He didn't matter. As he stood outside alone, he felt like cold water had been poured over his head all over again.

She stopped responding to his messages and receded into her inner circle. Of course, the gossip mill went into full swing and the aftermath of it all began to affect his career, something he'd been afraid of all along.

He lost opportunities. He was dropped by an agency that repped the big wig comic. Steve was told by various comics, including Roger, that the woman was trash-talking him all over the scene. Steve would have loved to know how the story was being spun so that it was affecting him this much.

In comedy, good opportunities were very few and far between, and now he was having them deliberately taken away by people he barely knew simply because he'd defended himself. None of it made sense to him. In life, you were supposed to be rewarded when you stood up for yourself, but not here it seemed. Here in this world, you had it all taken away if you offended the wrong people, it didn't matter if you were right. One misstep and it was all over. You could be banished to the cornfield if you angered the wrong person.

Showbiz and comedy were steeped in cancel-culture well before it went viral. The longer Steve was around, the more he noticed that revenge was the main motivator behind doing comedy. Most didn't do it for the enjoyment of it at all, they did it to get back at people who'd crossed them. Since Steve had made waves and hadn't played the game, they'd gone out of their way to cancel him, just because they could. After all, there was no room in comedy for anyone who dared go against the grain.

CHAPTER 27:

ALT RISING

S TEVE CONTINUED TO DO SPOTS AND WAS STILL A regular on many Rififi shows but he felt more isolated now. After retreating into a hole for a couple of months, he was contacted one afternoon by a friendly Comedy Central exec who offered him a gig hosting a TV show they were launching. The guy's name was Jack, and he said he was a fan of Steve's from *The Invite Them Up* CD, calling him his favorite on the album.

Comedy Central was going to start airing raunchy movies late at night completely uncut with all the dirty parts intact. Steve would appear during commercial breaks and provide commentary.

Steve shot the show over three days in Brooklyn. They provided him with his own trailer and everything else that he needed, just like he was a star or something. After it aired a month later, many people contacted him about it including old childhood acquaintances and even a girl he used to have a crush on at LaGuardia. He liked the attention a great deal even if he pretended he didn't care. He felt like he'd been given a higher credit line in the comedy world.

A huge TV credit had given him some much-needed new buzz and it meant he could stick around a bit longer and maybe even get acknowledged by the likes of Aziz again and maybe more alt groupies. He was hot again, at least for the moment. Showbiz was a roller coaster ride and you had to hang on for dear life the whole time, it seemed. Even the star-fucker had texted him out of the blue, but he refused to fall for her bullshit again. He actually resented her fair-weather attention now.

Soon after the Comedy Central exposure, he taped a couple more TV appearances on MTV and Fuse. Then he was asked to audition for a VH-1 show and became a regular on the pop culture show "Best Week Ever." Mulaney and Kroll, who were now flying high, were some of the show's most featured stars. Nick's Geico Caveman show had fizzled immediately which was a good thing for Nick. It had gotten his foot in the door, and he was now doing movies and TV show appearances. Mulaney was now writing for SNL.

Aziz returned from LA where he'd been for a few months shooting an NBC TV show and threw a party at UCB. It was a huge event. The party of the year. He was on the cusp of stardom and there was just a vibe in the air that it was just a matter of time. He was now officially set to host the MTV Awards making him New York Alt comedy's newest "it" boy replacing Demetri Martin who'd been the guy for about two years.

Demetri had been the guy expected to blow for a while now and had just been featured in the starring role in a major studio film about Woodstock. Unfortunately, the film bombed and didn't propel him the way he'd hoped it would, and now Aziz was dubbed the next big thing to come out of the alt scene. "Human Giant" was renewed for a second season on MTV and now this tiny unassuming kid was a comedy god.

Steve hadn't seen Aziz in months. He bumped into him as soon he walked into UCB. Aziz was standing alone leaning against a railing by the bar, sipping from a cup.

"Hey Aziz, how are you, man?"

"I'm good, man. Good," Aziz said, not looking up from his cup while taking another sip.

"What have you been up to?"

"I was in LA. I just shot a TV show."

"Cool. I saw some episodes of Human Giant. It's really funny."

"Glad you liked it," he said, still not looking at him, and then he walked off.

Aziz approached a more successful and important comedian named Jon. Steve felt his body tense up. Aziz wasn't exactly being mean, but Steve still felt ignored. Aziz hadn't meant anything against Steve personally, he was simply a shark and success was his food. And he was hunting for another hit of success that Steve couldn't offer him.

Aziz didn't even seem that preoccupied with women. Success and fame were his drives, and he was going to get them no matter what. He appeared to have the whole thing planned out and once he got where he needed to be, he could do whatever the hell he wanted and there would be no more consorting with anyone not on his level.

Nothing could touch him once he was at the top of the showbiz ladder. Absolutely nothing could stop his inevitable ascent. Nothing. The worst part of Aziz's dismissal of Steve was what it represented. Steve wasn't important enough for him to treat well anymore. How people treated you in comedy was a direct commentary on where you stood. He was still in the game, but he was riding the bench a lot more these days it seemed.

So Steve stood alone, leaning against the row of seats, trying desperately to appear unbothered and aloof. He scanned the room. Twenty-somethings drank and danced without a care in the world. Movie stars were milling about trying to act like they weren't movie stars although they relished the attention they received. Many comedians he had started with back in the day, who had only focused on getting accepted by the clubs, were now contacting him. This space was now one of the most popular places to be in comedy, a basement under a Gristedes.

Across the room, the star-fucker talked to an up-and-coming comic. She leaned in close to him, making sure that her breasts were on display. She glanced over at Steve who looked away. He was kind of terrified of her now. She was dangerous. There were pitfalls all over this place and he knew he had to be more careful.

Steve spotted a movie star sitting nearby smoking a cigarette wearing jeans and a loose-fitted hooded sweatshirt. Steve had met the guy back in 2001. Steve's brother-in-law's sister was college friends with him. This movie star was always hanging around the scene. He was one of those celebs that liked comedy but also seemed to like being the big fish in the pond. He was like the coolest alumni of their high school who came around now and again.

Over a year earlier, Steve had written a screenplay and asked his contact (his brother-in-law's sister) to the star to pass it on for him to read. Once she handed the script off, she informed Steve that the movie star said he'd get into contact with him after reading it. Steve never heard anything after that. Now the guy was mere feet away talking to a scenester named Joe.

Joe was a friendly guy and an okay comic whose main talent was knowing celebs. If there was a celeb in any room, he'd sniff them out immediately like a dog finding a piece of ham. Joe drank from a red cup and laughed loudly while talking too closely with the movie star, making it clear to everyone that he knew him. It was a laugh Steve was used to hearing in this scene, completely inauthentic and obsequious. Joe spotted Steve and waved him over. Steve hesitated, but Joe waved his arm again and Steve decided he had no way out, so he approached the two.

"Hey, Steve. Long time. What you been up to man?" Joe asked, smiling.

"Not much. Just ya know. Same bullshit."

"Hey, do you know Lum?" he said motioning to the movie guy.

"Ummm...not really. Hey, I'm Steve."

"Steve's a really great comic," Joe said. "He's done my show a few times."

"Hey man," the movie star said while taking a drag. He shook Steve's hand quickly as if he had to do so against his will. He was polite but not welcoming.

Steve sipped his drink and stood there awkwardly. He'd had it with being snubbed by people in this bullshit phony ass scene. What was so great about famous people anyway? Why did everyone want to be famous so badly? What was wrong with everyone? He was drunk and mad, a great combination. He wasn't exactly seething, but he was annoyed, and he could feel a slight wave of anger flow through his body like it had many times in the past. It was similar to what he'd felt when he beat the hell out of that kid in kindergarten. And it was similar to the feeling he had when he went after the douche in the audience who had heckled him at that crap, open mic years earlier. He got nervous since he knew once this feeling took hold, he would cease to be in control anymore.

The voices in his head were telling him that this phony movie star was a dick who had screwed him over and that Steve couldn't let him get away with it. The voices were angrier now that they were drunk. Steve felt himself losing control and finally listened to the voices. Taking a sip of whiskey from the cup, Steve informed the movie star that they'd actually met a few times before and had a mutual friend. He glanced at Steve.

"Oh yeah? Who's that?" he asked with his eyes narrowed.

"Kelly Dandridge," Steve said, deadpan.

"Oh yeah, I know who you are," he said, nodding, his eyes a little wider now as if he were remembering something embarrassing.

"Yeah. I wrote that script that she gave you," Steve said, not moving on and feeling the wave stronger now.

"Yeah, right," the movie star answered taking a drag and looking away.

"What script?" Joe asked.

"Oh, um. He wrote a script, and my friend gave it to me," he said looking at the floor. He wanted to get away and Steve knew it. Joe didn't press the issue since it was clear the movie star was uncomfortable about it and Joe knew not to displease the stars in a room. Without celebrities, Joe would have no 'in' with the women there. Knowing famous people was his ticket to endless sex.

"So, back to the script, did you like any parts of it? I mean specifically, did any scenes stand out to you?" Steve asked.

"Ummm...I didn't read it, man. I'm sorry. I get so many scripts."

"Really? You didn't read it? None of it?"

"No, none of it," the movie star said looking up at Steve with tight eyes.

"Why not?"

"I don't know, man. I guess I just didn't get around to it. I'm pretty busy ya know?"

"You're busy, huh?"

"Yeah. I am," the movie star said, staring into Steve's eyes.

Steve straightened his posture. The movie star was about five inches shorter than he was. Steve could have beaten the shit out of him easily.

"Yeah, well...." Steve started as he took a step closer.

Just then, Susi Lee walked up dressed in a tight black dress and black leggings.

"Hey, Steve," she said, smiling.

"Susi! Hey!" Joe said, putting his arm around her aggressively as if she were his girlfriend.

"Hey, Joe."

"You look hot, girl. Lum, this is Susi. Isn't she hot?" Joe said.

"Yeah, she's something else," he said.

Susi smiled and stood still. She seemed uncomfortable as Joe kept pawing at her. Steve turned his head back to the movie star who was no longer staring at him. He just stood there drinking and the tension was gone. Steve was no longer angry. He'd been distracted just in the nick of time. Beating up a movie star would not have helped his comedy career.

He wanted to leave the place but was unable to for some reason. He must have liked the punishment. The whole comedy scene in general was full of masochists. Doing stand-up in itself was a form of self-abuse. No normal person would ever want to do stand-up. This was a roomful of freaks.

The movie star quickly excused himself and walked away while flicking his cigarette onto the floor with abandon. Joe shot Steve a look of befuddlement and went right back to hitting on Susi. Joe had a rep for hitting on all the new young comics. He was successful about half the time. Susi didn't seem too interested and kept looking over at Steve almost like he was a life raft. Steve smiled at her and shook his head. The wave in his body faded away. He was glad the movie star had walked off. He didn't think he'd be able to resist mentioning it again.

A month or so earlier Steve had watched the movie star's last film. He was completely shocked when he saw a scene right out of Steve's script. It wasn't exactly verbatim, but the concept of the scene was almost identical. Steve chalked it up to yet another shitty showbiz story. He had a lot of them now and they weren't as funny as he used to find them. He had enough war stories to fill an entire book.

It was common for a comic to have his ideas lifted from them. After all, what could a comedian do if someone above them stole a concept from them? Nothing. There was no copyright or trademark on a comedy bit and someone like the movie star knew they could take advantage. Steve had convinced himself that maybe he'd imagined the whole thing, but the movie star's reaction seemed to confirm his suspicions.

Steve was plenty drunk now and the place was making him feel bad about himself.

He talked with some comics he liked. Greg was there. He was with Sam from the Whitest Kids, and they got high in the green room with a bunch of annoying improv people who wouldn't stop cracking jokes. This short blond guy with a mustache, who was wasted, kept jumping on the couch in the green room laughing. He and another improv dick were doing Pacino impressions trying to outdo each other. Two young girls were eating it up which only encouraged them. The mustache guy bumped into Steve as he stumbled off the sofa after losing his balance.

"Easy Tom Cruise," Steve said, making Greg and Sam laugh.

"What?!" the guy said.

"*What*?" Steve said mocking him.

"Who the hell are you, man?!"

"I'm nobody," Steve said.

"You got that right!" the guy yelled, raising his beer in the air.

"What?" Steve said.

"You are nobody! Pal!!!" the mustache said, making his friends laugh.

Steve saw the freckle-faced kid from little league and a wave flowed through him. This guy was going out of his way to humiliate him. Steve made his hands into tight fists. This shrimp was going to get it. The comment was just a dumb schoolyard taunt, but it had hit home. His opportunities were drying up and his rep was in severe danger of expiring unofficially.

He was close to becoming what he'd seen years before at the clubs. A lot of those older guys stuck in the comedy clubs had at one time been on the track to stardom, but their train got derailed somewhere along the way. He didn't want to wake up at forty-five and realize that it was over and he was the last to know. He still had some clout. He was still sharing the stage with the biggest names in comedy. The problem was that he was now the least successful one on the lineup. His status as an up-and-comer was gone and now he was just a comedian who had been around for a few years and didn't have a hit TV show in development being produced by Judd Apatow.

"Can you just watch where you're going? I don't want to be part of your improv exercise," Steve said, loosening his fists.

"Improv exercise?! What a fucking dick!" the guy yelled, causing his nerdy UCB friends to break into hysterics.

One guy laughing had a long beard and a fat belly with a Marvel t-shirt on. Steve wondered where these dorks had gotten their endless well of confidence. This didn't make sense. He'd grown up just blocks away from there in a New York where guys like this would have gotten pummeled for acting this way. Something wasn't right here. It was like he was part of some nerd cult, and he was on the bottom.

The obnoxious fat guy left the green room and his posse of geeks followed. Steve went to get another drink, but the bartender wasn't around. He was pissed and spotted Susi dancing on the stage area. About twenty people were dancing to "You're So Vain." Everyone was lost in the song, and a few comics had their shirts off and were gyrating. Susi made eye contact with him and smiled warmly. She waved him over with her tiny finger and Steve sort of danced his way over jokingly.

He stood in front of her and danced as she moved closer with a warm look on her face. He smiled as the song played and grooved with the rhythm. Everyone on the stage was completely in the moment and Steve suddenly found himself out of his head and enjoying the moment. He felt free for the first time in a while. Nothing else mattered. He wasn't thinking about the pot of gold but just enjoying the rainbow. He figured if the mustache ever fucked with him again, he'd beat the hell out of him.

CHAPTER 28:

NEVER SEEN

STEVE MET WITH A COMEDY MANAGER WHO represented some of the best around. He had a good rep unlike some managers in comedy who were despised by industry insiders. Steve had worked with managers in the past, but none had shown much interest in pushing him out there and none had shown any interest lately since his heat was all but gone. He had about as much buzz as a dead cellphone.

The guy managed Steve's friend Zach from The Whitest Kids U Know. It was Zach who had recommended Steve since he was a fan.

The manager was a slightly round, rugged, guy's guy with a beard, who spoke bluntly. He acted as if he was the Buddha of comedy and went on and on about all the celebrities he knew. Steve was sitting across from the guy at his desk watching him talk on the phone.

"Yeah man, I know right. I fucking loved it. It was fucking crazy right," he said never looking at Steve.

"Yeah, I roomed with him while I was there. He was fucking cool man," he said and then laughed loudly as if he'd just heard the funniest thing ever said in the history of life.

"Ha-aa-aa! Ha-aa-aa! You piece of shit! Fuck you! Yeah, man! That chick's tits are huge!" he said.

Steve was still. He wanted to leave. At one point, he was about to, but he knew that would look awful, so he just listened to the guy babble for about ten minutes. It was clearly a power move. He had to make it clear to Steve that he had a lot going on and that Steve was no priority for him and that he was doing Steve a favor. It was refreshing for Steve to meet yet another person in showbiz who was full of complete shit.

"Alright, dogger, I'll talk at ya. Yeah, bro. I'll see you at the funeral," he said and hung up.

The funeral? Someone he knew had died? He didn't seem real upset about it. Steve felt like he was on a hidden camera show. The manager let out a long dramatic sigh and put his hands on his desk. Then he finally looked at Steve as if he was noticing him sitting in his office for the first time.

"Ya know, I just roomed with Billy Baldwin during the Montreal Comedy Festival. He didn't have his own room for some reason, and he crashed on the sofa in my room. It's weird because he keeps calling me wanting to hang out," the guy said, not even greeting Steve.

"Oh, cool," Steve said, nodding, trying to act interested that the guy kind of knew a Baldwin brother who Steve couldn't give two shits about. He was bragging about hanging out with a Baldwin brother, a bad Baldwin brother at that. The guy then tooted his own horn over and over about all the deals he was making over at Comedy Central. It wasn't a meeting as much as it was just a chance for the guy to brag. Finally, when they got around to talking about Steve he simply commented on Steve's age and race.

"You're a 36-year-old white guy, there are a lot of 30 something white guys? You're like in the worst position possible."

Steve had heard this critique many times from comedy bookers, festival scouts, and agents. He was just a white guy. Yeah, sure he was funny, but who cared? What did this critique even mean? Was he supposed to not be a white guy? Was he supposed to wear blackface and transition into a woman? The message was always clear, being funny wasn't important, and being who he was wasn't going to work. He had a flash of the slick comedy manager he'd met in Hollywood a year into stand-up. He was right after all. Funny meant almost nothing in this business.

The manager took a couple more phone calls during their meeting and at one point commented that Amy Schumer was hot to the person on the other end and asked if they could introduce him to her. He mentioned the funeral again, it was for Richard Jeni who had committed suicide days before. The manager later told Steve that he used to represent Jeni but hadn't been able to do anything for him in the last few years since he wasn't hot anymore. Jeni was forty-nine and had been one of the biggest comedians in the world a decade earlier. He'd shot himself in the face. The manager kept mentioning how sad it was even though he didn't seem at all torn up about it. Steve left the meeting bummed out. The guy blew him off and told him if he had anything for him he'd give him a call. The female receptionist led him out.

The following night, Steve was booked on Crash Test. He was supposed to have been on the show a month earlier, but Aziz had asked to reschedule him since Zach Galifianakis had hit him up at the last minute. Now he was being bumped on shows. When he went up at the end of the long show, Steve didn't give a fuck. He killed since he was loose as all hell and had no interest in getting the crowd to like him.

By the end of his set, he was destroying. He had the set of the night, and he knew it. He was tired of trying to get people to like him. He was approached by a few women after the show who asked for pictures. Yeah, his set was good. A thin blond with a big chest gave him her number and told him she wanted to see his next show. Steve was trying to get her to meet up with him later when he was approached by a young and energetic man with a long nose.

"Hey man, I'm Scott Rogowsky. I did a few shows with you a few years back. We met a few times. I wanted to talk to you about something."

"Hey man, yeah, how are you?" Steve said, watching the busty woman leave.

"You killed it, man. You always kill. I wanted to maybe discuss the possibility of producing your album."

"Yeah?" Steve said, a bit miffed about the blond leaving. He let it go since she had wide crazy eyes and seemed a bit unstable the way she laughed at everything a bit too loudly.

"Yeah, man. I'm a huge fan. You wanna talk about it? Lemme buy you a drink," Scott said.

"Let *me* buy *you* a drink dude," Steve said.

"Oh, man! Steve Collin is going to buy me a drink?! This is too much!" he said.

"Yeah. Life is beautiful huh?"

"Yeah, man!" Scott cackled.

Steve went to a bar down the street and listened to the affable and charming guy fresh out of Johns Hopkins University. He was full of energy and laughed a lot whenever Steve said something. He had goofy energy but was a real go-getter and more importantly he was a fan of Steve's.

He told Steve how disenchanted he was with the world of stand-up comedy. Scott wanted to be a comic but quickly realized it wasn't for him since it was full of sharks. He didn't have the patience for stand-up comedy, and he didn't think it was where his talent lay.

"Your set on *Invite Them Up* is by far the stand-out set. You did better than all those guys on it. Way better than Aziz and Birbiglia. I always wondered why you weren't more famous."

Steve heard this sentiment all the time now and had grown to hate it with a passion. When Scott said it, he felt the blood leave his head and his stomach got tight. Why wasn't he more famous? He never knew how to respond to that. The words from the Aspen woman rang in his head "so close....so close." He hated when these words attacked his psyche. He wasn't in charge of the entertainment industry. Plus, he'd had obstacles thrown his way in the form of blackballing. Comedy was a tough business that took many down with it. Steve knew now how naïve he'd been to think comedy was about being funny.

Scott told Steve he wanted to be a producer now and start a label. This album would be his first project. It was going to be marketed as the first full-length comedy album from the breakout stand-up from the *Invite Them Up* album. This, he guaranteed, would make them take notice again and give him the attention he so richly deserved. Of course, Steve ate up this kind of talk. He was still relatively young, 36, and maybe still had a shot.

He immediately thought of the girl who had cheated on him when he was seventeen, and how this would show her. Where the hell had she come from? He hadn't thought of her in years. Why were these things still hanging around in his mind? He pictured her hanging herself for ever being stupid enough to let him go.

He'd all but forgotten about that 6-year-old kid in the back of the station wagon. That kid was still in the back of his mind, but all that mattered now was getting recognition, otherwise what was the point of any of this or anything for that matter?

CHAPTER 29:

THE UNDERRATED

S TEVE PREPPED HIS ACT FOR THREE MONTHS FOR the album taping at Pianos. He was still able to get on the biggest shows in the city, but most people he'd started with were migrating to the West Coast to cash in their comedy chips and become rich. There was a whole new class behind him comprised of younger and hungrier comics. Stand-up comedy was a booming scene again. UCB Theatre was now a full-on industry full of 20-year-olds hoping to become the next Aziz, Demetri, or Hannibal, or whoever the fuck was the latest hotshot. Kids were flocking to UCB to become the next big thing.

Steve focused on getting his hour to where he wanted it to be. He worked at it harder than he'd ever worked on his stand-up before. The set was coming together until one night at Rififi he had a particularly rough set. Nothing was hitting and a guy was talking during his entire set. Steve finally addressed it and the audience turned on him when he became angry. At one point, a few people in the crowd began shouting at him that he was an asshole. He was in the right, but it didn't make any difference. Once the crowd turned you couldn't get it back no matter whose fault it was. He'd crossed over the fragile anger threshold that transforms a comedy set into a tirade.

At the bar, he got more deflated when he heard who had gotten into the Montreal Comedy Festival, a success that had always eluded him. Apparently, a newer obnoxious comic had been accepted. Steve had never even been asked to audition for Montreal since the head of booking the festival was a vindictive prick who hated Steve. The guy had decided early on that Steve would never be a part of the festival. The guy was a notorious prick known for making racist and sexist comments at comics. He used his status to sleep with comedians and was a horrible human being, but there was nothing anyone could do about it. He was one of the comedy gatekeepers and if you wanted inside, you had to play by his rules. Comedy was grand. Steve was so happy he'd chosen to pursue it.

All Steve had any control over was how funny he was. That's all he felt he had at this point, so he threw himself into his set knowing he had nothing to lose anymore. If he was going to be ignored, he'd make sure it wasn't because he was bad, it was because they were plain wrong.

The day of the taping came; Sunday, April 11th. He walked over to Pianos slowly with his long set list in his back pocket. He had it memorized but brought it to have as a superstitious ritual. He always brought his notes onstage as a security blanket and also as an unofficial nod to what he'd first observed that first night at Largo when Mitch Hedberg and all the others brought their notes onstage. If the greatest comedians of the last ten years used notes, then Steve could too. His notes made him feel relaxed which was important in comedy.

The critique from club comics that alternative comedians were lazy because they always brought their notes onstage, was a bunch of shit. Steve brought his notes onstage because he was constantly doing new bits every time he performed. That was the antithesis of laziness. Most club comedians prattled off the same act over and over. Steve knew he could kill with the jokes he'd been doing for seven years every night but what was the fun in that? Steve treated stand-up like he treated being funny in school, he wanted to be loose, not too polished, and just have fun. Why were notes so frowned upon onstage anyway? If they helped you and made you more relaxed, then what was the problem? No one faulted the New York Philharmonic for having their music sheets in front of them while they played. When you went to see a doctor, they had a chart in front of them reminding them of your medical history, no one yelled at them about it. "Hey! You didn't memorize my lab results?! You can't do that! I'm telling your parents! I don't care if it helps you do your job better! You get an F!"

When it came down to it, Steve was better when he had his notes with him up there. It was him and his notebook against the world.

Steve was introduced by Greg Johnson after a couple of the Whitest Kids U Know did sets. The Whitest Kids were nice enough to let their Sunday show be the venue for Steve's album taping. He had become good friends with all of them and they supported him. He walked up in front of the packed room of about 70 people. The encouraging crowd laughed at his first joke. Then he spotted Mike Ferrari in the crowd. He immediately flashed back to the station wagon when Mike had shined the flashlight on him.

"Ladies and gentlemen, Steve Collin!" he heard Mike say as his friends laughed.

He got lost for a moment onstage looking at the lights. Had all of this started in that station wagon? What if that moment had never happened? Would he be here now? Was it even a good thing that he was here now? He suddenly let it all go and relaxed into his rhythm in a way that he hadn't expected, and he felt light on his feet.

"The other day, someone was reprimanding me about drinking and doing drugs. They said 'the thing about drinking and doing drugs is that once they wear off you still have the same problems you had before you started.' I don't agree with that. I find that when I drink and do drugs, and it wears off, I always seem to have a whole new set of problems than I did before when I started. It'll be like 'Man, I'm naked at the zoo handcuffed to a dead hooker. This is not a problem I had last night. How am I going to get my car out of the ocean? I didn't even own a car last night nor do I live near the ocean. My friend was wrong. I have a whole new set of problems that I didn't have before I started taking drugs.' "

When this bit received an applause break, he took his time and didn't try too hard to be funny which often tripped him up. He did an hour and was surprised at how quickly it flew by. Some jokes he did were only about three weeks old, but they got amazing responses. He knew when he left the stage that he'd done it.

Scott told him he'd killed it with a huge smile. Steve barely even remembered what he'd done up there. People were congratulating him left and right. He spoke to Mike and his wife for a few minutes.

"Great job, man. That was amazing," Mike said.

"Thanks. Thanks for coming. Ya know, it's funny...I was thinking about that time at your birthday party, in your parents' car. Do you remember that?"

"Yeah, I do. Joe mama!" he said, smiling.

"Yeah. That's right," Steve said crinkling his brow. He suddenly felt better. He often wondered if that moment had happened or not. It sometimes felt like it only lived in his head.

After a few Makers loosened Steve up, he brought up the Oscars. Mike of course remembered Shirley

Temple and said that he must have told that story about two hundred times.

"That's one of my go-to party stories. People are always gobsmacked when I tell them I was at the Oscars," Mike said.

They discussed how they each remembered it and their stories matched up almost identically. Steve wondered though why the same moment had such different effects on them. Mike had simply chalked it up to being a cool experience whereas for Steve it stirred something that became almost an obsession to prove himself and get attention. It culminated in this moment where he'd just recorded a comedy album.

Oddly, he wasn't happy. He envied Mike in a way for being able to move on and not get caught up in the attention like he had. Being creative at times felt like a curse to Steve. He hadn't been able to completely accept his artistic side, and at times he wished he hadn't been so funny young, not in an arrogant way either. Being funny was often difficult and draining and doing it for an hour straight depleted him.

Mike picked up the tab for a few drinks, hugged Steve, and promised to keep in touch, though they wouldn't.

After Mike left, Steve got a whiskey and tried not to worry about his set or pick it apart which was, of course, impossible.

He had received a lot of attention that night which made him uncomfortable. This had always been the most confusing part to him about comedy. He spent his life trying to get attention and when he received some, he didn't know how to react. It was like he didn't trust the positive reactions, only the negative ones. This was a common comedian trait.

Ari Shaffir had once told him that a hundred people could tell him he was great and he wouldn't believe them, but if just one person said he sucked then that's all he could focus on. Deep down, you knew that the one who said you sucked was the one person who really saw who you were. That one negative comment exposed you as a fraud, which is what most comedians felt they were. It was only a matter of time before everyone else found you out. He'd once heard a reputable comic say that when he was killing at MSG all he could see were the hundred or so people scattered throughout the arena who weren't enjoying themselves. Steve found it odd that you never saw that happen on the flip side. Like for example if you went to see a sad or dramatic play in a huge theatre there wouldn't just be fifty random people laughing the entire time.

He ordered another whiskey as he pondered whether this observation was funny enough to write down. He wasn't sure.

He talked to a few women after the show who showed no real interest in him. Outside, he took a few pictures with Scott for the album, and they then smoked a joint. Roger and Jacqueline were there to support him. They went on about how he'd killed it. Jacqueline was now a fan of Steve's and told him the album would be an instant classic. She commented that he was one of the best she'd seen in the last few years, if not *the* best. Steve had confidence in his ability but the idea of him maybe being the best seemed ludicrous. Was this all some dream he would wake up from? Was it possible that he was the best? This shy kid who'd grown up just a mile away from where they were standing? Steve could only focus on the people in his life who had ignored him. If he was the best, then how could anyone have overlooked him?

Two months later, the album was released. There were five reviews. The first review released by a comedy blog was scathing. It didn't outright say that Steve was terrible, but it said that he'd said "like" and "ya know" too much. Now that's all Steve could hear when he listened to the album. Fuck. The guy was right. Steve sucked. The review said Steve was funny at times but, for the most part, wasn't anything special. Nothing special, yeah, Steve agreed when he first read it.

About a week later, Steve read two more reviews from some reputable comedy blogs. These reviews were more favorable. A popular comedy magazine that had given him a favorable shout-out in their *Invite Them Up* album review called his solo album a "great follow up to his short set on *Invite Them Up*. Maybe one of the best albums of the last year or the last five years."

Steve was more relieved than he was happy. Scott informed Steve via email that the album had been voted one of the Top Comedy Albums of The Year by a magazine alongside Nick and Mitch Hedberg, a fitting bookend. He thought of the night at Largo when he could barely get a seat in the place and watched Hedberg kill. He was now being associated with the very comics that had first informed his comedy style and motivated him to keep going. Steve knew it was now only a matter of time before he got the success he deserved. He was feeling himself again and waited patiently for things to fall into place.

CHAPTER 30:

EAST VILLAGE GOES TO HOLLYWOOD

THE NEXT FRIDAY AT RIFIFI, STEVE WAS BOOKED ON Greg's show which had become more and more popular every passing week. A new guy from Chicago was in the lineup named Kumail Nanjiani. Steve had met Kumail and his wife, Emily, briefly a month earlier at UCB. They were very friendly and Kumail was set to go to Montreal in a month. He was the latest "it" comic and there was major "buzz" around him, at least that's what everyone kept telling Steve.

Steve heard a loud booming voice from the right side of the room. It belonged to a douchebag with blond, short-cropped hair wearing a black button-down shirt. The guy was practically yelling while Kumail was onstage, but Kumail didn't address it.

Steve knew the guy would likely become more of a problem in the room if no one addressed it. One thing about alt-comics, most were completely frozen by hecklers. Most alt-comics were former nerds terrified of confrontation.

Kumail plowed through, his voice getting shaky as the blonde guy talked louder. The blonde guy knew that no one would engage him. Steve despised bullies. If something uncomfortable was happening in any room, he immediately picked up on the vibe. He often thought of what Chris Rock had once said about comics being ultra-sensitive to everything around them and how it was a torturous way to live. Steve realized now that his comedy skill derived from being sensitive as all hell. Too sensitive, he often thought. It took him years to get over things, like the kid in kindergarten whom he beat up after anger took over his body like the black smoke in the show "Lost." That had been the very first time the rage appeared to him like an outside force. Steve walked out to the bar area to calm himself down before it was too late.

The show was packed, and the biggest comedian in the world at the time was there standing at the dark bar alone with a serious face that conveyed annoyance. He was set to perform on the show. Greg walked up to him and tried to shake his hand. The bigwig comic looked up at him and put one hand up as if to stop him from coming closer and asked him to "stay the hell away" from him.

Steve had heard the frequent weird rumors swirling around about the bigwig and his sexual fetishes. He was said to have a peculiar habit that he liked to do in front of female comedians. It was an unconfirmed urban legend. Steve wasn't sure what to believe. He assumed it was partly true since he'd heard the story so many times and it was always the same no matter who told it to him. The consistency made it seem credible.

One thing he had come to realize over the years was that all his idols in comedy seemed unhappy. Success didn't necessarily bring joy. The only famous comedian that had been polite and open when he met them was Colin Quinn. He'd treated Steve like a normal human being, an equal. Everyone else had been a prick. When Steve had known comedy icons before they became icons, they were always much friendlier.

People in showbiz were way more genial on the way up. After they got to the top of the ladder things always shifted. Showbiz was about being nice until you didn't have to be nice anymore, like in the movie "Roadhouse" when Patrick Swayze's character said; "I want you to be nice...until it's time to not be nice."

He wondered if happiness would come to him even if he did become a major comedy force one day. The idea that he'd reach his goal and still be unhappy terrified him more than anything. Because after that, there was nowhere else to go. Maybe it was better to always be chasing happiness like it was a concept that was still out there.

That night at Rififi, it dawned on Steve that maybe happiness wasn't waiting around the corner. Seeing his favorite comics miserable even after achieving their dreams made him uneasy. He convinced himself that all he had to do was make it in comedy and then, he'd be okay.

"Dude, the crowd is weird tonight," Greg said staring at the bar.

"Really?"

"Yeah, that one guy won't stop talking."

"Yeah."

"Dude, did you see Aziz on the MTV Awards?"

"Yeah. It was pretty good."

"I thought he blew. A lot of people did."

"Really? I mean...I thought he did all right. I mean considering the crowd. I'd be super intimidated to do something like that."

"I mean, whatever. I guess I'm sort of sick of hearing about him. It's like who fucking cares?"

Steve smiled.

"Did you see Chris Blanks yell at me?" he said smiling slightly.

"Yeah. What happened?"

"I don't know man. I guess he's a dick or something."

"Did it have to do with that chick?"

"Kristy? I don't know man. I don't even give a fuck about her. Is he like in love with her or something?" It so happened that Chris and Greg were both sleeping with the same woman at the same time, even Steve had also slept with her.

Steve chuckled. The idea that the bigwig would be more into a woman that neither Greg nor Steve cared much for was amusing in a weird way.

Kumail finished and Steve was introduced by Greg. The blonde douchey guy was still talking, emboldened by the fact that no one was calling him out. Steve thought about the freckle-faced kid on his baseball little league team when he was 10. The guy reminded him of the kid who was always mouthing off to people. He agreed to give the guy a couple of minutes to calm down. After that, he wasn't sure what he'd do but he knew he wouldn't let it continue.

Steve started with a few short jokes to get the crowd going. His favorite tactic for dealing with someone talking was to be so funny that they had to stop because the laughter would drown them out. In this case, with every laugh Steve got, the guy got louder. The guy wanted everyone to pay attention to him. The laughs Steve was receiving were a direct threat to him. This was common at comedy shows. The still-young social media culture was making it so that everyone just had to be the center of attention at all times even if they were sitting in an audience.

This guy felt entitled to be the one everyone was watching. It didn't matter to the guy that he was sitting in the fifth row of a comedy show. He was going to be seen dammit! This was what the world had come to. It amazed Steve how many people wanted attention so badly that they would go out to a show and completely ruin it. Wouldn't it be easier to just become a comedian and go onstage yourself?

Steve got angrier and angrier the louder the guy got, and it was clear this would inevitably hit a fever pitch. Something had to happen to end this. After a laugh died down, Steve stood there not saying anything. The sound of the guy laughing at something his friend was saying sent a wave through his body. It became clear that this was about to go down. The rage was now taking over like it had that time at the open mic years earlier. That hadn't ended well but once he went over the cliff it was out of his hands.

"Dude, what the fuck are you talking about that's so funny?" Steve asked.

The guy didn't acknowledge the question just like the kid from little league had done to him years earlier.

"This guy is the only one who can't hear me in here," Steve said. The crowd laughed. "Dude, yo. What's up?" Steve asked.

He went on talking loudly, ignoring Steve aggressively. This was a big mistake. It was time to not be nice. The girl next to the douche tapped him on the chest lightly. He finally turned and looked at Steve.

"Why the fuck is it so quiet?" the guy said.

"We're all waiting for you to shut the fuck up."

"Well, maybe if you were funnier, I'd listen."

And just like that Steve had been pushed.

"How the fuck do you know if I'm funny or not?! You're not even listening."

"Fuck you! Just do your dumb act and leave me alone!"

"I'm trying to do my dumb act, but I can't because you won't shut the fuck up!"

"Pfffffttttt!" the guy said kind of dismissing the whole thing.

"Fucking clever. It's always the stupidest, most uninteresting people that talk the loudest. You ever notice that? The people who have nothing to say are always loudest. Like this dick."

"I'll kick your ass!"

"You'll kick my ass? Well, I'm going to be done in five minutes, but I can wrap it up early and see what happens."

The crowd was laughing, but the tone had shifted and now there was a sense of danger. Steve took a breath and told the guy to just go to the bar if he wanted to talk and the rest of the crowd yelled at him to shut up.

Suddenly the douchebag started laughing uncontrollably at something his friend whispered to him. He was convulsing and laughing wildly. He was clearly laughing at something about Steve. Steve went right back to the 10-year-old version of himself. He was being mocked by a bully. Steve hated bullies and made the decision years earlier to never bow to a bully even if it meant being killed. He'd rather die than let a bully get the best of him.

"What the fuck are you laughing so hard at? Did you just see your penis for the first time?" Steve found himself saying.

The crowd laughed at this and something amazing happened. The douchebag just got up and walked out. Steve had won the encounter. He saw a flash of the punk red-headed kid in little league whom he'd first zinged with this line. The line had proven to be an omen of sorts. That asshole kid on the field had been his first heckler, and the first one he'd taken down. All those punks he'd grown up around in Manhattan had sharpened his comedy skills. Growing up in '80s New York, you had to be able to hold your own, not unlike a comedy set.

After his set, Steve went to the bar, and Lindsay the pretty and friendly bartender handed him his Makers on the rocks without him even having to order it. A young good looking writer for SNL walked up. He was very fresh-faced, and preppy looking and wore a button-up clean pressed blue shirt. He looked like he had just gotten back from sailing for Harvard, which he most likely had.

"Hey man, I'm Colin Jost. I've seen you here before. I'm glad you called that guy out. He was talking all through my set," he said staring at Steve, not breaking eye contact.

"Thanks. I didn't want to, but I can't ignore that shit when it's happening. I get too mad sometimes."

"Yeah. I hate having to deal with that kind of shit. You're from here?" Colin asked Steve.

"Yeah. I grew up right near here."

"I'm from here too."

"Where?" Steve asked.

"Staten Island."

"Oh, cool. I've only been there once," Steve replied.

"Yeah, well why would you go there more than you had to?" Colin said grinning.

"Yeah, right. So you work at SNL?"

"Yeah. I started after I graduated from Harvard."

"Oh. I've heard of it," Steve said, nodding with a blank face.

"Yeah," Colin Chuckled.

"How is it?"

"It's great. I haven't been there long, but I like it. My ideas don't get on much."

"Didn't Katy Perry just perform?"

"Yeah, last month."

"Man, I love her. Did you get to meet her?"

"In passing. I pitched an idea to her, but she wasn't into it."

"Women love funny dudes, right? Who knows, a lot of hot women come through there. Maybe you'll end up married to...Ashlee Simpson."

"Yeah well, I'm just a writer. It'd be different if I was actually on the show."

Susi, the young pretty Asian woman of about twenty-three approached them, smiling widely. She was always put together perfectly, and she was extremely pretty but Steve never got the vibe that she was into him at all. She just had great energy and seemed earnest and not at all phony. Steve could sense an opportunistic climber and she was not one it seemed. He actually liked her.

"Hey, great job Steve," she said, sticking her hand out to him while leaning back.

"I love your material. You're a great writer. I wanted to ask if you would do my show next month here. It's a great lineup," she asked Steve.

"Yeah, of course, I'd love to," Steve said.

"You were really super funny," Susi said to Colin.

"Oh, thank you."

"Will you do the show?"

"Um....sure. I'd love to."

"Great. Here's a flyer. Are you on Myspace?"

"Ahh...yeah sure."

"Great I'll message you. I think we're friends. I'm going back in."

"Who's on now?" Steve asked.

"Michael Che," she said and walked off.

"Oh."

"Who's Michael Che?" Colin asked Steve.

"He's new. He's really good."

"Oh yeah?"

"You should check him out."

"Yeah, I'll do that. What's his name again? Michael Shay?"

"Michael Che."

"Got it."

"He has a really good show in Greenpoint," Steve said.

"Do you know his info?"

"Ahh...yeah sure," Steve said and took out his phone. He gave Colin Michael Che's email.

A woman who looked young with a narrow pale face and slender athletic body walked over and introduced herself to Steve. He'd seen her from the stage and noticed her staring at him with wide eyes.

"Hi, I just want to say I was so glad you put that guy in his place. I wanted to strangle him so badly. What a douchebag! My name is Vicky."

"Oh, thank you, Mickey," Steve said.

"No, not Mickey! Vicky!" she shouted leaning into him.

Steve bought her a drink and they took a seat at a table in the corner next to Todd Barry who was talking quietly and closely to a young blond woman. The bar filled up after the show let out. Steve talked to a few of the comics before he left with Vicky and went back to her apartment. They ended up in her narrow cramped bedroom with her twin bed in the middle of the room like an island.

There were stuffed animals all over the bed, and on her dresser, there were a few framed pictures. One picture was the prerequisite girl picture of four girls in a row smiling each with one arm out ahead of them. Every woman Steve had hooked up with had this photo in their room. Another ubiquitous one was a photo of the girl jumping and in midair on a beach somewhere. They all thought they'd been the first to have this idea.

She took off her top and wiggled around and fumbled with her bra. She lost her balance and fell off the bed with a thud. Steve sat up and asked if she was okay. She was on her stomach on the floor trying to pick herself up. She asked him to grab her hand and help her up. Steve did so and took her cold hand. She was wobbly on her feet as she climbed back onto the queen size bed.

"I just want to tell you that I have a boyfriend sort of."

"Okay."

"I mean. We're not that serious, but technically we're engaged."

"Okay. Cool."

"But seriously, I never do this," she said. "You wanna do anal?" she asked.

Steve didn't care that she was engaged. A lot of the women he hooked up with of late were in relationships. It was actually kind of his demographic. He didn't seek it out and he didn't care. He *did* later judge them for cheating. It was crazy how many dudes out there had girlfriends and no idea that they were blowing comics after comedy shows. It was almost like they didn't consider it cheating if the guy was a performer.

Eventually, she passed out on top of him and started to snore. He wanted to leave but couldn't without waking her up. Finally, she kind of moved onto her side of the bed and looked like she was about to fall out of the bed. He wrote her a note with his number on it and apologized for leaving but said he had to get up for work.

As he walked out of the apartment on the west side, he felt drained. These random encounters seemed like a dream on paper but left him feeling empty inside.

It was so cliché and stupid. He'd completely forgotten that years earlier he was lonely most of the time and had to work to get a woman to sleep with him. He thought of that trite Kid Rock song where he crooned about trivial encounters with numerous women that left him empty inside. Steve had always thought the song was laughable yet here he was finally understanding Kid Rock's lament.

His head pounded as he entered the subway station on Park Avenue. He was tired more and more lately. He thought it was just from the late nights and drinking and drugs and short winter days, but it was more from the constant chasing of happiness. He always felt just a step behind happiness. As if in any room he entered, there was a ghost of happiness that had just disappeared. He'd been chasing it for so long and he still wasn't any closer to it. He kept telling himself it was out there and he just had to get to it. It couldn't outrun him forever. He thought of the dull Kid Rock song.

CHAPTER 31:

MISTER INDEPENDENT

ONE NIGHT, STEVE PERFORMED STAND-UP ON A SHOW at UCB put on by a hot new sketch group with an internet following. The theme of the show was that the guest comedians had to do brand new material. This was meant to make the show feel more dangerous and organic. It sounded hard but was a breeze for Steve. He reveled in doing new bits, making it a central theme of the show completely took the pressure off. It was a win/win situation. If you bombed, it was understandable since you had never done the jokes before and if you killed you came off as a total genius to the crowd. He went on after Maria Bamford who had a solid set. He'd seen her many times and was a fan. A year earlier he would have been nervous to follow her but not anymore. He was an actual presence now in his own right.

Steve went up and started with a joke he'd actually told once before, so he was cheating slightly. It was about how one time he was watching a movie he didn't like and in one scene the characters were watching a movie that was a movie he'd rather have been watching. It did well, which he thought it would since it was a strong premise that people could relate to. Everything else he did was brand new.

He did a lot of jokes he'd written over the last year but had never gotten around to telling onstage. Steve had notebooks full of jokes in his dresser. Most of his jokes never got performed. He wrote bits all the time and wrote them all down. Many of his bits were great but he simply didn't have time to do them all. There just wasn't enough time. It bummed him out many times that he was so prolific since it made it hard for him to focus on a tight set. A comic needed to hone a tight set over time to book a late-night appearance. He'd thought that constantly writing was a good thing, but it started to feel like yet another obstacle. It was like his brain never shut off. Since he'd discovered stand-up, it was like a floodgate had opened and thoughts wouldn't stop pouring out.

His set at UCB went well. He'd even heard Maria Bamford laughing. When he came off, he stood in the back and was congratulated by a young female comedian he'd been hooking up with off and on lately. She asked him if all those bits were really new. He told her they were, and she shook her head, impressed that he'd done so well with brand new material. The comic was young and pretty although Steve wasn't that into her which he knew was crazy since she was most likely out of his league. Years earlier she would have blown him off like those women at Luna once had. Comedy had made him much more appealing to women, which he enjoyed, but also sort of resented deep down.

As he was leaving to walk over to McManus Bar, he was approached by two audience members, a female with glasses and a slightly overweight bearded male, both were in their twenties. The bespectacled female was tall and a bit gawky. She smiled widely as she walked over gingerly, as if not wanting to scare off a cat.

"Excuse me. Great set. Just great. Can I talk to you for a second?"

"Ahh ... yeah. Sure," Steve said expecting her to ask him to perform on her show.

"I'm Rachel. This is Michael," she said, shaking Steve's hand.

The man stood about a foot behind the woman. He was dressed in a heavy winter coat with a fur collar and fidgeted with his hands. His head was down, and he was slumped over.

"Have you ever acted before?" the woman asked Steve.

"Um...yes. I have, as a matter of fact, I have acted," Steve answered.

"Do you know who Abel Ferrara is?"

"Yes, I do actually," Steve answered.

"Really? Well, would you be interested in auditioning for a film we're making?"

"Oh. Um...what is it like a short?"

"No, no. It's a feature. Low budget, but a feature," she said.

"Oh, really? Um...I mean yeah. Sure," Steve said.

They exchanged emails and phone numbers and as he watched them walk off down Seventh Avenue, Steve figured he'd never hear from them again. It did turn on the woman he was with though. He was set. He'd killed at UCB and was just asked to possibly star in a movie. The woman could barely keep her hands off of him the rest of the night. They went back to her tiny apartment, and she told him she wanted to have a three-way with him soon. She said she had a few women she could ask. She'd mentioned this before, so Steve took it all in stride. He figured she was trying to get him to hang around a bit longer. After they had sex, they lay separately on their side of the bed not touching and he thought of the Kid Rock song again.

Steve woke up to a text from the bespectacled woman at UCB asking him to come and read for the lead in the film. He didn't give it much thought. He hadn't really thought about acting in years and thought that ship had sailed. He'd wanted to be an actor years earlier mainly because he loved movies but acting never really appealed to him on a deep level. And once he discovered stand-up, acting seemed vacuous for some reason. He thought it was funny when famous actors would comment in interviews about how hard acting was. Steve thought that was crap. He'd seen babies act in movies before. If a baby could also do your job, then it was probably not a hard job. A baby couldn't be a doctor or a lawyer or a stand-up comic. Also, a stand-up comic with no acting training could pass as an actor but an actor could never just decide to do stand-up and hold their own. So, yeah, acting wasn't hard. Being a fireman was hard. And stand-up was harder than both. Stand-up was harder than most things actually.

When Steve went to the audition a week later, he wasn't nervous at all. The woman and man from the UCB show were there, as was a younger blond man with a friendly face, the casting agent, and an Asian man with thick gelled back hair. They were all smiles when Steve entered the room and the woman brought up his stand-up show and how impressed she was with Steve's presence.

Steve read with the good-looking Asian guy who had already been cast in a supporting role. Steve did a couple of scenes and they laughed. He didn't leave feeling one way or the other about it. He didn't care, which was of course when things aligned for him.

Two days later, he was offered the lead in the indie film produced by a reputable New York director who'd done legit projects. He accepted the job and started filming just two weeks later. The shoot lasted the entire month of July. It was sweltering hot most days making it extremely hectic and grueling. The director of photography and director were cinephiles obsessed with camera shots and lenses so it would take hours to set up a shot. Steve was required to be present almost every day of shooting and there weren't any trailers, so Steve was often forced to lay down on the ground wherever they were shooting. It was much harder than he'd anticipated making a film would be.

The production was shoestring, and Steve knew it would most likely never see the light of day much less ever get released. So much for his big movie debut which was proving to be less than glamorous.

On the second to last day of shooting, Steve had a meltdown of sorts. His frustration had been building for weeks and he knew he was going to blow if anything pushed him. It was particularly hot this day in July and Steve was over the whole 'waiting around' culture of filmmaking. Steve wasn't happy with how the film was going and as he sat on the sidewalk on Tenth Street and Avenue A waiting three hours to do a scene that consisted of him walking up to a falafel stand and placing an order, he finally became restless.

He felt his mind going to that place of rage that it sometimes did. He had flashes of the kindergarten incident. He could still see himself clearly, slamming the kid's head into the lunchroom wall. His first memory of losing control of his anger.

Part of his frustration was that his film debut wasn't what he'd dreamed of as an impressionable kid. He often felt embarrassed about being involved with the project. Another affliction he suffered from was a feeling of constant inferiority. No matter what happened or how he did in life, he still felt less than. Now he felt it deep down and he had to combat it. He decided to throw a tantrum. He stood up and asked the director what was taking so long. The shy and socially awkward director told him they were setting up the shot.

"Why is it taking so long?" Steve asked.

"Well, we have to make sure the lens is correct and that we have the light," he answered.

"I mean, it's fucking boiling hot and I'm wearing a down vest. Don't you have any sense of the people waiting around in this heat all day because you guys can't get your shit together?!"

The director and DP looked up at him with wide eyes and blank stares. They looked completely dazed. Steve could feel the tension in the air and also knew he was losing control of himself. He was in one of those situations he'd often found himself in where he knew he was in the right but somehow, he was alienating everyone around him with his temper. He didn't want to alienate anyone.

Most of the time, Steve just wanted to belong somewhere, but he never felt he quite did. He couldn't understand why either. If only he'd felt more included as a kid maybe he wouldn't be 35 years old laying on a hot sidewalk waiting to shoot a film that had no budget. He was most angry at himself for letting his life get to this point.

"Why is everyone just staring? I've been sitting here for hours waiting for one shot that doesn't even matter! I'm sick of this shit!" he yelled, throwing his messenger bag down onto the hot and filthy sidewalk.

The DP just looked away and the director shook his head. Steve was powerless in everything in his life. He had no power over anything, but he knew he could get their attention this way.

"I'm done. I'm not doing any more of this movie," he said walking away and holding his arms out dramatically.

"Wait, Steve...what?" the director said.

"I'm done! This is bullshit! You guys are ignoring me!!!" he yelled and knew immediately what had triggered him. He walked off quickly and turned the corner. He ran up to First Avenue. His heart was pounding, and he was short of breath like he had been that time his mother poured water on his head. He finally stopped at the corner. He was drenched with sweat and felt like he was going to faint. He leaned against a brick wall and tried to catch his breath.

After walking around the neighborhood for an hour, he calmed down and finally returned. They decided to cut the scene and pick it up the next day. Steve had now had his movie star diva moment and he didn't like it like he thought he would. The more things he experienced, the more he discovered he didn't actually know himself.

At the end of the grueling shoot, the director and his girlfriend, the man and woman he'd first met at UCB, told him they'd let him know when they had a cut of the film. They assured him it would be finished in a few months. He wasn't sure that it would come out like he hoped but at the very least he could tell people he was the star of an actual film. Maybe it was a good thing that no one would ever see it.

CHAPTER 32:

COMICS RAPPING

S TEVE WAS PUTTING TOGETHER A RAP ALBUM AT this point and had secured a few cameos from other comedians such as Hannibal Buress, Joe Derosa, and Ted Alexandro. He'd secured Hannibal at the last minute since they were friends and Hannibal liked Steve's comedy. It was clear though that Hannibal was the next person to break and was doing a cameo on Steve's album as a favor. The old guard was being pushed out and the new was taking over, an inevitability in life but especially in comedy and showbiz. The funny part was that the new kids who took over never realized that one day they'd be pushed out too.

In life, and especially comedy, nobody went quietly. Jim Gaffigan even did a short comedic bit on the album begrudgingly after Steve cornered him after a show.

Steve took the comics who'd appeared in his video to a bar to buy them all drinks. Joe DeRosa, Ted Alexandro,

Rob Cantrell, and Hannibal Buress all joined Steve at a bar near the place where they had shot for the day. It was called McKenna's on West 14th Street. As they got drunk in the emptyish bar, they started talking about comedy. This was an inevitability when a group of stand-ups hung out and drank together. You could dance around it and avoid the topic for only so long until it finally infiltrated the dialogue. What started as a debate over the best rapper of all time, soon shifted until they were listing their top three favorite comics of all time.

"Do they have to be current or can it be anyone?" DeRosa asked, leaning forward in his chair holding a beer that looked about to spill.

"It can be anyone," Ted said.

"Okay, okay fine. Carlin of course is number one, Rock, then Chris Blanks."

"Carlin's first?" Steve asked.

"Yes! Of course. Who the fuck else would be first?" DeRosa exclaimed, raising his arms in the air.

"He's not even in my top ten," Steve replied.

"Jeez. Who's your number one? Carrot Top?" DeRosa asked.

"So because I don't like Carlin, I like Carrot Top?"

"Yeah, I forgot, you're the guy who thinks Eminem is the greatest rapper of all time."

"Let's see. Number one, Nick. Number two, Eddie Murphy," Steve started.

"Yeah, that's good actually," DeRosa said, putting his head down.

"Number three...Collin," Steve said, smiling.

They laughed.

"Number three? Man, have more confidence in yourself dude!" DeRosa said.

Rob Cantrell gave his top three next. His number three was a tie he said between Richard Pryor and Bill Cosby.

"Cosby?" Steve asked with narrow eyes.

"Yeah. You don't like him?"

"I mean. I've never really seen his stand-up."

"You've never seen him? So how can you judge? She-e-e-sh Collin," DeRosa said, slamming his hand on the table a bit too hard.

"I've seen bits of it. I hated his TV show. Besides I heard he's supposed to be like a scumbag....with women I mean."

"I've heard that," Ted said.

"What'd he do?" Hannibal asked.

"I don't know the details, but apparently he's been accused a few times. Google it. Maybe there's an article about it," Steve said.

"Yeah, I'll do that. He does seem like a self-righteous prick with all the shit he says about black kids," Hannibal added, sipping his beer.

"You guys ever heard the Blanks story?" Cantrell asked.

"Yeah," they all said in unison.

"Who'd he do that to?" Ted asked.

"I don't know. A comedy duo, apparently."

"I'm friends with Blanks and I've opened for him a lot on the road. He's a good guy. I think it's bullshit," DeRosa said.

"You think so? How come I've heard it so many times? The story's around," Steve said.

"Trust me. It's bullshit."

"I don't know. Maybe. There's a rumor that he's done it to other female comics. I'd really like to know what actually happened."

"What're you? The fucking New York Times?!" DeRosa exclaimed, finishing his beer and taking out a cigarette.

Steve had discovered rap music in 7th grade when a classmate from Hollis Queens, the home of RUN DMC, provided him with mixtapes from Hot 97. Steve immediately became enthralled with the new sound and was hooked. Something about rap resonated. It was cool, new and the bravado was amazing. These guys had confidence out the ass. Nothing was going to bring them down. They were the best. Steve liked the idea of telling everyone how great you were with no apology. This would again become a big part of who he was. Growing up in New York City in the '80s, you were going to need some bravado to get through it. It was dangerous out there and you couldn't look weak or else you'd be eaten alive.

Steve entered UCB theatre walking past the long line of twenty-somethings. Whiplash had become one of the best shows in the city. He was asked by the young woman working at the box office what he was doing there. He told her he was on the show, and she looked away while raising her eyebrows as if he'd insulted her.

UCB was becoming almost cult-like, and the improv/ stand-up divide was even wider. He was suspiciously asked three more times in the green room who he was by the overweight guy with glasses who worked there. The guy was a creep and rumors were swirling that he regularly sexually harassed women at the theatre.

There was a newer comedian also on the Whiplash that night who Steve had never officially met. He was a charming and talented 27-year-old black guy who had just put out an underground rap mixtape. He had come up in the UCB circuit in a trio that made comedy videos. They were following Human Giant's lead and they had become a sort of sensation on the improv scene.

Steve sat in the green room near Jim Norton, a club comic who he'd never seen at UCB before. His girlfriend was on the show. Norton sat still with a scowl. He looked down, not talking to anyone. Steve then spotted the rapper/comedian walk into the small green room with a couple of younger women who worked there and were most likely 19-year-old UCB students. Steve introduced himself to the guy when he passed.

The rapper guy smiled and shook Steve's hand with his mouth open and his eyes blank. Steve had been told by numerous comedians how friendly and down to earth, the guy was. Steve decided to ask him about doing a cameo on his rap album since the guy rapped under a different persona. There were only so many comedians in the scene that rapped.

"Hey Ronny, I'm Steve Collin. We've done a few shows together, I'm friends with Mara."

"Hey man, yeah, cool," he said, shaking Steve's hand but looking away immediately.

Steve felt he was interrupting the guy's progress with these comedy groupies/performers.

"I have a random question. I'm doing this rap album with this label, and I have a bunch of comedians doing short cameos on it. Like Hannibal is doing a verse and Rob Cantrell."

"Yeah? Good for you man."

"Yeah. Ummm....I know you rap so I wanted to ask if you might consider doing a verse on..."

Before Steve was even done asking, he jumped in and cut him off.

"Yeah, I'm pretty busy dude."

"Oh, okay. Well, it wouldn't take long. I could coordinate around your...."

"Yeah, like I said, I'm busy. Good luck with it."

"Yeah, but I was wondering if...."

"Hey, dude, he's not interested," one of the female groupies said getting between Steve and the guy.

Steve was taken aback.

"What'd you say?"

"You heard the lady," the guy said.

"Jeez. I'm sorry but it's a free country. This is America," Steve said.

"What'd you say?" Ronny asked with a serious expression.

"It's a free country."

"No, after that."

"This is America."

He smiled at Steve and turned his head, looking off into the distance for a second. "Look, man. I'm just not into it. But seriously, good luck," he said, looking at Steve with a softer expression. He put his arm around one of the girls and took out a joint.

Steve stood there for a second and then walked out of the green room and sat in the back of the theatre to watch Amy, the young, blond comic on the rise, perform. How dare he turn him down. A few years later, the guy would become a Golden Globe winner and Grammy-winning hip-hop star. The alt scene was cranking out big names all over the place and he felt his turn was coming. His time was coming. It was his destiny. This is America after all.

AN ALT ORAL HISTORY
PART FOUR: LAST LAUGH

"Rififi to Close, the Laughter Dies Tonight!"

— Gothamist

"I had a lot of opportunity success and then it went away which almost felt more normal in a way because I was like oh I always suspected nobody liked me. Every now and then people will say 'no offense but you look like Janeane Garofalo'. I'm like 'well, none taken'. Then when they realize its me they say 'Why did you quit acting?' Which is like getting punched in the face."

— Janeane Garofalo

Comic

"It was like this great thing and then it was over. I was amazed at how quickly it went away"

— Roger Hailes

Comic

"I was glad I got to perform on *Invite Them Up* just before Rififi closed. I'd heard all about it before I moved to New York,"

— Comedian who became a Marvel star

"I came to learn that I wasn't riding the alt scene's cresting wave but rather catching its crash as the gentrification which had already forced the closure of Luna Lounge soon claimed the lives of Rififi, Mo Pitkin's, and other stalwarts of downtown comedy, pushing the community out to Brooklyn and Queens and many of the comics out to LA where they became the stars we know them as today."

— Scott Rogowsky

"That last night I remember Eugene got on at the end and started breaking things. It really did feel like the end of something."

— Steve Collin

Comic

"It definitely was a blow to the alt scene when Rififi closed."

— Antonio

Rififi Manager

"When Rififi became a Buffalo Exhange at first I didn't care because I thought it was a chicken wing place. it wasn't. So yeah, sad to lose a spot like that."

— Kenny Zimlinghaus

Comic

""It seemed like every huge comic of the next generation was there. The lineup was insane. Mulaney, Kroll, Jenny Slate and just everyone After that it felt like the alt scene had lost its center. There were still alt shows but you could feel a shift happen afterwards,"

— Chris Jurek

Comic

CHAPTER 33:

THE NIGHT THE LAUGHTER DIED

T HE LAST NIGHT AT RIFIFI WAS KIND OF A SHOCK TO everyone. It came out of nowhere, sort of. There had been rumors that the place was going under due to the soaring New York rents but, when it finally happened, it was jarring. Steve had suspected for a while that the place could not have been doing very well since there was barely ever a cover charge and most of the comedians drank for free every night. New York City was growing more and more expensive every month and it was an inevitability that a place like this would have to close. It had become the centerpiece of the alternative comedy scene that had taken shape in the last five years and turned into a burgeoning scene. The UCB was in full swing filled with college kids who wanted to be improv stars. UCB only had three stand-up shows, one of which was Aziz's Crash Test, even though Aziz was no longer running it.

With Rififi closing down, everyone showed up for the last bang. John Mulaney, Nick Kroll, Jenny Slate, Anthony Jesselnik, Pete Holmes, Kumail, Eugene, Bobby, Carl, Stephanie. Everyone drank up any alcohol left in the place. It was shilled by Lindsay the cute bartender who was always in a good mood.

Steve was slated to go on in the middle of the show. He felt more comfortable than he'd anticipated he would be. He'd become a staple in the scene. His solo album, while not a huge moneymaker, was a critical success and had garnered him even more respect in the alternative scene. He now embodied the scene in a way. He was respected for his talent but wasn't a commercial success. He wasn't "a sellout" so to speak, at least that's what he told himself often.

In three years, his debut album would become a "cult classic." In the meantime, Steve still felt like he was trailing everyone else. He didn't have any current TV shows or movie deals like many of his peers.

He got drunk on free Makers at the bar as was his routine. The energy in the place was kinetic and oddly positive. Though Steve wasn't aware of it, this was an important transitional night for him and the others. Things were going to change after this. It was a graduation of sorts, and most would go off in different directions. They would no longer have this place to keep them connected. It was like they were getting off the island on "Lost."

Steve drank and tried not to think about the future or even the next day. It was much like the New Year's Eve scene in "Boogie Nights" when the '70s ended. Nothing would be the same after this.

It was the summer of 2009 and the lineup in this hole in the wall bar featured some of the most defining names in comedy for the next decade. Future movie stars, TV icons, and stand-up gods who would one day sell out arenas performed in front of crowds of people. The show was free that night featuring a lineup that would cost thousands of dollars to witness in just a few years.

Every comic that went up did a riff on Rififi closing. Although this was the official last night of the place, there had been a few fake closings in the last six months. Steve went up after Mulaney, now a god in this room. Mulaney destroyed with some new bits and got off. Steve went up to raucous applause. He stood in front of the packed room for the very last time and paused before he started.

"So, Rififi is closing huh? Well, as they say, tenth time's the charm." The line got an applause break and Steve did a loose 10-minute set.

When he was finished and went back to the crowded bar, he told himself this wasn't really the end of anything. He would still do stand-up, of course. After all, Rififi was just another venue. Its closing didn't mean anything in the end. He told himself he didn't even care about the place. It was probably better for him that it was closing its doors finally. He almost believed what he was saying in his head. He sipped his whiskey at the bar for the last time. He was in full aloof mode, his default defense mode when he felt afraid and alone.

Eugene went on at the end of the show. The place had thinned out considerably. There were about fifty people left and it was just after 1 am. Eugene had a large pint glass full of liquid and ice cubes in his hand, He picked up the mic stand and hit the wall on the left side of the stage. The wall chipped a little with each hit. He kept at it while laughing. He then smashed the mic stand on the floor repeatedly and threw his glass against the wall causing it to crash into many pieces. It was very punk rock which felt fitting.

"It doesn't fucking matter anyway! We're all fucked! What're you all gonna do now?! It's fucking over man!!" Eugene yelled.

He picked up the mic stand again and hit the wall even harder. He was no longer laughing. The audience that was left cheered him on. He then invited everyone onto the stage to cheer with him. Everyone rushed the stage jumping up and down. The stage turned into a makeshift mosh pit. Steve just watched from the audience trying not to get swept up in the moment. He took another sip. He was wasted by now. This wasn't a big deal at all. Who cared in the end?

Back at the bar, he saw that the place was almost empty except for a few. Greg, Sam from the Whitest Kids, Roger, a newish comic and friend of Greg's named Ken, and Nick. Lindsay the bartender was dancing behind the bar to the Modest Mouse song "Float On." She had on a black skirt, a floral print top, and had her hair pinned up. He watched her as she wiggled her body slowly. She turned and smiled.

"Oh, I didn't think anyone was watching," she said.

"Yeah. Sorry."

"Do you want one last round?"

"Yeah. Will you join me?"

"Yeah. Of course, I will," she said and poured two tall pints full of the last of the whiskey in the place.

The song "Wonderwall" started to play.

"Today was gonna be the day that they'll never throw it back to you!" Sam sang while holding his glass high in the air.

"By now you should've somehow figured out what you're not to do!" he continued. Soon everyone else in the place joined in and sang along.

"I said may-beeeee! You're gonna be the one that saves me! And after allllllll! You're my wonderwaaaaaalllll!!"

CHAPTER 34:

IN THE WILD

THE NEXT YEAR, STEVE STILL DID STAND-UP BUT HE felt like he was treading water again just like he had when he started in LA. It was 2010, and the alternative scene had all but disappeared. There were a few alternative shows around still, but the center of the scene had been obliterated. Like the Empire's death star had been destroyed. He felt like an athlete who had been let go by his team but was still finishing out the season. He was now floundering in a post Empire world.

He got a few TV gigs here and there on terrible TV shows. The type of shows someone does on their way out of the business. With Rififi gone, a lot of the alt scene had completely dried up, and getting into clubs was a lot harder now since the comedy scene was even more flooded with new comedians.

Steve was asked to audition for the Cellar by his friend, Kurt Metzger. The Cellar was *the* club in the city and probably the country. Steve had all but given up on the clubs years earlier when he'd been rejected by them over and over. They all gave the same critique. He was just a white guy with nothing special about him that stood out. Kurt had recently opened for Steve at a college show at Bard and was now a fan. He told Steve that he just had to audition. He practically begged him to audition, telling him he'd kill it there and he'd be a Cellar comic.

The night of his audition, Steve felt confident about his set which was composed of all his "A material." The Cellar was tightly closed off to new comics. Even the entrance was small and hard to enter. There weren't many spots to go around and most who performed there had been there for over ten years. The vets weren't going to give up their stage time to some alt comic. The Cellar felt like the major leagues of comedy. Some of the biggest names in comedy were there every single night. It had palpable energy that Steve felt as he approached it on MacDougal.

He wasn't addressed by any of the frowning comedians as he stood in front. The small female manager was short with him when he told her he was Kurt's friend. The host didn't even ask for his name or tell him where the light was, a common courtesy extended to new comics at any club. He had been a presence in the alt scene, but here he was at zero again and they made sure he knew it.

The surly host of course got Steve's name wrong when he introduced him, either out of spite or just to be disrespectful. Steve went up and had a good set. A strong set. The audience was good, not great, but they were good. He didn't feel like he'd killed but he'd done well and definitely hadn't bombed. That's all you were really being tested for in a club audition. You had to prove you could hold your own as a comic among the regulars. The guy before him, a Cellar regular, didn't do any better than Steve had.

One joke he told a few minutes in received a luke-warm response so Steve quickly went into his next joke abandoning the flailing bit. He got them back with his next one, a tried and true bit about people telling him why they could never live in New York City. The bit killed and so he relaxed. He then saw the hallway light go on out of the corner of his eye. It was not easy to spot. He wondered why the host hadn't told him where the light was since it was so hard to spot. He wrapped up his set and ended on a pretty good laugh. He felt good. The set was about a seven. Not bad. He'd done what he was supposed to.

When he walked upstairs, he spotted the man-ager sitting at the infamous "Table" that would soon become folklore and was off-limits to mere unpassed mortals like Steve. Steve found it odd that she was sit-ting at the table. He'd just finished his set, how had she gotten up there so fast? A famous comic and a good-looking young woman he'd seen at Rififi sat across from the manager at the cramped table with dim over-head lighting. The manager was smiling as she sipped on a half-empty glass of red wine. She looked up at him with a dirty look as soon as he walked up.

"You went over the light. I cannot pass you," she said haltingly, glancing at him and then looking back at the table.

"What?" Steve asked not sure he'd heard her correctly.

"You blew the light by five minutes, you cannot do that here. I cannot pass you," she said loudly as if she'd had it with him.

Steve stood completely still, the blood rushing to his head. He turned his face to the side not sure how to walk away from the most awkward situation he'd ever been in. Was she done talking to him? He had no idea how to proceed. The famous comic at the table looked up with a blank face, his mouth frowning, and his eyebrows raised. Steve had practiced his set numerous times and knew it was a tight five minutes. There was no way he went five minutes over the light like she was claiming. He felt light-headed. He knew everyone must have been staring at him knowing he felt like a loser on the inside. He frantically went over her comment. He may have gone over by twenty seconds at the most because the host had refused to tell him where the light was. The host had clearly sabotaged him or at least tried to.

"Did you um...just say I went five minutes over the light? That's not true," he said looking down at the table.

"What's that? What are you saying? I'm a liar?" she said, leaning back slightly.

"No, I know what time I went on and it wasn't ten minutes ago," he answered.

"Well, you ran the light, and I cannot pass you if you don't follow the rules. You didn't follow the rules, so you do not pass," she said, looking away.

She started talking to the famous comic and didn't look at him again. Ignoring him. The famous comic stared daggers at him, signaling him to sulk away now. Steve felt the knot in his stomach and tapped his foot lightly on the floor to release some of the tension that was killing him. The famous comic held his stare on Steve defiantly. Steve looked him right back in the eye until the guy turned away and leaned towards the young woman, talking in her ear awkwardly.

"Okay, but I didn't run the light," he said and then turned and walked off.

He felt a wave through his body. His thoughts started in on him. Telling him he was nothing and a loser. They told him he'd made a fool of himself. He felt everyone staring at his back. They all knew exactly what had happened. The walk through the Olive Tree was excruciating. He walked outside in a daze.

He stopped just outside the club a few feet to the left. A brunette female approached him and told him he'd done a good job. That made him feel a bit better, but he couldn't even say thank you. He was too shook up. She seemed to be flirting with him as she smoked a cigarette. Steve wasn't in any mood to try and pick up an audience member. He was still feeling the adrenaline rip through him.

Comedian Dave Attell approached and introduced himself, offering his hand with a lit cigarette dangling from his lips and a black, wool hat on. Steve was nervous, so he asked him for a cigarette. Dave Attell asked his name and made a quip about Steve's set.

"Boy Steve, you blew it in there tonight," he said.

Steve looked up at him.

"I'm just fucking with you, man," he said, smiling after reading Steve's face.

Steve finally left and got a drink down the street at a fancy-ish wine bar with expensive drinks. Going to an expensive place was a way of punishing himself, his version of cutting.

After a few Makers on the rocks, they played the song "I Dreamed a Dream." He saw his mother in the back of their Cadillac singing along with her eyes closed. He closed his eyes to drive it away, but it stayed and jabbed at him. Now he knew how his mother had felt. For years he'd almost dismissed her experiences, but now he knew her grief and forgave her. In that wine bar, he knew she was just a human being. And unfortunately, he was just a human being also.

As he sat there, he became terrified. He pondered turning into a typical bitter person who once had a passion for something but lost it along the way. Maybe it was inevitable? Maybe he was destined to be unhappy. He'd seen numerous TV shows growing up about how you can do anything you wanted if you just put your mind to it and worked hard. Just follow your dreams was the great advice he'd constantly heard spewed out to stupid kids. It turned out sometimes your dreams didn't want to be followed and would call the cops on you and have you arrested for stalking them. Steve felt like he was in comedy jail ever since Rififi's demise. He had to figure out a new plan. He hated to admit that maybe just maybe it was all over for him. Times had changed and the industry wouldn't wait for him. He felt like he'd been shot at the Cellar. He was nothing there to them. He didn't think he had the energy in him to go on.

Maybe the moment in the station wagon wasn't as important as he'd once thought it was. It was just a fleeting moment that didn't mean anything in the grand scheme of things. Maybe not everyone was destined for great things. Maybe some people weren't "special." Maybe this had all been one big mistake.

On the subway ride back to Brooklyn, he placed his earbuds in and pressed on an Eminem song. He often turned to the angry rapper when he was in a low place. Eminem always helped him get his swagger back, something he desperately needed right now.

"By the time you hear this, I will have already spiraled up. Had a dream I was king when I woke up still king!"

Eminem rapped with pure rage, but it just wasn't doing anything for Steve, not tonight. He closed his eyes and listened to Eminem's voice full of frustration and rage after having been ignored his whole life. His rage was so strong that sometimes his voice would crack during a verse. You could hear the pain pouring out. Eminem was another Gen X'er marginalized by the world around him and had finally detached from it as a survival technique. He'd adopted the quintessential Gen X attitude of "I just don't give a fuck." Eminem made a career out of acting as if he didn't care what people thought. Steve wished he were like that.

Though they had different backgrounds, they seemed to share the exact same view of the world, the exact same insecurities, and most importantly, the exact same anger. Somehow this small white kid from Detroit who had been told by everyone growing up he was nothing special had turned his flaws into great strengths. He didn't just accept what everyone had told him about who he was. They were all wrong and just couldn't see how special he actually was. The world was wrong, and Steve found himself suddenly feeling a bit better. Maybe just maybe he also had something the world was just too blind to see.

Oddly, Steve had been more confident in his abilities as a six-year-old than he was now as a full-grown adult who had been on TV and been celebrated as a comedian. Somehow, the kid in the station wagon telling a bad knock-knock joke had more swagger than the adult version of himself. What had he lost and when? He'd worked to develop an aloof attachment, but now the detachment had frayed into desperation. He'd learned on that very first audition for the Fame school that showbiz can smell desperation a mile away.

Nothing washed off his back anymore. Now everything clung to his back and refused to let go. His anger
was out of control as of late. It was all getting to him,
but he didn't want to admit it. He'd been told no, over
and over, and he was starting to listen. He decided it
didn't matter if anyone liked him or not or if he sucked
or not. He was done seeking approval. If you didn't
like him that was your fucking problem. He wasn't
just going to slink away quietly. Fuck comedy, fuck
people, fuck fame. Fuck even Bill Murray who wasn't
that funny anymore anyway. Well, that may have been
going a bit too far.

As the F train headed outside onto the raised platform in Park Slope, a small group of loud teens entered
Steve's car. Steve heard them over his music but didn't
turn to look. He knew better having grown up in New
York City in the '80s. The last thing you wanted to do
was to make eye contact with a posse of rowdy teens
on the subway at night.

They hooted and hollered, trying to bait someone
into engaging them. They wanted someone to tell
them to be quiet and that would be it. He heard as they
moved closer to his section of the train. He simply sat
back staring ahead nonchalantly as if in his own world.
He heard them play fighting with each other and in his
periphery could see them just mere feet away. Uh oh.
They were going to make sure he acknowledged them
and that's when they'd have him. Steve wasn't tough
but he was great at acting tough. He was also great at

not showing vulnerability. Groups like this preferred the easy marks. They wrestled and cursed and ever so slowly moved closer.

"What the fuck bro! I'll fuck you up!" one yelled at the other.

One of them fell hard in front of Steve laughing hysterically. He wore a faded Mets cap. His laugh was high-pitched, sinister, and irritating as hell. Steve looked at him as the guy laughed and didn't get off the floor. The teen with long black curly hair and a tattoo on his arm looked at Steve and laughed harder.

"Yo bro! That was mad fucked up bro! Right bro?!" he said to Steve.

Steve simply nodded his head slightly and stared back. The kid jumped up and put out his hand.

"Yo dog! Put her there flaco!" he said in a sarcastic mocking tone.

Steve just smiled at him and didn't offer his hand. This kid was trying to rile him up. Steve was in no mood for this kid or his asshole thug friends. He hadn't been in a scenario like this in years and knew all he could do was act stoic and unreactive. As long as he didn't appear scared then they'd likely move on.

"Yo! You leave me hanging like that?! That's fucked up white boy! You racist!"

Steve could see out of the corner of his left eye that the other two were inching closer. Steve didn't flinch. The long-haired kid stood in front of him staring. Steve looked up at him not smiling. They stared at each other for about five seconds. The doors opened and one teen screamed directly into his face. "Fuck you bitch!" and they all ran out.

A week later Steve did a show downtown. A newer comic named Brett, who'd been at the Cellar that shitty night, informed Steve that the manager had walked out of the room thirty seconds into his set. It seemed that unless he'd had an ace in the hole at the Cellar, he had no chance of passing. It seemed as if Metzger had sandbagged him.

"I heard you just did all your alt stuff when you auditioned," Ari had said to him a few nights later at Stand-up NY on the Upper West Side.

"My alt stuff? What does that mean?"

"Yeah, Big Jay told me that you went in there and acted like it was an alt room and dicked around."

Steve hadn't seen Ari in years but remembered his "shtick" was to blurt out rude comments to elicit some angry reaction. Ari considered it daring and amusing to roast people with insults, a brand of comedy gaining momentum in New York City at the time. Steve was ultra-sensitive and didn't take well to Ari's style of humor. Steve chose not to engage.

By now Steve was used to being labeled an "alt comic" by other comics. He hadn't considered it an insult until recently. There seemed to be a backlash of sorts to this looser style that had been all the rage eight years earlier. The truth was that Steve could do comedy in any room. Jim Gaffigan, Hannibal, and Todd Barry were all alt regulars who could exist at the UCB and the Cellar without changing one word of their act. Alt crowds weren't averse to jokes and punchlines they were just averse to hacks and weak premises which were abundant in clubs. Not all club comics were hacks but a damn sure lot of them were.

Steve knew that his reputation was preceding him now and he was going to be shut out of the clubs. He went back to doing what he could and ignored his "alt comic" label that he now despised.

It was funny the different rivalries and camps that existed in comedy. It was hard enough to do comedy without other comedians sabotaging you too. Comics always seemed to make things way more difficult than they needed to be. The club comics looked down on the alt-comics and the alt-comics looked down on the club comics. It was like they were the bloods and the crips. It was so fucking absurd to Steve to witness a passive-aggressive gang war fought almost entirely behind the other's backs. There were rumors and gossip instead of drive-by shootings.

After Ari stopped baiting Steve, he told him he was visiting from LA to record a special at the Knitting Factory in Williamsburg. Ari had been passed over by Comedy Central and pretty much the entire comedy industry for close to twelve years. He'd been told over and over he was too dirty and not accessible enough. He was also a white guy which didn't help his case. Being a white guy in comedy was the worst thing to be. His only real exposure had been a video that went viral of him and Joe Rogan calling out Carlos Mencia for stealing jokes.

Ari told Steve about what some of the comics from back in the old days were doing now. Steve asked if he'd seen James Painter lately.

"Dude, Painter? I don't know what the fuck happened to that guy. He fell off the face of the earth."

Then Ari told a story about James getting into a fistfight at the Comedy Store with Bobby Lee after Painter smeared shit on his car. Painter had never shown his face there again. It had been over five years since any comic had seen James. Ari had heard rumors that he was doing drugs again after being sober for years. Steve had tried to find James on the internet for years to no avail. It was weird to not find anything about someone on the internet, especially someone who had been a comedian for years. He wondered if he'd ever see him again. James had become a sort of urban legend in the LA comedy scene.

It depressed Steve to hear that James had quit and disappeared. It reminded him just how fragile comedians were in the end. One misstep and it was all over. It could happen to anyone, and Steve knew he was just a few bad weeks away from falling into a pit he might not be able to climb out of.

Ari offhandedly mentioned he'd just started something called a podcast. Steve had heard almost nothing about this new medium. He knew they were like radio shows but not really since anyone could record them at home. Comedian Marc Maron had recently started one and was getting a slight career resurgence from it. Ari was slowly becoming a podcast presence. Joe Rogan had a podcast also that Ari was now a frequent guest on. Podcasts were more common in the LA comedy scene than they were in New York, and they weren't completely ubiquitous, yet. Steve wondered what a podcast even was. It sounded like nothing the way Ari described it. I mean who wanted to hear Ari talk for two hours every week? Or any comic for that matter?

The eventual rise of podcasts flooded the stand-up scene even more than before. Now anyone with two hundred dollars could start a radio show in their room and call themselves a comedian. Instagram was on the rise too and soon anyone could post a short video of themselves on their phone and gain a huge following.

Of course, it helped if you were hot and had huge breasts. The definition of what a comic actually was became even broader and blurrier with every new platform and app. It now seemed like everybody *was* a comedian. It was a comedy boom except that in this new boom being funny meant even less than ever before and being good at stand-up was an afterthought. The most important thing was a big following. It didn't matter what you did to get the following, the endgame was the following by any means necessary. Now it was literally a numbers game.

When he'd started in 1999, stand-up was barely on TV, now it was everywhere, TV, the internet, and on your phone. TV was now the *least* popular medium for comedy. Steve had mentioned to a young girl a month earlier that he'd been on TV recently.

"Who the hell watches TV?" she responded with a blank expression.

Ari broke out just months after Steve ran into him. His podcast was what finally did it for him.

CHAPTER 35:

THE DISAPPEARANCE

THE EMERGING COMICS OF NEW YORK AWARDS were being held at a new comedy venue called Comix. The upscale club was located in the meatpacking district. The plan for the new venue was to make it a downtown alternative type of club that could also be a mainstream club. Like a cooler hipper Caroline's minus the tourists. More and more comics were being plucked from alt obscurity by the industry gatekeepers. Comix was another signal that the alt scene had been monetized. It was a big fancy spot with overpriced drinks and gourmet food. Not exactly Rififi. This was Rififi's supposed replacement and it was like Disney had appropriated alt-comedy and punk rock had been bought out by AT&T.

The ECNY's had been going for about three years. They'd started out small at the UCB Theatre as an ironic joke and underground show. They were meant to be a parody of awards shows but now they were sponsored by Comedy Central and other corporate entities which drained the show of any irony and enjoyment, filling it instead with stuffy white male execs who seemed to hate laughing at comedy.

Steve was nominated for an award, not Best Male Stand-up, of course; an award he'd been passed over for every year even though he was a regarded comedian. The award he was up for was "Best Comedic Video." Just being included in the awards was supposed to be an honor and a sign that maybe his career was close to being back on track.

Just a year earlier, he'd started recording rap songs as a joke, so he was surprised when he heard rumblings in the scene about how he'd lost his mind with his side rap project. But a video he'd shot had gotten him to the awards show and he was actually favored in his category.

Steve immediately observed that the whole thing was being taken way too seriously. There was a fancy long red carpet with a press line just like at the SCOOMIE Awards years earlier in LA. Steve was all decked out as a rapper even sporting a fake gold chain, black knit cap, and black sunglasses at night. He waited on the carpet tapping his foot quickly with his hands in his jeans' pockets. He was behind another nominee who was being interviewed named Kate McKinnon, who jokingly grabbed the mic from the interviewer.

Steve did a quick 30-second interview, in which the interviewer got his name wrong, and was hurried inside by a pushy female producer with a scowl. No one behind the scenes of comedy ever seemed happy. It was apparently a miserable experience for all involved. He grabbed a whiskey at the bar to calm himself. He was way shakier than he thought he'd be, but he knew he could lean on alcohol. It always got him through these things. His nerves were always an issue in situations such as these. He was anxious that he might lose but he was even more nervous that he might win. He sipped his whiskey and felt it numb him. He glanced at the angry female producer who was now pulling someone's arm over to the room entrance, and he realized that he wasn't enjoying himself and hadn't in years.

Comedy was now officially not fun anymore. It was a job. A job that barely paid him.

He stood at the crowded bar and stared into the wall mirror behind the bottles. The bar was pristine and full of top-shelf liquor. He watched everyone arrive in the mirror's reflection. They were all dressed up like it was a prom. The show had only been around a few years but now it was an actual event with various press attending.

He noticed the slimy asshole Montreal booker sitting at a dark booth in the corner donning his signature fedora that made him look a lot older, although he was going for the opposite effect. The booker was sitting close to a young female who Steve assumed was a newer comic. The Montreal booker was pawing at the girl's curly dark hair in a creepy fashion. It was clear the guy was making her uncomfortable but didn't care. Steve sipped his drink and let out a sigh. The whole thing bummed him out.

He went into the room and watched the host Jon Friedman do his opening monologue. Steve acted happy whenever people won and applauded as if he was delighted for them. No one in the room was actually there to support anyone, they were there to be seen and praised themselves. It was like a support group for people who had been ignored by their parents. Hannibal Buress won Best Male Comedian. Myq Kaplan, Best Emerging Comedian, beating out Kate McKinnon. Kristen Schaal, Best Female Comedian. No surprises at all really. All the current "hot" comics won down the line. Steve sipped on his fourth Makers in his uncomfortable metal seat with a thin cushion.

When Steve's category finally came up, he felt his stomach drop as it always did when there was attention on him. He hated attention while simultaneously craving it like a heroin addict. It was a hellish feeling. A young improv girl with dark hair and glasses announced the nominees and when Steve's clip played, the crowd roared. It sure seemed like the room was pulling for him to win. He adjusted his hat and sunglasses and got ready to go onstage. He wasn't being cocky; he just didn't want to be unprepared.

When the hip improv girl channeling Janeane Garofalo announced someone else as the winner, Steve sank into his chair slightly and completely collapsed on the inside, wanting to disappear into thin air. He was frozen. He couldn't believe it. He felt like everyone was staring at him to see his reaction, though they weren't. It surprised him how personally he was taking the loss. Now he knew how all those Oscar losers must have felt. Losing at an awards show was pure torture. It got even worse when he saw the winner; the short mustachioed prick from the UCB whom he'd had a run-in with weeks earlier in the green room. The pudgy improv guy ran up and grabbed the award aggressively. He jumped around, making a scene.

"Yeahhhh!!!" he yelled while holding up the award. He then did a backspin onstage. Steve watched horrified. What the fuck was this guy doing?

As the next award for Best Variety Comedy Show was presented, Steve wanted to walk out and never look back. He knew he couldn't since that would be seen as rude and obvious. He'd be seen as a sore loser. He had to sit through at least ten more minutes of the show before ducking out. He was miserable and beat himself up the whole time. The winner for the next award was the king alt guy he hadn't seen in a few years. The guy confidently waltzed onstage wearing a nice black suit. He had a scowl on his face and rambled on for over five minutes as if he'd just won Best Picture at the Academy Awards.

Steve ordered another drink from the waitress since the alt guy's win and speech depressed him royally. Not only was Steve an award loser but now he was a *drunk* award show loser who had to watch everyone he hated win awards. He couldn't even enjoy being drunk now, one of the only things that seemed to make him happy these days. All the days had slowly become one long blur to him. He went to the bathroom while the rocker Andrew WK presented an award for "Best New Comic."

While he was downstairs, he ran into a pretty brunette woman who worked at the club. She showed him where the bathroom was. Wearing sunglasses and being drunk had completely disoriented him. The pretty brunette was friendly with a wide smile and asked about the bulky cool Sony headphones hanging around his neck. She seemed genuine and not like typical comedy club bookers, who were usually, rude, white, male, failed stand-ups, who took their anger out on young comics. Though she was not his usual type, figure-wise he liked her. She had good energy that wasn't common on the comedy scene. He'd heard the woman was engaged from a friend, but he'd later heard her make a flip comment about the relationship being "so totally over" to another comedian. Steve left without hitting on her since he felt he'd lost his mojo after the award loss.

Instead, he sat at the bar and ordered a double whiskey. He didn't get any drinks on the house from the balding, fat, male bartender, a far cry from Lindsay at Rififi. He couldn't believe they were charging him at an awards show, especially after he'd lost. What a fucking joke. The pretty female booker walked over holding a big set of endless keys and told the bartender not to charge Steve. She smiled and Steve thanked her. He was intrigued.

"I'm sorry, have we met before?" Steve asked flirtatiously.

"Oh, you already forgot about me, have you?"

"Well, I've met a lot of very interesting people tonight. Plus I'm wearing sunglasses."

"Yeah, I noticed that. That takes a lot of confidence. I like your outfit. It's cute on you."

"Yeah? Thanks. Not everyone can pull off a gold chain and sweatshirt. I like your outfit too. It's um...tight and shows off your um....ya know...body."

"So how's the show going?" she said bailing him out.

"It fucking blows."

"Oh, I'm sorry. Why is that?"

"Well, I lost if you can believe that."

"Oh, that sucks. I'm so sorry," she said frowning.

"Me too."

"What can I do to make you feel better?"

"You could give me your phone number."

She smiled at him and put her head down.

"Hmmm...I'll think about it."

"Yeah? Well, don't think too long. I might not want it later," he said, feeling confident despite his loss.

She walked off smiling. He liked her now. It was rare that someone in the comedy world was nice to him, at least someone that he couldn't do anything for. The fact that she had more to offer him yet was still nice perked him up a bit and his heart raced.

He turned to his right and spotted the young comic, Susi, whose show he'd now done at Rififi a few times. She leaned against the bar in her black dress and smiled at him.

"How's it going?" he asked her.

"Pretty good. I'm sorry you didn't win," she said.

"Yeah, well it was all rigged. How'd you make out?"

"Oh, I wasn't nominated. I just came by to hang out with John and Jesse," she said raising her eyebrows and leaning back a bit.

Steve talked with Susi for a few minutes. He noticed she was bouncing her body up and down as she spoke. There was a definite anxiousness that people had at comedy events. They weren't the Grammys or anything, but they might as well have been with the way everyone was on edge. Susi walked off after getting her vodka soda. She seemed like she wanted to get away, not because she didn't like Steve but because she was uncomfortable. She was still new to the scene and Steve was a known comedian in New York anyway. He then remembered how tense he'd felt that first night at Rififi around Birbiglia. Feelings of inadequacy were something every comic had in common. The feeling of not being enough seemed to be universal in funny people. Things like the ECNY Awards brought out people's insecurities even more and placed them on full display.

On his way home from the ECNY's, Steve stopped off at a bar on 14th Street, stumbled to a stool, and ordered a Makers. He was hammered now just bordering on shitfaced and figured he'd go all in. He'd reached that point where there was no turning back from his drunkenness. He was feeling sorry for himself and needed to shut down his brain for a few hours. A 20 something-year-old brunette wearing a tight black top and tight jeans sat a few chairs down the sticky bar from him. She had a drink in front of her and stared at him with sultry eyes that said she was high on something. Steve waved at her, and she stared back.

"Hi," she said with a blank face.

"Hey. I think you have something on your nose," Steve said.

"No, it's a birthmark," she said wiping at it with her hands.

"Oh, I couldn't tell from this far away. How's your night going tonight? Are you drinking things?"

"Am I drinking things? I just wanted to get out of the house."

"Yeah. Cool. I like that attitude. I like where your head is at," he slurred making her smile.

"You're funny."

"Yeah? I am funny! I am fucking the funniest motherfucker!"

"Why are you wearing sunglasses inside, funny guy?"

"I ahh....I just was at an awards show. I was nominated for this award thing."

"Oh, cool. Did you win?"

"I did not win," Steve said smiling and pointing his finger like a gun at her and winking.

"I fucking lost and then this asshole I hate won right after me. It has not been a good night. Hell, it hasn't been a good past two years. My mom died."

"Oh. I'm sorry. When?"

"Um....twelve years ago."

"Oh. Well...sorry."

"It wasn't your fault. Or was it?" Steve said squinting his eyes.

She smiled and got up and sat next to him. He told her about the show and how he'd had to sit through the whole thing after having lost. He drank some more and bought her a drink. She ordered the most expensive tequila the bar had. She was cute and had a great body. Her breasts looked large under her tight black lace top. She kept touching his arm and smiling. He got the vibe she would sleep with him which made him feel a bit better.

He started babbling about comedy and how political it all was and how he was sick of it and was going to quit. He went on and on about his album and how funny it was and how unfair the business was. He talked about being at the Oscars and meeting Shirley Temple. She listened to him as she sipped her expensive drink and didn't interrupt. Sometimes she didn't look at him as he talked but rather stared straight ahead. He didn't care or notice since he was completely gone now. He felt better getting it all out of his mind. She seemed most impressed by the Shirley Temple story.

The Beastie Boys song "Sure Shot" was playing over the speakers. Steve rapped along to the song drunkenly misremembering most of the lyrics now that he was feeling the whiskey on a whole new level. Steve finally leaned in to kiss her at the bar and she let him for a few seconds. Then she pulled away slightly and put her hand on his knee gently.

"So, can we go somewhere?" she asked him.

"Ummm....sure. I mean. You wanna go to my place? I live about ten blocks away."

"Well, can you get 100 dollars?" she asked staring at him.

"What?"

"Can you get 100 dollars?"

"Can I get 100 dollars for what?"

"Um...to ya know, go back to your place?"

"What? You're a fucking hooker."

"Shhh-h-h-h-h!" she said pulling her torso back with a sour expression and arched eyebrows.

"What? I was just going to say you're a hook...."

"Shhh-h! Be quiet!" she said louder hitting his chest a bit too hard.

"Ow. Ummm....sorry. But there's like no one in here," he said looking around only seeing a guy at the way end of the bar.

"I like you. I want to go home with you, but I need 100 dollars. I could go somewhere right now and get 200 dollars from someone."

"You could?"

363

"Yeah."

"It's like 3 am on a Wednesday. Where can you get someone to pay you 200 dollars at this hour?"

"Look, can you get it or not?"

"I mean I gotta say I'm not real happy about this. I mean you could have told me this like an hour ago. I wasted like three great stories on you. I whipped out my Oscars story for nothing. I mean the Oscars story is my big closer and I didn't even need to use it on you."

"Look hon, let's find an ATM and then get a cab to your place."

"Did you ever see 'Pretty Woman'?"

"Yeah, I did."

"Remember that movie? Julia Roberts was like a hooker. Disney made that movie. Disney! They made kids' movies and then they made a movie about a damn hooker!" he said and took a sip of his whiskey. He was borderline blackout drunk.

Next thing he remembered they were at an ATM down the street, and he was trying to put his card in the slot. He realized what he was doing and then asked her if she wanted to get another drink. She told him nothing was open and then told him to hurry up. He had his card in his hand and put it in his pocket.

"What are you doing?" she asked.

"I have to go."

"What?! What do you mean?"

"I mean....I...."

"You fucking asshole! You're not going to pay me?!" she yelled.

"Pay you for what? We didn't do anything. You hustled me."

"Come on baby. I want you," she said getting close to him and touching his crotch.

"Oh, hi there. Good argument. Okay. I'll do it. You've convinced me," he said.

He walked back towards the ATM and then started to run down the street. He heard her yelling after him. He saw a taxi with its light on and waved at it furiously. It stopped and he got in. She ran up to the cab.

"You fucking prick! Where's my money?"

The cab pulled off and she chased after it for about twenty feet yelling. Steve looked back. The cab driver was looking in the rearview mirror.

"Man, grandmothers huh?" Steve said and the driver, a young Indian guy, chuckled.

CHAPTER 36:

THIS IS THE BAD PART

O NE NIGHT THE FRIENDLY BOOKER FROM COMIX PUT together a comedy show at a restaurant she was now managing. She was a bit flirty in her email, so Steve thought maybe she would sleep with him, another incentive to do the show. He hadn't had a girlfriend for a while and was getting tired of having to chase women. She had asked Steve to host the show which he agreed to do since she offered to pay him more for it. The showroom was packed with about fifty people.

Janeane Garofalo was on the bill along with Christian Finnegan and a somewhat iconic '80s comic who'd been famous for a few years in the '80s. The '80s guy was strange. He lurked around the comedy scene trolling rooms for young male comics to sleep with. The guy had a rep for being unstable and toxic. Steve had once seen him use the N-word onstage at Rififi. He was constantly spouting off his credits from 1988.

Steve did some time up-front and then the first few comics went on. He was waiting for one comedian to finish when he was approached by the '80s comedian. His hair was curly and messy, and he was wearing a blue sweatshirt with a wave logo on it. His eyes were wide and dark. He looked not there completely. He had eyes like a shark, a shark with no soul.

"Hey you, host guy! I got something to tell you," he barked at Steve not even looking at him and waving him over.

"Okay, so listen dude, when you bring me up, I want you to say that I was on the Tonight Show, co-starred in the movie 'Punchline' with Tom Hanks and Sally Field. I have a new talk show with Robert Klein, Tom Hanks, and other guests. It's produced by Tom Hanks and it's going to be streaming online for three months...." He rambled on for what felt like five minutes babbling his intro incessantly like a psycho. Steve thought the guy was kidding at first but soon realized he was dead serious and expected him to remember this impossibly long intro. Steve was about to go up onstage to bring this guy up and he was throwing him a five-minute monologue to memorize. The show was in the back of a burger restaurant. What the fuck was wrong with this guy?

"I'm not going to be able to remember all that," Steve finally said, chuckling slightly.

"What do you mean you won't remember it? I should have known you wouldn't be professional. Fine, here," the guy snapped at him and handed him a typed-up piece of white paper with three long paragraphs on it. Steve shook his head and sighed audibly.

He walked onstage and thanked the comedian who had just performed. Then he looked at the paper and started the crazy '80s comic's intro. The comic walked on stage behind Steve while Steve was still introducing him and paced back and forth. Steve turned and looked at him.

"Well, this next comedian is walking behind me on the stage right now for some reason," Steve said causing the audience to laugh.

The '80s comedian stopped in his tracks and laughed loudly and sarcastically. Then he grabbed the mic from Steve's grip with a violent tug.

"Ohhh! Yeah, good one! What a guy!! Let's hear it for your host, whoever the fuck he is! How are you guys tonight?! You ready for some *actual* comedy now?!" he said while pushing Steve off the stage.

The comic began with hacky jokes about ethnic stereotypes. "Fine Asian men don't have small penises! Fine! Fine! Yes! Jewish people occasionally pick up the check! Fine! Fine!" The audience looked very confused, and no one laughed. Steve recognized it as the bit the guy had done in the '80s movie "Punchline." It was literally the same act. The guy hadn't written any new bits in 30 years? It was unbelievable. What was this guy doing? Steve remembered him from TV from back when he was a child. He'd thought the guy had it made. He'd been on the Tonight Show with Johnny Carson and was now in a burger restaurant bombing with the same act from 1987. Showbiz was a fucked-up business.

When Janeane Garofalo went on earlier she'd also seemed somewhat acerbic and bitter. She repeatedly commented on how poorly she was doing with the crowd. When Steve told her he was a longtime fan, she looked down at the floor smiling and made a self-deprecating remark. He remembered when he'd seen her at Luna about six years earlier and she was the queen of the place. Now Luna was gone, as was the alternative scene's epicenter. She had even joked onstage about being a "has been." The crowd chuckled uncomfortably, not sure whether to laugh or not.

The '80s comic bombed for twelve minutes straight, regularly berating the crowd for not laughing. He commented that he was the only good comedian on the show because he was "real" while the other comics were fake.

"You people suck. I'm gonna bring back your host who isn't funny at all," he slammed the mic into the stand and walked off like a kid who'd just been sent to bed without dessert.

The audience applauded out of awkwardness, and because they weren't sure what had just happened in front of them. Steve took the mic as the tepid applause stopped. A thick tension just sort of hung like a dark cloud raining piss.

"Okay give it up for my motivational speaker," the audience laughed nervously. Steve watched as the comic walked out of the room.

"Man, that was amazing. He fucking killed. He's better than all of us here, clearly," Steve said.

"Man, that guy needs to chill out or at least find a new coke dealer. That guy must have gotten rejected from Scientology. Tom Cruise said he was just too intense." The crowd was beginning to relax and laugh a little more.

"By the way, 1987 called, it wants its comedy back," he added.

Steve made a few more wisecracks which brought the room back. He'd fixed the vibe and introduced the next comic, a friendly young guy named Jermaine Fowler who was new to the scene. When Steve walked offstage, the '80s comic was standing in the back with a frown. Uh-oh. Steve's stomach sank. He'd somehow pulled some sort of David Blaine magic trick. Steve had watched him leave. The '80s comic stared daggers at Steve who just smiled back at him awkwardly.

"You're an asshole," he said to Steve.

"What? What's wrong?" Steve said, trying to look confused. "I was just kidding around," Steve added. But it was too late. The guy had hate in his bulging eyes that looked black, up close.

"How dare you say anything to insult me! You've done nothing compared to me! I was on the Tonight Show! Johnny Carson loved my comedy! No one likes your comedy at all! You're a nobody! I was the only good comedian on this shit show! Better than you or anyone else! I was the only one who was real! I'm not some phony alt comedian!" he said loudly, drawing attention from the audience.

Steve just let him have his rant which went on and on like the intro he'd forced on Steve. He sounded like an old man yelling at some punk kids to get off his lawn because he was angry with the world. It reminded him of when Chevy Chase re-emerged as an unfunny old talk show host. Hell, the '80s comic wasn't even writing new material anymore. Steve loathed comedians who never wrote new jokes. It was unfathomable to Steve that this guy was doing the same material twenty-three years later. How pathetic. Why would you want to still do comedy if you weren't writing anything new?

The guy had thrown the term "alt comic" at Steve as if it were supposed to mean something negative. This guy represented the old guard of comedy. To the '80s comic, Steve represented the new class that he perceived to have taken it all away from him. The reality was that no matter who you were, your time would pass eventually. There was no running away from that fact.

After the guy laid into him for about two minutes, Steve finally spoke up.

"I'm sorry, but you fucking bombed hard, man. It's the MC's job to bring the crowd back after a comedian completely eats shit," Steve said.

"I bombed! Yeah right! It's because the crowd was stupid! I'm better than everyone here!"

"Yeah, that's what the problem was. You're just *too* good."

The comments he made were delusional at best and psychotic at worst. It amazed Steve how crazy show-biz and comedy made people. It seemed that falling from grace in showbiz was a lot worse than in any other career. Steve was now witnessing comedy icons on their way back down the ladder and they weren't happy about their descent into normalcy. Maybe, just maybe, praise from strangers *wasn't* the answer to his problems. This '80s comic at one point had all the success, but was he happy? He looked like some raving serial killer as he ranted on about a set in a hamburger restaurant. Showbiz sure wasn't what Steve had experienced on that surreal night at the Oscars. He recalled that even Shirley Temple had seemed uncomfortable that night when he'd met her.

The '80s hack finally stormed off in a huff and slammed the door shut as he left. Just another comedy lesson kids. Comedy is not fun...at all.

CHAPTER 37:

THINGS TURNED OUT DIFFERENT

S TEVE AND HIS NEWLY DUBBED FIANCÉ HAD BEEN living together for almost two years in Brooklyn. Their apartment was small, and he still did stand-up, now grasping at the spots available to him, which were very few now. He was on the cusp of his 40th birthday which he'd been dreading. There was a right and wrong side of 40 in showbiz. The industry didn't exactly embrace older people. New comedians seemed younger and younger every year, especially now that it was easier to develop your own following through social media.

She walked into the apartment around 3 a.m., a common occurrence lately. She worked at a night-club in Manhattan and Steve was often asleep when she got home. He heard her fumble with her keys in the kitchen. He kept his eyes closed and pretended to be asleep, another common occurrence now. He had done the same thing as a kid when he heard his mother come home late.

She slipped into their bed, and he lay there facing the other way towards the open window. They had been drifting apart for months but he'd stayed in the relationship long after it was over. It was the only stable thing in his life, and he felt he needed it to get himself through everything. Stand-up wasn't his future anymore but rather something he was hanging onto just like the relationship. A lot had changed in the last four years.

She'd hinted around about getting married six months earlier and so they got engaged. For a while, it felt like he had one thing in his life he could count on. But now he barely saw her and neither one of them was trying anymore. As Steve lay awake in bed, he felt a knot in his stomach. He denied what was happening and didn't want to admit it was over even though it was painfully obvious. He had a sneaking feeling that something was going on behind his back. He didn't want to face that hard fact. So instead, he closed his eyes as tightly as he could, just like he did as a child.

A joke suddenly popped into his head, and he made a mental note of it as the joke unfolded in his mind. *I saw an ad online that a woman put up offering the "full girlfriend experience." I paid her a hundred bucks and, when I showed up to her apartment, I walked in on her sleeping with my best friend. Then she blamed it on me, broke up with me, and then stole my dog. I definitely felt like I had a girlfriend again.*

Steve did a show at a bar in Williamsburg, Brooklyn run by a young comic named Andy. The guy was friendly and had hung around Rififi the last year that it was open. The audience was made up of young hipsters dressed in jeans and vintage T-shirts. Steve didn't know one comic on the show. They were all in their first three years of comedy. Babies. Steve went on toward the end and opened with a joke in which he used the word "fat."

"You ever have someone dump you and then do something nice like marry someone fat?"

The joke got barely any reaction other than some loud groans. Steve was thrown by their animosity right out the gate. He went into another bit which was one of his most tried and true and it barely garnered a response. He knew he was in trouble and got rattled. Suddenly he was thinking too much. *If you think up there, then you're dead.* One misstep and it's over. He did another joke that seemed to anger them further. It was a joke about Bill Cosby, who'd been taken down months earlier by the internet with a push from Hannibal Buress. The crowd groaned again. They were great groaners. Steve felt a wave of anger inside. His joke was attacking Cosby for being a creep, but the crowd was angry he'd brought up something they didn't like in pop culture. The crowd didn't seem to understand nuance.

He later did a joke about Caitlin Jenner which they hated. He knew they'd hate it and did it to intentionally piss them off. The joke wasn't mocking Jenner in any way. It was simply an observation about what had transpired and to comment on something Jenner had said in an interview. It didn't matter anymore. That's what comedy had become. If you talked about certain topics they didn't like, the crowd turned on you and you were immediately ostracized.

The crowd was king now and they dictated everything you could talk about. Aloof, detached, smart alecks were officially not in fashion anymore. Nerds had dominated the comedy landscape for a long time now and Steve's heavy sarcasm was considered too acerbic and mean-spirited.

Suddenly he saw a young girl, about twenty-one, talking to her friend in the front loudly. He angrily commented about how they were so sensitive. The young girl continued to talk and pretty soon, Steve felt the wave stronger now. He looked at the young girl.

"What're you talking about?"

"What?" she said with a pained face.

"I said..." He started and looked out at the audience. The lights were bright and, in his eyes, but he could make out some of their faces. They were all stone-faced. He was now at a critical moment. He thought of the 80s comic who had lost it onstage months earlier.

"I said... never mind. I'm done. You guys have been great," he said and picked his notebook up off the stool.

He'd caught himself before it got really weird. A 25-year-old woman with a long face, a ponytail, and wearing glasses who'd been doing comedy three years went on next and killed. She opened with a bit about how guys were always trying to sleep with her and how annoying it was. Steve heard later that she was taping a Netflix special in a month.

He got a drink at the bar because he didn't want to go home. No one was there anyway. His fiancé hadn't been home before 3 a.m. in months. Their relationship was hanging by a thread. He had no idea what to do as he sat there drinking. His drink was no longer for recreation, he now needed it to get through the night. That scared him, but he was at least feeling better now about his awful set. The drink gave him some temporary peace. No one from the show approached him about his set.

He left and stopped off at another bar down the street in Greenpoint where they gave a free pizza with every drink. He drank more whiskey and flirted with a short-haired brunette woman at the bar who was wearing a blue flannel. He bought her a couple of drinks and she seemed interested in him. The last thing he remembered was being asked to leave the bar for smoking.

Steve woke up fully dressed and walked to the bathroom. His head was pounding, and his face felt cold and inexplicably wet. He could barely open his eyes which felt glued shut. He immediately knew his hangover was going to be brutal and he'd spend the entire next 24 hours beating himself up for drinking too much. In the bathroom, he reached for his toothbrush before being distracted by his reflection in the mirror which made him burst out crying. His face was covered completely on one side with blood. He had three huge cuts, one above his left eye, one on the bridge of his nose, and one more under his right eye. His breathing became heavy, and his body shook. He collapsed onto the floor of the small bathroom which had no rug and was freezing.

After frantically washing all the blood off, he lay in bed having a terrible realization. He was a complete mess and had no idea what to do. The kid in the station wagon's face flashed in his head as he continued to cry. The sobs were heavy and painful. He wondered if he'd ever be able to stop. He'd let that kid down. He would have been so disappointed to see who he'd grown up to become.

He pushed the image of the kid away with everything he had. The station wagon kid was a bit hazy in his mind now but was still haunting him. The image was getting fuzzier these days. The alcohol and pills were meant to erase him forever.

After she saw his cut-up face later that night, Steve's fiancé told him it was over. He was blindsided but only because he was completely ignoring what had been happening between them. Being drunk most nights didn't help his perception skills.

"What's the problem?" Steve asked in his boxer shorts.

"We're broken, aren't we?" she asked rhetorically.

"Ummm....well, I don't know," he said.

"We are broken," she said once more.

"What does that mean? What's the problem?"

"We're broken," she simply repeated, stone-faced, not looking at him as she sat on the unmade bed.

"Okay. But what do you mean?"

"It's broken. We're broken," she said, her arms now folded as if she didn't even want to be talking to him. It was clear she'd been planning this for weeks.

He went to the kitchen and poured himself a big glass of Ketel One with ice. That would help things for sure. For two more hours, he tried to get her to tell him what went wrong but she never did, and she moved out a day later. He wasn't positive but something told him she had another place to move into and that she'd set up a whole new life in the last couple of months. He was the final loose end to tie up or cut off. He did what he usually did. He drank incessantly and hoped maybe things would somehow magically come together.

A week later, a completely distraught Steve went to a nearby bar and drank about eight whiskeys to escape everything. He saw flashes of his mother when she told him she was sick. He'd thought maybe if he'd gotten married then she'd be proud of him. As he sat alone in the bar, drunk, he felt like he'd screwed up yet again. He had no comedy career to speak of, and no one close to him. Starting from zero all over again, he had no idea what he was going to do. He saw himself in the back of the station wagon and teared up right there at the bar. The kid looked sadder this time. He caught a glimpse of himself in the mirror behind the bar. He had bandages over the cuts on his face. He looked....broken.

Just then, a song came on that reminded him of his heartache. It was one of those cheesy love songs that you hear a million times and don't even like. The song had never meant anything to him before but now, it made total sense. He got choked up hearing the singer cry out his feelings. He felt like every song was speaking directly to him now, the way you do when you're an open, exposed nerve and can no longer outrun your emotions. The song hit him right where he lived which embarrassed him since the song was outrageously ordinary. Still, he was done fighting right now. He was exhausted and sometimes you just have to accept that being alive is somewhat embarrassing and hackneyed.

Later that night his legs gave out and he fell hard on the scratchy gray carpet on the bedroom floor. He was positive he was dying. Before he lost consciousness, he prayed right there on the floor that he would at least go to heaven. Could he at least have that? Just then, a joke popped into his head. He made a mental note to remember it and passed out.

Steve woke up in the hospital and was told that he'd passed out because his blood sugar had spiked out of control. The nurse said he'd come close to dying. The unfriendly ER doctor told him coldly that he had Type 1 diabetes and that he needed to adjust to his new life.

The man was cruel with the news. He had no bedside manners. His attitude said, "fuck you, I'm a busy doctor and I don't have time to hold your hand and guide you through this, you pussy!" He was like the guy from the hospital drama "House" minus the charisma.

Steve spent eight nights in the hospital getting his strength back. He was visited by his sister, his father, and his old comic friend Jacqueline Novak. They talked about comedy and Rififi and reminisced about their first meeting years earlier. He told her it was at Rififi while she remembered it being at B3. She said she was writing a one-woman show about her sex life and how it shaped her. He told her a joke he'd recently written about blow jobs where he found it funny in movies that a prostitute would offer a blow job to a man for 15 dollars. That always seemed way too low to Steve. A blow job was like the best thing in the world and you're charging 15 dollars?! That cost less than a movie!

She told him that his first album had inspired her stand-up. She said it made her work harder at it since he'd seemed to be such a natural.

"Were you funny as a kid?" she asked, sitting by his bed.

"Yeah, I was actually really funny."

"That doesn't surprise me," she said.

"Why do you say that?"

"I don't know, you just seem to have a naturalness about it all. Like trying is beneath you or something. Dare I say...aloof?"

Steve lay there in his hospital bed and thought of "The Natural," the film he'd seen one night in his room as a kid.

"Things sure turned out different," he said out loud, realizing what the character felt.

"What?"

"Nothing. I was just quoting that movie 'The Natural'."

"How'd you expect them to turn out?"

"Not like this, that's for sure."

"You'll be okay," she said, smiling.

She was always positive which made him feel a lot better. It cheered him up that she'd gone out of her way to visit him.

"Ya know, I always remembered this quote by some German poet, I don't remember his name. *No doubt the artist is the child of his time but woe to him if he is also its disciple or even its favorite*," she said.

"What does that mean exactly?"

"I think it means that just because you don't feel like you got the recognition you should have that doesn't mean you're not good. I know this doesn't mean much in the long run but to me, you're one of the best I've seen," she said.

"Thanks."

"I mean it."

"I appreciate that."

"You'll be out of here in no time and right back onstage," she said.

"Yeah, I guess," Steve said, nodding slowly and looking at the wall.

"You can't stop. I mean, it's a part of you now," she said.

"Do you like doing it still?"

"I don't know. I mean I wouldn't say I like it, but it's like I have no other choice, ya know?" she said.

"Yeah, I know."

"What about you?"

"I don't know. Not really," he said quietly.

"You don't? Why not?"

"I don't know why I'm even doing it anymore. Now it just feels like this thing I'm doing because....because I decided it was what I had to do. It's funny. I don't like it but it's the only thing I never gave up on. That and masturbating," he said, making her chuckle.

"I know what you mean but you're really good at it. It's like effortless to you."

"Effortless? I wish. I spent years trying to make it look like I was barely trying. It's the hardest thing I've ever done in my life."

"I've seen so many newer comics totally rip off your style."

"Maybe I need to just take a break or something. Catch my breath."

"I get that. I went through the same thing two years back. Comedy's like a war you have to keep fighting," she said.

"I guess I'm tired of fighting. What made you want to do comedy?"

"What do you mean?"

"I don't know. I mean, we're all so caught up in it, we spend all our time pursuing it. But I feel like no one thinks about why they're doing it in the first place."

"Hmmm...." Jacqueline said, turning her head to her right with her mouth closed and crooked.

"I was into performing when I was a kid. I used to do these shows in my living room all the time. I wanted to be a dancer at first. Then at Georgetown, I auditioned for this sketch group that my friend was in. I liked doing it. It was like a rush and opened me up in a way."

"When did you first know you were funny?" he asked.

"I think it was when I was around ten or eleven. Some kids were dancing onstage, and I went out and did this funny routine."

"Really?"

"Yeah. It killed. I remember it felt good. I liked the attention. What about you?"

"What?"

"When did you first know you were funny?"

Steve stared ahead blankly. He saw the station wagon. The flashlight was shining on his face. He didn't answer.

"I don't know. I can't remember specifically," he said, looking down, trying to erase the station wagon from his head.

"I know it's going to sound like some bullshit, but I really do think you're one of the best I've ever seen."

"Thanks. I *am* great," he said, smiling and laying back on the uncomfortable bed.

He wondered why he felt so hollow whenever people praised him. Many people had commended his talent before, even some of his idols, but it was never enough. He always imagined that he'd one day get to a place where he was finally happy if enough people told him he was good. It was like Ari had told him years before. You never believe the people who praise you, you only believe the ones that insult you.

The ones that put you down are the ones that really see you. He thought about how his father hadn't seemed impressed when Steve was at the Oscars as a child. He'd been the only person that didn't seem to care. Steve never forgot that.

"I think I might have to...take a break," he said quietly, looking forward. He knew he meant it and that made him sad.

"I never thought I'd be so tired at 40," he said paraphrasing the movie "St. Elmo's Fire." So many of his clever quips seemed to come from pop culture. He sometimes wondered if he even had a personality. His persona seemed to be made up of an amalgam of various personalities he'd seen on TV or in movies. He'd been raised on pop culture and, for the first time, wondered how it had shaped him. Yeah, he needed to take a breath. The thought both relieved and terrified him. Who would he even be without stand-up? What would he chase without it?

A week later, he was discharged and sent out into the world with a new identity. Steve the diabetic. He dropped thirty pounds and was now injecting insulin to level off his blood sugar and keep living. One thing was for sure, he wasn't going to let anyone hurt him ever again. He'd let someone get close to him and it had almost killed him. Now he *really* couldn't let anyone in again. It was a matter of survival now. He would never make himself vulnerable again. He knew that if he got close to someone again, he might not survive.

CHAPTER 38:

PLAYING WITH ONE HAND

S TEVE WOKE UP, HOPPED OUT OF BED, AND GOT dressed. Then he checked his blood sugar which was at a good level. Now constantly conscious of maintaining his health, he had quit drinking six months earlier. He was no longer doing stand-up, he'd finally decided to move away from it. It had been almost two years since he'd walked onto a stage. He hardly heard from any of his comedian friends from his old days, anymore. He had reached out to a few but none of them had returned his messages. He didn't take it personally since they felt like former camp friends who had moved on to different lives.

Now, when he was mentioned in the comedy world, he was talked about as some sort of distant memory by other comics. He once picked up a copy of AM New York and read an interview with a comedian he'd known years earlier. The comedian said he used to like comedian Steve Collin who'd quit years ago and that he had no idea what he was doing now. Steve was talked about like someone who had disappeared out at sea.

"I remember Steve Collin had this great bit about horror movies. Man, it was great. Whatever happened to him? He was hilarious," Pete Holmes commented on his now widely popular podcast.

These comments made Steve cringe at first, but they soon didn't affect him anymore. As time passed, he still thought about comedy. It would never completely go away. Jokes and bits still came to him but he didn't write them down in a notebook anymore. He didn't carry a notebook anymore. He dreamt that he was onstage a few times. Sometimes he even dreamt about that first TV spot.

"If you think up there, you're dead." He heard Tom Cruise saying from his TV. He sat up and looked at the screen then lay back down on his bed.

The 10's were not like the aughts. The alt scene was all but gone and stand-up was a completely new land-scape. There was a new class of comedians all vying to become the next Aziz or Mulaney or whoever the fuck they all wanted to be that week. UCB was no longer an alternative scene, it was now a booming business, like the Amazon of comedy.

One day, while waiting in line at a Dunkin Donuts, a woman in front of him took forever to leave the counter area after paying. As she fumbled with her huge bag, he chuckled to himself. He had done one of his first bits at

The Love Below at B3 about this very scenario. Then he remembered Romey, Roger, Nick, and Neal.

A few days later, in the same Dunkin Donuts, the Irene Cara song "What a Feeling" played through the speakers quietly. He was immediately back in the Dorothy Chandler Pavilion. "Welcome to the big-time kid!" he heard Nicholson's sly voice in his mind.

"I have a joke!" he heard his six-year-old high-pitched voice echo. He could still remember how it felt when everyone immediately quieted down, and the focus was on him. It was a feeling he'd come to know well over the years. The feeling of an audience directing their attention and not yet sure what to think of you. That moment where you have only a few seconds to prove that you're funny.

He could still hear the laughs he got in the wagon. He could hear Mike Ferrari's cackle. He almost hated the moment now. If only he hadn't been funny as a kid, then maybe he wouldn't have put so much effort into this whole comedy thing. Many restless nights he lay awake alone in bed cursing that moment. For years, he tried to forget the moment as best he could. He'd tried drinking the memory away, but it just seemed to gain strength. The kid was mocking him now and would never go away. It was like the kid was waiting for something.

One sleepless night, Steve wiggled around in bed for over an hour. Then suddenly, an idea for a joke popped into his head. This still happened now and again since the comedy joke portal had been open for so long. These days the joke would usually just eventually fade away like a cloud passing slowly. But this joke held on and wouldn't go away no matter how hard he ignored it. The joke put itself together in his head seemingly without any effort from him. It was as if the joke already existed, and he was merely the medium through which it was breaking its way out of some alternative universe. It was like the joke was yelling at him to write it down.

Just write me down and make me alive! The joke yelled. Jeez! *I'm already a finished joke! Just put me into the world, you lazy jerk!* The voice yelled and, suddenly, he realized that the voice was that of his six-year-old self.

He opened his eyes and sat up in bed.

Please! Steve! Please! Write it down! The voice said. He saw a flash of his young self on his knees on the floor pleading with him for a split second. He wasn't sure why he'd seen it. He tried to pretend that he hadn't, but he had, and it scared him. He looked around the room as if someone else were standing right by him. Was he finally losing it?

He got up and ran to his cluttered desk covered in bills. He found a pen and tried to scribble on the back of the Time Warner envelope. The pen didn't write. He tossed it to the floor and found another one nearby, a blue one from Chase bank. He wrote furiously while the joke was still in his brain. The joke involved ski masks and the idea that it was strange that those were sold legally in the world since they were used only for

390

illegal activities. Whenever you saw someone wearing a ski mask it was always a red flag for horrible things about to happen. He laughed out loud as he wrote.

He wrote it all out and when he was done, he felt sweat dripping down his cheeks. He looked it over. Then he continued writing what was going through his head. Most of it was weird and unintelligible but at least these thoughts no longer existed solely in his head.

After writing it down, he closed the notebook and turned the light off. *Fine, ski mask joke, I did what you asked of me. Now can I go back to being miserable and cursing all my life choices?* he thought to himself.

The joke was out of his head now and alive in the world. He had in a way exorcised a joke demon. He'd been repressing joke tendencies for a year or so now, but he knew that wouldn't stop the jokes from coming and some of the jokes inside would refuse to simply go away. That joke portal he tried to shut again opened wider that night. He rolled over and closed his eyes and drifted off to sleep quickly without crying for the first time in months.

He showed up at the deli a little early. He was working a job downtown on Wall Street having finished law school and passed the bar on his first try. He was now working alongside a bunch of boring attorneys who had no sense of humor. He'd met one young stand-up fan who was earnestly impressed with Steve's background as a comic. The guy wanted to be a comic and kept asking him for advice. Steve was hoping he might be able to live out the second half of his life with some peace and maybe a little more dignity. He sat there in the deli's backroom and waited for the man who had contacted him a week earlier out of the blue over social media.

James, his former acting professor from college, walked in and Steve spotted him before he saw Steve. The man was older and greyer and a little heavier but still looked the same, pretty much. He'd always been stocky but now he was softer. James was one of those people who looked old young, so he hadn't aged much in the last twenty years. He smiled warmly and shook Steve's hand. Steve immediately remembered him all those years earlier. He was very soft-spoken, calm, and Zen.

"I saw you on TV a few years back. Are you still acting?" James asked him, smiling and sipping on coffee.

The question stung, just as it always did when someone asked that question. He was trying to move on from all of that and didn't feel like explaining, once again, why he'd stopped. It embarrassed him every time someone brought it up. He just wanted to leave all that behind. That felt like another life now. He didn't want to even acknowledge that it had ever existed. It even now seemed a sort of immature lark he'd once been a part of when he was young and naïve. It was almost as if he'd been in a cult and finally escaped.

"No, not really," Steve said, trying not to go into the details while picking up his sugar-free Peach Snapple.

"Are you auditioning for things?" he asked further, not letting it go.

"Um...not really. I mean I was a little bit. Not anymore."

"Why not?" James asked, seeming surprised at Steve's lack of success. Steve took it as a compliment even if it was an indirect way of asking why he wasn't more successful like people had asked him for years. James wasn't being judgmental about it though, he appeared genuinely curious.

Steve recalled how cocky he'd once been in his young college days when he strutted around as if he were already a star. Now he felt old, worn out, and in pain. A lot, physically and mentally. He'd become okay with finally accepting his life without the attention he'd always felt he needed. With alcohol out of his life, he had more clarity. He didn't need that attention anymore.

"Ummm....well. Not that much. I did some stuff but ya know, things kind of happened."

"What happened?" James asked. It was a blunt question that came out sharply. A question Steve asked himself on those sleepless nights when things were especially quiet, and his thoughts were no longer drowned out by whiskey and other substances. What *did,* the hell, happen?

"Well, things didn't go the way I thought they would," Steve said, picking at the Snapple label.

"They usually don't."

"Yeah, I know that now. Although it took me a while to, ya know, learn that," Steve said, still fidgeting with the bottle label.

"Are you thinking about getting back into it?"

"Into what?"

"Showbiz. Stand-up."

"Now? Ummm...no, I don't think so."

"Why not?"

"Well, I...I'm older now. I...I just don't think I could ya know....make it."

"Make it?"

"Yeah. Ya know become like famous or whatever people do it for."

"Do you miss stand up?"

"Ya know, I still remember when I did it that first time in your class," Steve said, avoiding his inquiry.

"Yeah. I remember that," he said, smiling.

"I was thinking about that the other night when I couldn't sleep. That was the very first time I ever did stand-up. It was the very first time I killed onstage, that is. After that, it was over. There was no getting away from it. I was hooked in a way, without even realizing it."

"You were the best in the class. You were the best in any class I ever had actually."

"Yeah. I was good at it. It's funny how that all came about. It was almost a total accident."

"How so?"

"I don't know. I mean, I sort of fell into it in your class. It was just this thing I did and somehow it never went away."

"Yeah? You were good at it. I remember."

"Yeah. I guess I was," Steve said, nodding his head smiling.

"So why'd you stop?" he asked, sipping his coffee loudly.

Steve's body tightened and he narrowed his eyes. He didn't want to get into it. He just wanted to detach and not care the way he always had. It was so much easier that way. He was a Gen X'er after all. The ignored children who were now completely ignored because of the Millennials who now demanded all the attention. The next generation of comedians behind him were getting all the easy breaks now, not his generation.

"I got distracted for a bit and felt I needed to step away. The problem is that in that business they don't wait for you to figure your shit out. Once I got my bearings again everything seemed to have moved on without me," he managed to get out.

"Why don't you try again?"

"Yeah. I don't know. I mean, I don't know if I can still do it."

James was silent. Steve just sat there uncomfortable with the silence.

"Why did you stick with it for so long?"

"I guess because I liked it. That's all it was really. I was good at it since I can first remember."

He saw a glimpse of the station wagon.

"But then..."

"What?"

"I don't know. I stopped liking it somewhere along the way."

"You were a natural. I always remember that," he said.

"Yeah."

"You can't give up something that's natural to you. That's just not possible, no matter how hard you're trying to. You were born with it," James said.

Steve looked up at him sharply. James' face was still, his eyes warm and his expression was bright. Steve felt he was looking directly into his mind. What the fuck? Steve had been trying to forget all this shit and now this guy he hadn't seen in twenty years was shaking it all up again. What the fuck was his problem? Couldn't he tell that Steve didn't want to talk about this shit?

"Do you feel like you still have something to say?" James asked him quietly. Zen master.

"I don't know. I mean....yeah. I do actually. I just don't know how to say it," Steve answered quietly looking at the saltshaker on the crooked tabletop.

James didn't say anything for about five seconds, but the silence felt like it lasted longer.

"As long as you know what you want to say and are honest about how you're saying it, then no one can touch you," James said in a quiet almost hypnotic voice. Steve stared at James as he sipped his coffee. He could still see the station wagon and was on the verge of spilling the story out to James. He'd never mentioned that story to anyone who hadn't been there. Telling it to someone else almost felt like a betrayal. The story was his and belonged to him. To tell it would make it no longer his. It would make him way too vulnerable to tell it.

Eventually, Steve had to get back to his boring job. He and James promised to meet again. He didn't want to think about comedy anymore. It had almost broken him the way he'd seen it break so many others. He'd pulled away from comedy to feel safe again and figure out who he was without it. The alcohol that helped him detach was no longer a crutch he could rely on. Now he just had to deal with the feelings as they arose.

One night, Steve tossed in bed until he finally turned on the TV and flipped around. He passed by a Pete Holmes comedy special on HBO. He watched for a few minutes, but it made him even more depressed. Pete made noises and smiled a huge smile. He tried not to take it personally, but it still stung to see him perform. He finally stopped on an old episode of "MASH." His father had served in the Korean war and had been obsessed with the show. It was on every weeknight in Steve's house.

The episode involved a soldier who'd been shot in the hand and lost all feeling in it. He tells his doctor that he's a concert pianist and now with only one hand he won't be able to play ever again. The doctor later tells him about all the successful pianists that could play certain pieces with only one hand. At the end of the episode, the distraught man starts playing again with one hand. It reminded Steve of all those '80s TV shows where every life problem was solved in 22 minutes.

He went scavenging for some Ambien in his closet. He thought he had some left over on the top shelf, instead, he stumbled upon an old photo album in his closet. He flipped through it and found a picture of himself in the first grade. It would have been around the time of the station wagon incident. His eyes were bright and his hair lighter, and he wore a shirt with the number ten on the front. Surely there was a part of that kid still in him. In all likelihood, the kid was completely gone. He put the picture down and went to the bottom drawer of his dresser. He took out his elementary school yearbook and flipped to the back where each sixth-grader had to say what they wanted to be one day. A few read: "I want to be a doctor because I like to help people." "I want to be a fireman." He spotted his. "I want to be a comedian because I like to make people laugh."

There was a stack of small, old, comedy notebooks in there also at the very bottom of the drawer. He slowly picked up the top one with a torn blue cover. He looked at his scribbled writing inside that was barely legible even to himself. The entire page was covered in scratch. He read jokes he'd written long ago; some he had forgotten completely. There were about ten blank pages at the end of the notebook. Steve found a pen and began to write down funny thoughts he'd been ignoring for two years. He wrote for an hour until he finally fell asleep.

CHAPTER 39:

REQUIEM FOR AN ALT COMIC

S TEVE SAW A BUNCH OF POSTS ON FACEBOOK ABOUT a female comedian who had taken her life. It was the friendly, petite, Asian girl, Susi Lee, who was always so pleasant and smiling.

It pissed him off how many comics on social media were quick to jump in with a post about it that was really about themselves. It felt hollow to him the way people used her death to get some attention. Steve hated social media yet, at the same time, was hooked just like everyone else. Susi was only 29 years old, younger than he'd thought. He hadn't seen her in years but remembered she was beautiful, funny, and had so much going for her. Whenever someone killed themselves, people always said the person had so much going for them but this time it was actually true. It rattled him when he heard about her suicide. It now seemed like it really *could* happen to anyone. Susi had never seemed down, ever. He felt it very well may have happened to him if he'd stayed on the track he'd been on years earlier.

One night, he dreamt again about that first TV spot taping. He was anxious as he waited to go on, dressed in only a tiny white towel. He paced back and forth and waited. The anticipation was unbearable. It felt just like it had when it happened. Those moments just before he went onstage had always left him shook. He woke up just as he was walking onstage. The host bringing him on was Mike Ferrari as a child. It was then that Steve realized he was only a child walking up to the mic.

Months later, Steve received a text message from his old comedy friend Kjell from back in his LA comedy days. Kjell was now living in Minneapolis doing stand-up, another addict who just couldn't quite stop. He told Steve that comedian Brody Stevens had hanged himself. Steve had known Brody briefly in LA years ago. They eventually became pretty good friends. He remembered Brody always being positive and friendly, something rare on the comedy scene. Steve hadn't seen him in over ten years, but the news made him break down and cry.

> *"Ya know, man, you're one of the reasons I started doing stand-up. You were my favorite starting out. I lo-oo-ve your first album. I and my friends always play it. Are you going to do*

another one? Anyway, I would love to have you
on my show sometime. It's down on Rivington
and we get good crowds. Let me know man.
Thanks – Julian."

Steve received the Facebook message from a young
comic. He'd received similar messages regularly back
when he still had something to offer people. A lot of
people contacted him back in the day about how good
he was and what fans they were. A downtown legend is
how he was often described. But after his alt cachet had
gone away, the messages had disappeared too. This message from Julian stood out since the guy had nothing to
gain from praising Steve. The guy seemed genuine, and
Steve immediately liked him since deep down Steve was
still a comic at heart and thus completely susceptible to
flattery, just like Birbiglia had been years earlier.

Steve heard wheezing coming from his father's bedroom. He walked into his father's room to check on him
before he went to sleep. The health aid slept in a rocking chair right by the bed. He watched as his father lay
there with his mouth open and his gaze aimed toward
the large flatscreen TV perched on the wall. The volume was low, and Steve noticed the TV was playing a
re-run of a show he'd appeared on a few years back on
TRU-TV. It was one of those dumb talking head shows
that Steve had felt almost embarrassed of. Steve stared
at the screen and saw himself come on with his name
below his image: STEVE COLLIN-COMEDIAN

Steve turned to his father, now bedridden, thin, and frail. It almost looked like you could see right through his body, he was so skinny. His breathing was labored all the time now and every breath sounded like it may be his last. His father stared at Steve's image on the screen with no reaction whatsoever. Steve realized his father had no idea it was him on the TV. He recalled the time in the movie theatre when he'd heard his father laugh loudly at the movie trailer. Steve stared down at his father who no longer looked like his father, and it finally hit him that it was nearing the end even though no one wanted to admit it, including Steve who always had a hard time letting go.

He said good night to his father while squeezing his hand, then kissed him on the forehead. His father looked up at him with a blank look. He told his father he loved him, just as he had for the last couple of weeks. He knew he might never get another chance to say it. When he turned to leave, he noticed a bound manuscript on the cluttered desk in his dad's room. It was full of short stories by his mother. The aide had been reading them to his father. He flipped through some.

"Born Funny" one was titled.

> *"He was seemingly born funny. You were laughing so young. I just remember that early on I could sense you were different. You had a unique way about you almost like you were in your own alternate universe that only you understood.*

Your expressions. I remember another mother commenting when you were less than three months old that your expressions were hilarious. Like you just had this innate sense of humor. Born funny. I was afraid for him. I knew he had a gift but wanted to protect him. I shouldn't have though. When you have something special, a gift from somewhere else, nothing can ever really take that away no matter what."

Steve finished the story that he'd never even known existed before. Born funny. He smiled to himself and felt like maybe she'd seen him after all. He watched as his father slept, his breaths were more relaxed when he slept which was a relief to Steve.

CHAPTER 40:

AN ALTERNATIVE ENDING

S TEVE RECEIVED A MESSAGE FROM GREG FROM THE Rififi days. He provided a link to a New York Times story detailing many alleged sexual assault accusations against one of Steve's favorite comics. The Me-Too movement was just beginning, and various comics were getting caught in it. Nick, the bigwig comic who had frequented Rififi, apologized in the media but didn't stay away from stand-up for too long. People attacked him for coming back so fast, labeling it selfish, but Steve knew better. It simply came down to the fact that once comedy was in your blood you couldn't just stop completely. It was like heroin. You had to do it gradually.

Nick, the bigwig, wasn't being a prick when he started doing stand-up again, he was simply an addict who'd relapsed. There's no rehab for stand-up comics.

Right after Nick, other comics started dropping like flies. Another former alt scene comic, now a movie star, also got caught up in a sexual assault scandal. He was now commenting on Steve's Facebook page again.

"Hey, Steve! How are you doing?" one message from him read.

This was from a guy who'd completely ignored him to his face five years prior. There was a shift happening in the comedy landscape again. The old guard was being pushed out and they weren't going down without a fight. Even Aziz got wrapped up in his own weird controversy. He survived his better than most, but the incident was still an asterisk on his current legacy. Aziz was like the husband caught cheating whose wife now had him by the balls.

That's how it is in comedy and showbiz. One misstep and you're gone. Things could go south fast. Aziz was clearly willing to do whatever he had to do to get back in. He was like a shark who wouldn't just let all that attention and fame go by the wayside. Who would he be without it?

Steve thought of that bitter '80s comic who'd yelled at him years earlier for insulting him after his set. He reminded him of the faded starlet Norma Desmond in "Sunset Blvd." The world was changing faster than ever now.

Nothing was how it was when Steve had started in 1999. The internet and social media had turned everything on its head in comedy. Anything could happen. Everything could change in an instant.

Steve even thought about trying stand-up again simply because he missed it and for no other reason. He wouldn't be looking to become a star or to beat out others this time around. He knew however that stand-up was fickle and after being out of practice for so long he would have to suck again for a little while if he wanted to be good again. He literally had nothing to lose anymore. He wondered if he should actually try it again. Who knew? Maybe he would. It would be different now that he was sober.

One day while bored at work Steve googled himself as he often did purely out of habit. A review of his album "Lou Diamond Phillips?" He was amazed he hadn't noticed it when the album was released. He looked at the date and the review was a brand new article. It was by a website called The Comedy Nerds and the post was part of a series called: TEN CLASSIC COMEDY ALBUMS YOU SHOULD KNOW. The idea behind the series was they dug up obscure comedy albums and gave them some hype. The glowing review singled out one of Steve's bits as one of the reviewer's "top five comedy bits of all time." It made Steve feel good but at the same time depressed him a bit. There was a link at the bottom of the page to an Onion AV Club article. He clicked it and discovered that the *Invite Them Up CD* had been voted one of the "Top Comedy Albums of the Decade." He looked at the album cover and was immediately taken back there. For a second, he could smell the stale beer in the place. He found an old picture someone tagged of him at Rififi looking off-camera. His expression was blank as he stared ahead not seeming to focus on anything. It reminded him of his mother's expression when he caught her staring out the window.

Steve left a meeting downtown on Third Avenue and walked down 11th Street without even realizing where he was. He found himself in front of the old Rififi location nine years after its closing. It was now a Buffalo Exchange store that sold designer clothes at discounted prices. He peeked through the window and saw racks of clothes. The store was brightly lit and there was some neon decor. No sign that Rififi had ever existed there. *The times they are a-changing* he heard Bob Dylan singing in his head. He suddenly recalled Lindsay the bartender dancing to Modest Mouse behind the bar with her arms over her head as the place emptied out. He could feel the ghosts of the place still hanging around. He could almost hear the place whispering to him. He spotted a t-shirt hanging on a rack that featured the words "OH HELLO" featuring animated faces of Nick and John.

It was as if the whole alternative movement had been washed away and there was now a corporate store in its place. He thought of all that had transpired right there in that very small space where a few women were browsing for leggings. They had no clue the star power that had passed through this place. They had no idea that stars had actually been born in the very spot where they were standing.

Some of the Rififi regulars were now the biggest names on the planet. They were the ones who were shaping comedy for the world and the beginning of it all was gone. There was no tangible proof the place ever existed. It felt like Rififi and alt-comedy had been a video store edged out by time. All that time he'd spent there was gone and there was no record of it. That made him sad.

He walked away slowly and headed West on 11th street and came upon an ad for a film being released featuring Amy's smiling face.

Steve walked on and tried to get the whole thing out of his head. But instead, he saw a flash of the station wagon. He saw it more clearly now than he had ever before. Cramped and dark. About five kids, him in the middle.

As he walked forward with the wind hitting his scruff, he wondered if it had all happened. Whether any of it had been real. It all ironically felt like an alternate universe. With every passing step, it felt further away.

As he walked a joke suddenly popped into his head. He stopped walking and made a note to remember it since he knew it was good. He ran across the street to the CVS and bought a small loose-leaf notebook for $1.99 and a pen for one dollar. When he got outside, he jotted down the joke and smiled to himself.

It wasn't just good, it would kill and he knew it. Once at home he sat at his desk and started scribbling in the notebook.

I must have been six years old. I was coming back from Mike Ferrari's birthday party. His parents were driving us in their brown station wagon. Everyone was telling jokes in the back. I was afraid to tell one, but I desperately wanted to be the center of attention. I remembered a joke I'd heard before and though I was terrified I informed everyone I had a joke to tell. The entire station wagon became quiet and the five kids in the back stared straight at me, waiting for me to say something funny. My stomach in knots, I began my first comedy performance. "Knock knock...."

AUTHOR BIO

Tom McCaffrey is a writer/comedian/actor from Manhattan. He has appeared on Comedy Central numerous times including; "Premium Blend", "Shorties Watching Shorties", "The Secret Stash Movie" and "AtomTV". He also appears on the "Invite Them Up CD/DVD Compilation" produced by Comedy Central Records. This album was named one of the "Best Comedy Albums of the Decade" by the Onion AV Club. His last comedy album "New York Funny" debuted at #1 on iTunes in 2019.

Tom's other TV credits include appearances on: Hulu, VH-1, Tru-TV, Animal Planet and CNN. His stand-up album "Lou Diamond Phillips?" was named one of the 'Top 10 Comedy Albums of 2008' by Punchline Magazine.

His feature directorial debut, "Adventures in Comedy" featuring Janeane Garofalo, Jim Gaffigan and Michael Che (SNL) was distributed by the reputable Comedy

Dynamics. It premiered at the Annapolis Film Festival. He was the lead role in the indie film "Happy Life" Executive Produced by Abel Ferrara (Bad Lieutenant).

Tom was a writer and producer for the Comedy Central show "Masters of the Universities". He has contributed to the column "Say Something Funny" in the Onion and was a contributor to The Onion News Network. He was featured in the Random House book "Rejected".

Tom was featured in photographer Seth Olenick's coffee table book "Funny Business" which features some of the hottest people working in comedy today; Judd Apatow, Jon Hamm and Paul Rudd are featured. Tom has blogged for The Huffington Post, BarelyPolitical. com and contributed to TimeOut NY and the NY Daily News. In 2012 TimeOut NY nominated him for "Joke of the Year".